TANGO NOVEMBER

It was around half past five (GMT plus two) on a cool, wet morning, the 119 settling steep, sitting elegantly back on its tail. So far it had made a perfectly normal approach: the synchronized green-red-green of the warning lights visible to the ground in patches where the cloud thinned; their blip fading from a distant radar screen as the plane descended below the profile of the hills; the 15000-pound turbofans a slow whistling roar over a sleeping stone village. But the last nine minutes of many lives were already counting down. The 119 was Tango November, the black headline all round the world in tomorrow's newspapers.

Tango November

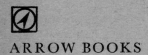

ARROW BOOKS

Arrow Books Limited
3 Fitzroy Square, London W1

An imprint of the Hutchinson Publshiing Group

London Melbourne Sydney Auckland
Wellington Johannesburg and agencies
throughout the world

First published by
Hutchinson & Co. (Publishers) Ltd in 1976
Arrow edition 1977
© John Howlett 1976

Made and printed in Great Britain
by The Anchor Press Ltd
Tiptree, Essex

ISBN 0 09 914850 1

For all those who helped

Contents

Prologue

Mike Duckham left home as light faded on a warm September evening. He slipped away as he liked to do quietly and with a minimum of fuss, though little Clara had come running from the nursery following him downstairs, repeating goodbyes in her sing-song voice. She would not be hushed, stretching to open the front-door latch and standing on the gravel to call fare-wells at five-second intervals as the car backed out of the garage.

Mike had been laughing from the driving seat but when Julia ran from the house to gather up Clara those endless good-byes were sing-singing in her head and she touched wood on the door lintel as she carried the child back inside. She remembered for ever the heavy sweet apple smell of that evening; the white car with its whiter exhaust smoke moving away down the drive; Mike's hand waving out of the window.

It was a wrong 'un from the moment he signed in; three night sectors after a four-day rest; a delayed plane; the voluble weari-some George Raven for Flight Engineer; and a sour-looking Peter Nyren standing in for a First Officer who was off sick. 'Sorry,' said the Rostering Officer. 'There's no one else available.'

They sat around with the girls in the Crew Room listening to a series of bad knee-slapping George Raven jokes. When Dispatch confirmed the delay Mike Duckham left the others and retired to his office to clear up some of his paperwork. He should have been sociable, especially with Peter. It was an obvious occasion to patch up their quarrel, but Mike was tired and flat. He'd lain in bed all afternoon without even approach-ing sleep, and now his eyes were drooping and his neck begin-ning to ache. Off-duty he'd have felt like a stiff drink.

G-FETN, 'Tango November', had been held up in Germany. A false fire-warning during a military charter flight into Stuttgart had meant checks on the number two engine, and by the time the plane returned to base at Gatwick its schedules were running over two hours adrift. Distant girls in the terminal building coped with frayed tempers and the particular anger of one youthfully dressed not-so-young man on his honeymoon. Departure was further delayed when Duckham requested another report on that number two engine. The log entry at Gatwick repeated the German engineer's: 'Checked for hot gas leaks. Fire wire checked. Ground run and found serviceable.'

Tango November was an American-built 119, a T-tail design with the three engines grouped at the rear, similar in size and configuration to a Boeing 727, in silhouette to a Tupolev 154 – a good-looking monster, shining under the airport lights as Duckham walked out to climb on board. He smelt the weather. It was a humid still night and no doubt they'd be back in time for some early-morning fog. The old Death's Head fighter pilot grinned somewhere in Duckham's skull: '*If* we get back.'

Flight GC 523 taxied out for take-off at 01.25: a crew of nine and 181 passengers: two holiday charters totalling 87 bound for Sicily; 40 members of an Italian society from New York already in the twelfth hour of their journey; and a Residents' Club booking of 54 for Malta.

Soon after take-off the company radio came up with information on one of the holiday passengers, Mr Julius Janius, the honeymoon man. They had found out who he was and requested Duckham to give him a bit of the treatment. Mr Janius had been a well-known young tycoon in the far-off Swinging Sixties. Once they had reached cruising level Duckham moved back into the cabin. The senior hostess indicated the honeymoon couple with a discreet nod of the head, and Duckham stopped to address the man by name.

'I'm sorry about the delay, Mr Janius' . . . and the bullshit worked its usual magic – the name, the fact of being singled out from the crowd. Mr Honeymoon was very mollified, his new young wife very impressed.

Tango November had flown a Seaford One departure climbing to 29000 feet over the French coast. A wrong 'un. Twenty minutes beyond Rambouillet the Flight Engineer noticed oil temperature rising on the constant-speed drive to the number one generator.

'Switching essential power to number two generator.'

'Trouble?'

'Oil temperature. I've taken her off the bus-bar.'

A minute later the Engineer spoke again. 'Temperature's still up, skipper. Tripping the CSD.' Number one generator was disengaged irrevocably now – useless until it was serviced and reset on the ground.

'White rabbits,' said the Flight Engineer. 'Looks like we got a duff battery as well. It's charging too high.'

A wrong 'un. As they passed the coast-line over Genoa they were given the weather report from Sicily: Taormina-Peloritana was covered; runway visual range down to six hundred metres; cloud base at two hundred feet – the bare minima required.

'*Greyhound Tango November, you are clear to the beacon Kilo Lima at flight level one one five.*' Air Traffic Controller at Taormina-Peloritana. His English was broken but his voice was clear.

'*Roger, Taormina. Descending to one one five.*'

The T-tail 119 was moving four miles above the Mediterranean at 450 knots south-east into the mocking clarity of a clear dawn sky, ninety tons of silver bird sinking slowly towards an isolated bank of cloud on the horizon.

The Italian voice in the headset dropped formality: '*Good to hear you, Greyhound.*'

The Flight Engineer slapped his knee and laughed. 'Blimey! He really can talk English.'

'*Sorry we're late, Taormina. Can we have the weather again.*'

'*Stand by, Greyhound.*'

The Engineer laughed again. 'He's licking his finger and sticking his hand out of the window.' Flight Engineer George Raven, thirty-nine years old, ex-RAF, voluble to a fault.

'*Taormina weather at o three hundred GMT. Light rain. Wind one four zero at five knots. Cloud base at two hundred metres. Runway visibility at six hundred and fifty metres. QNH one zero zero six.*'

'*Thank you, Taormina.*' Thank you for nothing, Duckham thought.

'He's creeping the RVR up. He'll push it to seven hundred if he wants us in there.'

George Raven, sideways on behind the pilots, hadn't stopped

chattering all night, but for once Duckham shared his senti-
ments. He still wasn't sure where he would put down. Twelve
months ago he'd have given up this border-line visibility and
settled for Malta. Visibility in Sicily was bound to clear after
sunrise.

But twelve months ago he hadn't been a fleet captain, and
the finer points of airline economics had never influenced his
decisions. They were nearly three hours late tonight, and there
was a large party waiting in Malta for the return flight to
Gatwick. If he went straight to Malta now there would be no
room to take the new party on board, and that would mean a
couple of extra legs flying between the islands. Another two
hours' delay compounded for Saturday's schedules.

'There's a nasty echo waiting for us.' The Flight Engineer
was chirping again, one eye on the weather radar. 'It's that
bloody volcano, that's what it is. The biggest tit south of Mont
Blanc and north of Kilimanjaro. It picks up all the dirty
weather that's lying around.'

Duckham looked at the scattering of white storm dots on
the radar. He knew the island from hairier times and remembered suddenly and briefly one moment of terrified panic in
a Mosquito thirty years ago. It had nearly killed him once, that
mountain.

'It's a lousy runway if it's wet.' The Flight Engineer, feeding
some more bad news to Duckham's insides.

'Approach and descent checks,' said Duckham to shut him
up, and the three men took up their cards.

'Seat belt signs.'

'On.'

'Radio altimeters.'

'On. Decision height set.'

'Flight instruments and transfer switches.'

'Checked and set.'

'Air condition and pressurization.'

'Set.'

'Fuel.'

'Set for landing.'

The checks went on, voices, eyes and hands reacting mechanically. Duckham took up the let-down chart for Taormina–
Peloritana. 1943, he was thinking. His first year of operational

flying. Out over the Med. They'd been shooting up trains on the Italian mainland and a 109 had chased them home – home being one of the recently captured Sicilian fields. Sigonella, was it? They had flown into a bank of cloud to lose the Messerschmitt then found it so rough inside they'd forgotten all about the mountain.

Peter Nyren called out an altitude check from the seat beside Duckham: Five hundred to one one five.' Duckham nodded but one half of his mind was still wandering.

Ten feet above the trees they'd been when they came out of the cloud, both of them sick with the turbulence, and flying straight for that mountain. This would be the first time in thirty-two years that he'd been back on the island.

'One one five.'

Duckham reacted automatically, easing back the wheel: 'Check. Levelling at one one five.'

The tower spoke again. *'Greyhound Tango November. Runway visibility clearing to seven hundred metres.'*

George Raven slapped his knee again. 'What did I tell you! They want their landing fees tonight.'

'Roger, Taormina. We'll give it a try.' Duckham pushed reminiscence away and buzzed the galley. Stella Pritchard came quickly through the door to clear empty plates and coffee-cups. A swift breeze of scent and she was gone.

Idiot, thought the young P.2. I haven't even said hello yet.

First Officer Peter Nyren, twenty-seven years old, a graduate of Hamble Flying School, 1547 hours' flying time, and unlike George Raven silent but for procedure since they had left Gatwick two hours ago. It was the first time he had flown with Duckham since one happy and hilarious trip to Malaga ten weeks ago. But their relationship had changed radically and for the worse since June.

'There's the mountain,' the Flight Engineer sang out behind him, and Peter looked up briefly from his instruments and through the side window. They were over the northern isthmus of the island now, 1000 feet above the level of the volcano and fifteen miles or so to the north of it. Peter had seen it once before, two weeks ago, smoking lazily into the sunshine. It looked harder now, a white-dusted cratered lump silhouetted against the dawn sky, protruding a few hundred feet clear of the dark storm clouds gathered to its north and west.

A blue light flashed with a repeating bleeper. Nyren jumped at the noise and had to refer to his chart before confirming position.

'Outer Marker. Kilo Lima.' He wasn't concentrating and he knew the captain would have noticed his delay. Duckham didn't miss much.

'Greyhound Tango November to Taormina. Checked on Kilo Lima and taking up the hold.'

'Roger, Greyhound. You are cleared down to seven thousand feet on QNH one zero zero five.'

'Roger. Cleared to seven thousand feet. Confirm QNH.'

'QNH one zero zero five.'

Pressure dropping, thought Duckham. That storm centre moving nearer?

The plane was banking into a long starboard turn, its rate of descent now perceptible to the 181 passengers in the two sections of cabin. Their imminent arrival at Taormina had been announced and three of the uniformed girls were moving up and down checking seat-belts. Two hostesses were securing the trolleys and containers in the forward galley. The senior hostess was packing away the duty-free boxes in the tail galley. She was given an OK through the door from her number two and she called the flight deck.

'Seat-belts checked. Both galleys secure for landing.'

Duckham acknowledged. He looked up for a moment through the window at the primrose-dawn horizon. By way of a farewell, for five seconds later the cloud enveloped them and they were blind, back into the darkness, on their way down towards unseen mountains. Thirty-six years of flying experience did little to diminish the apprehension that began to tighten Duckham's stomach and accelerate his pulse. 'It's none or a crowd,' his old RAF instructor used to tell them. It was beginning to look like a good crowd on this flight: one duff generator; a doubtful battery; Peter Nyren sitting there like a broody hen not quite on the egg; a wise-cracking wiseacre of a Flight Engineer who wouldn't stop talking; a plane load of delayed and disgruntled tourists. And now, a storm, marginal visibility, a bloody mountain, and a half-arse airfield which only the

P.2 had ever flown into before. Serve the moody bugger right if I made Peter fly it in, Duckham thought. It was Peter who now warned him of their approach to clearance.

'Five hundred to seven thousand.'

'*Greyhound Tango November approaching seven thousand.*'

The airport voice was casual and confident: '*Roger, Greyhound. Reclear down to four thousand for ILS on Runway two nine.*'

'Roger. Cleared for ILS on Runway two nine.'

'*Call me when procedure turn complete.*'

'*Roger.*' Duckham looked over at Peter Nyren. 'Time me fifty seconds. Gear down and landing checks.'

'Spoiler switches.'

'On.'

'No smoking signs.'

'On.'

'Anti skid.'

'All green.'

'Five hundred feet to four thousand feet. Ten seconds to fifty seconds.'

The approach turn had taken them out over the sea. It was time now to head themselves back at the island and the airfield, hopefully to find the Instrument Landing System.

'Gear down in three greens.'

'Four thousand feet.'

'Levelling out at four thousand.'

'Localizer alive.'

A voice laughed in Duckham's ear. 'Miracle number one.' George Raven was swivelled round to monitor the letdown.

'*Established on the ILS. Four thousand feet.*'

'*Roger, Tango November. Call me on Outer Marker.*'

Nyren called out as they picked up the landing system on their instruments. 'Glide slope alive.'

The Raven laughed again in Duckham's ear. 'Miracle number two!'

'Shut up, George!'

They were on the glide path beamed up at them from the airfield, the magic eye that would, all being well, guide them down to the threshold and the moment when they made visual contact with the runway. The blue light and bleeper activated again.

'Outer Marker.' Peter Nyren paused to check on the letdown chart. 'We're two hundred feet high.'

'Sod it! It checks out on my side. I'd say it looks good. Confirm glide slope your side.'

Peter confirmed: 'Check on the glide slope.'

The Flight Engineer muttered again behind Duckham: 'Bloody marvellous. I bet they changed the slope and forgot to tell anyone.'

'OK. Let's have a bit of hush. *Tango November over Outer Marker*.'

'*Roger. Tango November, you are clear to land*.'

Tired staff on the apron at Taormina–Peloritana began to hear the approaching whine. They had been waiting five hours for this one delayed flight – two fuel attendants, a tractor-tug driver, six baggage handlers, four immigration officials, a couple of policemen and the travel couriers with their bus-drivers.

It was around half past five (GMT plus two) on a cool, wet morning, the 119 settling steep, sitting elegantly back on its tail. So far it had made a perfectly normal approach: the synchronized green-red-green of the warning lights visible to the ground in patches where the cloud thinned; their blip fading from a distant radar screen as the plane descended below the profile of the hills; the 15000-pound turbo-fans a slow whistling roar over a sleeping stone village. But the last nine minutes of many lives were already counting down. The 119 was Tango November, the black headline all round the world in tomorrow's newspapers.

Part One

I

'*Taormina calling Greyhound Tango November* – ' The call was repeated twice through shattered headsets before the radio faded on the flight deck.

Two minutes after impact survivors started to move and cry out in the wreckage. Of the 190 passengers and crew less than half were yet medically dead. The senior hostess in her folding seat at the back of the plane found herself able to move. The left side engine under the tail had torn into the fuselage on impact, smashing the galley bulkhead against which she had been sitting, cutting a space open for her to fall into, still strapped to the broken wall. No one around her seemed conscious. The shouting was further forward. It was three and a half minutes after impact when she had freed herself from the straps and the wreckage. She tried to activate the left-side rear emergency exit, but the tilt of the fuselage had jammed the exit against the ground outside. The ventral staircase that let down under the tail was smashed and locked solid. The right-side emergency exit was tilted too high for her to exert the necessary pressure to open it. She started to crawl forward on her hands and knees around bodies and a jumble of loose and broken seats. 'Is there anyone there?' She repeated the question over and over, crying to herself for all those motionless and distorted people. She remembered their faces row by row, some of them angry, some of them forgiving, a couple of them drunk, most of them eventually asleep. Fire, she was thinking to herself. She could smell paraffin.

Kerosene from ruptured fuel lines was draining slowly into the accumulation of wreckage at the tail. Five minutes after impact the fuel level rose high enough to make contact with the left side engine. The fuel ignited and progressively through the next ten minutes passengers between rows 31 and 22, immobilized by injuries, began to choke or burn to death. The senior hostess, still crawling forward through the debris in the cabin, had reached row 23 before she finally succumbed to the fumes. She died, unconscious, a minute and a half later.

In the mid section of fuselage the tilt of the plane had thrown cabin wreckage against both left-wing exits, and none of the passengers between rows 13 and 19 were in a fit condition to clear these exits. Their only chance of evacuation was through a gap where the fuselage had split just forward of the main bulkhead in the mid-plane toilet. No one saw the gap and the only people to escape from this wing section of the 119 were the air hostess Stella Pritchard and a five-year-old girl called Trixie. They had both been thrown through that gap as the crash occurred.

In the darkness and the confusion there were only isolated cries of distress or pain. Two passengers in the forward section of the fuselage had escaped without major limb fractures and the noise they were making in the attempt to free themselves convinced everyone else that a rescue party was already at work. But fourteen minutes after impact the heat of the fire below the tail created enough draught to counteract the lateral ventilation of the north-westerly breeze. The poisoning effect of carbon monoxide with the cyanide from burning plastics began to spread from row 21 forward to the fuselage break and the presence of cyanide in the atmosphere made it impossible for anyone to hold their breath or control their respiration.

The realization of fire in the narrow fuselage created panic among the conscious survivors, a deformed, contorted hysteria of people trapped, gassed and unable to move. It was in that ugliness and with that fear that most of them died.

Air Traffic Control in Catania had been alerted by telephone from Taormina and they raised the alarm for a missing plane some nine minutes after impact. A coastguard helicopter and an Italian Air Force Sea King on exercise were both diverted to search.

The smoke of the fire was finally spotted by the coastguard helicopter thirty-four minutes after the crash. Fifteen more minutes passed while the helicopter moved inland and up the long slope of the mountain. It was flying dangerously near to its own altitude limits and proceeding with appropriate caution. Forty-nine minutes after impact the wreckage was positively identified, and the helicopter landed as best it could on the rough lava. An air hostess and a young girl were found clear of the wreckage and apparently still alive. They were covered with blankets to await stretchers. The Air Force Sea King arrived a few minutes later. Marker flares were lit and the pilots joined the coastguards in their attempts to clamber into the wreckage.

Twenty miles away in Catania police woke the Procuratore Generale and informed him that a major disaster with fatalities had occurred. The Procuratore detailed an elderly and senior Magistrato to take charge of rescue and investigation. The Magistrato issued an immediate request through the Prefettura for assistance from NATO air force bases.

Sixty-one minutes after impact the first heavy rescue and fire-fighting helicopters arrived overhead, an Italian Air Force Boeing-Vertol 114 and a USAF Sikorsky S-64 Skycrane.

Tino G. on his first visit back to his parents' homeland was bent double and buried under seats and other bodies, his own body broken and in pain. He could feel the warm wetness of blood down his legs and could sense unknown hideousness where his bent-up stomach was holding wounds together. He hoped no one would ever realize how long it had taken him to die and he wondered if anyone would find the fragments of the autographed guitar he had been holding between his knees.

The words of a song were running through his head without their tune which he could not remember.

> '*Sweet dreams and flying machines*
> *in pieces on the ground.*'

2

The night Duty Officer in the Department of Trade and Industry glasshouse on Victoria Street read off the telex at twenty minutes past six on that Saturday morning. The message followed the outlines of ICAO protocol, but the facts were sparse, and the Duty Officer checked for further information with Reuters and Associated Press before dialling up the Duty Senior Inspector at his south London home. It was 06.17 (GMT plus one hour) when Ralph Burden picked up his bedside phone.

'There's an accident AFTN, sir.' The Duty Officer read out the details on the telex: a 119 belonging to Greyhound and registered in Britain had crashed on the slopes of a mountain in Sicily. 'I checked with the news agencies. There's no indication of damage or casualties.'

Burden's duty list was lying under the telephone, and he made his own calls without stirring from bed, alerting two members of the standby team for departure and dictating messages for the RAF pathologist and dentist at Halton. As an afterthought he left word with the night staff at the undertakers in Edgware Road. Four calls in seven minutes, clipped, unapologetic, naked for the lack of facts.

The PBX operator at Halton was having more difficulty with his messages. The dentist had gone away for the weekend, and the pathologist wasn't answering. The operator listened to the ringing tone for two minutes, then used another line to check the number through the exchange. Mac Pherson, the operator was thinking with a grin, hung-over with drink or sex.

European headquarters for Greyhound Flight were temporarily accommodated in crowded offices at Gatwick, where the busy end-of-season Saturday had been in disarray all night. Tango November had left for Sicily and Malta nearly three hours late, and there were four holiday charters throughout Saturday that looked like inheriting the delay. The Flight Coordinator had been searching for a possible switch-round among their seven 119s variously engaged in Europe and the Near East. Flight Coordinator and computer between them were just about cracking the equation when the Crewing Officer took an outside call in the next office and banged with pale-faced urgency on the glass partition. Associated Press were asking for the crew and charter details of a crashed plane in Sicily. It was Greyhound Flight's first notification of disaster, and within a minute their entire switchboard was blocked by incoming calls from the other press agencies and newspapers.

A 'disaster-procedure' team was hastily improvised and an office and telephone lines borrowed from a neighbouring airline. But it took twenty minutes to obtain confirmation of the accident from Italy, and no one seemed able to give them an assessment of casualties and damage.

The disaster team began to contact the travel companies who had contracted the charter, and the families of the nine crew members involved.

Julia Duckham was in the kitchen when the telephone rang. She'd been up early expecting her husband back any time for a meal. His bed was already made up in the black-painted dressing-room he used for day-time sleeping. He had called last night from the airport to tell her about their delayed departure and to warn her he would be back later than expected.

'You'll never guess who I'm flying with.'

'Not Peter?'

'The P.2 went sick and Peter's on standby. If he wants to make friends I might bring him back for breakfast.'

Why bother with him, Julia had thought, but she'd prepared enough food just in case. One of Michael's early-morning specials, neither breakfast nor supper: a cress soup, kidneys, bacon, eggs, sausages, tomatoes, a bowl of autumn raspberries from the garden, and a glass of wine to help him sleep.

Even at seven in the morning the sound of the telephone caused her no anxiety. The superstition of the evening before had long since passed away, and she assumed the call was Mike to say he was on his way from Gatwick.

But she didn't know the voice on the line at the other end, a soft Southern States American drawl trying to establish the need for calm optimism. 'Mrs Duckham, I am afraid there has been some kind of an accident . . .'

She was in no way prepared for it, not on this particular morning with the sun slanting across the garden, Mike's meal spread in readiness around the kitchen and the children pattering and laughing upstairs. She shouted out loud in alarm and disbelief.

*

Peter Nyren's next of kin was his widowed father, the elderly vicar of a thin village congregation in East Sussex. The vicar's reaction to the bad news was almost professional.

'I'm sorry,' he said. 'Oh dear, I'm so sorry,' as though the soft-voiced American needed his comfort. He replaced the receiver without saying another word.

It was seven in the morning and the enormous Georgian vicarage felt cold and empty. Canon Ash Nyren walked to the end of the garden, through the broken lychgate and the overgrown graveyard to an even colder church.

The village women heard him on their way to apple-picking half an hour later, the church organ grumbling away full of discord from arthritic fingers and uncertain legs.

Twice before in his life early morning messages had brought death to a household. Once at seven years old when an elder brother was killed at Loos; the second time when his then only son had been killed flying gliders into Arnhem. Eighteen years old; a future cricket blue, they'd said; first-class brain. A fine boy. How many doomed boys.

Later in the morning the old man remembered to pray.

3

In Washington it was twenty past one in the morning, and Larry Raille's bedroom telephone woke all four members of the family. 'British registered Greyhound 119 in Italy,' the National Transport Safety Board night operator told him, and Raille, with a glance at his frowning wakened wife, moved the phone into the kitchen to make his calls. 'We've a party Monday don't you forget,' her scowl had told him. 'Eight guests and all from NASA.'

Another twenty-two and a half hours, thought Raille, and someone else's name would have been pencilled in on the roster. He had arranged to keep Sunday and Monday free. Raille placed telephone calls to Rome and London and asked the operator to keep his line plugged up. It was the third 119 'incident' in two months and he had no intention of playing Washington ear for any political lobby. In California it was not yet bed-time and in California there were many thousand jobs dependent on the long-term future of the 119. The 3 W plane they had called it at first, for its greatest sales potential was thought to be with the Third World. 'Easiest plane in the world to fly,' a company test pilot had told Raille at someone's party. And a mildly drunken company salesman had entered on cue – 'Even a monkey could fly it' – before lurching across the room to buttonhole an African air attaché.

Larry Raille frowned at the memory. Washington was a difficult place to maintain constant professional objectivity. But cadre pride kept the more susceptible regulars of the National Transport Safety open-minded about such things. Only the politically appointed Board members were sometimes suspect, and Larry hoped that this time they would leave without one. The investigation would already be complicated enough: an Italian crash; an American plane; British registration – three nations with a legal claim to participation.

'Is it a bad crash?' The eldest Raille boy was standing pyjama-ed in the kitchen door.

'No one seems to know.'

'You're going to miss the party.'

'It looks like it.'

'You could ask someone to go in your place.'

'That's not the way we work, not unless we're ill.'

'You could be ill.'

'I'm not an ill kind of person.'

'Gee! Mom is really going to be mad – ' and the boy's eyes were gloomy with apprehension as the open line came to life again: a disorganized Italian Air Force clerk from Rome, fluent in English, but otherwise ill-equipped to answer Larry Raille's queries.

There was nothing specific about damage, casualties or apparent scenario of disaster, except that the site was accessible only to helicopters. 'There are reports of survivors inside the plane,' the clerk told him. 'But the plane is also on fire.'

Not very cheerful, thought Raille. The poor old 119 could have done without another gruesome crash. 'Albatross', the world press were beginning to call it. Ninety people had been killed only three months ago shortly after take-off from Nairobi.

Half past one. It was the wrong half of the clock for transatlantic flights. Larry looked at his time charts. Italy was on Eastern European time. Even if he found seats on a non-scheduled charter they'd hardly make Sicily before the next nightfall. There seemed no point in waking anyone up yet.

But another voice appeared on the open line.

'Colonel Parker for you sir. USAF Travis.'

That lobby's been working fast, Larry thought. They don't like this one.

'Got seats for you on an exercise flight,' Colonel Parker told him. 'Three seats. We'll have your team over in Sicily in five hours.'

'That would be a great help sir.'

Three seats and five hours to Sicily? Probably the new swing-wing bomber, the 'B1', or whatever they were calling it.

'Can you get 'em all over here inside a half-hour?'

Half an hour? He hadn't even alerted them yet. He looked down the address list on the duty roster. He'd have to pick the men who lived within shouting distance of the Travis air base: one man for his Italian and the second for his knowledge of the 119. Both of them promised to be at Travis within thirty minutes.

Raille dragged his bags from the wardrobe: three ready-packed bags, a hot weather bag, a cold weather bag and an equipment case. The plane had crashed on a mountain. He threw some heavy clothes into the hot weather bag and checked the climbing gear. His wife didn't even turn to watch. A year ago she'd have been up out of bed and packing for him.

He called good-bye to her when he was ready.

'I'm not putting it off,' she said. It was the party she was talking about. 'I'm not going to make a fool of myself. Not after six months cultivating them all. I'll do the talking whether you're here or not.'

Larry Raille had no doubts on that score. She'd missed out on the moon. But by all that was New England holy she'd have her man on Mars or thereabouts, carved into the history books.

4

Tango November had set a multitude of telephones ringing in Rome that morning as officialdoms tried to rouse themselves from summer slumbers or disguise the extent of unauthorized weekend absenteeism. There were also warnings for people whose interests might be served or threatened by the fact of the disaster: those who suspected that they could be making money; and others who wondered if they shouldn't be preparing lines of retreat.

In the midst of high-level fluster and bluster one very unimportant call was made to a cheap two-roomed flat out in the concrete jungle along the Tuscolana, half a mile or so short of Cinecittà. 'Sharlie' Barzizza was woken by the ringing, and when no one else stirred he got up himself to answer it. There were six of them on mattresses around the room, eight if you counted two girls who had stayed the night. The mattresses radiated haphazardly towards the centre of the room, each one surrounded by the owner's pile of clothes, records, books and suitcase, and in Sharlie's case his cameras.

The phone was in the kitchen, the single luxury the tiny flat had permitted itself. More of a necessity than a luxury, for five of the six mattresses were hopeful and underemployed young actors, and Sharlie a hopeful but impoverished photo-journalist – one of a new generation of Roman *paparazzi* struggling to make a living now that cosmopolitan dolce vita had moved elsewhere.

The call was for him. 'An aeroplane has crashed on Etna,' the voice said stuttering on its l's and n's. 'A 119 full of tourists.' It was Citto from back home.

'So what am I meant to do? Jump in my helicopter?'

'It's your mountain, old son. And the only big story we'll get ourselves near this side of Christmas.' Citto Risarda from the Catania newspaper that had published Sharlie's first pictures.

'I'm busy here,' Sharlie lied.

Citto ignored him. 'I'll ring Air Sicily at Ciampino.'

'I don't want to come home.'

'They'll take you down on a cargo flight.'

Sharlie put the phone down and stared out through the windows at a tired end-of-summer morning already hazy with dust and filtered sunshine. Soft, lazy September was somewhere else beyond the dirty city or these weed-ridden concrete suburbs. Saturday. Today and tomorrow were reserved for hustling pictures of soldiers and their girl-friends up around the station and the barracks and the nearby streets and piazzas where the buses from the provinces set down their passengers. 'Develop and print while you wait' was the gimmick, and Sharlie used a tiny dark-room behind a chemist's shop hired out by the half-hour. But it was a hard way to make the week's bread.

An air crash on Etna. Mongibello. 'Your mountain', Citto had said, for Sharlie had lived his childhood in the shadow of its gently smoking cone. He remembered the violence of the eruption as he had photographed it one winter's night nearly a year ago: the explosions of flame and stone from the crater; and, a long way below, that slow oozing of molten lava from a wound on the mountainside. Citto had taken him up there within hours of its starting and they'd seen the rocks still buckling apart as the lava exit elongated itself.

The shapes on the bedroom mattresses were still fast asleep, only one of the visiting girls awake, winking at Sharlie as he stepped over her to return to his corner. He wondered whether she'd come and lie with him if he beckoned. They were all actresses or models, the girls who came here, most of them happy enough to hook a tame photographer to do their portfolios for them. He sat on the mattress and looked over at her, but she'd turned over and gone back to sleep.

Sharlie pulled out his camera bag. He didn't really want to go back to bed, not in this fug of sweat and sex. Anyhow it'd take him an hour and a half to walk into town unless he had money for the tram. By Saturday morning it was usually a question of choosing between a tram or coffee.

Nine o'clock Air Sicily flew from Ciampino, he thought, and Ciampino was only twenty minutes' walk down the road.

News had travelled in inverse ratio to distance. Twenty-five miles from the mountain journalists in Catania had read of the crash on the tape machines from Rome. When they rang the hospitals for news of casualties the hospital staff knew nothing of casualties or crash. 'In fact,' said a receptionist, 'don't send anyone here. Everyone's gone away for the weekend.'

The News Editor of the local daily had assigned four reporters to cover various aspects of the crash. The investigative role was given to Citto Risarda, tubby, polite, apparently innocuous as he peered at everyone through thick lenses. But since the Alitalia crash at Punta Raisi he had become a minor expert on the shortcomings of Italian airports – shortcomings usually well concealed. At Punta Raisi they were trying to blame the dead pilot.

A couple of hours after the crash Citto's battered old Giulia was squealing up the hairpins off the *Statale* 185 and through the sci-fi perimeter fence of Taormina-Peloritana. The airport was quiet, uninhabited it seemed, gleaming in the early morning sun. The rain had shone up the tarred joints in the tarmac, had cleared the air and given body even to the dust-coloured earth in the shrubbery around the car park – waist-high sprigs of oleander. The shrubs were the only clue to the airport's age, for everything else, concrete, tarmacadam, metal shutters and dirty glass had been baked into premature age by the sun and the wind on this high plateau. Citto left his car at the main passenger entrance and walked round the outside of the terminal building. Every door was locked and only the distant throbbing of an engine suggested the presence of man or men's creatures.

Citto was not surprised. The crash had occurred in the province of Catania and rescue was being organized from Fontanarossa and Sigonella. This new airstrip was over the border in Messina province and there was little they could offer in the way of assistance or equipment. The night shift would have packed up when Tango November was posted missing, and the day shift on a Saturday didn't start here until half past eight.

He peered through barred glass at the departure concourse: two flag-carrying airline desks repeated for ever in two large wall mirrors; a marble floor; half a coloured glass mosaic; empty patches of brick that should have been decorated with pictures or friezes. The young architect who had won the local *concorso* would hardly recognize his masterpiece. The contractors here lacked finishing power. Even the clocks had stopped, reading twenty to six in identical lines endless through the looking glass. Rome money had paid for these buildings. The runway and aprons, financed from Brussels, had been more carefully completed.

Citto listened to that distant diesel engine splutter and fade. A few moments later a lorry pulled away from behind the maintenance buildings and on to the road beyond the car park – a dirty black oil tanker just near enough for Citto to read the top line of its Catania number-plate. He turned back to his car resigned to a thirty-minute wait before anyone would arrive to answer his questions.

The tanker crept down the hairpins and joined the main road in a crashing of gears. A young red-haired man with a flushed and fleshy face and an oil-stained suède jacket nursed the heavy monster down into the valley and back towards the small town at the foot of the hills. He parked the tanker on a wide dirty pavement and walked along the main street under the balconies back to where he'd left his green and luminous orange Ferrari Dino in the Agip Garage on the east side of town. Flavio Consoli.

5

The plane lay halfway up the mountain broken-backed on a ridge of black lava at the end of a splintered swathe through thin chestnut and scrubby pine. Smoke from the burning tail section flattened suddenly half a mile wide through the rocks and trees as the Skycrane manoeuvred to aim a final load of foam. Death and damage done, the fire surrendered, and the giant helicopter side-slipped away looking for a landing patch. On the ground rescue teams moved back towards the wreckage in clumsy scrambling movements over the corrugated black pumice.

Tino G. heard them returning. He waited for the sound of

their feet on the ladders, then resumed his low and painful cry.

Bowed old Turi heard him. He'd been listening to that intermittent cry since he had first arrived, and the cry hurt him because he could do so little to help.

Turi Pennisi had been picked up from the road nearest to the accident site by one of the early police helicopters. He was Medico Condotto, the local state doctor with a multitude of responsibilities covering life, death, disease and sanitation through a half-dozen villages and hamlets under the volcano. For two hours he had worked in the shattered fuselage, directing rescue with the Air Force medics, until he was sure there was no one left alive except that voice trapped in the mess at the front of the aeroplane. Thirty-four survivors had been evacuated, many of them close to death, and Turi did not give them much hope for survival in the butcher-shop hospitals along the coast. Not on a warm September weekend. One of the ferrying pilots had told him that they had already run out of both blood and plasma, and that an SOS had gone out to the ships in Catania harbour for sailors to volunteer transfusions.

Turi's coat pulled and flapped in a gale of rotor blades. Grappling hooks had been lowered from the huge helicopter overhead. They were going to try to prise a hole open near the smashed cockpit in an attempt to speed the rescue of that trapped voice. One of the blackened sweating policemen gave Turi a swig at a water-bottle. Considering the inaccessibility of the wreck Carabinieri and Air Force had seemed quite well organized in operating their standby procedures for earthquakes or eruptions. Both teams were now deployed by the elderly Magistrato who had legal charge of salvage and rescue.

The grappling lines tightened and the wreckage began to part in an unearthly shrieking of metal. The Magistrato helped Turi squeeze himself into the widening gap. 'Check the bodies of the crew if you can find them – three of them.'

'If they were up front they'll be dead.'

'I have to have official confirmation.' He wasn't too sure of himself, this elderly Magistrato. He was following textbook procedures.

The engineers from the helicopter had calculated well. They had told Turi that the front exit and the corridor between galley and w.c. would be impacted upwards, but still relatively clear, and sure enough on one side Turi could sense a possible way into the wrecked cockpit. On the other side he felt the wall of accumulated debris where seats and bodies had built up against the front partitions of the cabin. Four seats, one on top of the other, had jammed across the aisle behind the galley, and the trapped voice was pinned somewhere inside that giant sandwich. It was six hours since the crash, and bodies were cooling. Turi moved his hands from flesh to flesh. He found a braceleted wrist that moved suddenly, rings on stiff fingers – a severed arm that fell across him as he let it go in sudden horror. Then below it he found a leg, still warm, and as he touched it the voice cried again for help somewhere just below him.

Turi called out: 'You hear me?'

Tino G. heard the voice, muffled but very near, an Italian voice talking in careful English. 'I am a doctor,' the voice said. 'You must tell exactly what you hear to me. You hear me touch your leg?'

Hear? *Sentire*. He means 'feel', thought Tino G. 'I think so.' His words were breathless.

'You have much pain?'

'My chest.'

The boy was bent double, his feet and head on Turi's side in the wall of wreckage.

'I can't breathe properly.'

'Your mouth and your throat it is clear?'

'My chest.'

'You not talk. I give you morphine for the pain.'

Turi had found one of the boy's arms and followed it back to the shoulders. 'We have to free you out of here very careful. It take a long time. You understand that?'

'Yes.'

'I am going away to tell the engineers how to free you. You understand?'

'Yes.'

Turi listened to the boy's breathing. It was short but it was strong. 'You must not be afraid. I come back. I not leave you. What is your name?'

'Tino G.'

'G?'

'It's a nickname.'

'I come back soon Tino G. OK?'

'OK.'

Turi pushed himself back to the hole and called to the engineers telling them how the boy was lying. They would have to use jacks and hacksaws to shift the wreckage millimetre by millimetre and Turi told them he would stay inside with the boy. The Magistrato asked him again about the cockpit crew. 'I must have confirmation.' Turi squeezed feet first into the concertinaed chaos of the cockpit. He could see nothing in the darkness but he felt three bodies, cold and very broken. Then moving sideways to turn himself Turi found a fourth body with them, dead like the others, and even more broken. A woman.

The drama of the fourth body brought the salvage operation to a halt. The Magistrato forbade any more movement or evacuation of bodies from the wreck, except the work directly concerned with freeing the trapped boy. All other evidence was to be preserved intact for technical and forensic examination.

Only two men were allowed to continue: officials detailed by the Magistrato to search for the so-called 'black box' flight recorder. The two men left the scene later in their own small helicopter, their canvas holdalls heavy with salvage or equipment. But no one actually saw whether or not they had yet found the 'black box'.

An hour or so after Turi's unexpected discovery the press agency teleprinters began to carry the dramatic news of a flight-deck intruder and the possibility of an attempted hi-jack. An addendum to the drama was the confirmation that all members of the Tango November flight crew were dead.

*

There'd been little for Julia to do except wait. She had sent the children next door with a request to keep them away from the radio or TV. She had rung up Mike's first wife in Richmond, her stepdaughter's school in Kent, her own sister in Guildford. She could tell them all so very little. 'No one knows what has happened.'

She had seen Mike alive, seen him injured, dead, shattered beyond recognition. She'd seen him laughing as he had laughed waving from the car last night; brooding and worried as he had sometimes been during the nine months past. She saw him crying as once he had cried when their love and her physical contentment had finally coincided.

She told herself Mike would have rung or telegraphed if he'd been alive. She heard little Clara's sing-song goodbyes of the previous evening. And each time the telephone rang she thought she knew. But every time she was mistaken. Once it was her sister, Pam, driving up from Guildford; then her stepdaughter's school to say she would be sent home in the afternoon; finally a cheerful ironmonger in Woking to say that a spare chain for the lawnmower had arrived. Julia saw Mike again, driving the lawnmower like a racing car in and out the borders, and up and down the orchard.

She thought of 190 other families also waiting in this agony.

Then, just as she heard Pam's car turning in the drive, that soft Southern States drawl phoned her from the Greyhound office at Gatwick, definitively, conclusively. When Pam came upstairs the two sisters cried for the memories of two separate loves.

6

Taormina-Peloritana came slowly back to life, personnel, buses and cars gathering for the Saturday-morning traffic: four holiday charters from Germany and Scandinavia; and Air Sicily cargo services from Rome and Bari. They would be the last flights into the airport for some time. The ministry in Rome had already announced the closure of Taormina-Peloritana to all commercial traffic – 'until the cause or causes of the crash have been reasonably established'. The atmosphere at the airport was accordingly muted and no one particularly anxious to discuss the crash.

Citto Risarda watched the activity from a stone bench in the arrivals hall, moving every now and then for a hesitant stuttering word with one or other of the airport officials. He was told that there were no records available of radio conversation with the doomed plane, and emphatically no record of malfunction in the landing aids at the airport. The clocks, Citto noticed, were in operation again and back on time.

When the first charter flight arrived, a DC-9 from Bremen, he followed the two pilots to their coffee break at the bar and talked with them in stumbling English. No, they told him, there had been nothing wrong that morning with the landing approach. The ILS glide path was operating normally. 'But then,' the German captain said, 'you would not expect anything wrong on a warm sunny day.'

'So you say this is a safe airport?' Citto asked.

The German laughed and held up a hand. 'You want I count the safe airports south of the Alps and Pyrenees? We make not even one hand of fingers.'

'So you say it is not safe?'

'I say already – on a warm sunny day is like parking my car. Now you tell me what was the weather last night.'

Citto shrugged. 'I don't know. In Catania it was fine. Around the mountain the weather changes every ten kilometres.'

The pilots finished their coffee and turned away. Citto persisted. 'What happens in bad weather?'

'Once I land here in a storm. Next time I go some place else. Your mountain he is like a bad animal in a storm.'

The two pilots returned to their DC-9 for the journey home, and Citto wandered outside on to the veranda enclosure. An Air Sicily Viscount was settling in to land, and Citto watched it through binoculars. The whole operation looked so simple, the plane and its shadow meeting with light puffs of smoke and scarcely a ripple on the wide white runway. That lump of volcano was far away, not more than a hill with a pretty plume of smoke, and a scattering of innocuous-looking clouds.

The Viscount was the morning flight from Ciampino and Citto moved back into the building in the hope of seeing Sharlie. There were half a dozen journalists who had hitched an unauthorized lift down from Rome, all of them making a beeline for the telephones, anxious no doubt to arrange a passage to the scene of disaster. Sharlie was behind them, unshaven, definitely leaner and hungrier, but still carrying the

same battered plastic bag of cameras and lenses. Sharlie
Barzizza. Barzizza had been just a kid when they'd first known
each other, Citto a young cub reporter and the boy another
potential delinquent from the Catania waterfront, until he had
discovered his natural talent photographing a street fight with
a stolen camera. Citto had placed the pictures with his newspaper and thereafter shared stories with him, using him for the
paper whenever the staff photographers were unavailable.
Nine months ago they had climbed the mountain together and
Sharlie had made big money with his pictures of the exploding
crater and the lava flow. After that he had bought new cameras
and gone north to make his fortune in Rome.

The boy wasn't waiting at the baggage counter. The camera
case and one duffle bag were always, as Citto remembered, his
only companions. Citto caught up with him outside: 'Sharlie!'

The boy turned, the look in his eyes defensive until he saw
who it was.

'Were you in the middle of another job?' Citto asked.

There was the slightest hesitation before the boy replied. He
had, thought Citto, contemplated telling an untruth. But he
grinned instead and said no. Citto guessed that things in Rome
hadn't been going too well. The Levis were threadbare, his
shoes splitting.

Sharlie laughed again. 'I just jumped on the plane and came
as I am.' He had seen Citto's once-over up-and-down assessment
of his appearance. He indicated his clothes. 'I didn't have time
to change.'

The other journalists were moving from the telephones and
towards them at the door. Citto drew Sharlie aside. 'I've got a
ride up on to the mountain.'

Sharlie was still defensive. 'What's your deal?'

He wouldn't have asked that question nine months ago. He
wasn't believing his good luck. That was another sign of hard
times.

'Just a friendly thought,' Citto replied. 'You give us first
refusal on the pictures – and me ten per cent if you make your
million out of them.'

'A million?' Sharlie laughed. 'I could do with a couple of
thousand right now.'

'You still got a chance. No one's been in there yet, not as far as I know, and the first good pictures out are going to sell all round the world.'

'What's the ride?'

'Army helicopter. A friend of a friend. A favour returned for favours past received.'

'Whereabouts on the mountain?'

'Somewhere between the Citelli and the Val del Bove.'

'Rough country.'

'That's why no one can get in and out, except by air.'

Christ, thought Sharlie. I hope I don't run out of film.

7

The interior of the plane was dark and cramped and hot and stinking, and Tino G.'s midriff still trapped tight in an inter-locked maze of seat frames. It felt to the boy as though his body was being held together by that wreckage and he was convinced that when they finally freed him his various components would fall apart like a broken machine. At least his two extremities had been freed and his breathing was now easier. The Italian doctor was still with him, encouraging him now to talk and keep himself conscious. Tino G. had been telling him about the journey, remembering everything in the clearest detail, sur-prising himself with his own clarity of mind. He had thought that after accidents people were meant to forget things.

They had left from Kennedy in a big DC-10, plush and ugly, like the inside of a large and badly designed cinema. They were pushed out somewhere in England in the middle of the night. Like refugees they'd been treated while they waited for a delayed connection, abandoned in a large airport hall with no-where to sit and children crying and mothers going bananas and the bar shut up for the night until they made a big enough fuss. Then in the second plane a pretty girl hostess fixed him a drink and told him to sing because she saw the guitar. So he'd sung them a pair of his own songs and earned himself another drink from the Brooklyn family in the seats behind him. That was the family with the little girl who'd been playing hide and seek while they came down to land. The pretty hostess had to go looking for her because they were all meant to be strapped in. Then something happened and they were climbing again, flying all ways it seemed. People were getting scared. There was a storm, they said. Then they came out of the cloud and it was clear and there was a big red sun rising out of the sea. All the people in the aeroplane started clapping. 'The sun was so big and round and perfect,' said Tino. 'And such a colour. Like a hole in the world.' Then down they fell again and there was the pretty girl sliding around and other people screaming. And then the bangs. He had been sitting facing backwards with the guitar between his knees and the force of the crash had broken the seat and the belt so he tipped back heels over head. After that he couldn't move no more.

Tino G. was freed at midday. He cried out once with pain when they finally moved him, and old Turi swore at the men to be careful. The boy had been bent double but his back was not broken and they unfolded him slowly on to a stretcher. His midriff was a mass of wood splinters and blood. Turi couldn't make out what had caused the damage until one of the other men produced one half of a smashed guitar from the sandwich of wreckage.

Turi had been with the boy for three hours and he stayed with the stretcher now as they scrambled it up the lava slope to the waiting helicopter. At first the boy had looked about him, at the world outside that dark nightmare of wreckage and bodies: at the sky; at trees; at the shape of a mountainside; at the sweating, tired faces watching him. But before the helicopter took off Turi could see the boy's consciousness fading, the colour of his skin changing, and a sudden mist of sweat over his face. Turi held the helicopter two minutes while they put the boy on a saline drip, and then told the pilot to make for the nearest town at the foot of the mountain. It was a smaller hospital, inadequately staffed and equipped, but they would lose another twenty minutes flying him into the city. Something had gone badly wrong. After six hours of great resilience the boy had suddenly relapsed into deep shock. Probably one of those splinters, Turi thought, shifted by the inevitably crude movements of rescue and causing some bad haemorrhage inside him. It was almost impossible now to find the boy's pulse. The heart was racing and the blood pressure very low. One of the medics was holding the boy's legs high and Turi using the oxygen mask on him. The co-pilot radioed details of the boy's condition and police stopped traffic in the streets outside the hospital to make a landing area for the helicopter.

Turi knew the waiting surgeon – a competent man by local standards, but elderly, and already exhausted with emergency operations on earlier survivors from the crash. At least they'd organized a roomful of potential blood donors to cover all but the more obscure blood groups, and the elderly surgeon had opened the boy up within five minutes of arrival to find the suspected haemorrhage. A lacerated liver, they told Turi as he left the hospital. Turi wondered if it wouldn't have been wiser to take the risk of the longer journey and go for the larger hospitals in the city.

He walked out into the hot sunlight and returned in a taxi to his village and his own patients neglected since that early morning.

Turi need have had no qualms about his decision. There were twenty-nine casualties from Tango November in the larger city hospitals but only three qualified doctors to cope with them. An offer of medical assistance from a NATO base had been rejected earlier in the day by hospital administrators unwilling to admit inadequacies in their weekend staffing arrangements. Of the twenty-nine victims four had already died, and twenty-three were 'critical' or 'dying'. The two exceptions were the air hostess, Stella Pritchard, and the young girl found with her, neither of them yet conscious of their good fortune.

8

Thirty miles away up the coast five men were gathering for lunch on a restaurant terrace overlooking one of the small bays to the north of Taormina.

The youngest of them, a fleshy moist face, was the last to arrive, announcing himself with a roar of green and orange sports car and a swirl of gravel. Flavio Consoli had changed his oil-stained suède jacket for a white suit, the combination of white suit, black eyebrows and dark red hair silencing a table of young American women as he passed by. He turned to look at the women each in turn before joining the other four men on the edge of the terrace. His father, the Avvocato Consoli, was the only one to nod a welcome. Two of the others were politicians who had been driving since early morning to make the meeting. They were not tolerant of unpunctuality in the young. The fifth man was obviously a subordinate. He sat apart from the others keeping his silence until he was asked to talk. When he did speak it was in a low but very clear voice, a voice used to making itself immediately understood. Captain Duckham would have recognized the voice of the Air Traffic Controller from the tower at Taormina-Peloritana.

He answered questions about events that morning, describing in detail the conversations he had had with the crew up until the moment he had given clearance for landing.

'And the airport instruments were all functioning?'

The controller shrugged. 'There was a bad storm. ADF beacons without a VOR – that's all there is. They could have been all over the shop.'

'That's just a theory.'

'Yes sir.'

One of the politicians joined in. 'You are sure about the ground conditions?'

'Visibility was marginal. It was up to the pilot to decide.'

Avvocato Consoli had a suggestion. 'It is a possibility that this plane was in fact nowhere near the airport. If its own instruments were at fault, for example.'

The ATC shook his head. 'The plane passed right overhead. I don't know what happened. I think he went for the factories.'

The Avvocato stood up from the table. 'Another of your theories. I'd be grateful if you kept them to yourself.'

Just how 'grateful' was explained to the Air Traffic Controller as Avvocato Consoli walked him back to the waiting airport car.

When the Avvocato returned to the lunch-table he did his

best to reassure two nervous politicians. 'The young man will not misbehave.'

One of the politicians smiled. 'That's obvious. It's Rome I'm more worried about.'

'I've spoken with Rome this morning.' Consoli poured wine for them all. 'Rome will be all right. The Ministry's short-handed. Their senior investigators are all out on a couple of military crashes up north. They can only send technicians.'

'Where does that leave the investigation?'

'In our court. The technicians will come. But our local Procuratore is holding the reins, with one of his older Magistrates.'

'The Americans and English will be sending investigators.'

'They won't be down till tomorrow. And they can only work on what evidence is available. If I make myself clear.'

'What about flight recorders?'

'We can be confident that flight recorders will not be found on this occasion.'

Waiters served lunch, but only young Flavio seemed interested, attacking his shellfish risotto with delighted appetite. Silence was broken once during the meal as a train passed on the single-line track below the restaurant terrace. Under the noise it made, the two politicians alone could hear what the Avvocato had to say.

'We're lucky the plane crashed where it did. The Procuratore in Catania is a personal friend.'

The politicians nodded. The implications of such a friendship did not need elaboration.

They passed from pasta and rice to fish; from fish to fruit; from fruit to coffee, Flavio slowing with his digestion, his eyes dulled like those of a satiated python. Then as his father paid the waiter, Flavio asked a question across the table.

'I don't understand how you can be so certain about the flight recorders. Surely they would show if the plane went for the factories?'

No one bothered to answer him.

The Avvocato and one of the politicians departed in a chauffeur-driven car on a mission of persuasion to Messina, the second politician in the opposite direction home to Palermo. Consoli's fleshy young son watched them drive away, then tipped the car-park attendant to look after his sports car until the evening. Flavio had seen the four young American women grouped around a sun umbrella on the beach below the railway.

9

For all his preparations and intuition Avvocato Consoli had been mistaken in two of his assumptions. Both American and British investigation teams were already on their way to the scene of disaster – the Americans courtesy of a hastily improvised USAF proving flight; the British courtesy of Greyhound Flight (Europe).

In the absence of a standby aircraft of their own the Greyhound Flight Manager had chartered a BAC-One-Eleven for the ninety stranded passengers still waiting to return from Malta in Tango November. This relief plane had been routed via Sicily to convey company representatives to the crash, and travel facilities on the plane had also been offered to the Accident Investigation Branch of the Department of Trade and Industry: Ralph Burden with two AIB Engineers; and, if they arrived in time, an RAF pathologist from Halton, his aassistant, and two operatives from a London firm of undertakers specializing in the identification of aircrash victims.

Take-off had been delayed to wait for the medical team and in the interval a box of files had been delivered to the plane by the Greyhound Safety Officer – personnel details of the Tango November crew. Access to such files was now the legal right of the official investigation, and Burden, as accredited British representative, signed a receipt.

Pink and blue the files; hostesses and flight crew. Burden opened each file quickly and briefly: Pilot Officer Peter Nyren; Flight Engineer George Raven. Burden knew neither name. He looked at the photographs in the cabin crew files. Pretty girls all of them, in neat tight jackets and buttoned skirts. The Captain's file was underneath.

Michael Edward Duckham. The shock of recognition froze Burden for a moment. He looked again for the details. They were unmistakable. Duckham, M. E., born 1922. 'Dixie' Duckham, no more, no less. D.S.O., D.F.C. with two bars. 23 Squadron: one-time hard-drinking, womanizing crown prince of north Norfolk. The absolute fighter-pilot prototype, prematurely lined young face, sunken eyes, and a head that never stopped moving side to side over each shoulder like a nervous bird. Definitely an image for the adulation of younger members of the Squadron. Burden did not need the filed photograph to picture him. 'Dixie' Duckham. You silly old sod, he thought, breaking all rules of objectivity. You come all that way and through all that war and down all these years, just to fly into a ruddy mountain half a step short of retirement. I should walk off this job, Burden thought. Telephone the chief. Tell him I know this Duckham. Or knew him. The chief wouldn't worry about that, though. It was thirty years ago. You don't know people any more after thirty years.

'Your colleague has arrived, sir.' The steward was leaning over him. Burden looked at his watch and out of the window at his elbow. They were two minutes off the promised departure time and Mac Pherson had appeared trotting briskly across the apron, an Indian assistant trailing behind him with a heavy instrument case. Even the journalists hushed as Pherson banged loudly up the steps and into the cabin. He entered bearded and huge and announced himself, as was his habit, in thunderous tones: 'Dr Pherson.' He grinned as he saw Burden. 'Bloody man put the chopper down in some field wrong side of the motorway.'

Burden stood up, bent under the luggage rack, to shake hands. 'Good of you to break a weekend, Mac.'

Pherson subsided into the gangway seat and kicked himself backwards with his feet testing the seat mountings. 'Hope this rotten little soap-box doesn't fall.' He turned to Burden. 'Couldn't find a dentist. He'll fly out tomorrow. What's the story?'

Burden passed him the sheet of notes attached to his formal authorization. They summarized the circumstances of the accident: hour, date, place, company, plane –

'Another 119? Time they grounded the bloody things.'

His silent Indian assistant installed himself in the seat across the gangway.

'That's Sanju. He's training with us,' Mac explained, not very *sotto voce*. 'Jolly bright little chap. Do him good to see a bit of blood.'

The plane moved and Ralph Burden stared out at the tarmac as the One-Eleven taxied to take-off. He remembered suddenly the judder-tail grass track take-off of the Little Snoring Mosquitoes. It was Dixie Duckham who had led Burden into the night sky on Burden's first active mission, talking him into position as Ralph strained to keep the silhouette of the other plane in sight. 'Take it easy, sonny' . . . the two years' difference of age in those days had been a lifetime. 'Drop her back. I know you love me. But you're more than halfway up my backside.'

Mac was busy telling Burden some story. Women or booze. Ralph heard not a word. While Sussex dropped away below them Ralph felt instead the dancing tracer of a Junkers smacking through the fuselage below him, and heard Duckham's voice shouting in his headset: 'Left foot down! Throw it around!' Burden had been paralysed with fear, frozen in the sky. The voice afterwards had been sweet and acid: 'You got three lives up here, sonny and you just lost two of them.'

Michael Edward Duckham, Fleet Captain for Greyhound Flight Europe. Age fifty-three, 18711 hours' flying time. 779 days of his life in the air, one twenty-seventh part of his living to date.

Ralph Burden's mathematical brain could cope with statistics in a file, but was not sure it yet wanted to reconstruct memories of this one-time fellow combatant. A pilot always has a reasonable chance in a forced landing with a better seat and a better harness than the poor old passengers. Come this evening, Burden was thinking, and I might be talking to Duckham in a hospital bed.

But the One-Eleven Captain came on to the public address two hours into the flight and put an end to wishful thinking. 'There has been a message on our company radio regarding the list of casualties. The dead are now estimated at around one hundred and sixty. That includes all members of the flight crew.'

A few minutes later the One-Eleven Captain appeared in the cabin and introduced himself to Burden and Pherson, leaning over the empty row of seats in front of them: 'Dixie Duckham wasn't it?'

Burden nodded. 'You know him?'

'Met him once or twice. Nice man.'

'No more indications of what happened?'

The Captain shook his head. 'Nothing that we've heard.'

'Do you know the airport?' Burden asked him.

'I've been in and out most of the summer. You'd better come and sit in with us. Get the general layout. Though it seems they're trying to divert us.'

'Any reason?'

'I expect they'll close the field for a few days. They get a bit hysterical after an accident, you know, shutting everybody up in prison and impounding everything. That's what it's like in Spain anyhow. I pranged a car there once. You'd never believe the hoo-ha.' He stood up to go. 'You coming up front?'

Pherson shifted his bulk and his tray of breakfast sandwiches to let Burden squeeze past. 'Don't let this clown anywhere near the steering wheel,' laughed Mac. 'The last time he did it he dropped nine tons of dried milk into the sea.'

Burden followed the Captain forward, past the subdued Greyhound party, and through the end door into the cockpit. He shook hands with the P.2 and settled into the jump seat.

The Captain grinned over his shoulder at him. 'What did he mean, "dried milk"?'

'Dried milk and bananas. Vital military supplies. I put a Hastings down in the sea. One of the landing-strip islands in the middle of the Indian Ocean.'

The One-Eleven pilots wagged their heads sympathetically and asked no more questions. Burden's embarrassment was too obvious.

1953, Burden was thinking. A Hastings C.1 on a night flight from Singapore through the tail of a tropical storm and trying to land in the dark. Over-tired and blinded by the storm, the inquiry had suggested afterwards. Extenuating circumstances they'd been trying to give him and he had accepted it on day one of the inquiry. Day two, and after a night lying awake with his conscience, he had gone back and told them, thank you very much but such excuses were not really valid. It was error of judgement. Eventually he had worked it out for himself. The landing-strip ran straight off the beach without approach lights and the runway lighting cross-bars were accordingly shorter and fewer than normal. It had been a late night landing with no hut or hangar lights to give an alternative visual reference. Someone who didn't know the strip could assume they were higher than they really were on approach. On that particular occasion Burden's co-pilot had been sick from the storm and Burden had excused him the routine read-off of altitudes that would have told them something was wrong. They had 'landed' a hundred yards short of the beach, soft as a feather, with an hour to unload some of the bananas before the Hastings finally decided to sink. Not surprising that the prang and its diagnosis had obsessed Burden. It effectively ended his flying career. A couple of years later he had entered the AIB as a crash investigator.

'If you can't beat 'em, join 'em –' The One-Eleven Captain was grinning over his shoulder at him. Thought-reading. But the headphones called and Burden was spared further conversation.

Greyhound Special, Sierra Sierra. Turn right to one four zero to take up approach for Catania Fontanarossa. Taormina-Peloritana closing to commercial traffic from 14.00 hours.'

'*Roger Control. Our estimated time of touchdown at Taormina 13.50. Request permission to continue with approach. We are non-commercial with Government personnel on board.*'

The Captain winked at his First Officer. 'The weather's all right. They can't shut the door on us, not unless they park lorries across the runway.'

The headphones replied after a long delay. EEC or NATO goodwill had triumphed. '*Greyhound Special. Continue approach on one five zero for Taormina.*'

They were over the tiny volcanic islands around Stromboli, each island with its capping of cloud. Inland on Sicily they could see cumulus gathering against the north and west flanks of Etna. Burden scribbled on his note-pad: Kilo Lima at one one five. The checking-in point for the hold was at 11 500 feet over the Outer Marker beacon, giving a reasonable 700 feet and 25 kilometre clearance from the mountain. The descent pattern circled the Outer Marker and the approach turn swept eastwards out to sea and back over the coastline on heading 289°. The Outer Marker beacon was crossed for the final time 11 miles short of runway threshold at 5000 feet. The final approach followed a long valley, wild and rough with ridges and ravines, but the airport was over 2000 feet on a plateau at the end of the valley and the glide path 3000 feet clear of any danger. Distance from Etna was maintained throughout the approach at around 25 kilometres and high ground around the airport was no more of a problem than skyscrapers in a city approach. Considering the terrain it was a safer approach than many of the Alpine airports, or the seaside wind-traps at Naples and Palermo.

The runway was plainly visible from six miles out, wide and long, carved out of the plateau. It seemed that whole ridges had been flattened, slopes ironed out, ravines filled in, and the equivalent width of two or three motorways laid out over a length of two miles. Smaller taxiing roads led from either end of the runway to the airport buildings half a mile to one side. It had been an enormous feat of engineering at goodness knows what kind of astronomical cost.

The One-Eleven came in, dwarfed by the size of the landing area, the touchdown scarcely detectable on the smooth runway. A nice piece of Italian road-building, thought Burden.

'Feels lovely.'

'Perfect until it rains.' The Captain laughed. 'They forgot to put in any drainage. First time I landed here in the wet the water knocked two flaps off.'

They taxied round towards the buildings and Burden turned to the side window to keep the distant volcano in his view. It looked almost innocuous, the profile broken on one side with cloud and on the other side with smoke from the crater. It was only the near horizontal angle of the smoke that gave a clue as to the mountain's 11000 foot altitude and the extremes of wind and weather around its central craters. Burden wondered where on those slopes the crashed plane was lying.

The One-Eleven drew up by 'International Arrivals' as casually as a car drawing up outside a house. The ventral stair of the rear exit was down almost before they had stopped, and as Burden said good-bye to the pilots the two of them were already into their pre-take-off checks preparing for a swift turn-round.

The Captain gestured apologetically at Burden. 'If they're shutting up shop at 14.00 we've got six minutes.'

Burden closed the door on their activity. Cowboys, the computer half of his mind might have said of another crew, but he liked the way these two had flown, methodical, unfussed and good-humouredly arrogant. Definitely ex-RAF.

A wall of heat hit Burden on the stairs at the back of the plane. Ninety-three degrees in the shade, after fifty-six at Gatwick. A bronzed and shirt-sleeved Italian Air Force Captain was waiting for them with a helicopter on the apron.

They squatted on metal benches and took off one minute after the One-Eleven, Burden watching their 130-knot shadow as it moved like a tiny cloud over a hilltop village, a green valley of orange or lemon trees, eroded ridges, and the dried-up bed of a winter torrent. He'd never been on Sicily before. It had the scrubby white-rock biblical look of Crete or Cyprus. That is, until they came out on to the seaward slope of the volcano where, in contrast, the mountain contours were rich and green, endless cultivated terraces falling some fifteen miles down from the tree-line to the shore, chestnut woods on the higher slopes, citrus, vineyards and a multitude of villages lower down. To the north of the mountain and perched above the sea Burden identified the hilltop resort of Taormina from his map. To the south where the land flattened the coast was dominated by the city sprawl of Catania. The Italian Captain touched his arm and pointed.

'Taormina –' The rest of the words were lost to Burden, but the Captain was gesturing bed and sleep with his face against the palm of one hand. Taormina was presumably to be their accommodation base. It looked an unhealthy long way from the scene of operations.

They were under the volcano now, rising evenly with the slope like a gigantic cable-car.

'Lava!' A sudden bellow from further back in the hold where Mac was gesturing like an excited schoolboy stabbing a finger at a window. They were passing over a black corrugated ridge of solidified lava that had flowed in some recent eruption from high on the mountain bisecting and burying everything in its pyramid-shaped path. The pilot swung away momentarily to show them where the lava had changed course, surrounding but not quite entering the highest of the mountain villages.

'*La Madonna!*' The pilot shouted back at them with a smile. Whether the tone was deprecating or adoring Burden could not tell. The Captain explained that the village priest had marched out to meet the advancing lava with the Madonna and the statue of the Patron Saint from the church. The lava had obediently altered course and only one house had been destroyed.

Burden called across to the Captain. 'How high is the crash?'

The Captain showed him the spot marked on the map. 'A thousand six hundred metres.' Over 5000 feet.

'Like so—' The Captain described the attitude of the wreckage pointing southwards, tangential to the mountain, and about eighteen to twenty miles distant from the airport. A long way off course on any possible approach or overshoot.

A road moved into sight below them, zigzagging through the chestnut woods, glittering and moving like a river. A road jammed solid with vehicles reflecting in the sunlight. It was a sudden shock to see so many shining cars in such a lonely place and Burden remembered the time it had taken the AIB inspectors to work through the queues of sightseers on the evening of the Trident disaster at Staines. Sure enough the jam below them was interspersed with the occasional flashing blue lamp of an immobilized police or Red Cross car. Columns of coloured human ants wound and undulated through the lava ridges and the trees – the sightseers from the cars. But the crashed plane was too far for them to reach on foot and by the time the helicopter banked round to land the countryside was once more bare and uninhabited.

Burden caught a glimpse of the wreckage before they descended: a trail of damaged woodland and the plane fairly compact, still more or less contained within its natural length and width. A low-speed crash. On the lava slope above it white sheets had been laid to mark the only vaguely horizontal patch of ground clear of the trees. The Vertol put down slowly to join the other two helicopters already on the site.

The elderly Magistrato, hot, tired and ill at ease, met them with his attendant Carabinieri. He was unsure how to treat these new arrivals and whilst he could realize the importance of their technical inquiry, he still felt he had to safeguard the priority of his own legal investigation. He warned them through an interpreter that no technical evidence was to be removed from the site, and told Mac that all pathology and identification would have to be done under police supervision. But at least Mac's status was not queried. The Italians had not yet found a local pathologist prepared to take charge of the 170 bodies.

The Magistrato detailed Carabinieri to keep an eye on the Englishmen, then clambered thankfully into a helicopter and left the site to return to his office in the city.

Burden and his party paused on the ridge above the crashed plane to film the general picture before moving in closer. The plane had hit a low ridge of lava that protruded from the general woodland and scrub. The fuselage had split on the major bulkhead just forward of the wing, the front half shunting up at an angle along the gradient of the ridge, the rear half grounded and badly fragmented on the lava. The left side wing had disintegrated in the trees just prior to the main wreckage, and the right side wing was broken into four sections scattered over the lava ridge. The attitude of flight seemed to have been left wing low, and the grounded fuselage was tilted at that same angle. A hundred-yard trail of wreckage and luggage stretched out behind the tail where the lava protrusions had ripped the cargo holds under the cabin floor as the plane slid to its final position. The fire had started at the rear of the cabin where roof and walls had been destroyed but had worked forward with steadily decreasing effect until by the wing section there was little evidence of burning. The T N of Tango November were the two surviving if blistered registration letters at the root of the tail. Golf Foxtrot and Echo had disappeared with the central engine through the fuselage and into the blackened ruins. Only the twin-tone magenta-and-black Greyhound strip remained unmarked rising with that high white soaring tail towards the unshattered unburnt rudder and stabilizers thirty feet above. Forward of the fire and the break the cabin was relatively intact except for the odd buckling and peeling of fuselage skins. But the sharp end was hopelessly smashed, a telescoped broken nose of cockpit piled at all angles into the lava. Somewhere in there, thought Burden, is whatever is left of Dixie Duckham.

Citto and Sharlie watched the new arrivals from the juniper scrub twenty yards or so above the wrecked plane. Sharlie was changing a film in his camera, and Citto scribbling notes for a paragraph of prose that he hoped would accompany some of his friend's pictures.

'So different from a car crash,' he had written. 'The car is intimate, the smashed car an obscene reminder of how near we all are to sudden death or disfigurement. The broken airplane instead is the shattering of a myth; the frailty of an apparently infallible technical sophistication, a reminder, for those who need reminding, that only birds can really fly.'

The two of them had been there now for nearly three hours, virtual stowaways on a military helicopter, and tolerated only so long as they kept their distance from the wreck. Official access to journalists had not yet been granted, and with the arrival of the investigators, journalists were not likely to be admitted until tomorrow. Which gave Sharlie an eighteen-hour advantage with his pictures. He had taken over ninety exposures of the plane from all possible angles and their tame Air Force pilot had told them he'd be leaving in ten minutes' time.

Citto was watching the investigators. They had unloaded themselves and their baggage from the helicopter and were pulling boots and boiler-suits over their clothes before they moved down the slope towards the wreckage. They were all a bit wild, as befitted mad Englishmen. There was a tall bearded giant of a man striding out with great ferocity, a turbanned Indian shadowing him like a slave; but the boss here was undoubtedly the old worn face with the thin mouth and the sharp eyes, peering about him with great suspicion as though he expected to find the wreckage already desecrated.

Police, soldiers, Air Force personnel and the two truant journalists all watched as the Englishmen, clown-like in boots and boiler-suits, split up around the broken-backed fuselage. They seemed like a parody of anxious tourists with their bags of camera equipment and their haste for pictures. One of them perched suddenly with pad and pencil like a sketch artist in a ruined temple.

Above them the cloud crept lower and the sun disappeared.

Lunch-time and afternoon news on Italian radio and television emphasized the presence of that fourth body on the flight deck of the doomed plane. It was generally assumed, with the usual reservations, that the crash had somehow resulted from an attempted hi-jacking. Terrorist specialists were already on their way south from London and Munich, dispatched by Scotland Yard and Interpol. Though there had been no exchange of views and no collusion it was nonetheless clear to various authorities in Rome, and subsequently in Catania, that a 'hi-jacking' solution would satisfy many influential parties. After all an aeroplane, an airport and a major charter flight company were all at stake.

'Naturally it's pilot error,' said one off-the-record voice on a telephone conversation from an unnamed embassy. 'But I'm sure you'll find the poor guy had someone's gun stuck in his back.'

Early indications suggested there would be no straightforward solution to this particular 'incident'. Left alone it would end up as one of those half-explained crashes. A little innocent arm-twisting here and there was instinctive and inevitable.

A helicopter pilot was rung later that afternoon by the Avvocato Consoli.

'Have,' the Avvocatoa wondered, 'any oranges been found?'

'Both of them found and both disposed of,' he was assured. 'Dropped from a great height into impenetrable undergrowth.'

Consoli thanked the pilot, assured him that his work would not be forgotten, and privately hoped that the man had chosen undergrowth well away from any road or mountain path.

One trail of evidence had already been laid, albeit unwittingly, by a dirty black oil-tanker parked on the outskirts of a small town in the valley below the airport.

Citto was hurrying with Sharlie and his rolls of film to a dark-room in Catania, but when he saw the lorry he stopped for a closer look. It was pulled up on a wide dirt sidewalk. Citto walked round it, sniffing at the off-loading pipes coiled untidily along the chassis. It smelt like petrol. Certainly not the kerosene that fuelled jet engines.

Sharlie joined him on the pavement. 'You want a picture of that thing?'

'With the number-plates.'

'Breaking some law is it?'

'It was up at the airport this morning.'

'So?'

Citto grinned and shrugged. 'I'm just a compulsive collector of useless information.' He picked up a scrap of paper lying in the gutter and rubbed oil and dust from the offside door to reveal the owner's name: 'ETNOLIO, Fuel Distributor', with an address in one of the larger villages on the slopes of the volcano.

It would have been an exaggeration at this stage for Citto to have claimed a theory. But there were two small details beginning to nag him: this lorry on its refuelling mission that early morning, and those dead clocks set on 05.40 in the airport buildings. Tango November had crashed, they had been told, 'some time between 05.35 and 05.50'.

I I

Passengers though they were, the 'go team' from Washington crossed the Atlantic the hard way with oxygen masks and on hard sit-up USAF scanners' seats. And for all their trusty official positions they were politely kept off the flight deck throughout the five hours from Washington to Taormina. The bomber and its equipment were far too hush-hush. The only concession to their job in hand was on landing approach at Taormina when they were given visibility through a side window and the letdown procedure was relayed on their intercom.

Not that the Colonel had been anything but courteous. He seemed to Larry Raille a very senior man to be flying an ordinary transport mission, and it was plain he had higher priorities than driving on this particular trip. In fact he spent a long time with Raille back in the radar hutch making a rather bad hash of a psyching job, talking at great length of the many virtues of the 119 – 'the most important sub-Jumbo medium-range transport in the history of aviation; the standard multi-purpose plane for the 1980s.'

'No need to worry about the Italian officials,' said the Colonel with a nod and a wink at Raille's impassive face. 'They want to extend their manufacturing licence on military helicopters. They're not going to play Jack and the Beanstalk with us.'

The Colonel could have saved his breath. Raille, a very non-political animal, was concerned only that the lecture had effectively ruined any chance he might have had of sleeping.

His two 'go-team' colleagues had slept heads down on the chart table. They were all of them bleary and tired when they stumbled down the ladder on to the blazing afternoon tarmac at Taormina-Peloritana.

Cloud was still creeping contour by contour down the mountain, and all but one of the helicopters had been withdrawn. Apart from the Carabinieri and an Air Force salvage team Burden's men were alone, scattered over Tango November still photographing , annotating or sketching on their pads. Burden was in the burnt-out tail section of cabin, his face covered with a mask against the smell, showing two groups of Carabiniere how to label the carbonized bodies, how to plot their position on a plan, how to roll up the remains intact into plastic sheets.

Pherson was doing a similar job with the unburnt bodies in the forward cabin helped by the silent and ever attentive Sanju. They were working as fast as they could in the cramped conditions unravelling the jumble of human and structural debris, plotting each tiny piece of aircraft, body, or clothing on to a plan, trying to penetrate into the cockpit area for the evacuation of the bodies inside. They had been told that the local doctor who had supervised the morning's rescue operation had arranged temporary facilities for autopsy and cold storage in a nearby village and Mac wanted to begin pathology on the flight crew that same night before deterioration had progressed too far.

It was after two hours of work that he finally called out to Burden: 'I think we've found your buddy, old man.' He led Ralph on hands and knees into the dark cavern of wreckage that had once been the flight deck. The windows were lost in folds of the crumpled fuselage and Mac was using lamps to illuminate the salvage. Burden saw both pilots from behind, still strapped in, their heads at odd angles and crammed down into their seats so that they seemed like stunted dwarfs. The cockpit had shrunk, stove in on three sides, and the two men were embraced grotesquely by the instrument panels and controls.

'No point in looking at him,' Mac told Burden. 'There's nothing much left of his face.' Mac gave him instead Duckham's passport, and Burden nodded recognition of the photograph. He stared at the back of that head and neck: the hair was thick but greying, curled round below the ears, the remains of a headset hanging loose. Burden retreated from Duckham's death.

'Looks to me as though he knew he was coming down,' said Mac. 'His hands and feet are right for landing. And he went for his fire levers.'

Burden nodded again. He was seeing a young fighter pilot barely twenty years old at the end of an evening's briefing, left hand held high with his navigator's right as the crews walked out and separated to their planes. He was hearing Dixie Duckham's voice calling to them all in the darkness: 'We all have to die and we only die once. Enjoy it, my friends.'

Somewhere above them a helicopter was manoeuvring slowly out of the cloud, the Vertol carrying the American investigators. Burden climbed down from the wreckage turning up the slope to meet them, his mind still trying to relate the image of the twenty-year-old fighter pilot with the grey-haired body in Tango November. He heard his name called and came out of his dream. He saw Larry Raille on the lava above him and he waved a greeting.

He'd never worked with Raille but he'd met him at a couple

of ICAO conferences in Montreal – a 'jigsaw' and 'crossword' man who loved the fitting together of evidence and the satisfaction of reconstruction.

'Any miracles?' Raille asked.

'It's going to be a bastard,' said Burden.

'No clues?'

'Not even a recorder.'

'Broken?'

'If they're still under the tail they're smashed. And if they're not in the tail they've been pinched by the local sheriff.'

'Any Italians from their Air Ministry?'

'They haven't got a team together yet. They've only sent a few technicians. I'm afraid that means the local judiciary have rather taken over.'

They picked their slow way down the slope towards the wreckage. Raille gestured with one hand, miming the landing approach of a plane. 'Low speed, and all set for landing. Was it still dark?'

Burden laughed without humour. 'You won't believe it, but no one really knows what the visibility was like. It wasn't dark, but there could have been cloud cover.'

The investigators gathered by the crashed remains of the flight deck, Mac towering over all of them as he climbed down from the wreckage. Burden and Raille agreed on the composition of groups and read out their deployment of manpower. The Italians themselves would organize and man the groups investigating weather, air traffic services, and the post-mortem on evacuation and rescue. Witness statements would be collated by a combined team. Raille would be in charge of site investigation and specifically attached to systems group. The examination of structure, power plant, and maintenance records would be largely made up by specialist engineers from the manufacturers concerned, due to arrive next day, and they would come under Raille's general supervision. Mac was in charge of human factors group, the aero-medical and crash injury aspects of the investigation. Burden was to head operations group, investigating the history of the doomed flight and flight crew. Again Ralph Burden wondered if he shouldn't opt out of that particular job. Memories of Dixie Duckham had seemed to hang over him all day like ghosts of ill omen.

Raille was asking Mac about the bodies of the flight-deck crew and the supposed hi-jacker.

'Give us another hour and we'll have them out tonight.'

'Maybe you need some more men?'

Mac shook his head. 'There's only room in there for two of us.' He turned back up his ladder to rejoin Sanju in the tangled remains of the cockpit.

The other men were breaking up in twos and threes around the wreckage forming the groups within which they'd be working for the next few days. The two chief investigators walked together back along the slide of wreckage and down into the avenue of splintered trees, Raille busy with his camera clicking off a methodical round-the-clock picture of the whole disaster area.

The avenue of damaged scrub and woodland tapered away to their right as they faced it from the tail of the plane.

Burden described an angle with one forearm: 'Left wing down. The line of damage on the outside of the arc is very regular – until the wing breaks. It must have been in one heck of a turn.'

'Away from the mountain.'

'We're at five thousand feet here. That's the check-in altitude on the Outer Marker. He could have been at normal approach height on a correct heading and the only thing wrong being he was fifteen miles too far to the south. He comes out of the cloud, sees where he is, tries to bank, and he can't make it.'

'Anything's possible at the moment.'

'It'll be damn near anyone's guess if we don't find a flight recorder.'

'You really think the Magistrate pinched it?'

'We didn't get here till after two o'clock. They had time enough to find it.'

'Why would they do that?'

'To let everyone know how important they are.'

They reached the end of splintered death row and turned to view the distant plane.

'Poor son of a bitch,' said Raille. 'He must have seen what was happening to be turning like that.'

Dixie Duckham, thought Burden. Trying to fight his way out of the mountain.

12

The elderly Magistrato, sticky and dirty from the scene of disaster, was back in his office reading up textbooks and old reports. But there were few precedents for him to draw on and no colleagues along empty Saturday afternoon corridors to share the burden.

The Magistrato in the next room would have been the ideal choice today – a young man from the north who had done his national service in the Air Force. Turin he came from, and he was appropriately self-confident and energetic. So after two hours at a deskful of books and papers the elderly Magistrato rang him at his home, with apologies, suggesting his participation: 'Your technical experience could be useful.'

The younger man agreed. He was not one for false modesty.

Disgruntled representatives of the world press were gathered in the bar at Catania Fontanarossa Airport, their numbers growing with the arrival of each flight. Notwithstanding the chaos of extra traffic diverted by the closure of Taormina-Peloritana the authorities had set up their press office at the airport and what little information existed was being released there. Access to the crash site was promised the next morning and there seemed nothing more to do except wait. The few intrepids who had set out cross country by car and by foot returned defeated; the flying of private planes and helicopters had been banned in the area until further notice; short of parachuting off the top of the mountain there was no way of reaching Tango November.

They had been allowed to question the men in charge of the rescue operation and at the end of the afternoon the Air Traffic Officer who had been on duty in the control tower was also produced to read a statement.

It had been, he assured them, an entirely normal and satisfactory landing approach until the final moments before touchdown, when the plane had seemed to veer away. After that he had had no further communication with the pilot. There had been no Mayday call and the coded 'hi-jack' signal had not been used. Visibility at the time had been poor but quite safe – cloud cover at 1000 feet, and runway visibility at 900 yards.

The statement did not quite coincide with what the officer had told Consoli and the politicians at lunch-time. Nor was it a completely full account of what had happened that early morning. But the journalists were not given a chance of elaborating on the statement. It was regretted, explained an Air Force officer, that since the Traffic Controller was a military official, he could not be allowed to answer their questions.

Cameras and lights were switched off and the journalists turned back to the bar muttering darkly about the evasive Italians.

Sharlie's pictures had come out well. He had used the dark-room at the newspaper office, giving them in return, and as Citto had suggested, the first and free choice of pictures. Thirty of the best exposures had then been sent on the wires to Rome where an agency would sell them for Sharlie to newspapers and magazines all round the world. On the phone the agency had been disappointingly cool. After all the boy had never made much money for them before. 'You're probably too late,' they warned him. 'Someone else is bound to have got something out.'

Sharlie tried to shrug it off in the car afterwards. 'Bloody hell! I thought at least I'd get a pair of new jeans out of it.' He pulled Citto's driving mirror round to look at himself. 'The family's going to be surprised. I mean turning up like a tramp when I've been writing them how well I was doing.'

Citto retrieved his driving mirror. 'I'm sure they're not going to bother much about your clothes.'

Sharlie's mother had not been home at her two-room tenement on the waterfront, and without a key the boy was stuck. Citto was driving him out to his grandmother's place in one of the fishing villages under the mountain.

'You didn't have to bring me all out here.'

'What would you do? Sleep on the pavement?'

'My mum'll come back sometime.'

'She's gone off for the weekend.'

'Where?'

'How should I know? It's *vendemmia*. She's probably picking grapes somewhere.'

They drove on in silence past the lumps of the Cyclops standing forlorn in a yacht-pocked sea. Polyphemus and Odysseus – both would have chosen blindness in the face of this twentieth-century riviera ribboning unplanned and unbeautiful along the coast, Citto was thinking.

'I told her I was going to send her money,' said Sharlie. He was still thinking about his mother. 'I never had enough to send.' He laughed. '*Paparazzo!* They're all Romans. Like a bloody Mafia. No room for new boys. And she thought I was going to make my fortune.'

Sharlie's mum was a working woman. A tough little lady fighting her life on a factory floor somewhere out near the city airport. A widow, Citto wondered? 'My father was a sailor,' Sharlie had told him long ago. But the 'was' had never been explained.

This grandmother out in the fishing village came from the father's side. Nonna Lisa. She lived in an old fisherman's house on the black lava rocks a stone's throw from the sea: a pergola courtyard, one room for cooking and eating, and two rooms for sleeping. Washing was done behind a curtain in the courtyard. Her husband had been a fisherman and these few square yards of habitation had been her world for fifty years. Her only son had been Sharlie's sailor father, and her daughters were variously married in the fishing villages along the coast, or the farming villages higher on the mountain. The children of one of them were here now, a teenage son and daughter and two younger kids, and when Sharlie walked in he was welcomed back with a great shouting and laughing which Citto watched smiling from the car.

The boy needn't have been self-conscious about his clothes. They were all far too surprised to see him to worry about what he was wearing. But Sharlie was still worrying. When they were hauled off to admire a cousin's new motor-bike Citto could see the despair of desire and envy behind Sharlie's raptures. It was a 900 cc Desmo Ducati with drop bars and a fancy black and red paint job on the tank – the fastest beast on two wheels that ordinary money could buy. Even Citto felt a pang for it, but then Citto had long ago persuaded himself that he had the wrong physical shape for bikes.

'Do you like motor-bikes as well?'

Citto turned round. It was Sharlie's girl cousin who had spoken, taking him so much by surprise that he didn't even answer her question. She looked at the motor-bike with disapproval.

'It's a crazy way to spend money.' The girl was very slim and serious with a long El Greco face, and Citto watched her in amazement. Where had she come from? A couple of years ago he used to visit here but there'd only been kids running around. She smiled at him.

'You're Citto.'

'I'm afraid I don't know you,' he stammered in reply.

'I'm Laura. I remember you used to come out with Sharlie. You were on the mountain the time he took the pictures.'

Sharlie interrupted, glad of an excuse to turn himself away from the motor-bike. 'We've been up on the mountain today. I'm working for a big magazine,' he said flamboyantly. 'They sent me down to cover the crash. I had to leave in a hurry. That's why I've come without presents.'

Why was he lying, the clown? There was no point.

The girl looked at Citto. 'Have you seen the aeroplane?'

'Yes.'

'Is it terrible?'

'It is sad to see it – I mean if you think aeroplanes are beautiful it is sad to see one so smashed.' He was still stammering like a fool.

'And the people?'

'I didn't see the people.' Citto couldn't take his eyes off her. She was so grave.

She turned back to Sharlie. 'Turi was up there.'

'Who's Turi?' asked Citto.

'Our doctor at home. We live up on the mountain. He was called to help in the rescue.'

'What's his full name?'

'Turi Pennisi.'

'And which is your village?'

'You're not to go and see him and ask a lot of questions. He won't like that.'

Sharlie interrupted. 'It's the same village where your dirty black oil-tanker came from.'

'He won't help you,' said the girl. 'The doctor doesn't like newspapermen.'

'Not many people do.' Citto smiled and turned to go.

'Come on down the harbour bar,' said Sharlie. 'I'll buy you a whisky before you go. Come on, you others,' he added in a shout. 'I'll buy you kids ice-creams.'

Sharlie pulled Citto outside and down the road before the others could organize themselves to follow.

'For Chrissakes,' he said. 'Can you lend me some money? Just until they pay me for the pictures.'

The clown now needed to finance his lie: maintain his successful image, his *bella figura*. Citto fished out three tens for him. 'Tell them the truth, you idiot. It's much easier in the end.'

The others were behind them now and they all walked together down into the little piazza around the harbour. The children disappeared into their haunts and hideaways amongst the dirty concrete blocks that formed the seaward side of the harbour jetty, their shrieking unnoticed in the general hubbub. A three-wheel Vespa truck piled high with new mattresses was blaring pop songs at full volume through a loud-hailer while the driver drank coffee in the bar at the end of a fruitless day trying to sell bedding around the inland villages. He'd obviously left the music on as a public service for the village. No one seemed to mind. Citto wondered if they even noticed. We notice very little, he thought. We live with noise; with the ugliness of the new villas along the coast; with refuse piled on the shore as though dustbins and dustcarts had never been invented. Even old Nonna Lisa would throw the fish-bones and leftovers from supper into one of the gullies on the lava rocks and when challenged would reply: 'The high sea in the winter will clean it all away.' What are we, Citto wondered. Tired, lazy, uncivilized?

Two fishing boats came chugging into the harbour, cutting their engines and drifting on to the beach. Two families gathered round their tired men to help winch the boats up out of the water on to the gritty black sand. The fishermen heaved the baskets of fish on to the roadway and left them there, returning to straighten and stow their lines and nets. The grandfathers of the families, too old for the sea, took over the catch. It was their job to barter with the merchants waiting in their trucks. Sardines, *bonita, occhiata, sarago* and some nasty-looking eels. One of the boats had landed a large dentice, steely blue and pink, with a flesh and a taste as delicate as salmon. Not a prize to be wasted on the merchants. The old men laid it on a trestle stall, sluicing its still-moving gills with sea water, shouting its qualities and its price over the cacophony of pop. Their shouts ignored the villagers for the price was too high. The old men were angling for the Saturday evening cars out from the towns for the home-made ice-cream in the harbour bar.

Citto and Sharlie drank their whiskies, Citto watching the fish auction, Sharlie watching Citto.

'You think something's going on, don't you?'

Citto didn't reply. He was listening to the old men with the fish.

'The aeroplane. You think something's happened and someone's doing a cover-up.'

The fish sold at 25000 lire, and Citto turned away with a smile. 'I never said nothing.'

The mattress merchant drove his noisy Vespa truck away up the hill on to the plateau of citrus above the village, the blast of pop music fading into the evening scent of *zagara* from the lemon trees.

'Some things are best left alone,' said Sharlie. 'Especially round here.'

13

Up on the mountain the investigators were lifted out by helicopter as darkness and cloud descended. They hadn't yet accomplished more than a general assessment: photographs; sketches; first impressions. The only 'discovery' had been made by Raille when he dug through ashes and twisted metal to expose one end of the central number two engine. He had found the turbine blades intact, which virtually established that that particular engine had been shut down at the time of impact. It was too late now to carry the search any further. The investigators left the wreckage fading in mist and guarded by a none too wide awake platoon of Carabinieri. Forty bodies were loaded with them into the two Vertols: the three crew members; the supposed hi-jacker; twenty of the burnt bodies from the tail section; and sixteen torn victims from the tangle up front. Another fifteen bodies had already been evacuated. A hundred souls were left in various states of disintegration and decay, appeased only by collective blessing from a local priest earlier in the day.

The helicopters landed after only ten minutes' flying, one after the other at either end of a wide piazza in the highest of the mountain villages, the noisy intrusion bringing a crowd of inhabitants young and old from the bar and shuttered houses up and down the narrow hillside streets. The piazza protruded at the edge of the village, built out over the slope in a long scenic balcony, a promenade with stone benches, a straggly palm and oleanders, obliterated now in a hurricane of dust and scrap paper and old men's hats. The rotors turned in slow motion as Pherson supervised the unloading of his plastic sheeted bodies, then the helicopters rose again leaving Mac alone with Sanju and the row of bodies, a priest hurrying from his church steps hands aloft to keep the villagers away from such an undignified and naked display of death.

The departing helicopters left a sudden silence as the village stood watching the bearded and boiler-suited giant who had so suddenly descended with his strange cargo and his turbaned companion. They watched from the edges of the piazza in slightly aloof silence, as though they did not wish the newcomers to think that they were not used to unusual visitors. Only by the village bar was there conversation, for one of the huge Vertols had ripped off a dozen telephone lines on its way down and a local Carabinieri was trying to figure out whose lines were damaged.

Mac squatted on his instrument case and wondered if anyone knew quite what they were waiting for. He roared across the square towards the bar holding up two fingers: '*Deux bières.*' No one moved. '*Bière!*' He shouted again and raised a hand to his mouth in the gesture of drink, but his colonial approach cut no ice here. They'd seen them all coming and going since the time of Odysseus, Greeks, Italians, Spanish, French, with plenty of roaring bearded Macs and Jocks in occupation the last time war had passed them by. The quiet Sanju walked to the bar and bartered for the beers with a one-pound note.

Two lorries were edging down one of the streets into the square, hooting furiously to move the crowd.

An elderly, much bowed little man climbed down from the first truck directing the driver towards the row of plastic shrouds in the middle of the square. Mac stood up to meet him.

'Dr Turi Pennisi.' The man announced himself and shook hands, looking up sideways at Mac from under bowed shoulders. 'You wish to make autopsy.' And he indicated the bodies.

Mac nodded and thanked providence for the man's English. 'Tonight?'

'It's important to look at four of them tonight.'

'Tomorrow we find a better place to work, but tonight we can work at my surgery.'

The backs of the two lorries were open – refrigerated meat trucks. The little doctor had improvised well.

'I represent the Magistrato for the moment. You have papers for these bodies?'

Mac handed over a sheet of paper given him by the police up on the mountain. The little doctor counted the bodies and the numbers on the paper. Then the three of them stacked the plastic bundles inside the two trucks and squeezed themselves into the cabs with the drivers. The villagers watched them drive away up the narrow street on to the main road that joined these higher mountain villages with the outside world below.

Turi's house stood on a sloping street in the middle of a larger village, where it seemed that the entire population was racing noisy miniature motor-bikes and tiny Fiats. Impossible in such a place to be discreet, though the doctors tried to disguise their crude plastic bundles with blankets before carrying them from the lorries into the house. Turi's surgery was in the front of the house and they could see through the shutters the crowd sauntering from the bar in twos and threes to examine the strange meat trucks.

The four flight-deck victims were laid out on Turi's tiled floor, and Mac began his preliminary examination. Two of the bodies were reasonably intact, only marred by an unpleasant flattening distortion to their skulls and faces: the two pilots held well by their seat harness but disfigured by the upper instrument panel telescoping down on top of them. One of them had an arm flung high over his head, an instinctive flinch as the plane had crashed; the older man was in a normal sitting posture but much damaged about the hands, forearms and legs. Mac had made a sketch plan of the cockpit and the technical investigators would eventually work out which controls the Captain had been operating to suffer such injuries. Left hand on the wheel, right hand on the fire levers, Mac thought. Passports in the men's jackets confirmed the names and Mac entered them both on Autopsy Forms as positively identified: Captain Michael Duckham; Flying Officer Peter Nyren.

There was no evidence in either man's pockets to suggest illness or drug addiction. The older man had a packet of Disprin tablets which would have to be analysed, but they were foil-sealed and Mac was quite sure they were genuine. He looked at a photograph in the Captain's wallet: a pretty English face in a pretty English garden – Mrs Duckham, Mac presumed, for there was a baby in her arms.

Sanju helped Mac as they separated the bodies from belongings, laying the two pilots aside for full autopsy when the preliminaries were over.

The Flight Engineer and the mysterious fourth victim were in more of a mess. The Engineer seemed to have been torn from his wretched swivel chair, suffering multiple flailing injuries to his head and his limbs. If they hadn't killed him his back had been snapped where the floor had buckled upwards catching him trapped between his seat and that of the Captain in front of him.

The cockpit intruder had a shattered forehead; her right arm was missing, torn off at the shoulder; the left forearm was impacted into her jaw where she had flung it up to protect her face; both her knees were fragmented, and most of the frontal area of her body was badly bruised. But for all her terrible injuries Mac had found her unentangled with the main flight deck damage, and depending on where they eventually located the missing arm, it was possible that she arrived on the flight deck as a result of and after the crash impact. Such evidence, negative or positive, was obviously vital to any hi-jacking theory.

The Flight Engineer's documents tallied with Mac's crew list: George Raven, aged thirty-seven and unmarried. Next of kin was a brother in Australia. The intruder instead had no jacket or handbag and therefore no documents to suggest identification. She was dark-skinned and what little remained of her features suggested Arabic, or certainly Mediterranean origins. There would be trouble about identification here, thought Mac, and the possibility could not yet be excluded that this young woman had interfered in some way with procedure on the flight deck. Mac scribbled in his notebook: 'F/E moving to keep intruder off flight deck?'

Turi watched the huge bearded Englishman move dispassionately through his preliminary examinations, and remembered the battered bodies, some of them still alive, in the confusion of wreckage that morning. Turi had had his share of traffic accidents, increasingly so in recent years, but he had never experienced quite such grotesque disfigurements as he had seen on this occasion. Nor had he through thirty years of practice ever succeeded in distancing death. Death in his own villages had always meant the deaths of people he knew, often his own patients with the connotations of loss and sometimes of failure or inadequacy on his part. But even the deaths of total strangers disturbed him more than he cared to admit. Especially this kind of ugly, violent, wholly indiscriminate, wholly fortuitous dying. He supposed the English pathologist had seen it often enough, but he still admired the man's absolute detachment.

The Indian assistant had covered the table with rubber sheeting and Mac warned the Italian: 'It's going to make a bloody mess of your surgery.'

Turi shrugged.

'Just these four. That's all we need to do tonight.' Mac grinned. 'Just in case your Magistrato pinches the bodies.'

They lifted Captain Duckham onto the table.

*

Ralph Burden was thinking about Mike Duckham over his supper. 'Dixie' to Burden, and even after thirty years Burden could still hear the dry impeccable-even-when-drunk, so wholly self-confident Harrovian arrogance of that voice. 'Raffles Burden – survivor supreme,' the voice had mocked one evening. 'You know, chaps, it's extraordinary. Most bloody awful pilots got themselves killed pretty quick. Two sorts of chaps got killed – your gay young bloods swanning all over the sky, and your bloody awful pilots who couldn't hold their sticks straight. But this bloody awful pilot' – and here the voice raises tone as the eyes pick out Burden – 'he came back every time. Plane all pulped ready for the paper mill, the bloody pilot still looking for his stick.'

Duckham had been very drunk. VE-Day plus a week or so. Yes. He had been very drunk and the next morning he had not only apologized but had walked Ralph twice round the airport perimeter trying, it seemed, to find excuses for his behaviour. In retrospect, many years too late, Burden recognized his despair. 'Actually you see, none of the chaps I knew are around any more. I don't know what I said about you last night but what I can't work out is why *I* am still alive.' He had laughed heartily, mocking himself for a change. Dixie Duckham. They were going to get to know each other well in the next few days.

Burden looked round the hotel dining-room. The meal was over and the guests leaving in ones and twos. Burden wished the other members of his team had been with him in the same hotel, but they were scattered all over the little town. Taormina, the Italians had told them, was in high season, hotel accommodation limited – though Burden noticed with not a little irritation that the Americans had managed to get themselves fixed up in a luxurious palace of a hotel, some old monastery on the other side of town.

He walked out afterwards into the glow of the evening and the scatter of lights up and down the alleyways and narrow streets. It was a pretty touristy town, full of hotels and pensions and the odd discreet nightclub down leafy stairways advertised with photographs equally discreet and unharmful. But Ralph Burden was not after entertainment. He tried in vain to find his way through the maze of steps up the hillside to the even smaller pension where his engineers were billeted. Defeated, he sat at an outside table in the main piazza drinking expensive malt whisky watching the crowd grouped round a coin-operated telescope. They were training it on the mountain as though they could see through the darkness the glow of the crashed plane, or a cloud of flying souls ascending.

Later, back in his bedroom, Burden sat down at the table and opened the Greyhound personnel file. 'Michael Edward Duckham, born Rangoon 1922.' Rubber planters, Burden guessed. Ralph Sinclair Burden, he thought to himself as he started to make notes. Born Sanderstead 1924 into a family of grocers.

The child of Empire Michael Duckham had been: occasional voyager on the P and O, habitué of a half-dozen prep-schools in Kent and Sussex. Why so many changes? Burden wondered. Did it denote a wild childhood? Over-anxious absentee parents? Poverty? A wild childhood, Burden decided. Duckham had been removed from Harrow after only three years and had re-surfaced in a London crammer, passing out with enough qualifications to have satisfied the bespectacled scrutineers at ACSC. Air Crew Selection Centre, St John's Wood, a kind of half-baked extension of boarding school with its lock-up and communal rules. But then schoolboys they all had been. Except for the odd screwballs – the ones who had climbed out at night to chase the WAAF girls down Baker Street or the nurses up in Swiss Cottage. Was that where Duckham had learned his womanizing, or had it all been just a legend?

Michael Edward Duckham. Initial training wing in Newquay Grading school and Tiger Moths in Worcester. Classified as a pilot. Six weeks kicking heels in Heaton Park, Manchester, waiting for a ship, then EFTS and SFTS variously around Canada. Back across the Atlantic in one of those coldly comforting North Atlantic convoys. OTU on Mosquitoes in Scotland. It was all very familiar. Burden had trod much the same trail eighteen months later.

'Attached to 23 Squadron December 2nd, 1942. Embarked for Malta December 11th. First active mission January, 1943. Shot down off the coast of Malta February, 1943. Missions recommenced March, 1943. Awarded D.S.O. following low-level sorties during the Allied invasion of Sicily.'

Sicily. Burden wondered how many times Duckham had been back on the island since the war.

'Crash-landed at Castelforte (Monte Cassino front) April, 1944. Invalided home. Rejoined the Squadron July, 1944 at Little Snoring, Norfolk.'

Burden smiled to himself. He could remember the very moment: the slightly raffish hero of whom so many stories had been told, leaning on an unnecessary stick, surveying them, the newcomers who had joined the Squadron during his absence. No, Burden hadn't exactly liked Duckham, though the impression had in no way affected a mild attack of hero worship.

'D.F.C. March, 1945. Transferred to 29 Squadron September 25th, 1945. Transferred back to 23 Squadron September, 1946.' Of no significance those transfers; the Squadron had been disbanded for a year. Burden instead had left it for good, moving to Transport Command and re-training first on Dakotas then on Hastings. Burden looked again at the photograph on the file. Dixie's face had filled out. It probably carried less lines than the twenty-four-year-old fighter pilot thirty years ago. Burden wondered if that head had still ducked and swooped over its shoulders. The temperament must have changed or he would never have been appointed Fleet Captain. He'd been a strangely uneven character in those far-off days. Meet him outside, walking down the lane, and he'd have a smile and a chat. But catch him in a crowded mess or pub on a bad day and he could turn the mob·on you for no apparent reason. You'd see him·some evenings waiting for a night mission, eyes roaming the room searching out a victim, and closing in for a kill. But it wasn't the best time to judge a man, when he'd come back from a lay-off after injury. He had been shot down twice already and was living, as the Squadron medic would have said, somewhere along the razor's edge. One winter's night he'd returned with a dead navigator beside him and a plane so shot to hell you couldn't even make out its true silhouette. Everyone had thought that that would finally tip him over. But oddly enough he'd come the other way, as though the incident had focussed him again. It had been the successful combination of his next three missions that had earned him his D.F.C. He had even mellowed to his juniors – until that drunken outburst in the early days of peace.

'Married July, 1946, in Mereworth Parish Church, Deborah

Poynton-Stevens. Divorced 1951. Married August, 1952, Norwich Registry Office, Angela de Waal. One daughter born 1958. Divorced 1967. Married September 21st, 1967, Guildford Registry Office, Julia Ann Dutton. One son born 1969. One daughter born 1971.'

He'd had some bites at the apple. A screwball.

Ralph Burden. Married Mary Howard 1957, Selsdon Parish Church. Marriage petered out *sans* drama *sans* everything over many years. Separation 1974.

Burden weighted down his papers with an ashtray and put away his pens and pencils. Mary had gone to live with a sister in Ibiza where, by all accounts, she was busy making up for lost sex. Another screwball.

Ralph washed and undressed and carefully thought of nothing in particular. But lying in bed later with the darkness he dreamed old nightmares: pipe smoke from the mess drifting on the evening air; Mossies lined up in rounded silhouettes against the open Norfolk sky ready to shadow the bombers on some long night raid deep into Germany; the drone of twin Merlins drumming through the wooden frame. Fear, continual fear, that drew youth from the mind and body like sap from a wounded tree.

14

The elderly Magistrato had returned home to shower away the dirt and smells of the mountain and the plane. He already felt better. He had left his younger colleague in the office poring over reports and plans. Shared responsibility was more comfortable.

But his sense of satisfaction did not last long. The Procuratore Generale telephoned him at seven o'clock with a string of questions. He already seemed to know a great deal about the accident and the day's events.

'*Tutto con calma si farà*,' he said. 'We can't rush this kind of investigation.'

He was not at all pleased to be told of the younger Magistrato's participation.

'Too much technical knowledge is often a hindrance,' he said after a long and rigid silence. 'Our eager young colleague will be feeling sorry for the pilot.'

The elderly Magistrato, still damp from his shower, sensed pressures, local wheels and whispers. He hated these oblique conversations, for he knew he would fall in with them. He was vulnerable to pressure.

'We are all on trial,' said the Procuratore. The Procuratore Generale who had too many friends, too many smiles and too much protesting of his own incorruptibility. Though in a sense he was correct. There was never corruption as such; no open collusion; no crisp persuasions received under the table. It was far more ancient and sophisticated. More like a well-drilled football team: when the ball came to your feet in a given situation you sensed the play and you knew instinctively where to move and how to lay it off.

The Dino was travelling south along the old *Statale* 114 at speeds mostly in excess of 100 miles an hour. The young man in his now slightly soiled white suit did not believe in motorways and his midnight rendezvous was well away from any main road. The afternoon had passed pleasantly if stickily on that hot beach with three of the four American women making a heavy play for him in their awful Italian. At dusk he'd offered to drive them back up the hill to Taormina, one at a time he explained, for the Dino was an impractical car. But his choice of first passenger had proved correct. The lady had opened his trousers while he was still manoeuvring out of the darkened car park, and by the time they reached her hotel he was in no mood to think of the others. They were probably still on the beach waiting for him. Another day, he thought.

Tonight Flavio would play poker with friends and tell of his afternoon's adventures. He could stay out till dawn if he wanted, for his father had taken the afternoon flight to Rome and was not returning until Monday. His mother would not tell tales. She couldn't bear the noise they caused.

A blue Alfa waited in a darkened garage on the inside of a tight bend listening to the six-cylinder roar of Ferrari approaching down through its gearbox. The Dino snaked into the bend and accelerated past them in a haze of rubber and racing oil – 160 kph, the police driver had calculated with grudging admiration. But both traffic cops had seen the number plate and the driver killed his engine with a shrug of resignation.

'Come on. Give him a scare,' his mate said. 'We can radio a car further up the road.'

'And all of us get two days' pay docked? He's more trouble than a gangster.'

The Dino was an hour late for its rendezvous and Capo Tomacchio in his van outside the cemetery muttered an unheard oath as the young man climbed without apology out of his low cockpit. Tomacchio watched in silence. He was playing the subordinate tonight, an unaccustomed role. But then he was a worried man; his lorries were at stake.

The young man pulled a dirty suède jacket from the boot in the front of his car, walked across the road to the van and dropped the keys of the petrol-tanker through the open window. He had an envelope of money in his hand.

'How much?'

'Five hundred for the fuel. We go halves.' Capo Tomacchio had thick eyebrows in straight short lines; eyes on the small side watching for competition; his heavy face creased around the nose into a perpetual sneering challenge.

Flavio nodded, peeled off the money and patted him a thank-you on his arm.

'Any trouble?' the older man asked.

'No.'

'You moved fast this morning.'

'They rang me from the airport as soon as the power failed. It wasn't the fuel. It was the taps all set wrong. The emergency tank ran itself dry.'

'My fault last week, I suppose. I was in a hurry. I was running late.'

The young man moved away.

'Is everything going to be all right?'

'Why shouldn't it be?'

'A whole bloody airplane's come down, that's why. There's a hundred and fifty people dead. What did your father say?'

'He's got bigger problems than this. He's gone to Rome.'

'Well he's involved with us whatever happens.' Tomacchio paused. 'He is involved, isn't he?'

Flavio gestured impatiently and turned away without answering the question.

Tomacchio called after him: 'If it was my mistake I'm sorry.'

The young man turned from his car with a lazy, limp smile. 'If you want to make amends you'd better talk to your daughter for me.' The green and orange Dino screeched a U-turn on the road, completing it in a slide through the gravel by the cemetery gates.

Capo Tomacchio listened to the roar departing. One daughter he had – an only child, like Flavio Consoli. Giuseppina. The young couple would never be short of money. But that greedy young man had never explicitly talked about marriage, and if he'd ever suggested anything else Tomacchio would have taken his shotgun to him – influential father or not.

Citto Risarda was running about a day and a half ahead of the official investigators. He had covered fifteen villages in four hours. Fifteen village bars had given him most of the information he needed and in the early hours of Sunday morning he parked his old Giulia outside the perimeter fence at Taormina-Peloritana and waited for the last of the lights to die in the private Aero Club behind the control tower. He plotted last night's storm on a map, relying on the accounts, not always consistent, that he had picked up in the bars. Cloud and rain had covered most of the mountain but the storm itself had been restricted it seemed to a narrow triangle on the north and west of the mountain, between Linguaglossa, Bronte and Randazzo. Heavy rain or lightning strikes had caused power failures in some villages at varying times during the night. By early morning the storm had apparently been centred somewhere around the Maletto on the south-west flank of the mountain.

Citto stared out through his dark windscreen at another cloud-covered night. He had the basic facts, no more, and he wondered if his theory was really worth this amount of trouble. After all there were official investigators who were paid good money to unravel the mysteries of this Tango November. Still, the clocks had all stopped at 5.40. Could other systems have failed at the same time?

Lights went out and the airport slept with only one security guard prowling somewhere with his dog. Citto removed the bulb in the interior lamp to avoid showing light when he opened the car door, then slipped out, torch in hand, to take an investigative stroll. The night was close and still even at this altitude, the airlessness eerie and uncomfortable. There was nothing to feel on the skin, no sounds in the ear and only the occasional pungency of a squashed centipede to bring any scent to the nose. Citto walked across the vast and empty car park past the façade of the Aero Club where he had first seen the dirty black oil-tanker that morning. He turned once when he seemed to hear footsteps on the gravel; he even saw shadows move along a wall. But he had the innocence of inexperience; he didn't know when to retreat.

He found interconnected fuel tanks at the base of the control tower where the lorry had been parked. The two feed pipes were labelled, 'Petrol' and the two sheds next to the tanks labelled: 'Generator – All Circuits'; 'Generator – Emergency Circuits'. Citto retired with a smile. Part one of his hunch had proved correct.

15

A group of intrepid sightseers, like hounds with their noses in the wind, sniffed out Tango November in the small hours of Sunday morning. Their discovery was entirely fortuitous for they had been wandering in the woods and on the lava lost since night had come. Now they smelt stale fire smells, and, as they worked their way nearer, the more specific stink of burnt plastics and paraffin.

There were seven of them in the group, three girls and four boys. They moved the last hundred yards in silence and the girls stood guard on the ground as the boys climbed the ladders into the unburnt front half of the fuselage. The Carabiniere sentinels were fast asleep.

A quarter of an hour later the sightseers heard a helicopter approaching and saw searchlights descending slowly from the sky. The boys jumped down with their loot and the party scrambled away still unseen into the woods. They had collected a rucksack full of British and American passports, wallets and purses, wrist-watches, assorted rings and cameras, and one packet of male contraceptives which they shared out and used later in the morning when the sun had warmed the pine needle dust.

The nocturnal helicopters brought newcomers: efficient men in dark suits on a macabre mission. They moved quickly in the searchlights with their briefcases and their bags of equipment.

16

Day and night was all one long confusion in the hospitals, a vigil of waiting journalists in reception halls, a shuttered darkness in the wards, a floodlit nightmare in the operating theatres. Of the thirty-five survivors ferried off the mountain only fourteen were still alive. Of those fourteen six would die before morning, two from undiagnosed internal bleeding, one from an undiagnosed blood clot in the head, and three on the operating tables while tired and understaffed teams tried to keep them alive.

The five-year-old girl, her arm in plaster, wandered up and down a darkened hospital ward calling for her mother. In a smaller room nearby Stella Pritchard recognized the voice from the depths of a drugged sleep. 'Trixie', they had called her. Yes, it was the voice of Trixie, who had somehow obscurely saved her life. Yet when Stella awoke she was aware only of a car accident, and terrified to know who had been in the car with her. Her parents in their Morris Traveller, or Mike in his white Volvo? Two Italian nuns listened to Stella's questions without understanding her alarm. Their strange soothing talk only increased her fear, driving reality even further away. But late in the evening her pain returned and the nurses dispatched her once more with morphine, back into the limbo where Trixie's voice remained her only link with what had really happened.

Twenty miles northwards in a small town hospital up the coast Tino G. was lying in an operating theatre with a tune stuck obsessively in his mind, his body connected to a variety of artificial aids, tubes sticking in and out of him all over. He could see them quite clearly reflected in the glass of the huge lamp above him and he wondered why the doctors wasted so much time and energy. The clarity of mind he'd had when trapped in the wreckage had gone. It seemed to him that life was fading out of him like the colour from a piece of coral taken from the water.

His liver had been stitched up, a damaged gut bypassed, and a tracheotomy performed to help his breathing. But when his condition continued to deteriorate the surgeon diagnosed kidney failure following the earlier and sudden loss of so much blood. In the absence of a kidney machine a continual process of peritoneal dialysis was theoretically cleansing his abdominal cavity and by that early Sunday morning the deterioration had been momentarily arrested. The old surgeon was snatching some sleep on a couch in the rest room. He had already described the boy's condition in a bulletin as 'hopeless'.

Guitar, harmonica, percussion and a bit of piano. Tino G. hoped he wouldn't die with that tune lost in his head without words or title.

A small group of journalists waited in the lobby downstairs. Someone had wired from New York that this Tino G. played folksongs in Greenwich Village.

Part Two

I

Tango November hadn't moved. Broken-backed, she still sheltered her victims. But she looked unreal in this early morning light, as though a photographer had exaggerated each detail of disaster, as though the disaster itself, acceptable in yesterday's mist and cloud, was now somehow improbable and inexplicable.

A helicopter hung over the wreckage settling slowly to land – two Italian Air Force pilots, Mac and the turbaned Sanju. Mac and Sanju had slept at Turi's house, the helicopter picking them off the village football pitch at first light. The four flight-deck autopsies had taken half the night, without producing any spectacular evidence – no heart attacks – and Mac's preliminary tests indicated nothing abnormal in the contents of anyone's blood. Mac looked down at the crumpled 119 as they climbed out of the helicopter and wondered if that twisted mass of aluminium would ever reveal the secrets of its own death throes.

'Bloody soap-box,' Mac said out loud, thinking of the mess they had to face again inside the shattered fuselage. Floor, seats and belts, all no doubt legally within minimum required specifications, and all totally inadequate in a crash that should have been sixty per cent survivable. Gradual deceleration through the trees; energy absorbing factors during impact in the progressive collapse of landing gear and cargo hold; and finally a long slide to take off some more speed before the front impacted on the slope: it was possible, probable even, that maximum horizontal forces had been as low as 15g and calculable in thousandths of seconds. The human body could survive milliseconds of up to thirty times gravity but the seats, to comply with American and British safety standards, were only required to withstand 9g. Mac hoped that the medical evidence might lead to one or two severe paragraphs in the accident report. Too often the results were ambiguous or inconclusive. It was difficult at the best of times to produce statistics strong enough to challenge the accepted norms of civil aviation safety. Perhaps this time. Perhaps Tango November, at such high cost, would save a few thousand future lives.

There were already small groups of men moving in and around the wreckage, the other investigators ferried from their hotels, Mac assumed. But the faces were all strange to him, a mixture of uniforms, dark suits and dark glasses that suggested cops. Yesterday's Carabinieri were still there dishevelled and unshaven after a night in tents. They tried to stop Mac and Sanju at their cordon but Mac brushed them aside marching possessively towards the wreckage and his hundred unclaimed bodies. A couple of suits and dark glasses detached themselves to deal with him.

'Group Captain Pherson, Royal Air Force,' Mac roared, instinctively spoiling for a fight. But he realized immediately that he should instead have smiled and taken them under their arms or clasped them over their shoulders. Another pair of dark glasses arrived, summoned by a call.

Mac glared down at him from his twelve inches' advantage. 'We are helping your Ministry in Rome to conduct an accident inquiry as is obligatory under international agreement. That includes the identification, examination and proper disposal of bodies.'

'Naturally. But the Magistrato has also his responsibility. Death here' – the bodies, stiff, grotesque and smelling, hardly needed his dramatic gesture – 'that is our responsibility also.'

'Is the Magistrato here?'

The dark glasses turned and Mac followed him down a duck-board, past a half-buried engine and the scattering of burst suitcases and bags.

The Magistrato had been changed since yesterday. This one was younger, more alert, detached and inscrutable as Mac protested.

'I've been told I cannot continue to evacuate bodies.'

'All evidence is subpoenaed.'

'Another couple of hours,' said Mac abandoning aggression, 'and this place will be thick with American and English journalists. They're not going to be too happy to see bodies still lying around twenty-four hours after the accident.'

'There will be no access for journalists.'

'You can't keep them away for long. They'll question your motives if you do.'

The Magistrato watched Mac, a smile somewhere behind his inscrutability: 'You are looking for something in particular?'

'These bodies are my responsibility. Another day out in this sun and they'll be crawling off the mountain by themselves.'

'You have seen the body of the hi-jacker?'

'I have an autopsy report that is still incomplete.'

'Because part of the body is missing.'

'How would you know that?'

'These Carabinieri were helping you yesterday. They tell me the hi-jacker was taken out with her right arm missing.'

Mac nodded.

'Well — it seems someone has been here during the night. The arm has been found and taken away.'

'With half a bloody regiment here meant to be guarding the place?'

'Someone arrived in a helicopter with an official warrant. There was nothing they could do to stop them.'

'Did they see where the arm was found?'

The Magistrato shook his head.

'If we don't find out, we'll never know what this woman was doing.'

The young man handed Mac his card. 'All my telephone numbers, official and unofficial. I hope you keep in touch if you make a discovery.'

The Magistrato shook his hands before returning to his helicopter, and Mac hoped he was on the way to making a local ally. This set-up was beginning to look hairy.

2

Canon Ash Nyren pulled his Sunday newspaper from the letter-box. Even triple folded it was obvious which story dominated the front page. '170 Dead In British Charter Crash. Attempted Hi-jack Ends In Disaster.'

Ash Nyren laid the paper open on the kitchen table. 'Flying Officer Peter Nyren, aged 29.' There was even Peter's photograph on an inside page, a smiling, healthily tanned young man. Ash Nyren read the story he did not yet know, that Peter had flown as it were by accident, in place of a sick colleague. Somehow that made it even worse.

The Canon looked up at the grey clouds above his rain-wet garden. Why not me, old and of no further use; a life so inconsequential that only the church could offer a framework? Too young for one war, too old for the next. Why not me? Why always the young men?

Did Peter see death? Was he afraid? How long did his dying last?

The church was almost crowded this morning. His average congregation might reach the round half-dozen if the sky was blue. There were thirty or more today dripping from the rain, gawping and murmuring to each other like Christmas or Easter tourists. They had come to see him. Had they come to share his grief? To remember Peter? Or merely to watch? If they were looking for the manifestations of grief they would have wondered at his hymns. Most Sundays he had to play his own organ and today was no exception. What he had neglected to do was change the hymn numbers from last week and while he played one tune the congregation was trying in vain to fit the words of quite another hymn. They lapsed into confused silence and listened to his impassioned and untidy playing, and the occasional wafting rumble of his baritone.

'I am weary of my crying: my throat is dried: mine eyes fail while I wait for my God.' Ash Nyren read the text for his sermon. It was to be, it seemed, a sermon of texts.

'Thou turnest man to destruction; and sayest, return, ye children of men.' The Canon was quarrelling with God, the culmination of a long and bitter feud.

'Why art thou so far from helping me, and from the words of my roaring?'

His Church Council met later round sherry in the Rear-Admiral's sitting-room across the village green. The Rear-Admiral called the Rural Dean and the Diocesan Secretary, and it was finally agreed that Evensong should be conducted jointly with the neighbouring parish, and that the Canon should be flown out to Sicily as soon as possible.

All down the east coast of Sicily village priests that morning gave mass for the casualties of the air crash and offered special prayers for the survivors. Eight survivors were consciously alive: two American citizens, Tino G. and Trixie, the little five-year-old survivor of the family snapshot; and six British subjects, Stella Pritchard, a retired army Major and his wife from Malta, a young sales executive from Twickenham, a bachelor GP from Weardale in County Durham, and a shopkeeper friend of his from over the Derwent in Northumberland. The investigators were not surprised to discover that apart from Stella Pritchard and the little girl, all survivors had been sitting in rear-facing seats, Tino G. in row 1 at the very front of the plane, and the other five of them in row 12 just forward of the main bulkhead and centre fuselage toilets.

The sales executive and the Major were the only ones yet coherent enough to help investigators.

'Can't tell you very much, I'm afraid,' the Major was saying. 'We seemed to be going down, then we were going up again, then down again. Then it started bumping and – bang! We went arse over head. That's what saved us. Always sit with my backside to the driver if I can. That's what Transport Command do. And if they do it, it's for a bloody good reason.'

The Italians were having trouble understanding exactly what the Englishman was saying. The voice was too clipped, his mouth seeming hardly to move when he spoke.

The Magistrato asked him about the woman hi-jacker. Had he noticed her at all?

'Good Lord. Didn't know about a hi-jacker. They all looked like stewardesses to me. Tell you the truth I was a bit pissed. Sleeping most of the time. I expect my wife'll be able to tell you more when she's feeling up to it.'

'How long were you in the wreckage before you were rescued?'

'Felt like ten years. I don't know what it was really. Smashed my watch you see. So did Alec. He's in the room next door.

We were the only two bodies *compos mentis*. Everyone else was upside down and broken bones and all. We tried to break a way out, but then the fire started moving forward and we had to build a wall against that instead. Then there was first aid of course. Not much we could do really. Tear up some odds and ends and stop some bleeding.'

'How many people were alive?'

'Difficult to say really. We could only move in the space where we were. A couple of rows backwards and forwards. I straightened out my wife and some other bloke. They had broken arms and legs and things.'

Alec in the room next door was not in condition to help the investigators. 'He doesn't seem coherent today,' the Major had warned them. 'Quite all right yesterday. Worried about his friend I expect.' The Major didn't quite approve of the relationship he thought he had detected between doctor and shopkeeper.

The young Magistrato left the hospital with the impression that witness statements were not going to help the investigation. They had already interviewed the sales executive from Twickenham, whose account differed in almost every single detail from that of the Major.

A young surgeon in the second hospital gave the investigators even less hope. Two of his survivors were on the operating tables and in critical condition. The young surgeon had diagnosed respectively acute renal and hepatic failure, but could find no obvious cause in either case. He had requested a second opinion but the machinery through which his request had to be channelled was slow to react. A urologist was contacted by radio on his racing yacht somewhere south of Syracuse becalmed and unable to help. The general physician instead spent his weekends in a hill resort halfway up the mountain and it took him four hours to return into the city and pronounce judgement. It was a forensic more than a medical diagnosis. Both patients had had substantial transfusions of blood during the previous evening. The two transfusions, incompatible to each other, must have been interchanged.

'What can I do?' the young surgeon asked in despair.

'Peritoneal dialysis – and make an official request for a kidney machine,' replied the physician. 'When they both die make sure the blood counts are kept off the death certificate. Renal failure was due to severe shock. Hepatic failure to haemorrhage from a lesion.' And having thus organized the affair the consultant escaped back to his car in time to make the hills for Sunday lunch.

The little girl was sitting on the bed when Stella woke back into her pain and confusion. Drugged and only partially conscious she had recognized the girl's voice and remembered her name, aware of some strong connection between her and whatever had happened. But now, with her eyes open, even with the girl's face beside her, Stella could remember nothing. The girl's face, somehow familiar, increased her dread about a car accident. Was this a lone survivor from another car? The accusing face of a girl she had run over? The face whispered.

'Where's Mama?'

They had been together, one way and another, for twenty-four hours, Stella's face Trixie's only point of reference. It had been a normal face at first, laughing as it played a game, getting a little angry when the game went on too long. Then it had been injured and blood-marked; now it was repaired, shiny and dirty in patches all over. Trixie was conscious of what had happened, much more so than Stella, though her memory was equally dominated with dread. She was convinced that the crash had been all her fault, somehow a result of that game she had been playing up and down the airplane while everyone else was strapped into their seats. They had all been calling her; then this hostess had been chasing her; and finally her mother.

'Mama hurting,' she whispered. She still could see the plane all smashed and burning and her mother somewhere there inside.

3

The Dino was parked with one foot in the fountain, its tail drunkenly wide across the courtyard: the lady's coupé was comprehensively boxed in but the *signora* in the dark grey dress merely shrugged and returned indoors. She didn't want to wake her son. She would go instead to evening mass.

The gods smiled on her this Sunday. Ten minutes later her husband telephoned from Rome, and she was able to explain that their son was out on an inspection in the orange gardens, an insignificant untruth that neither of the maids would have dared to tell.

'Call him,' was the order from Rome.

This time she had to waken the boy, explaining quickly what she had told his father. But the young man's voice when it appeared downstairs was still thick with sleep.

'And what were you looking at in the orange gardens?' his father sneered. 'The sky or a peasant girl's arse?'

Flavio Consoli laughed. It was his only defence. The Avvocato loved his words to be appreciated. He told him now that he was to pay a call that morning on the Procuratore, his wife, their daughter and son. 'You will pay special attention to the daughter and treat her with respect and admiration.'

'She's just a fat little schoolgirl.'

His father took no notice. 'You will be invited to lunch and after making the correct gestures of reluctance you will join them and pay respectful attention to your host and make yourself useful in whatever way is possible.'

'It's Sunday.'

'When I come home tomorrow I want to hear word for word what has happened.'

'I have to take a tape recorder?'

'Are you stupid?' And after a pause. 'Yes, you are stupid, I know. A stupidity that comes with laziness and too much material comfort. And that is my fault.' Another pause and a voice that seemed to regret those harsh words. 'You have understood what to do?'

The young man nodded respectfully. Then remembered his father would not see the gesture over the telephone.

'Yes, sir.'

Avvocato Consoli was installed in his usual hotel behind the Piazza Colonna, his room old-fashioned with heavy furniture and noisy with its dreadful plumbing, but otherwise discreet and unostentatious. He dialled another number. The airport had telexed that morning. Some journalist had been hanging around late last night. There were precautions to be taken.

The telephone was answered.

'You will not remember me,' said the Avvocato. 'We met once or twice while you were sitting on an airport feasibility committee.'

The man did remember. The heaviness in his voice recalled old debts and favours.

'There was a twelfth man on the committee,' said Consoli. 'A civil engineer. He didn't like our project. He resigned and I wanted to make sure his name had been cleared from all records.'

'So far as possible it was done at the time.' The heaviness of voice drooped even further. 'It was a public inquiry and difficult to close all references.'

Consoli's voice was neither heavy nor threatening. Scarcely a murmur. 'I rely on you.'

The other man's affirmative grunt sounded more like a lamentation.

'Preuss was the name.'

'I'm sorry?'

'The twelfth man. He lives in Venice.'

Another affirmative grunt.

'Relying on you then.' Consoli hung up. Relying hell, he thought. Reminding was the operative word: if anything goes wrong you are also implicated.

Consoli dialled another number. There were a lot of nervous voices answering this morning. Civil servants. The politicians had all left town.

*

Ingegnere Preuss watched with a shiver as colour moved across the lagoon and the mist disappeared. Sunrise belated or otherwise, through mist or over a horizon: he had never lost the sense of tremulous and total solitude that the moment provoked. He had felt it as a boy standing hand in hand with his mother. He felt it now, standing alone on the eastern edge of his decaying city, listening to a jet whistling over Jesolo as it circled to land.

Preuss had all but forgotten about that air crash. The news of it had worried him yesterday. It would return no doubt to worry him today. He didn't really want to be involved, not after all the previous heartache and wasted energy. There was an awful lot of mess to be dug up if someone looked hard enough.

He would go out to the Lido today, he thought. One last bathe before the water cools. He had tickets that afternoon for one of the films at the Festival. A couple of his young students were coming along with him.

4

ETNOLIO was a large courtyard of buildings and oil tanks in the same village where Turi and Laura lived. The establishment was set back from the village street and hidden by a high wall. Citto remembered the building as a distillery producing a good brandy from the local vineyards and indeed the chimney of the furnace still survived, with the tall copper retorts in the steam house that now seemed to serve for lorry maintenance. The flat-roofed top of the storage buildings was the terrace of the main house, and a girl was standing there, leaning over the railings in a bikini talking with someone out of sight. Voluptuous and unashamed, Citto thought as he watched her: big breasts, masses of brown hair, dark skin. Citto walked in at the yard gates. The girl saw him and turned away back to her sunbathing, shouting at her unseen companion.

'Renzo! Someone to see you.'

A grimy mechanic crawled from under one of the lorries and

Citto asked innocently and with his inevitable stammer about the distillery he remembered.

'Sold,' said the young man in overalls. The family business it seemed had died with the originator, his sons too given to the soft life to apply themselves with the vigour and physical hard work necessary to keep such a business going. 'Ten men thrown out of work,' said the mechanic. 'And forty acres of vineyard grubbed up. They're building holiday homes for the folk from the city.' The mechanic was young and sharp, and the energy of his disgust suggested a Communist or a Fascist. But Citto was not looking for a political discussion. He glanced round the yard: four tankers, all of them in middle age, the oldest of them black and oil-stained, dirty and smelling as it had been the previous day on that wide dirt pavement outside the town below the airport.

Citto nodded at the lorries. 'Do you do contract work?'

'Maintenance you mean?'

'Delivery.'

The boy nodded. 'Nafta, petrol and diesel.'

'Are you the boss?'

'No.'

'So who is?'

'Tomacchio. Capo Tomacchio.' He was sardonic this young man, emphasizing the 'Capo'.

'Is he inside?'

'The Capo is out in the country.'

'Do you know where?'

'Turn right halfway through the village and right again above the bridge. First left at the top of the hill then stop the car and listen for shooting.'

'Hunting?'

'You could call it that. The most he's ever shot is rats and snakes.'

Renzo watched the tubby little man depart and wondered briefly if he could be a cop. Giuseppina reappeared on the terrace above. 'What did he want?'

'Looking for your father.'

Giuseppina was working on her hair, long lazy strokes of a brush. Renzo sat on the step of one of the lorries, lit the butt end of a cigarette and watched her.

87

'Mother's gone to mass,' the girl said after a while.

'So?'

'So you can come up here if you want.'

Renzo laughed. 'Some trouble I can do without.' He flicked away his butt end and crawled back under the lorry.

The countryside up on the hill was dry and scrubby, regimented into roads and building plots, with only two or three of the houses under construction and the rest of the site overgrown. It was easy to see how the terraced vineyard had been constructed, falling in a carefully interlocked pattern of walls and neatly built steps from the summit of the ridge down to the winter torrent by the bridge below. The carving up of building plots had ruined most of the walls, and only the bare outline was left of ten centuries or more of agricultural tradition.

Citto found Capo Tomacchio and his shotgun in a gorse thicket halfway up the hill, angry at the intrusion into his morning's duel with the three-legged hare that had been denying him since early summer.

Citto struggled through a stammered introduction. 'They told me in the village where I would find you.' He decided not to implicate the mechanic. He might turn out to be an ally.

'You have business with me?'

Citto was stammering a reply when the man cut in on him. 'It's Sunday you know.'

Reactions to his stammer were often Citto's measure of an interviewee or opponent. This Tomacchio gave no quarter. When a man was vulnerable he attacked. He was a bludgeoner.

'I'm an investigative journalist,' Citto said. 'Dottor Risarda,' and he named his newspaper. He was going to name everyone if he needed and all of them with their full titles – his Editor, his MP, his Cardinal, *professore, onorevole, eccellenza*. The bludgeoner had to be bludgeoned back in language he could understand.

'I'm writing an article about the new airport. I understand you do contract work for them.'

Tomacchio had a very level stare and Citto only his spectacles to hide behind. He took them off and polished them on his shirt front.

'You are mistaken.'

'One of your lorries was at the airport yesterday morning.'

'Which lorry?'

Citto read off the registration number from his notebook.

'The lorry was out on hire yesterday. I don't know where it went. It wasn't with one of my drivers.'

'But you know who hired it out?'

'If you think I'm coming all the way back into town with you just to fish a name out of a file —'

'It's a bit unusual isn't it? Self-drive hire.'

'Only way some of us can keep going.'

'So you don't undertake regular work for the airport?'

'You think a half-cock outfit like mine can muscle in on airport fuel concessions? They fight about such things in Rome, and there's sure as Christ no one fighting there for me.'

Capo Tomacchio broke his gun and reloaded. 'And now if you don't mind I'd like to get on with my Sunday.'

Citto slipped and stumbled his uncomfortable way out of the thicket and down through the thorny ex-vineyard, aware of the Capo's level stare — and the shotgun — watching him go. He was a bludgeoner all right, though he didn't seem uneasy enough to be hiding anything. But then maybe a bludgeoner wouldn't be uneasy whatever he had to hide.

Citto stopped on his way back through the village. The mechanic was closing up to go off for his lunch.

'Did you find him?'

'Yes, thank you.'

'Got a bag full of rabbits has he?'

'Not exactly.'

The young mechanic laughed.

'He was telling me he sometimes hires out the tankers.'

'Him hire them out? First I've heard of it. He must have liked your face. He even hates us driving his precious lorries.'

'I must have misunderstood him. I thought he said he'd hired one out yesterday.'

'That old black monster? He lent it to a friend for the day — and it came back in a bloody good mess too.'

'Must be an influential friend to gain a favour like that.'

'Consoli.' The young man glanced up at the terrace where the girl was watching them both. He spat into the grit under the wall. 'Daddy's little boy with his racing car and his women. It's his father who bought the vineyard.'

'Not a friend of yours?'

'I get told to clean his car sometimes.'

'What does he drive – the son?'

'A Dino. You've seen it around I expect. Luminous orange and green. And a horn that plays silly tunes.'

Giuseppina laughed from the terrace above them and Renzo scowled. 'She loves it. She gets taken for rides in it.'

The mechanic walked off to his lunch with a nod at Citto and nothing for the girl. A very severe young man. Not a severity of the right, Citto thought. Which must make him something of a black sheep in a village where, at a guess, forty per cent of the electorate voted for the neo-Fascists, and the remaining sixty per cent for the Christian Democrats. This Consoli was a Christian Democrat family way up the scale. Quite a different league from Capo Tomacchio. Citto couldn't see where the two coincided.

He looked up at the terrace above the old distillery. The girl was playing with a large chained Alsatian, throwing him a bone, teasing it away from him before he could settle with it. Citto had the feeling that her men suffered much the same kind of treatment.

Renzo was crossing the piazza when Citto caught up with him.

'Nice girl.'

'A bloody good hiding is what she needs.'

'From you?'

'From whoever decides to tame her.'

Citto steered him aside and into the village bar. 'Why not you?'

'I'm just a mechanic.'

'She fancies you though.'

'She fancies a lot of young men.'

'Do you fancy her?'

'What's it to you?'

Citto called to the barman for a couple of beers and they sat for a moment in silence.

'I'll pay for mine,' said Renzo when the beers came. 'That way I don't owe you anything.'

'I'm trying to ask a favour.'

'So ask it and don't bugger about.'

'I'm a journalist. I want to ask you questions about your boss and the business he runs.'

'How do I know you're a journalist?'

Citto pulled out his identity card and laid it on the table. 'Ring up the newspaper and ask them.'

And to Citto's surprise that's exactly what Renzo did, tucking himself into the corner by the door with the telephone and Citto's card. Citto wondered why at his age the boy was so cautious, but he was pleased all the same. It should make his answers that much more reliable. He wasn't the sort to elaborate or lie.

Renzo sat down again apparently satisfied and ready to talk, and by the time Citto left the village twenty minutes later he had a clear idea of how ETNOLIO operated and how the week's work was broken up into a timetable of collections and deliveries. One run in particular interested Citto: a midweek trip over the Peloritani mountains with an empty tanker and trailer to pick up petrol at the oil refinery in Milazzo. According to Renzo that particular journey was always taken by the Capo himself, and always over the mountains instead of round the coast on the autostrada. The mountain road passed within shouting distance of the new airport.

Flavio Consoli had performed his duties well: the Procuratore had been made a friend of; his fat daughter flirted with.

Lunch-time had been quite hard work as he concentrated on remembering the basics of good manners and charm. But his occasional lapses had been overlooked and after coffee the fat schoolgirl had offered compensations as they walked together through the Procuratore's orange groves. A discreet kiss on the cheek had released a great energy of virginal passion in the girl. She had given him her mouth, offered her huge and satisfying breasts, and rubbed her crutch hard against his thighs. At which point, thankfully, her brother appeared through the trees and difficult sexual decisions had been deferred.

The brother had been given a ride in the Dino; the Procuratore complimented on his orange trees; his daughter promised future satisfaction. Talk of the air crash was limited to careful generalities, though it seemed to Flavio that the many interruptions to the Procratore's Sunday, whether from the telephone or by visitors, had all been associated with some aspect or other of the disaster. One of the guests at lunch had been an elderly Magistrato in charge of yesterday's rescue, and afterwards, returning home in the car, Flavio used his pocket dictaphone to list the points he had picked up from conversation at the table – most important of them the name of the younger Magistrato who had apparently taken over investigation at the crash site. 'An over-eager young man', the Procuratore had called him, precisely the sort of detail Flavio's father would expect to be told when he returned from Rome.

Flavio flicked off his dictaphone and plunged a facia button for eight-track stereo, blazing a trail of six-cylinder megaphones and blared rock through sleepy afternoon villages. How would his father react to Tomacchio? he was wondering. Was it worth telling him? Just in case anything went wrong?

5

Undeterred by newspaper, radio and television pronouncements on the inaccessibility of the crashed aeroplane, cars had streamed up the narrow mountain roads all morning, funnelling into a series of two-lane traffic jams. The hopeful sightseers had not come unprovided for. They had brought their food and drink with them and by lunch-time the woodland roadsides were ankle deep in empty coke tins, paper, broken bottles, plastic plates, plastic cups, plastic knives and forks. Many of the families, as was their custom on weekend country outings, brought their household refuse with them in plastic bags and added these to the landscape.

The traffic jams were accompanied by a great deal of engine-revving and horn-blowing, and by midday the traffic police reported a large proportion of cars immobilized with overheating engines or flat batteries and unable to roll downhill and out of the way because of the crush of cars behind them. The combination of these stationary blocks finally froze the traffic jam solid.

When a cigarette end or broken bottle set the woodland floor gently smouldering the car-encased spectators stared through their windows at the wisps of smoke as though it was another entertainment laid on for their benefit. Ten minutes later and with a gust of wind the smouldering woodland floor burst suddenly into a wall of flame.

The fire made a steady 1500 metres in a band 100 metres wide across the slope of the mountain, cutting the road in two places and isolating thirty cars in the curve of a long hairpin. Towards the end of the morning the wind freshened and veered from south-east to north-west, turning the fire towards the trapped cars like an angry, unpredictable and suddenly noisy animal. Each gust of wind threw the fire forward fifty metres with a sharp explosive roar, and as overfed citizens fled from its path their cars disappeared into a blanket of flame.

An Air Force helicopter pilot at the crash site had radioed notification of the fire when it first started and a couple of French-owned CL-215 water bombers had been sent from Taranto where they were on temporary station after combating a series of forest fires in the Gargano. By the time they arrived the front of the fire had broadened to 300 metres and a north wind was threatening to sweep the danger downhill towards the villages.

The sight of the smoke and flames on the mountain enticed another few thousand sightseeing cars up on to the mountain surrounds. Two days too late the Carabinieri and the Polizia Stradale set up road-blocks to turn the cars back. The villagers on the mountain had seen the phenomenon before. They had watched the same faces gawping from cars as their woods and vineyards were burnt and buried during the last eruption. There had been resentment then against the sightseers and there was some grim amusement this time as news passed around of the burning cars and stranded city folk.

The investigators at the crash site paused in their work to watch when the water bombers arrived, loaded from the sea, attacking the fire like second world war bombers in their droning inexorability. They flew ten seconds apart, starting at one end of the fire with a dummy run to judge the wind.

Then the first plane dropped his artificial cloudburst, 1200 gallons in less than a second on the forward-moving front of the fire. Fifty metres of flame snuffed for a moment, and the second plane arrived straddling its drop slightly forward of the same area. When the wind regathered the fire for another leap the heart was gone out of it and the ground ahead of it soaked. It survived only in pockets – small bonfires in the undergrowth.

Six planes they really need, thought Raille as he watched the two tankers bank away towards the sea for a re-load. The turn-round would take at least twenty minutes and in that time the fire would recapture half of that lost fifty metres. They would need ten round trips to break the blaze and he doubted that they had sufficient fuel left for five hours' flying.

Not that the fire was anything more than a distraction for the investigators. There was no apparent threat to the wreckage and their own helicopter transport would be unaffected by the long pall of smoke that was now reaching out southwards towards the city.

Work in and around the wreckage had been exhausting in the full heat of the sun. Temperatures inside the forward section of fuselage had risen to over 140 degrees Fahrenheit and two investigators had already been evacuated with heat exhaustion.

In those conditions it was as well that death had at last gone from Tango November. A final load of bodies had been lifted out with Mac in attendance and, before leaving, Mac had joined Larry Raille in the concertinaed cockpit to explain how the four bodies had been lying when he found them, describing from his autopsy the precise significance of the injuries to Duckham's hands and feet. The two men decided that the Captain had been 'landing' the plane at the moment of impact. The flaps were set in landing configuration, and the distribution of undercarriage wreckage scattered back along the crash path through the trees made it clear that the landing gear was locked down. Only Duckham's right hand on the fire handle and the line of approach path broke the pattern of an apparently normal landing. As Burden had pointed out the day before, the path of wreckage through the trees described an unmistakable left-turning arc, and the plane itself had grounded in an attitude of left wing down, with the fuselage tilted. Duckham's shattered right foot braced on the rudder bar seemed to have been an attempt to counteract the bank, and suggested that the plane was, for an as yet undiscovered reason, partially out of control.

'What about the hi-jacker?' Raille had asked.

'No comment. I'll need to see the evidence for myself.' Mac's tone of voice had seemed like a warning.

He was an abrasive man, this pathologist, deeply critical about the aero-medical aspects of the crash. There'd be some sparks flying in his section of the report. 'Are you a betting man?' he had asked earlier in the morning. 'I'll lay ten dollars a head that a hundred and thirty of this lot were still alive after the crash.' It wasn't going to make pretty reading.

And pretty reading was worrying a lot of people. They had woken Raille at four o'clock that morning with a call from Washington offering him a replacement investigator. 'We heard about your wife's party,' the Washington voice had said. 'We'll fly you home for it. Someone else can take over the investigation.'

Raille could guess who the someone else would be. One of the Republican placemen who had arrived during the latter Nixon years. Someone who knew how to be discreet. Someone to take care of the 'albatross' 119.

Raille had politely declined the offer. They couldn't actually extricate him unless he volunteered. It was too late. He was accredited representative here, constitutionally independent, answerable only to his Board chairman. He had been sent out to reconstruct as exactly as possible the circumstances of disaster, whatever consequences they might have on jobs and votes. Make or break crash it might be for the 119, but if there was something wrong with the aeroplane now was the time to find out.

The teams from Seattle and Burbank had arrived. The power-plant engineers were grouped with their clean tarpaulins pegged out around the engines. Already they'd discovered the generator on number one engine disengaged and since the 119 didn't carry an emergency wind-driven generator Tango November would have been down to single generator operation when the number two engine had been shut down.

There was even the suspicion now that the shut-down itself

had been the result of an unnecessary fault – another false fire-warning. The fire extinguishers in one and three engines had been found only partially discharged before impact damage, the anti-fire precaution taken by Captain Duckham seconds before the crash. But extinguishers in number two engine had been fully discharged some time prior to the crash, though without apparent signs of a pre-crash fire or overheat.

Everything would now need to be subjected to the microscope and to film and X-ray tests for a proper analysis. Eventually each part of the aircraft would be fitted together jigsaw fashion with the damage on impact and pre-impact damage or deterioration carefully detailed. The mechanical and electrical systems would be reassembled and tested, and hopefully somewhere along the line they would discover why the sensing-element had indicated a fire, why the number one generator had been disconnected, and what effects, if any, both failures had had on the operation of the aircraft.

The most difficult reassembly job had been tackled by two of the Italian investigators, joined now by four engineers from the aircraft manufacturers. They were piecing together the two shattered wings, with the ailerons and aileron mechanism. The left side wing had disintegrated back along the crash path and there was scarcely a piece of it larger than a car door. The Italians had found the two small ridges in the ground that provoked the break-up. None of the trees were resistant enough to have caused such damage. In fact they had been scythed off like stems in a wheat field. But when the wing tip had hit a protrusion of old lava the structure had given way ten feet from the fuselage. They were lucky the break had happened so spontaneously, thought Raille. Considering the angle of bank the plane might easily have cartwheeled. The pilot must have been flying it to the last hundredth of a second to put it down so flat, and not just flying it but fighting it. It was a pity his efforts had been rewarded with so few survivors.

Larry Raille turned back into the concertinaed mess of cockpit. The flight deck had yielded one cryptic piece of evidence that morning: a scribbled note on the Flight Engineer's pad found torn and blood-stained among the debris on the floor – 'Battery high charge', the Engineer had written, if handwriting comparisons proved conclusive.

Everything else was now to be worked out through a painstaking dissection of electrical and hydraulic systems: bulbs to be examined for the stretching of filaments that would prove they had been alight at the time of impact; instruments to be photographed in ultra-violet to show up their original readings; wiring circuits to be tested and X-rayed for possible short-circuits; manual controls finger-printed to show which of the three men had been operating them and to establish whether the lady intruder had interfered in any way with the operation of the plane.

But dramatic solutions like hi-jacking were beginning to seem ridiculous. Already they'd discovered two technical failures, neither of them disastrous in themselves or even unusual, but potentially dangerous in combination, and combinations were what aircraft accidents were usually about. Raille had examined more than forty incidents in his time at the Safety Board, anything and everything from single-seat gliders to Jumbos, from a steward's broken nose in a heavy landing to death in a major disaster. On every occasion where evidence was available the investigators had found themselves dealing with combinations of circumstance: bad design; inadequate maintenance; weather conditions; human error; technical failure; fatigue or stress, both mechanical and human; above all, bad luck in a game where luck theoretically should play no part. Raille pictured this Captain Duckham for the first time – in the middle of a storm, minus an engine, minus a generator, perhaps over-tired, certainly over-stressed.

Raille used to fly Starfighters in the Air Force. More than once, with the combinations, it had scared him shitless.

Ralph Burden watched the conflagration through binoculars from his hotel balcony thirteen miles away. He thought at first that the smoke was Tango November, and he feared a repetition of an RAF accident in the tropics many years ago where wreckage had ignited spontaneously under the intense heat of direct sunlight. He took a compass bearing on the root of the smoke and plotted out the line on a map, but the line passed four or five miles clear of the crash site and Burden guessed with approximate accuracy that the fire was a result of picnicking sightseers.

He returned into his room and to a table that was slowly accumulating a weight of files, charts, diagrams, together with Burden's own notes. Greyhound's Safety Officer had supplied him that morning with flight information covering Tango November: the pay load and fuel take-off weights, and the records that brought Tango November's log book up to date. Maintenance records would be passed on to the Americans when they returned to their hotel that evening and Burden was checking quickly through them for any information relevant to his own investigation. He chronicled Tango November's delayed departure in his notes, tracing it back through Duckham's request for a recheck on the number two engine, the time taken to change cabin configuration from military back to normal requirements, and the initial delay and engine check in Germany. Until that trouble Tango November, in her seven months of service, had been relatively free of major faults and recent log book entries were largely taken up with items of cabin furniture: loose seats, tables and ashtrays; inoperative belts, a minor collapse in the overhead luggage rack. Burden made a brief note of them all. He had heard a tirade from Mac yesterday about conditions inside the cabin. A history of loose seats and belts could be relevant to his medical report, and it might not occur to the Americans to refer those sections of the log back to him.

Burden had sketched out the bare timetable of disaster on thirty sheets of otherwise blank foolscap; Friday evening to Saturday morning subdivided by vertical columns into half-hours and further subdivided into one minute sections for the last half-hour preceding the crash. Horizontal columns represented each member of the flight and cabin crew, the operations in progress, and communications with Air Traffic Control zones and airports, and, in case the flight recorders were found intact, entries for position, altitude, speed and heading. Burden had set aside two additional columns at the foot of each page to cover 'woman intruder' and 'hi-jack indications'.

A further four foolscap sheets dealt with biographical and professional summaries of the three flight-deck crew members and any relevant details concerning the six hostesses. For the moment only one of these pages had come to life, and Burden had deliberately set that page aside. He had spent the evening and half the night renewing acquaintance with people, places, and sensations long forgotten. Dixie Duckham would have to wait. He was too distracting. Perhaps Mrs Duckham would supply the perspective, if and when she arrived.

The Flight Engineer's biography was a great deal simpler, deceptively simple, Burden thought as he checked Raven's RAF record. A single man with no known commitments, he had been in the service until three years ago, leaving at the age of thirty-six. And yet in eighteen years of service he had made very little progress in rank or status. His RAF career was recent enough for Mac to be able to find out something about him from assessment records and Burden laid his file to one side.

Co-pilot was Peter Nyren. Born 1946; father Canon Ash Nyren; mother, Evelyn Mary, *née* Fawcett, died 1959; educated at the Dragon prep-school in Oxford, and at Radley; entered Hamble Flying School 1965, passed out 1968 with average to good results. Entered Court Line 1968 to fly One-Elevens. Recruited eight months ago for Greyhound and sent to the States for 119 training. Entered service with Greyhound ten weeks later.

Burden scribbled down the relevant details: age 29; Hamble; flying hours as at September 5th, 1847; six years on One-Elevens; eight months including training on 119s. There were two loose pages at the back of the file – a photocopy of a letter addressed to Captain Duckham, Fleet Captain Greyhound Flight, and the carbon copy of a reply. Burden glanced over them quickly, caught the words 'regret' and 'complaint', and took both letters out to read them more closely.

Peter Nyren's letter to Duckham had been written in careful long-hand and was the result, Burden guessed, of many rough drafts.

Dear Fleet Captain,
I am writing to you in your official capacity because I should like this letter and the nature of my complaint to be placed on record.

Strange, thought Burden, that these letters had been left in the file. No company liked to air its dirty linen, especially in the aftermath of a disaster.

At the time of my recruitment into the company I was given to understand that the seniority list would be as per normal practice based on length of service within the company. Indeed you yourself emphasized my early prospects of being appointed Captain. It has since become known that you are now recruiting 'senior' or older 119 pilots as Captains, offering them entrance at three, four or five increment levels. I feel that you have taken advantage of our friendship to foist this state of affairs on myself and the younger First Officers whom I represent. It would not be an exaggeration of my feelings to describe your action as a betrayal. I must communicate to you the prevalent attitude among my fellow officers, for you have so undermined our confidence and trust that your continued office as Fleet Captain could seriously affect labour relations in the company.

I greatly regret having to write to you in this vein after your earlier kindness and hospitality. In this respect I hope my good wishes to your family are still acceptable.

The good wishes at the end of such a letter sounded more like a threat than a blessing. Duckham's typewritten reply merely acknowledged receipt without reciprocating regret, anger or good wishes. The letters were both dated in the third week of July. Had the two men been in contact at all since then? On Friday night Nyren had been on standby. He had flown Tango November as it were by accident, substituting for another colleague on sick leave. Was that the first time Nyren and Duckham had flown together since the quarrel?

Dixie Duckham again. It was easy enough to imagine people quarrelling with him, but Burden had to remind himself that his own memories of the man were thirty years old.

He was relieved when the hotel desk rang him to tell him that they were serving lunch in the dining-room. He sat at his single table struggling with a plate of spaghetti and imagining in spite of himself how Dixie might have ridiculed him for his ineptitude.

6

Irrespective of technical opinion on site the office of the Procuratore issued a press release that afternoon restating the scenario of hi-jack, this time without the usual reservations.

When the younger Magistrato protested to his colleague about the release of ambiguous and unsubstantiated material he was told that the press release had been an unfortunate mistake too late to rectify.

Sharlie read the press release in mid-afternoon and rang Citto at the newspaper: 'Looks like it's all over.'

'We've only just begun,' Citto told him. 'Where have you been.'

'Looking for my mum.'

'Or joy-riding on your cousin's motor-bike.'

'Maybe.'

'Take it up on the mountain. There's a big wood fire burning. You might find some good pictures. I'll meet you at the doctor's house when it gets dark.'

'What doctor?'

'Pick up your lovely cousin. Take her with you. She knows which doctor.'

Sharlie's grunt was unenthusiastic.

I'm going to lose him, thought Citto as he hung up. Sharlie doesn't like being home. He'll be off back to Rome tomorrow.

Citto was shirt-sleeved and sweating, buried in the basement archives at his newspaper office. He had spent all afternoon with the card-index, records and back-numbers, tracing the respective histories of the Tomacchio and Consoli families.

Tomacchio was straightforward enough – country boy to small business owner in thirty years' labour. He'd been in trouble at the end of the war operating a black market in stolen drugs and equipment from a British army hospital on the far side of the mountain – sentenced to a year and a half inside and released on an amnesty after seven months. But he must have kept some of his money. He was running a small garage by 1950; driving his own lorries by 1955; advertising a transport business in 1959. A small-time hustler tough enough to look after his own limited interests. He'd bought that distillery three years ago, selling off the vineyards to a construction company. Which is doubtless where the Consoli *père et fils* had entered his life.

Avvocato Consoli was altogether more complex, the sort of man who travelled to and from his office in chauffeur-driven cars with police out-riders to protect him from would-be kidnappers. The family went back generations as local lawyers, estate managers and tax agents in the service of absentee landlords and rulers. The present head of family had established himself after the war with the Christian Democrats, a party organizer and local government dignitary. He had been rewarded ten years ago with minor office in Rome and had afterwards returned to Catania as what could politely be described the number one wheeler and dealer. Still a practising lawyer he had been associated with all large-scale development on the east coast of the island – everything from the oil refineries at Augusta to the autostrada and the new airport. He had doubtless fostered his close links with politics and administration at local, regional and national levels, and must have enjoyed unrivalled access to planning departments, not to speak of his professional participation in the distribution of official funds whether from Rome or from Brussels.

The newspaper had done a profile on him only a year ago on the occasion of some local party function. 'A modest man,' the reporter had written, 'whose emotions are closer to the countryside than the city.' The Avvocato lived on his own farm somewhere out on the southern slopes of the mountain.

Citto checked the telephone number. 62–58991. The area code was somewhere out in the orange groves near Paterno. He dialled the number on an off-chance, listening to the ringing tone a long time before someone answered.

'Casa Consoli,' announced a hesitant woman's voice.

'I'd like to speak with the lawyer, please.'

'I am afraid he is out. He's been away since yesterday.' The woman sounded genuinely apologetic.

'It's a matter of some importance. Do you think I would

find him at home if I visited this evening?'

'Oh no. I'm sorry. He's away until tomorrow.'

'Is there any number where I can reach him?'

'I could pass on a message if he rings.'

Citto tried guile. 'I was asked to meet him. Tomorrow.' His stammer made lying sound so innocent.

The lady believed him. 'At the airport you mean?'

'Yes.'

'Just a moment.' There was a pause while she looked for something. 'It's flight AZ 140. I'm afraid there's nothing written down here about when it arrives.'

'Thank you, Signora, I can find that out.'

'Who shall I say called?' she asked, but the phone was already dead.

What a strange and illogical series of questions, the lady thought as she walked back upstairs. Better not tell her husband when he returned home. He would only yell at her. She remembered he had told her specifically to tell nobody that he was in Rome. AZ 140. She'd given away the flight number. Always intrigue, she thought to herself. Always things not to say and not to do. Signora Consoli retired to the shuttered silence of her room. The maids had their half-day off and there were another two hours to live through before she could leave for mass.

Julia's hotel room was also shuttered and dark. She was lying on the bed, a jug of iced lemon on the table beside her. She hadn't asked for it, but the proprietor's wife had brought it up to her soon after she arrived. The taxi had dropped Julia at the bottom of the long flight of steps off which the pensione was situated. She hadn't even been able to cope with paying him, handing over her purse as he was explaining the tariff.

Julia Duckham had been scarcely conscious of effort at any stage of her journey from England. The children had been left with Pam; a car had driven her to Heathrow; an Alitalia hostess had met her at Rome and escorted her to the connecting flight for Catania; and at Catania the pilot himself had taken her from the plane to find her a waiting taxi. He had saluted her and stood back watching the taxi leave. The little freemasonry of airline pilots, thought Julia, helping each other or each other's families when things go wrong.

Reality was gone. At home it would be tea-time: Pam calling the children in from the garden; bicycles and pedal cars to be wheeled into the garage; raspberries, apples and spinach to be picked for the evening. Julia tried to think of the details but they were all broken. Little pieces of a nightmare that would soon reclaim her. She couldn't even bring herself to telephone and talk to the children as she had promised.

'*Devo vedere il corpo di mio marito, il pilota.*' The phrase she had accumulated with the help of her patient taxi-driver. 'I must see the body of my husband, the pilot.'

Hospitals, morgues, police stations, she had tried them all up and down the coast without success. What had they done with Mike? Was there anything left of him at all? I must see him dead, she thought, or I shall never be able to accept it.

There were pots of geraniums on her balcony, a buzz of voices promenading in the square below, smells from a restaurant. It was the sort of place they'd always promised themselves to go when Mike retired.

'Come on girl. It's an adventure.' She heard him say it, saw his encouraging smile, felt his chivvying arm under her elbow.

Like the very first time they'd been out together, the evening her air hostess sister had been stranded in a German fog. The two sisters had shared a flat near the hospital where Julia worked. Mike had arrived that evening to take Pam out, and had seemed almost relieved not to find her.

'Come on,' he'd said to Julia. 'Let's you and me go out, and do just the hell we please.' And they had. They had been to Bentleys for oysters and smoked salmon; then to Rules for pheasant; and finally across the Strand for treacle pud and cream at Simpsons. Mike's expensive joke of course. A bottle of wine at each establishment and a walk over Waterloo Bridge for their first very formalized kiss. A traditional seduction he had called it, though they were both too sloshed to do anything much more than giggle at each other by the time they got home.

'My God,' he'd said, next morning, 'but you're different from your sister.' He had nicknamed poor Pam the 'Prim and Trim', Pam who had been his mistress for six months and tormented by the fact that he was apparently inexorably married and with family. But that same first morning-after he had proposed to Julia and they hadn't even made love properly together. 'I offer you my life,' he had said, 'absolute and complete apart from my paternal affection and duties to my daughter.' And he had carried out the whole operation on his own without apparent melodrama. He met Pam that day and told her what had happened; he had led his wife through the divorce and had made it seem to her inevitable; he had even won the affection of his daughter for Julia.

Nine years ago they had begun, courtesy of a Trident grounded at the Lohausen Airport in Düsseldorf. To end here, with another aircraft, in another country, and for reasons as yet unknown.

For the first time Julia wondered how the crash had happened. She remembered Mike's bitterness when a colleague had been killed: 'You watch them, girl. You watch them make it pilot error. Dead pilots don't talk back.'

The hotel room was dark, Julia sitting in a bowed slump on the edge of the bed. It was very late, well past the dinner hour on the notice behind the door. Yet the proprietor returned to escort Julia to the empty dining-room. He sat her in a window, poured wine and left her alone with a trolley of cold meats and salad. She ate and drank mechanically, watching the lights in the piazza, with Mike's voice and gestures jollying her along.

7

Mac's bodies were organized. Numbered, labelled and bagged they had been stacked on makeshift shelves in four refrigerated produce wagons parked on a railway siding next to the fruit market of a small town at the eastern foot of the mountain. Turi had organized the operation with the local Carabinieri and he and Mac were now installed a mile away from the siding in a basement of the same small hospital where the elderly surgeon was still working, in apparent futility, over Tino G.

For the moment, and thankfully, no one else knew the whereabouts of the crash victims. Even the inhabitants of the town, crowding for their Sunday evening stroll in the main piazza, did not yet guess the function of the meat truck as it ferried its locked up loads to and fro between the railway sidings and the discreet service door at the back of the hospital.

Mac and Sanju had been joined by an RAF dentist and two representatives from the London undertakers, and the process of official identification was under way based in the majority of cases on dental or medical evidence, records telexed from England. Direct identifications were impossible. Most passports and wallets had been stolen, and even the bodies that had escaped burning were in no condition to be shown to relatives. Mac had experienced the unwillingness of husbands, wives, mothers or fathers to acknowledge the identity of a badly damaged body. They were better left out of the proceedings.

Mac's team had decided to complete the operation in two stages: identification first; autopsy only when relatives and authorities had been given official notification of death. The casualty lists published so far had relied on the names of passengers issued by the travel companies, and such evidence was not considered sufficient for any legal purpose. Mac reckoned that they had at the most two clear days before public opinion started to call for the burial or repatriation of bodies. He would have liked more time. He wanted full autopsies on each one of these victims, for only brute statistics in brutal detail would make any impression in the official report. He had limited himself so far to opening only three specimen bodies from the three different sections of fuselage and they had each of them confirmed his initial impressions on the survivability of the crash.

The body from the front section of the wreck had whip-lashed over the seat-belt. There was a tear in the meseantery of the small bowel, a common enough cause of death in commercial aircraft where lap-belts are worn without shoulder harness. Any slackness in the belt would have provoked the injury and the passenger would have haemorrhaged to death long before the rescue teams arrived. It was clear that none of the bodies from the front of the plane had been affected by fire or fumes. The break in the fuselage would have acted as a ventilator.

The body from the wing section of the plane had suffered

compound fractures of both lower legs where they had hit the row of seats in front. In addition he had bad bruising and swelling above his eyes where his head had hit the hard plastic cover of the pre-packed meal container in the head-rest of the seat in front. This passenger would have been immobilized after the impact, probably unconscious and certainly unable to escape from the ensuing fire. Apparent cause of death here severe burning of tissue in the lung, but Mac was sure that blood tests would also reveal a high level of cyanide from burning plastic materials used in the 119 cabin.

A partially carbonized body from the central rear section had extensive fat and bone-marrow embolism in the lungs, again indicating major ante-mortem bone fracture probably of a serious enough nature to immobilize. Carbon in the trachea and bronchi established the fact that this passenger had still been breathing when the effects of the fire reached her. The burned remains of a watch on her wrist showed distinctly lighter patterns on the dial where the two hands had been pointing. The time indicated was 5.50. If the watch had been accurate it suggested that the fire had reached this passenger and finally stopped her watch as much as eighteen minutes after the supposed time of impact. It was clear enough to Mac that if passengers had not been immobilized by wreckage and injuries inside the cabin many of them would have had ample time to escape.

Later in the afternoon a police driver arrived with an up-to-date list of survivors and twenty-three bodies collected from hospital morgues. At least the figures now tallied. The only missing numbers among the living and dead were the four flight-deck corpses, all of them in the hands of local legal authority in Catania. But the autopsies on pilots and Flight Engineer were at least complete, and only the fourth of the four, the mysterious lady intruder, presented any problem in that she had not yet been identified nor her missing arm located.

Two floors above Mac Tino G. was watching the red second-hand of the theatre clock. It moved slowly and spasmodically, jerking its way round, unsynchronized with whatever pulses now governed his consciousness. He felt he could have played one side of an LP in the time it took to move from twelve to twelve. He knew from the sweat-stained white-coated backs bent around his nether regions that no one present had realized that his eyes were open and his mind awake. He didn't want to trouble them. There was no point. He felt no pain and that thin red hand was moving far too slowly. He thought instead of his girl's face, oval through her long hair, sideways eyes grinning at him as they walked, and her shoulders hunched into a heavy coat. Just whistle and I'll come, she'd told him. But who would pay her ticket 3000 miles out here?

The plaintive notes of that tune came back into his mind: F sharp, E, D sharp, F sharp. C sharp, D sharp, E, D sharp, C sharp, B.

The simplest of melodies in dominant and tonic. A wandering travelling song: *jet plane, freight train,* and *early-morning rain.*

8

The charred scar of forest fire was still blowing sparks in the breeze. Sharlie had arrived on the mountain road, passing the road-blocks with the borrowed press-cards he always kept in his pocket, Laura behind him on the rear hump of her brother's racing-bike, nursing the bag of cameras and film.

The mountain road was now empty. Apart from the piles of refuse there was nothing left to suggest the queues of cars that had blocked the road earlier in the day. The evidence was scattered high up on the hairpin where the fire had passed: two fire-engines, groups of police and a long littered line of burnt cars. Sharlie parked the bike and walked up the road to take his pictures: metal skeletons of cars still glowing in the fading light, the ashfields of what had once been woodland and undergrowth. Sharlie walked through it, his shoes hot through cracked soles, scuffing clouds of dust and sparks. Then in a defile twenty yards from the main road he found wreckage that had survived the fire, mechanical capsules that must surely have been dropped by the crashing plane. Sharlie used a flash to photograph them in detail: two cylinders similar in shape to the self-inflating life-rafts that lined the upper decks of ocean-going ships. For some reason they had survived the fire intact, only discoloured by the heat and smoke.

Sharlie rejoined Laura on the road and they walked together back to the motor-bike as a helicopter passed low overhead: Larry Raille and his team of investigators returning from Tango November to their hotels in Taormina, and swooping, courtesy of the pilot, for a look at the remains of the forest fire. But from thirty feet up they couldn't make out any detail, and the two strange canisters remained undiscovered, but for Sharlie's camera, until the police retrieved them later that evening.

The two cousins freewheeled downhill in the chilly dusk and stopped at the first bar for a hot coffee.

The barman served them watching Sharlie: 'You're a journalist.'

'How do you know?'

The man shrugged. 'You must be a journalist to get through the road-block.'

'They lost a lot of cars up there today.'

'Serve them right. They shouldn't come gawping at other people's misfortunes.'

Sharlie drank his coffee. 'You think anyone heard the aeroplane crash from the village?'

'People higher up might have heard.'

'Who'd have been up in the woods at that time of the morning?'

One of the villagers joined in from behind his newspaper: '*Cantallaluna.*'

The barman nodded. 'That's possible.'

The other man put down his newspaper. '*Cantallaluna.* He came down with a sackful yesterday. I saw him on his motor-bike on the top road.'

'You didn't talk to him?'

'He didn't stop.'

'Has anyone talked to him?' Sharlie turned to the other men in the room who were listening and watching.

'Who's seen him?' answered one old man. 'I haven't.'

Sharlie paid for their coffees and they returned to the bike.

'How would we find *Cantallaluna*?' asked Sharlie.

Laura shrugged. 'You'd have to choose the right sort of day and catch him in the woods in the early morning.'

Sing-to-the-moon. The origins of his name went back many generations. His family had been cart-drivers, riding their loads at night and singing their way through the mountain villages. *Cantallaluna.* The name was still appropriate though he had no need to drive carts or lorries any more. He made a good living from the mushrooms in the woods high on the volcano, picking them in the early morning and putting them on the aeroplane for Turin or Milan where they'd fetch around 10000 lire a kilo.

If he had been up on the mountain picking on Saturday morning he could have been very near to where the aeroplane had come down.

'We'll find him one morning,' Laura said.

Someone will, thought Sharlie. Not me. For he still believed he would return to Rome next morning.

The village slipped into evening as Mac and Turi came home: harvesters returning from the vineyards; young men calling for young girls and walking them to the little cinema at the top of the street; children being yelled to bed, and the smell of someone's pasta and beans leaking out of a backyard and over the roofs to tease Mac's empty stomach.

Mac had sent Sanju with the day's report to Taormina. The monosyllabic Indian was well-enough equipped for the conference table, and Mac in his present state of exhaustion could not face one of those interminable multi-national pow-wows. Not that he ever liked to attend the evening pooling of evidence until he had his own answers cut and dried. That missing arm was beginning to worry him.

The doctor's doors had not been barred tonight. There were two cars and a motor-bike parked outside; a taxi-driver in one of the cars, a lady in Turi's waiting-room, Sharlie, Citto and Laura on his terrace.

'Bloody journalists,' said Mac. 'I can't talk to them.'

But it was Turi for whom Citto and Sharlie were waiting, and Turi who had to evade their questions by attending to his duties in the front of the house.

The lady in the surgery was no patient. '*Devo vedere il corpo di mio marito, il pilota.*'

Both Turi and Mac recognized the pretty English face from

the photograph in Captain Duckham's wallet. The pilot's wife. It was clear from her confused questions that she had not yet succeeded in tracking down her husband's body.

'I don't think there is anything for you to see,' said Turi.

'I've seen bodies before.'

'I examined the flight crew last night,' Mac told her. 'But the police took the bodies away this morning. I am afraid they have a legal right to their own medical examination.'

'You make it sound as though they were criminals.' The woman was angry and confused.

'You would expect the same after a car crash,' said Mac.

'They told me you'd be able to help me. They said you would know where he is.'

Turi was more accommodating. He knew where the police would keep their sensitive medical evidence: 'It's an easy enough place to find. But I still say there is no point for you to see your husband's body.'

'I didn't come here to sit in the sun,' the lady said.

'If we did find him,' suggested Mac, 'we might find our hijacker's missing arm. Why don't we all go into town?'

Turi would have to come, thought Mac: the *medico condotto* to give the escapade some spurious official validity. And Sharlie, too, for his cameras. Citto was less lucky.

'I only want photographs for my own purposes,' Mac told him. 'We'll be in bad enough trouble without turning the whole thing into a newspaper story.'

9

Turi, Mac and Julia left in the taxi and Sharlie met them an hour later at a prearranged rendezvous in the centre of town. They walked into the building after only a perfunctory challenge from the policeman at the door. Turi was still carrying a pass issued to him yesterday by the Carabinieri at the crash site and that, together with Mac's RAF warrant, seemed to satisfy the guard. Once inside there was no one in the corridors or on the stairs to query their movements.

They came down stone steps into a cold vaulted cellar, Julia suddenly afraid at what she might find. One of the rooms was lined in white tiles and furnished with a long cold-store cabinet of giant drawers. The bodies inside were oddly shaped and covered by plastic sheets.

Mac took Julia by the arm. 'There is nothing for you to see. There is no point in looking.' Death is ugly and irrelevant, he would have liked to explain.

'Captain M. E. Duckham' – a label in Mac's handwriting. He watched Julia raise one corner of the plastic sheet. She found a pair of feet cold and hard, one white, one bruised blue and ugly like part of a desecrated statue.

'Please,' she said. 'Please show me.'

Mac took the sheet from her and folded it back. In that moment only pain and disgust kept Julia from collapse. The body was naked and broken, even further violated by a scalpel whose long incision had been sewn up with thick crude stitches. The face seemed masked. What was left of it was torn down in folds over the chin like soft red rubber. Even the shape of the skull had gone, flattened, grotesquely framed by unnaturally coloured hair.

Mike. There wasn't much to identify. His stomach, hips, thighs, genitals. It was enough. She turned away to sit by herself while the two doctors pursued their own search.

Sharlie was watching Julia. He thought, I could have taken a terrible picture of her face in that moment with the body. An Italian woman would have shouted or screamed and demonstrated frenzy. This lady instead is sitting there frozen and composed as though posing for someone.

The doctors found the woman hi-jacker in a numbered drawer, her identification still unsolved. Her torn arm was lying grotesque between her legs, but there was no mark or label on it to show whereabouts in the wreckage it had been found.

Turi was looking at the arm remembering his cramped struggle to find the trapped American boy. The wrist was circled in rings of copper, silver and gold, and Turi recalled the jangle of bracelets when an arm had fallen across him in the wreckage of the plane.

'I think I know where it lie,' he said. 'I was trying to reach that boy and it fall on me. I hear these rings – '

Mac picked up the arm and jangled the bracelets. Turi nodded with a grimace. 'It was in the same mess where the boy was trapped.'

'The American boy with the guitar?'

Turi nodded. Mac was studying his salvage plan. Tino G. had been found well behind the line of the front exit in the middle of loose wreckage that accumulated against the galley wall. It was six or eight feet back from the flight-deck door.

'Was the arm loose or trapped in the wreckage?'

Turi thought for a moment before replying. 'Trapped. I move something and then it falls.'

Mac grunted. 'Problem solved.'

'How you mean?'

'No hi-jacker.'

'Why?'

'She lost her arm when the plane crashed, right? So she was in the cabin when the plane hit the ground.'

Mac was matching arm to body. There was no possible doubt that the two belonged together. Ligament and muscle damage were complementary and the skin pigmentation identical.

'I'd say she was out of her seat standing in the aisle – probably in a panic. When the plane hit the ground she was thrown forward at whatever speed they were travelling. A hundred and thirty miles an hour perhaps. She would have flung out an arm to stop herself and she lost it when it caught on the galley partition. She carried on minus arm and crashed through the door on to the flight deck. The rest of the injuries are consistent with extreme frontal impact – splintered ribs and sternum, broken hips, both knees smashed, the other arm flung up to protect her face and jammed into her broken jaw.'

Mac noted down what he could see of the woman's dental set-up. Many of the teeth had been broken by the arm but there were two clear characteristics that might prove identification if related to dental records: a gold crown on a molar; and a gold cantilever bridge involving a canine, dislodged by the arm but still in one piece. The bridge looked like American handiwork.

Mac called Sharlie to take pictures of the body and the dental fragments.

Sharlie saw the body of a young woman terribly disfigured, a severed arm lying loose between her legs, her jaws broken wide open, the trunk sewn together in clumsy stitches. No one would have recognized it, brother, mother, lover.

Mac held the flash-gun for him. The boy was looking very green.

'I need a tripod for this,' Sharlie told Turi. 'I can't even hold the camera still. I never felt so bloody ill in all my life.'

Julia watched them as the repeating blue tinge of the flash-gun lit up the cellar, and three silhouettes bowed like vampires or body-snatchers over the corpses. When the giant Englishman was satisfied he slid the bodies back into the cabinet. Turi took Julia by one arm and the trespassers returned upstairs, down the empty corridors and back to the taxi in the street.

Sharlie unloaded the film and handed it to Mac. Mac shook his head. 'You get them developed and bring them to me. I've got no facilities.' He shook hands with the boy and thanked him for his help.

Sharlie watched the taxi turn the corner and disappear. Those bodies had made him feel ill. He saw lights and cars and the bustle of people in the main street and walked down to find a bar on the Via Etnea. He needed a large whisky and ice to dispel his nausea. But the drink only made him feel worse. He left it unfinished and wandered back into the obscurity of the side streets towards his motor-bike.

They caught him at the corner of Via San Francesco.

He didn't even hear the car behind him, and only turned to look when the doors opened. He caught a glimpse of the rotating blue lamp as a strong arm twisted him face to the wall in the sunken alley beyond the pavement. They were in darkness, unseen by anyone, ignored from the main street for the flashing blue lamp that licensed the violence. He sensed two of them; faces he could not see, and voices that did not speak. They frisked him; lifted a heavy boot into his balls when he tried to protest; and grabbed the camera case he had dropped surreptitiously in the angle of the wall. He heard them pull out the cameras and film; heard one of them mutter at his colleague; then heard the film reels break open under someone's foot on the pavement. He turned his head. They were unrolling the film through the slots of a drain cover. Finally one of them talked.

'Who were you with?'

The heavy foot came back when he failed to reply. Sharlie wondered how brave and obstinate he was meant to be in the face of such interrogation.

'Who was with you?'

'I was asked to do a job.'

'Who asked you?'

'I thought it was official.'

The interrogator turned to him with a sneer. 'Come on, baby-face. Don't give me shit.' Soft and round this cop was. He had Sharlie's balls in one hand, squeezing them gently. It was obvious from his eyes he was enjoying it. 'A smart boy like you always knows who he's working for.' He had pushed Sharlie back to the wall and was leaning close to him, tobacco and garlic breathing into his face. Sharlie felt the man's hand pull down his zip and move inside his trousers fondling his cock. He hit out at him instinctively, saw the man weave his head aside, smile and look to his colleague.

The colleague nodded. 'He's assaulting you.'

The soft round cop flicked his fist twice into Sharlie's face, back and forth so fast that the boy didn't even see it. But he felt the pain, blood warm in his mouth, and his tongue deep in a pit where one of his teeth used to live.

'What car were they in?' The man patted Sharlie's cheek where the tooth had broken. 'You want to lose all of them, pretty boy?'

The pain had made Sharlie cry. He didn't want to show himself crying. He mumbled a reply.

'You make it sound like a love scene if you whisper.'

'A taxi.'

The man's hand was back inside his trousers churning around for a reaction. 'What sort of taxi?'

'From Taormina.'

'What sort of a car?'

'A Lancia.'

'Colour?'

'Dark blue.'

No more was said or done. The hand was withdrawn,

disappointed, and the two men vanished in their car while Sharlie groped around on the cobbles retrieving his cameras and the broken pieces of film cartridge. He spat blood and the broken tooth into his hand and wondered whether it was anger he was shaking with, or just fear. He also wondered what trouble there would be for the others in the taxi.

But the two cops were not in luck. Their mission was not official enough to call out more cars, and the taxi had taken the inland roads to drop Turi in his village. The cops, burning rubber along the autostrada, found no Lancia and it was only much later in the evening that they were able to trace the taxi-driver and ask him questions about his passengers and their itinerary.

Citto and Sharlie met at the newspaper, the boy's face bruised and swollen, his voice thick and stumbling like that of a beat-up boxer after a bad fight. He told Citto of the bodies in the morgue and the cops nailing him afterwards. He was still shaking, his mouth bloodied and his face bruised.

Citto went over the details of both stories making Sharlie repeat the sequence of events.

'Where did you go afterwards?'

'I've come straight here.'

'You didn't go home to your mum?'

'Looking like this? She'd be out with a gun shooting cops.

'Did the English doctor leave an address?'

Sharlie took out a piece of paper with the name and telephone number of Mac's hotel in Taormina. Citto copied it into his notebook.

'Better go back to your Nonna Lisa. Get yourself patched up by your beautiful cousin.'

'Give them a fright, won't I?' Sharlie pulled what he could of a grin. 'Will the paper print the story?'

'Half of it. The bodies in the morgue. They'll blow the hi-jack theory but they won't print anything about the cops.'

'No. They never bloody well do.' Sharlie turned at the door. 'If you want my help you know where to come.'

Citto grinned. 'I thought you were going back to Rome.'

Sharlie fingered his face. 'After this? I want those bastards. They wouldn't have done this if someone wasn't hiding something. You want anything done you come and tell me.'

Citto followed him down the corridor and waved good-bye at the stairs. Then he called on his News Editor and repeated Sharlie's stories. At least Sharlie's earlier pictures had survived, the strange capsules on the mountain.

'Flight recorders from the aeroplane,' said Citto. 'People reckon someone's been trying to hide them.'

'Why should they do that?'

'Frightened of the story they might tell.'

'So what do we print?'

'The truth about the hi-jack body and pictures of the flight recorders.'

'Everything out in the open.'

'Almost everything. I'd like to keep going at it.'

'What's stopping you?'

'I'd have to go to Messina and Rome. Maybe even further.'

The News Editor waved his arm and laughed. 'Draw expenses and go. At least if you're not here no one can have you taken off the story.'

Citto left the office but without drawing expenses. He didn't want any written record of where he was going or what he intended to do.

He would need the early train to Messina, and, if he finished there in good time, the mid-morning flight to Rome from Reggio Calabria. Time for five hours' sleep he reckoned, before he packed his bags.

10

Julia Duckham felt the darkness closing in again. The woman on the flight deck had been a myth. The bearded doctor had told her that a hi-jacking was now excluded as a possible cause of the accident. It seemed to Julia that Mike would now be heading the list of suspects, with 'pilot error' the most probable result of any investigation. How unfair if his life were to end with such a lie.

Mac had guessed at one half of her anguish. He too believed that the odds were shortening against Captain Duckham. He would have liked to tell this pretty woman to go back home and forget all about the circumstances of the crash and the inquiry. She had a young family. He knew that from Duckham's file. She ought to find another man. Death was not to be lingered over, except as a medical equation.

He stared from the taxi window. They were high on lava cliffs above the coast, the whole sea covered it seemed with bobbing lights, like a procession of lanterns. The lady was also watching them.

'Fishermen,' Mac told her. 'The fish come up to the lamps, then they pull the nets in.'

She looked at him and nodded, and her eyes in the dark looked so sad and so lost that Mac wanted suddenly to take her hand and offer her some comfort.

When they arrived in Taormina he paid off the taxi and walked her up a flight of steps to her hotel.

'You've been a great help,' he said. 'I wish there was some way I could help you.'

'He was a good man,' she answered in a low voice. 'He really was a good man.'

Mac watched her cross the lobby of the little pensione, a forlorn, unhappy figure. He wondered for the first time what this Dixie Duckham had really been like.

A few hundred yards away in a different pensione Ralph Burden was asking himself much the same question. He had been interviewing the Greyhound Safety Officer about those strange letters in Peter Nyren's file. The American did not deny that the two letters were left there deliberately.

'Within the company it was a very public quarrel. Sooner or later someone would have found out. Much better for you to have the precise evidence, not hearsay and gossip.'

Burden nodded. 'That's a very commendable attitude to take. Some companies might have tried to cover it up.'

'You will find, Mr Burden, that our company will cover up nothing in the efforts to get at the truth.'

Burden turned to his notes. 'We will have to know whether Duckham and Nyren had flown together since the exchange of letters.'

The American shook his head. 'There was a tacit agreement to keep the two men apart until the quarrel was resolved. They flew together on Friday night because someone went sick. Nyren was on standby.'

Burden nodded. 'In your opinion was it a bad enough quarrel to have affected their mutual efficiency on the flight deck?'

'I am quite sure a Captain of Duckham's experience would not allow personal animosity to get in the way of good flying procedure. In fact I imagine when you listen to the voice recordings you will find they had already patched up the quarrel.'

Burden referred back to his notes again. 'Was there any particular reason why you recruited Duckham as your Fleet Captain?'

'Experience. Excellent safety record. Very safety conscious. And he'd had twenty years' flying on the European routes we were trying to set up.'

'He was responsible for most of your recruitment?'

'Yes.'

'Were there any problems with recruitment?'

'It was almost complete. He wanted one or two older pilots. They couldn't very well come in at the bottom of the ladder. That's what caused the quarrel.'

'Nyren claimed in his letter to be speaking for the younger pilots in the company.'

'I don't think they shared his vehemence.'

'So there was something personal about the quarrel?'

'They had been close friends. I don't know.' The American paused and grinned. 'He was quite a guy for the girls of course.'

'Nyren?'

'Duckham.'

Dixie Duckham, hard-drinking womanizing crown prince of Little Snoring. The young fighter pilot was like a ghost walking round them in the hotel bedroom. Burden stood up.

'That'll be all for now, thank you. We might have to go over some of it again.'

The American turned to the door. 'Mrs Duckham has arrived. I expect you will want to ask her one or two questions. She's staying at the Pensione Albert.'

Burden wrote down the name. The American paused at the open door.

'There is just one more thing. Again it's something I'd rather not say, but it's one of those things some clever journalist is going to dig up. I don't suppose it has any relevance at all, but it seems Duckham had something going with one of the hostesses on this flight.'

Burden stared at the American deciding suddenly that he did not much like him.

'Company gossip I'm afraid. Probably nothing in it. It was the girl who survived. She's in one of the hospitals. Stella Pritchard.'

The American closed the door and Burden heard the squeege of his soft rubber soles receding down the corridor.

I I

A sequence of chords and one line of melody had held the thread of a boy's life. If someone had suggested that to the masked man in the white coat he might almost have believed it. The tired surgeon was ready to believe anything. He'd been working over the broken body on and off for nearly two days by now almost willing death on its way. For until the boy finally died he could not bring himself to wash up and go home.

Then some time in the dawn of Monday the surgeon changed sides again. Some time during that night he had stopped anticipating silence from the monitor and started instead to listen for the rhythm of that pulse. To fight so long. Even the tired old man suddenly wanted this mess of shattered bones and body to defy the shadows in the corner of the theatre.

— see the silver bird on high —

The boy's mind smiled. Tino G. had found a verse of words
for that lost tune in his head.

> Hear the mighty engines roar
>   see the silver bird on high
> She's away and westward bound
>   far above the clouds she'll fly
> Where the morning rain don't fall
>   and the sun always shine
> She'll be flying over my home
>   in about three hours' time.

Part Three

I

The storms had returned, a frenzy of impenetrable rain that
flooded the roads and erased all apparent movement from the
sea. Families began to move out of their summer homes along
the coast returning to the city, or the towns and villages in the
hills. The gathering of grapes stopped in the vineyards, and
on the mountain where the forest fire had destroyed the trees
a slope of earth and loose lava slipped a hundred feet and
buried the road.

In the wreckage of Tango November the investigators
continued to search for their evidence, partially sheltered under
tarpaulins and wrapped in heavy oilskins. Plastic sheeting had
been taped over the left side remains of fuselage and tail, and
the reassembled left wing had been laid out under canvas on
a suitably flat and cleared area of scrub nearby. Engineers had
found traces of fuel and hydraulic fluid that had leaked, it
seemed, from damage in the wing. The fluid stains, too substantial to have been caused by accidental spillage, were found
on the insides of buckled sections and complementary on both
sides of fractured wreckage, establishing that the fluids had
been leaking before the plane broke up. The outside ten feet
of left wing and ailerons were missing from reassembly and a
search-party of two Italians and two of the aircraft manufac-
turer's engineers were kitting themselves out for a long and
uncomfortable hike. Aerial search had shown up no wreckage
and until the missing wing-section was found no one would be
able to pronounce on the possibilities of a mid-air collision,
or earlier impact with the mountain.

Raille laid out the large-scale maps and plotted Tango
November's left-turning bank, projecting it in a consistent
arc from the pattern of damage in the splintered trees on the
crash path. The search-party would have to follow the likely
path of that arc back across the mountainside in the hope of

finding the missing piece of wing. Whatever they found or failed to find, it seemed likely now that the doomed plane had already lost half its manoeuvrability some time prior to impact.

At least the flight recorders had been found and the younger Magistrato had already arranged to send them back to England for read-out and analysis. They had turned up rather mysteriously lower down the mountain, and the local authorities had handed them over that morning after Sharlie's photographs of them had been published in the newspapers. Without those pictures they might have disappeared altogether, for it was clear that someone in the local hierarchy was doing his damnedest to hide or obscure evidence.

Raille watched the four men move off heavy under the rain with their packs and bivouac tents. They had an uncomfortable time ahead of them, whether in the wet or in the heat and humidity that seemed likely to return afterwards. The arc they were following swept across the eastern flank of the mountain, through dry scrub and over fields of lava as wild, featureless and inhospitable as a moonscape.

There were only five investigators left now in the actual wreckage – Raille and one of the Englishmen with the engineers from Burbank and Seattle, three of them buried waist-deep in the blackened tail wreckage salvaging the engines. Raille could hear them at odd times during the day cursing the rain, the occasional blasphemy exchanged between the two Americans, or the Englishman's dry-toned scolding as they overlooked his careful rules of procedure.

Raille and the systems analyst were bent up double instead in the floodlit cockpit, oil-skinned surgeons with their tangles of wiring and disembodied instruments.

Number one generator u/s, number two engine shut down. The instruments were beginning to reveal part of the nightmare: weather radar, one HF set, galley power and two booster pumps all apparently switched off, and cabin heating and lighting reduced. The Flight Engineer must have been shedding load to protect that one surviving generator, though it seemed a lot of load to shed. Galley power and a HF set were usually sufficient on a 119. A single generator could cope with the remaining equipment. Unless there'd been trouble on the number three as well. That would have been stretching bad luck to absurd limits. Even safety regulations had to depend on some law of probability.

Raille turned his attention back to the number two engine. Only six weeks ago, after the Nairobi crash, the Safety Board had sent a recommendation to the Federal Aviation Authority for further tests and development work to be carried out by the manufacturers on the 119's number two power-plant. In twelve months there had been over thirty reported cases of fire-warnings necessitating in-flight shut-down. No one had yet come up with any answers though it was thought that lack of exterior cooling due to the position of the engine under the tail was causing distortion giving rise to hot gas leaks.

The FAA had passed on the recommendation but without any mandatory conditions, content to leave further research to the initiative of the power-plant manufacturers. A Washington solution for a corporation already in financial difficulty.

A whistle blew lunch-time from the helicopter higher up the slope. It was half past twelve. Sun up in Washington. In fifteen hours' time, thought Raille, his wife would be opening their front door to the first guests, her eyes carefully sparkling, her make-up superb, her New England manner impeccable, his booze flowing freely. She gave very good, and very expensive parties.

2

The rain marked the end of summer, however brilliantly the sun would afterwards return. It was time to think on serious things.

The young Magistrato returned to his office that morning to find a corridor full of waiting counsel. The judicial timetable had been altered and three prosecutions brought forward, unexpectedly and without warning. Why and how he could not find out. A week's work, he calculated, and at the end of the week no doubt another three cases would reappear. His participation in the air crash inquiry had been effectively curtailed without obvious interference or collusion.

The Procuratore Generale seemed surprised when his young colleague complained.

'Your involvement with the air disaster was only advisory. Merely to help settle some of the technical problems.'

'So far as I know I haven't solved a single technical problem.'

'These crash inquiries take years to sort out. We cannot allow our timetable to congest as a result.'

'My own timetable was very uncongested – until this morning.'

'I expect some lawyers have been complaining about delays.' The Procuratore referred to papers on his desk. 'Two of your prosecutions involve men who have been waiting trial in prison for nearly a year.'

'Then statistically they should count themselves among the more fortunate.'

The two men eyed each other in distant half-smiles.

'You feel you have something to contribute to the investigation?' asked the Procuratore.

'I feel it is too much for one man to cope with, however able and experienced.'

'There is really very little to do at the moment. We have to cooperate with the technical investigation and wait for their results.'

The young man nodded. 'We have to be sure that they have access to all the evidence. Someone tried very hard to hide the flight recorders.'

'We're making inquiries into that. It seems more likely they fell from the aeroplane during the crash. There is some confusion about the exact location.'

The young Magistrato could imagine what kind of confusion. He tried again.

'Will the hi-jack theory be officially abandoned?'

'It is not our job to officially abandon any theory. Everything must remain a possibility.'

'Including the malfunction of the airport or airport instruments?'

'Good heavens!' For the first time the Procuratore looked almost alarmed. 'Who's suggesting that?'

'It is another area for investigation.'

'Of course.' The Procuratore turned away. 'You can rest assured that our own side of the inquiry will be thorough. If there is fault to be found we will find it.'

The young Magistrato returned to his office. He had as it were staked his claim. If nothing else, they would at least be more careful with their evidence. He bound up his share of the Tango November files and referred them back down the corridor to his elderly and still reluctant colleague.

A mile away across the city a Christian Democrat delegate of the city council was speaking eloquently of the distress caused by the disaster. He suggested a series of three charity concerts in Taormina, Catania and Syracuse to raise money for the bereaved relatives and injured survivors. A Dutch orchestra due to play at the Opera House in Catania agreed to postpone its departure to perform at the three concerts, and a Japanese pianist who had given a recital of Ravel and Poulenc in the Greek Theatre at Taormina offered a concerto from his repertoire.

On the far side of the mountain shopkeepers and businessmen in a village near to the airport met with their administrative authority and decided to offer facilities for the burial of the victims. A representative was sent directly to the Prefetto in Catania and to the travel agency officials in Taormina and a plan for a mass grave was accepted.

Unfortunately for the village authority the villagers themselves reacted against the idea of mass interment, which seemed to them to offend the dignity of death. There was no room in the cemetery for anything else, they were told, but the administrators had not reckoned with the community's sense of outrage. Two reluctant families owning land adjoining the cemetery were approached by their own peasants. Language and threats were used that had certainly never been heard in quarrels over wage claims or conditions of work. The two families relented: a chestnut, a row of olives, and half a dozen lemon trees were sacrificed; a high stone wall was demolished and rebuilt by voluntary labour; the cemetery gained a half-acre of ground, and the municipality, at more expense than it had bargained for, was obliged to lay out dignified lines of headstones, gravel paths and ornamental shrubs.

Outside Sicily the crash had dominated headlines for only one day. When the hi-jack theory had been blown and the blood and tears washed away the accident lost its 'box-office' potential.

The journalists and film crews began to disappear and in their place arrived the insurance men with Monday morning briefs from London and New York anxious to settle damages and compensation before sentiment or anger escalated. There were a few million dollars at stake between airplane and passengers, and the odd hundred thousand or two to be saved by asking the right questions in the right quarters.

Mac was one of the prime targets for their polite but insistent requests for medico-legal information. Had husbands died before their wives? Was there evidence of natural disease in the corpses that might have shortened life-expectancy? Had there really been suffering associated with death?

There were a dozen such queries already waiting for Mac and Sanju that morning, five of them relating to the same two victims – Mr and Mrs Janius, the 'honeymoon couple'. Mac remembered the name. Julius Janius had been one of the whizz-kids of the sixties rebuilding the nation's essential industry. What angle of the market was it he had cornered?

Sanju had read the newspapers. 'Velvet linings for budgerigar cages. Diversified into luxury dog and cat foods; then into boutiques and discos; finally into land and property.'

Enterprising Janius. What an expense of energy; what wastes of productivity.

Who, the insurance companies were asking, had died first, Janius or his newly wedded wife? In the event of her surviving his death five companies would be obliged to pay out £50000 each to the widow. It didn't matter whether she had died four seconds after him, or forty years. If she had survived him Mrs Janius or her estate collected a quarter of a million pounds.

Insurance men and Interpol were working hard on that one, tracing the origins of those unusual policies. Many of Janius' subsidiary companies were having a lean time and with that kind of money at stake someone may have tried to sabotage the plane.

3

Cloud had covered Taormina for the first time since spring. Torrential rain turned the hillside alleys into rivers and waterfalls, washing earth from the flower boxes, the lizards from their walls and a summer's dust from the roofs and terraces.

Ralph Burden watched it from his hotel room, the windows thrown open to let in the sudden freshness of scent from the gardens next to the pensione. He was waiting for Mrs Duckham, trying to imagine what Dixie's third wife could be like, trying to make up his mind about the questions he should ask.

Statistics and a photograph in a file; two strange letters in the First Officer's file; second-hand and unreliable gossip; his own bad memories: it seemed to Burden the more he learned of Dixie Duckham the more confused his picture grew. Dakotas, Ambassadors, Viscounts, Comets, Tridents and 119s – Duckham had seen and participated in each phase of airline growth since the early 1950s, and after twenty-two years of commercial flying still had a clean and uncomplicated record. Burden wondered if that in itself might not be relevant. If his flying had always been easy he might no longer have had the reflexes for an emergency. Ralph Burden had never found his flying easy.

The reception desk called him to say that Mrs Duckham had arrived and he told them to send her upstairs.

A young boy had shown Julia the way to Burden's pensione, padding uncovered and unconcerned through the downpour while she tried in vain to keep herself dry under an umbrella. When she walked into Burden's room her thin dress was blotchy with rain, her legs splashed and dirty, her shoes flooded. She knew as he looked at her that he had thought, my God what a mess.

She's so young, Burden was instead thinking. She seemed almost as young as the birds Duckham was pulling thirty years ago. 'Quite a one for the girls,' the American Safety Officer had told him. Dixie had been known to lay them anywhere in those far-off days – under hedgerows on the airport perimeter, in the long grass of roadside verges, standing up against the wall behind a village pub. 'Raffles' Burden had preferred not to believe such stories. He didn't even get to kiss a girl until V.E-Day.

He apologized to this Mrs Duckham for asking her to come on such a day and sat himself down at his table. There was only the bed for Julia to perch on. He apologized again feeling awkward and ill at ease, then led her rather brusque and cold through the timetable of events on the day preceding the crash: when had her husband eaten; when had he slept; when had he left home for the airport.

It was the first time Julia had relived the scene: little Clara with her sing-song dirge of good-byes; the white car disappearing down the drive; Mike's hand waving. When had she last touched him, she asked herself. He had kissed her on the landing. When had she last heard his voice? What were his last words to me? She remembered that red rubber face in last night's morgue.

'How much did he drink that day?' the man was asking her.

Burden saw the woman tighten up. 'You don't have to answer that question. There are medical tests to establish blood levels of alcohol or drugs.'

Julia was incredulous. 'You make it sound as though he's a criminal. You talk of him as the guilty party. He is guilty isn't he? Unless something actually happens to prove him innocent.'

The outburst quite frightened Burden. 'I only meant to ask did he have anything to drink during Friday.'

'He had a glass of wine with his lunch. He always does when he has to sleep in the afternoon.'

'One glass of wine.'

'One normal glass of normal wine.' She was eyeing the whisky bottle on Burden's bedside table.

The rain outside stopped as suddenly as though a tap had been closed and Burden looked round at the open window. Out over the sea forked lightning ran slowly zigzag parallel with the horizon.

Burden stared back at his papers. 'There was a storm on Saturday. Not as bad as this. But they were very bad conditions.'

He had offered it as a possible and innocuous explanation but Julia was fighting on reflex now.

'That would be nothing new for him. He's been flying thirty-five years. He was in the war. He's done every possible sort of flying.'

'He must have had a good temperament.'

Julia did not reply. She was trying to tell herself to calm down.

'If one took a poll of airline pilots in the major companies your husband would have been considered among the very top pilots on safety and experience.'

Julia stared at her wet shoes. She could feel the damp creeping up her legs.

'It must have been a wrench for him when he left his old company. Twenty years, wasn't it, he'd been with them?'

'We've only been married eight years.'

'Have you any idea why he changed company?'

'He was offered a better job.'

'Did he need the extra money?'

'I don't know anything about the money.'

'His job with Greyhound doubled his salary. You must have known that.'

Julia stared at him. It's not only drink, she thought. It's going to be his salary. Three children. Two divorces.

'He had heavy commitments, I believe.'

'I don't know what you mean.'

'Two ex-wives,' said Burden. 'Three families to support.'

'What's that got to do with the crash?'

'Everything is relevant that concerns the state of mind of a pilot. He might have been worried or depressed about something. Distracted.'

There was a silence and when Julia spoke it was in a whisper. 'We were very happy. He liked me to keep house for him. He liked the way I cooked for him. He liked everything. We were very happy. There's nothing to hide.' She was crying, talking head down.

Burden felt inexplicable hostility. 'Then you must have been aware that he was having an affair. He was sleeping with one of the hostesses involved in the crash.'

She stared across the room at him and Burden looked away. He didn't even know why he'd said it. It was nothing more than an unsubstantiated piece of gossip thrown out by a company man preparing scapegoats. I can't apologize, he thought. It would make me seem absurd.

'The girl in question is the surviving hostess in hospital in Catania,' he said. 'Her picture has been in the newspapers.'

Julia replied in a calm voice. 'I haven't seen any papers.' Why has he told me? she was asking herself. Such a story was nonsense. Why is he pretending things? To make me talk? About what? What tales do I have to tell on Mike? We were happy. I was happy. Was Mike happy? Who is this girl?

Burden sifted the papers on his table. He started again. 'So far as you know he had no particular anxieties?'

She shook her head.

'His health was good?'

She nodded.

Could he still take a girl standing up, Burden wanted to ask her. How many times a week? How long could he keep it up? Did he have this hostess in the airplane loo? When Burden's Mary had left him ten months ago they hadn't had sex in ten years. Now he had heard she was having good times with the young men of Ibiza. A screwball. Burden used to imagine that ordinary women only suffer sex. Favours bestowed.

The tap had been turned on again outside, a wall of rain obliterating sight and sound. He was staring at it, the woman still perched uncomfortable and bowed on the edge of his bed. How long was it since he had asked her a question?

'Did your husband's responsibilities as Fleet Captain cause him any additional worry?'

'I don't know.'

'Was his behaviour different in any way after he changed jobs?'

'Obviously he had more to think about.' About what? she wondered suddenly. About air hostesses?

Her interrogator was staring at his papers. 'A long time ago he was a very wild young man.'

'I don't know what you mean.'

Burden looked up at her. 'Did you know he was called "Dixie"?'

She nodded.

'Did you get to meet any of his friends from the RAF?'

'"Dodo" Griffin.'

Griffin had joined the squadron a few months before Burden in 1944. Another wild young man. Another screwball. Dixie, Dodo, Raffles: what an absurd collection of names. Perhaps all flying men were mad.

'Did he get on well with his colleagues?'

'He had a lot of friends.'

'You met them?'

'He liked people to come round.'

'Did you ever meet a young First Officer called Peter Nyren?' Julia nodded.

'You knew him?'

'He was a regular visitor a few months ago. He and Mike were flying together a lot.'

'They were friends, were they?'

She paused before answering. It was a trick question, she thought. He wouldn't have asked that if he didn't already know something. 'They quarrelled.'

'Do you have any idea why?'

'Something about recruitment.'

'Was it a bad quarrel?'

'Peter was very bitter. They'd been good friends.'

'They stopped flying together after the quarrel, did they?'

'It all went back to normal crewing procedure. Friday was the first time.'

'Do you think it might have made things difficult?'

'Mike wouldn't have let it. He'd have made friends again before they even started. He was going to invite Peter round for breakfast when they got back.' Julia remembered the sunlit kitchen on that Saturday morning; the food ready on the table; a bottle of wine; the bed made up in the dark room; the children upstairs. She felt her heart falter, her whole body weaken.

'There was nothing more personal about the quarrel?' Burden asked the question but she didn't appear to have heard him. 'Was there a quarrel over the girl?'

'Girl?'

'The hostess.'

Julia shook her head in despair. 'I don't know anything about a girl or a hostess. I don't want to know.' She stood up. Her dress was sticking to her in patches where the rain had wet it. 'You're going to blame him, aren't you? You're inventing stories about him. And I don't want to hear them.'

She walked out of the room. The man had been trying her on. Mike was so quietly and totally in love with her. That is what he told her time and again. 'You have made sense of my life,' he would say.

Dejected tourists sitting in the reception lounge with their foreign newspapers watched Julia appear from upstairs and march defiantly out of the pensione into the rain, leaving them to guess at her pain and her anger.

It was with the freshness and noise of the rain that Stella Pritchard returned to the conscious world. She woke in gloom listening to the water cataracting out of broken gutters, and when the nurses wheeled a telephone to her bedside she was able to speak coherently to her aged father and mother far away in Harrogate.

Both parents were sternly stiff-upper-lip, anxious to explain why it had been impossible for them to travel out to her bedside. Stella did not need explanations; she would not have expected them to come. In fact she would have been very alarmed to see them at all. She would have believed herself to be dying, for her father only undertook dramatic, unscheduled gestures *in extremis*.

It was he who replied calmly and factually to her questions when she asked him what had happened. Stella, equally calm and objective under the influence of her father's voice, accepted his account of the air crash and her miraculous survival. He told her of the little girl who had survived with her; of the large casualty list: of the other crew members all of whom had died. She realized in that moment that Mike was dead. And Peter. She could not for the moment remember who else had been flying with them.

The nightmare of the car accident receded, still a suspicion, to the edge of her subconscious. She remembered instead chasing the little girl up the aisle of the airplane and the sudden thump of uncontrollable movement when they hit the turbulence. She began to remember other things: Mike picking her up in the evening on the way to Gatwick; the honeymoon couple self-conscious and self-important as the plane loaded two hours late; the American boy with the green eyes and the guitar and the soft smile. She remembered clearing coffee-cups from the flight deck and realizing that Mike and Peter were still silent with each other. She remembered thinking that's the fault of Peter brooding, the silly kid. But now the silly kid was dead.

Was the American boy also dead?

When the telephone call was over the little girl came into the room shy and afraid, her hand tight held to one of the nurses. Stella remembered her name.

'Hello Trixie.'

Trixie sat next to her on the bed, Stella's face still her only link with events past in her life. All other faces were strange and the language they spoke associated with her mother and grandfather both of whom had disappeared. She was in fact the only survivor from a Brooklyn family party of twelve passengers.

When Stella took her hand Trixie lay on the bed with her head on the pillow and refused to move.

Tino G. was alive, and the old surgeon had returned home. Tino G. was now to be considered a probable survivor. He was wheeled from the theatre and slid off rubber sheets on to clean white linen in a bed. His body was still perforated with rubber and plastic tubing, his every function monitored. But these functions now presented a coherent pattern. The specialists who had at last arrived from sailing boats and mountain retreats confirmed the obvious and wisely slipped away.

The nurses who had suffered with him arranged the room with flowers cabled from 'Corinna' in New York. Two patient journalists still waiting in the lobby were led upstairs and a photographer allowed one picture of a sleeping boy.

4

Flight AZ 140 landed with a prayer through a curtain of rain and in a cloud of spray. Disaster was vivid on people's minds, not least those of the pilot and the Air Traffic Controller in the tower at Catania Fontanarossa airport. But the DC-9 pulled up on the short wet runway with – well, a few yards to spare. The pilot, clammy and thankful, taxied right up to the reception buildings to save his passengers a long walk in the rain.

Sharlie was waiting under a Coca-Cola umbrella on the terrace outside the bar, well protected in his cousin's motor-bike waterproofs and armed with his Nikon and a telephoto lens. Citto had been very precise on the telephone from Messina. He wanted photographs of every face that left the airplane, with particular attention paid to any passengers associated with Avvocato Consoli. Sharlie knew Consoli well enough as a local VIP and he picked him out as he appeared down the steps of the aircraft. But the scamper through the rain from the air-plane to building broke up the groupings. Only afterwards as the arrivals waited for their baggage did Sharlie notice the two faces accompanying the lawyer, and the young man meet-ing them in his orange and green Dino. It was Sharlie's bad luck that the weather made his job so difficult. His inquisitive camera, inconspicuous outside on the terrace, was seen by more than one vigilant pair of eyes as he circulated inside the recep-tion buildings. His face, his clothes and later his motor-bike were carefully remembered.

Canon Ash Nyren had also landed from AZ 140. He had transferred planes in Rome but had omitted to check that his baggage changed planes with him. They had assured him at Heathrow that his suitcase was labelled through to Catania and that consequently he had no need to concern himself about it. He now watched luggage rolling out down the conveyor belt and being stacked up on the baggage counter which was situated for some extraordinary reason on the exterior of the building exposed to the rain. His fellow passengers claimed their pieces and hurried away through the downpour to their cars and buses, until he was left alone still waiting by the conveyor belt for his angular and old-fashioned suitcase.

Sharlie saw him there: a sunken face, a hook nose, a mop of greying blond hair, a priest's collar standing alone against the rain and the empty counter. It was a good picture and Sharlie did not miss the opportunity. But having secured his picture he went up to the man to ask him if he could help in any way.

Ash Nyren had no Italian, but he had travelled over most of Europe in his time and always succeeded in some form of communication through his Latin. Now with this boy he spoke slow Latin trying to soften the vowels to approach an Italian sound. 'My baggage is lost,' he told him.

Sharlie picked up the gist of what the old fellow was saying. 'I'll help you,' he told him. 'I'll fix it all for you.' He registered the old man's loss with the Alitalia desk then took him out to the Taormina bus, promising he would be in touch about the lost case by letter, *poste restante* at Taormina, for the old priest had no accommodation yet fixed and therefore no address or telephone number.

One good deed done, Sharlie returned to his motor-bike. Good deed number two was to stop off at the nearby factory where his mother spent her days. He left a message to say he'd be coming to see her that evening, then rode carefully back into town on the flooded roads and spent the rest of the afternoon shut up in the dark-room at the newspaper.

Consoli had been closeted with his son for three hours asking the same questions a dozen times before he was satisfied he had the full answers.

Signora Consoli sat on the covered verandah trying unsuccessfully to hear the conversation over the noise of the rain. She was afraid her boy might be in some kind of trouble. He had been silent over breakfast with her that morning and had most unusually driven to the airport to meet his father. Fruitlessly it seemed, for Consoli had arrived with two colleagues and the Dino could only carry one passenger.

The *Signora* walked into the house on the pretext of ordering a cold tea from the kitchen. To reach the kitchen she could legitimately pass, and linger, outside the study. She heard talk as usual of the airport, that monstrous undertaking that had dominated their lives for so long. She had been told countless times how that strip of asphalt and concrete had secured their family future, and she had decided that given the choice which she never was, she would have preferred to risk any future rather than live with such an obsession. But then Signora Consoli had never lacked for money. Her life had always been well lubricated. She did not, as her husband often told her, understand or appreciate money.

She ordered the tea and retired upstairs to her bedroom from where she could watch the two men whenever they approached the study windows.

Flavio Consoli had reported to his father the events of the previous day: holding hands with the fat schoolgirl; obsequious lunch with the Procuratore; the gossip exchanged around the table.

What, asked the father, appeared to be the prevalent attitude towards the disaster?

'Fear of scandal,' the son replied. 'Sicily must not suffer', was a phrase he remembered.

The Avvocato laughed. 'In Rome they were saying, "Italy must not suffer".'

The son dared a question of his own. 'Were you successful in Rome?'

'Do you know why I went to Rome?'

'No, sir.'

'Well then – you can have no interest in my success or lack of success.' The father concluded with firm advice: 'Act normally,' the Avvocato said. 'We must all act normally. Everything must go on as before. That is most important. After all, we have nothing to hide, have we?'

'No sir.' Flavio hesitated before replying, but his father did not notice. Capo Tomacchio and their little side-show, Flavio was thinking about. He'd meant to tell his father. But goddamn it, he didn't want his head yelled off. 'No sir, nothing to hide.'

It was a tragic exchange: bad advice, and a fatally evaded opportunity to confess.

Act normally. Flavio had intended cancelling the truck for

this particular week. That journalist had been poking round ETNOLIO and Tomacchio was uneasy. But the Avvocato had been adamant and Flavio, obedient and unintelligent, resolved to act as normally as he knew how – apart from an unusually attentive walk later that afternoon around the orange gardens with his father to assess the effect of a day's rain.

That evening Flavio telephoned Tomacchio and told him to do the week's run as usual.

'We might attract attention to ourselves by not doing it,' he explained.

'Bloody nonsense,' replied the voice at the other end. 'Lying doggo is what we ought to be doing.'

'My father said quite expressly we must act normally. Everything must go on as before.'

'*He* said that?' There was a silence and a grunt. 'Still seems bloody nonsense to me.'

Stupid ape, thought Flavio. He would go somewhere else for his lorries when this business blew over. In fact he'd have gone elsewhere long ago if it hadn't been for Tomacchio's delectable daughter.

5

In Rome there had been no sign of rain, not even of cloud. Summer prolonged itself lazily, the city centre still occupied by tourists, the boulevards and gardens of EUR empty, the fountains playing to themselves, halls of government departments silent, corridors deserted.

Yet Citto had found a few pockets of activity: two separate offices on the Quirinale with a flurry of official cars; hidden pandemonium behind a glass façade out in the Piazzale del Grande Archivio. Citto had been at work since midday, rebuffed not always politely or calmly at his every destination. But there was certain information that could not be refused him. The administrative and legal history of Taormina-Peloritana was available to anyone prepared to sit down and search through documents and reports. Citto was able to trace the airport from conception to ceremonial opening, and by careful cross-checking of the names and addresses associated with the undertaking he had mapped out the darker areas of confusion that seemed to link the corners of the spider's web.

In Messina he had discovered the consortium formed three years previously to promote the planning and building of the new airport. The names in the consortium were not unfamiliar: a pair of distinguished figureheads from Catania and Palermo; and an otherwise unholy alliance of construction and finance companies, most of them publicly respectable, but some of them known to Citto for their connections with Mafia families or Mafia money. That in itself was no surprise. Any sizeable undertaking south of Rome, be it *autostrada*, industrial complex or airport, would be influenced to some extent by Mafia finance or Mafia interests in local planning.

Once the airport plans had been submitted they were examined and authorized by a government appointed committee in Rome. It was this committee that now gave Citto his first tenuous lead. Documented at its inception as a committee of twelve, the final report was only signed by eleven names. The twelfth name had been carefully erased from all lists of attendance. It was obvious that the name had been there and any death or illness would have been recorded in the minutes. One possible explanation was that the man's evidence had been deleted from the report, and certain gaps in continuity within the final document seemed to support such a theory.

Citto showed the first page of the committee's proceedings to a Ministry clerk in the archives. 'There's a name missing. An omission. Could you look up records to correct the mistake?' I'd be very grateful, Citto implied – 100000 lire grateful.

The young clerk nodded. 'I expect it will be possible. I'll meet you tomorrow after lunch.' And he named the time and place: a car park in the Piazza Enrico Mattei at two-thirty in the afternoon.

That evening Citto found a cheap hotel near the railway station and shut himself into a dingy little bedroom with a bag of rolls, a carton of milk and a day's laboriously accumulated notes.

The Ministry clerk, home with his family in the sprawl of new housing beyond Monte Sacro, was having second thoughts about the favour he had negotiated with the stuttering little Sicilian. He telephoned a colleague and told him of the rendezvous he had made for the next day, but decided that if he heard nothing more about it he would proceed as agreed. 100000 tax-free lire would mean that he could take the family back south for Christmas.

Colleague rang colleague rang colleague. There were those who knew about that one-time committee, those who did not know. But eventually the one-time secretary of that one-time committee was given the news of Citto's unwelcome inquiry.

'I'm relying on you,' Consoli had told this Civil Servant. The poor man did not now know where to turn for advice. He should have ignored his fears and telephoned direct to Consoli.

He resorted instead to amateurs.

6

Sharlie spent that evening playing good son for his mother, inventing success stories about Rome for her neighbours in the old tenement block down by the waterfront. He'd bought his mum chocolates and flowers, and, when they had appeared to him inadequate, a silk scarf from a boutique on the Via Etnea that had knocked him back the last of his borrowed tens. If his agency didn't come up with some fees for the Tango November pictures he wouldn't even have money for the rail ticket back to Rome. Unless there was some more money to be made from selling pictures on the side. There had been a message waiting for him at home – another journalist wanted to see him. He had left a telephone number. Maybe he wanted to buy pictures.

And if he didn't buy? Well there was Citto to see him right again. He had a bad conscience about Sharlie's broken tooth.

When the neighbours all had gone Sharlie and his mother looked at each other across the kitchen table. Sharlie had told them he'd cut his face coming off the motor-bike, but mother and son didn't really fool each other.

'You working for that madman again?' She meant Citto.

'I'm freelance.'

'But he's telling you where to go and what to do.'

'He's a good journalist.'

'You're the only living thing I got in this world,' the mother cried. 'I don't want to be left with the priests and candles for the rest of my life.'

'I told you, I came off the motor-bike.'

'I live on this waterfront thirty years. You think I don't know the marks of a fight?'

Sharlie grinned at her and poured them both wine. She'd been picking grapes for pocket money at the weekend and the padrone had given her a couple of last year's litres.

'One day soon,' he promised, 'you'll have enough money so you won't ever have to go out and work again.' And he took her hand across the table and made her believe again in the dream.

7

Mac climbed the steps to the Pensione Albert past windows flickering in candle-light. A power failure was the only evidence left of the day's rain. The streets and alleys were already dry, the sky over Taormina was clear, and the moon out over the sea as sharp and white as a winter moon back home.

'Can we investigate the possibility of power failure at the airport on Saturday,' Larry Raille had asked round a candlelit table earlier in the evening. But the Italians had already thought of that possibility and they were able to report that Taormina-Peloritana had been supplied by generator power during the storms on Friday night and Saturday morning. Witness statements taken from staff at the airport confirmed that there had been no lighting failure at any time during that night.

All groups of investigators had met to exchange evidence together over supper in a private room at the San Domenico. Only the search party on the mountain was missing, encamped somewhere high and cold on the lava. Burden had taken the chair tonight and the meeting had been consequently swift and economical of words. Amazing, thought Mac, how fifteen years in the British Civil Service can concentrate a man's mind on the essentials – though he did also suspect that Ralph's thoughts had been focussed elsewhere for most of the time tonight. Dixie Duckham, Mac had guessed. He knew himself how hard it could be to meet old friends among the dead.

The Pensione Albert seemed well prepared for power failure with bottle-gas lamps in its small reception lounge. Mac asked for Julia Duckham and wrote down his name for the manager to carry upstairs. Signora Duckham, he was told, had spent most of the day in her room.

But she didn't keep him waiting, following the manager downstairs without a pause for patting up her hair or adjusting her face. She came into the lobby two large anxious eyes in that soft gas lamp, a face without make-up that seemed even younger than the night before; a crumpled skirt and blouse, and hair flat and matted on one side where she had been lying on her bed. The force of her emotion left Mac quite without words. She was anticipating God knows what: perhaps that her husband had somehow returned from the dead? Officially consigned to the dead would be nearer the truth. Duckham's Knightsbridge dentist had been out of town Saturday and Sunday, and the Captain's dental records had only just arrived. Not that there had been any doubt about his identification.

'We have the final results of some of the tests,' Mac said. 'I mean the blood tests and that sort of thing.'

She was watching him, her eyes suddenly vacant as though she wasn't even listening.

'I just wanted to tell you that there's nothing wrong with any of them. Your husband was quite all right. There was nothing wrong with him medically or in any other way.'

She nodded. Mac was convinced she had not heard him. But she thanked him.

'You are very kind,' she said. 'You are very kind to take the trouble to come and tell me.'

They were standing in the middle of the lobby facing each other like soldiers on parade. It was the hotel manager who rescued Mac, leading them aside to a table and two armchairs set into a white wall alcove.

'Everyone's trying to blame him,' said Julia. 'I don't understand what's going on.'

'They've been asking a lot of questions, have they?'

'Drinking; money; divorce. It's like they were adding things up against him.'

'I'm afraid it always happens. They have to ask. It doesn't necessarily mean anything bad.'

'He said things he couldn't have known anything about.'

Ralph Burden, thought Mac.

'He even made out that Mike had been having an affair with one of the hostesses.' She looked up at Mac. 'Do you know anything about that?'

'Good Lord no. I'm only the medicine man.' Mac did know. Burden had mentioned it at the evening meeting: two dozen words under the heading 'possible flight deck tension'. Some talk of a quarrel between Duckham and Nyren, and the possibility of the surviving air hostess being somehow involved.

'He even told me who the girl was,' said Julia. 'I can't stop thinking about it. All day I've been thinking, could he have done that? And why. Her picture's in all the papers.' She looked around the lobby as though there might be newspapers on the table. 'I even met her once. At a cricket match.'

Stella Pritchard. Mac had seen her medical report that morning. She was recovering at a hospital in Catania from head injuries, abrasions and shock. Condition satisfactory.

The lady was watching him as though waiting for confirmation, denial or advice. 'You see,' she said, 'we were very happily married. I don't understand.'

'Well then,' said Mac, 'if you were happy it doesn't really matter, does it? Whether he did or he didn't.' But it was not quite the moment, Mac realized, to deliver a lecture on the differing natures of love and sex.

'It matters to me,' she said. 'Perhaps it shouldn't. But I can't stop thinking about it because I don't know whether or not it's true.' Those large anxious eyes of hers were all over the place now, up and down the walls, all round the lobby, out of the windows.

'Why don't you come for a walk?' said Mac. Fresh air and exercise were his antidote to all trouble physical or mental. 'The rain's stopped.'

She stood up with him and followed him outside. He had the sort of voice and bearing that made suggestions appear commands.

They walked down the steps along a main street now lit by a scattering of oil flares. Apart from the occasional taxi the centre of the little town was free from traffic and the street silent but for the distant shouting of some kids and the slip-slop of sandals as tourists wandered up and down. Mac bought brandies standing up at one of the bars. He was telling Julia about the repercussions from last night's adventure at the city morgue: the flurries of angry cops jabbering away in Italian. He even coaxed a smile out of her when he mimed their agitation.

They walked on down the narrow steeper streets below the main road past faces they could not see, and mysterious shops and houses flickering in candlelight. He asked her about her home; where they lived; the names of her children; who was looking after them.

She answered him with something of the outside of her life – bits and pieces, but none of the secrets or the dramas: the house and garden in Virginia Water; Andrew and Clara; her one-time air-hostess sister.

They came out on the edge of the hill overlooking the narrow exit road that circled the lower part of the town. A car horn was blaring and headlamps picked out the erring pedestrian, an elderly man with a mop of light-coloured hair and a stooping plunging stride – Groucho Marx or an earnest horseman who'd lost his mount: Canon Ash Nyren, searching as he had been all afternoon for somewhere to sleep that night.

'Peter's father,' said Julia as she saw him.

'Peter?'

'Peter Nyren. The First Officer.'

'You know him?'

'He's very old. I should go and see him and make sure he's all right.'

But the Canon had passed on out of sight.

'You'll find him tomorrow,' Mac told her. 'I expect Greyhound are looking after him.'

'We went down to his village one day,' Julia explained. 'To play a cricket match. Everyone was playing except me. Mike, Peter, the Canon.' Julia paused. 'She was there.'

'Stella Pritchard?'

'It was a charity match. Men and women, and everyone called by what they did. Pilot. Doctor. Vet. There was a writer and a film star. She was the air hostess.'

'She's in a hospital in Catania,' said Mac. 'Maybe you ought to go and see her.'

'Why would he do it?' she asked in a whisper. She was looking at the moonlight over the sea 700 feet below them. She was trying to live the dream again where she and Mike were together in places they had always promised themselves to visit. But now there were too many questions in her mind.

'Why would he do it?'

'I didn't know your husband,' said Mac. 'Why don't you tell me about him?'

Julia looked at Mac. There seemed no threat in that question. Not from him. She opened her mouth to talk about Mike, but started suddenly and without warning to cry.

'Another time,' said Mac. 'You tell me another time.'

'You've been very kind. I'm sorry,' she whispered.

Mac took her arm. 'Let it all go. You go ahead and cry. You cry out loud if you feel like it.'

And with her head against his arm she did so, her whole body sobbing violently until emotion was exhausted.

Mac walked her back to the pensione, his own feelings toward this distressed young woman suddenly guilty and uncomfortable. He wanted to protect her, yet he would have to play the spy instead, telling Ralph Burden what she had been saying.

Power was back, street-lamps, and music from a radio or a juke box filling the silence.

Canon Ash Nyren watched the lights and sounds return. He was sitting on a hillside above the town. The evening was strangely warm, the ground almost dry and the Canon tired of his plodding inn to inn. Without suitcase or money he had been treated with suspicion by hotel clerks. No room, they had told him, and '*bacauda perdita est*' had not persuaded them.

Late in the evening he had seen a group of young American students climbing from an alley up a stone wall and under a fence on to a hillside of cactus. He had followed them, laying out his mackintosh some way from their rucksacks and sleeping-bags. For the moment he was neither cold nor hungry.

'A cricket match?' Burden frowned. 'How very odd.'

Mac caught Burden in his pyjamas and the older man was rather embarrassed.

'She's a very hysterical woman of course.'

Mac shrugged. 'I don't think so. She's obviously still in shock. I think she's coping rather well.'

'I suppose she complained about my questions this morning.' It irritated Burden that Mac had been gallivanting around with that woman all evening.

'No. She had no complaint. She's defensive about her husband, that's all.' Mac grinned. 'She's a pretty girl, isn't she?'

'For God's sake, Mac! There are occasions when such observations are tasteless.'

Burden heard Mac laughing all the way back to the lift. Mrs Duckham pretty? Burden had been thinking all day about the transparency of those wet blotches on her dress.

8

Far away in Washington Priscilla Raille's party had been a great success: the amount of drink generously calculated; the food visually sensational; the guests gossiping, joking and flirting with each other and with Priscilla.

Her choice of pander was limited. She needed someone influential enough to make or sway decisions and since the eldest and most senior of the Colonels had been paying her obvious attentions she made sure he stayed on after the other guests had gone home. They sat side by side on the couch talking rather drunkenly of the necessity of human understanding. She took his hand to emphasize a point, and he left the hand with her. They talked of health and of keeping fit, and Priscilla, in describing her palpitations, placed the Colonel's horny hand over her left breast. Thus encouraged he caressed her, and thus committed he kissed her. When he finally pulled her head roughly down into his lap she understood what task she had to perform. At least, she thought, being a military man he will be clean.

She was mistaken, and when he was finally through his spasms she was quietly but comprehensively sick in the kitchen sink while she freshened his drink.

Next morning he telephoned to thank her for the party. 'You can rest assured,' he said, 'that we have our eye on your husband. I'm told he is an outstanding engineer.' He arranged to drop in on Priscilla again that evening – 'just in case I have any news.'

The Colonel had found the favour unexpectedly easy. Inner administrative circles had been trying for two days to find some way of shifting Raille off the Tango November investigation. It hadn't occurred to them until the party that Raille might be tempted with a transfer to a job with NASA.

9

Sharlie left his mother in the early hours of Tuesday, collecting Laura from the fishing village at three o'clock. The rain had passed and the sky was clearing. It would be a good morning for *Cantallaluna*. They rode uphill fast and noisily through darkened sleeping villages, and when they reached the mountain road they stopped to wait in the damp silence. After ten minutes or so they heard another distant motor-bike and saw a headlamp zigzagging up the hillside towards them. Laura waved it down, and *Cantallaluna*, not overjoyed to have company, killed his engine to listen to Sharlie's questions.

'You'll lose me too much time,' he grumbled, looking over his shoulder at the lightening sky. 'If you want to talk you'll have to come with me.'

So they drove on behind him until they reached the earth slip beyond which Sharlie dared not pass with his cousin's precious Ducati. They followed *Cantallaluna* on foot, tailing the sound of his old-fashioned motor-bike as it bounced and roared its way over the boulders and up the hillside into the woods.

When they caught up with him he was already at work, bent double and running in quick scampers from one likely spot to another. Even in the half-light he could see enough to pick out the small humps of earth where the mushrooms were pushing their way up. He used one hand to hold the sack, the other to excavate round the hump, and when the two cousins joined him he handed Laura the sack to streamline the operation. It was comic opera: *Cantallaluna*, small and stocky, hurling out snatches of operatic aria, moving with extraordinary speed; Laura high-stepping fastidiously through the undergrowth behind him; Sharlie circling their darting movements as closely as he could, persisting with his questions.

The answers came in bits and pieces as the rhythm of the hunt allowed. Saturday morning? Yes – now where had he been? – over the ridge. He'd been able to move further from the road that morning because he wasn't hurrying to catch the aeroplane. The day's pickings had all been ordered by local restaurants. Saturday and Sunday lunches. He'd set out at half past three; started picking at maybe half-four.

The darting movements of the hunt took over for a while, the sack already beginning to bulge. He seemed to be finding them not in ones or twos but in half-dozens. 'It brings whole families of them out, a bit of rain,' he told Laura.

Saturday morning – yes. He'd heard the plane. 'Seemed like an earthquake at first. Then more like an eruption from the top. Not really a noise. The whooshing of air. The speed it all happened. It gave me a fright, I can tell you.'

Cantallaluna paused, swooping for another family of mushrooms.

'I didn't know what it was until I looked up. And even then. An eagle? It blotted my sky out and then it was gone. The real noise came afterwards. A terrible noise. The jet noise. But I can't say I heard the crash. What was it? Three kilometres away.'

The light was widening all the time, filtering from a pale sky into the trees. Sharlie started taking pictures. After all, *Cantallaluna* was the last man to have seen Tango November in the sky. Some paper or magazine might want to publish his picture. *Sing-to-the-moon.* He was worth an article in his own right, part of the folklore of Sharlie's mountain. *Cantallaluna* grumbled at them both for slowing up his progress. 'Seven o'clock the flight leaves. I have to be gone at six.'

Sharlie looked at his watch, then up at the sky. 'What time was it on Saturday morning?'

'When the plane passed? A half minute or so to five thirty-five.'

Citto had told Sharlie about the stopped clocks on the airport. 05.40, he'd said. The two times didn't seem to correspond. 'How can you be so sure about the time?'

'I always carry a watch because of catching the flights.' *Cantallaluna* was grunting, bending low to massacre another family.

'But you weren't flying them out on Saturday.'

'It's habit, isn't it. Knowing what the time is. The watch on my wrist is only a check. My real clock's up here.' He tapped his head behind one ear.

Sharlie panted along in his wake as he darted away, scrambling up a bank. 'What clock did you use on Saturday?'

Cantallaluna seemed to have disappeared into scrub, but he re-emerged both hands full of goodies like a bunch of fat fingers. 'Always check with the watch, don't I?'

The light grew from flat grey monotone to a depth of layers as the sun hit the tops of the ridges above them. *Cantallaluna* glanced at his watch and tied up his sack.

'I suppose you want some for your lunch?'

'Don't worry,' said Laura. 'We'll stay on and pick our own.'

'You know which ones are good and which ones are dangerous?'

'Well – if we make a mistake my grandmother will know. She's the one who'll be cooking them.'

'Your Nonna Lisa,' said *Cantallaluna* over his shoulder as

he hurried away. 'How is she? She's a good woman. Tell her I'll come and see her one day and she can cook me a nice *sarago*.' The voice was fading through the trees as *Sing-to-the-moon* hurried for his motor-bike and the early morning flight. He shouted again, almost out of earshot. 'She's a good woman. You tell her I said so. You tell her if she's tired of the sea I have a fire in my hut for long winter evenings.'

They heard the motor-bike bump-start somewhere below them. Laura was laughing. 'He used to pay court to Nonna Lisa when grandfather died. But the sound of the sea drives him mad, and Nonna Lisa wouldn't leave the house.'

The four members of the search-party woke that morning with what they thought was the sound of voices and laughter. But when they unsheathed themselves from sleeping-bags and bivvi tents they found themselves alone. In fact they had heard Sharlie and Laura, for the two parties were, at that moment, only 300 horizontal and 50 vertical metres apart from each other.

The four men set to work with the tiny Gaz fire, a can of water and powdered coffee. They'd had to call off the search as soon as the light went the night before, and after struggling with the tents and their soaking wet clothes none of them had felt like socializing very long over their cold meat and biscuits. They'd been fast asleep by nine o'clock. At least they would get their clothes dried today. It was a long slow game this search. The span of the 119 was 119 feet and they had to double that measurement on both sides of their line to allow for error. It had taken most of the previous day plodding under the rain to cover a mile, and today's ground looked even worse: thick scrub to start off with, and beyond it a maze of lava ridges rising up from the woods.

They decided to leave the tents set up where they were, and yesterday's clothes hanging to dry. They could then come back at lunch and strike camp for a longer trek in the afternoon.

Ash Nyren had woken with the sun on the horizon, already hurting the skin with its glare and heat. He felt untidy and dirty and physically uncomfortable. He didn't understand why he was here. Yesterday on the bus from the airport he had been asked whether he wished to see the body of his son. He thought the idea grotesque and he had told them so.

What would happen now? Peter would be buried and the Canon would return home. Someone had wasted a lot of money sending him out here. White stones in a wilderness.

In 1920 his father had taken him to a military cemetery in France. They had found his brother's grave on a warm summer's evening and his father had cried for the first and last time in his adult life. In 1946 Ash Nyren, alone, had tried to find the grave of his own eldest son. But there was no grave. The boy had just disappeared, his manner of dying unrecorded. Like Peter, he had fallen out of the sky.

Ash Nyren left the American students still asleep in their bags. He climbed off the hillside under the fence down the wall into the alley. The town was quiet below him, only the cats prowling the back-yards before the refuse-men came. How easy for cats, he thought. They can even make scavenging seem dignified.

The old Canon could not quite make up his mind about his retreat to the hillside last night. Had that been dignified? Should he not have made a fuss about his predicament?

He walked for an hour while the town awoke around him, and until he discovered a public convenience tucked away down some steps in the main square. When he re-emerged twenty minutes later he imagined himself albeit unshaven quite clean and tidy. He visited the *poste restante* – in vain, for that young man had not yet communicated about his lost luggage. Then back in the street a policeman approached him. When Ash Nyren verified his identity he was led across town to a comfortable looking hotel. But the Canon's hopes were not fulfilled. He had been brought here only to answer questions.

'Accident Investigation Branch, Department of Trade and

Industry,' an Englishman said at a bedroom door.

Strange place for a interview, the Canon thought. It felt even stranger when the man asked him of all things about a cricket game played earlier that summer.

'It is my fortune or misfortune to run the village cricket team,' Ash Nyren explained over coffee and buns. 'We had an invitation match for charity.' The old Canon corrected himself. 'Well not really charity, I'm afraid. Our church steeple. Yes. Somehow there are more important things than church steeples, aren't there? It was a Women's Institute idea. They call it "what's my line". The invitation team is named by profession. Doctor, Farmer, Solicitor – that kind of thing. Duckham was our Airline Pilot.'

'And Miss Pritchard – ?'

'Yes. Air hostess I believe they're called.'

'Do you remember when this match was played?' Burden's notes required precision.

'Early June. The last week of the rhododendrons I would think. They're a feature in the churchyard and the Vicarage.'

'Did Mr Duckham come down with his family?'

'Yes. His wife and children.'

'They stayed with you?'

'They had supper in the Vicarage and then drove home. It's difficult for me to have guests overnight.'

The old Canon was pinched and frail, an odd fuzz of white stubble on his face where he had not shaved. His clothes were crumpled. His shirt seemed dirty. Burden wondered where he had been sleeping.

'Did you form any impressions of Duckham?'

'He seemed very nice. Very pleasant. He brought a dozen bottles of wine I remember. That was very generous. I don't keep a cellar myself. Not since the war.'

'Good cricketer was he?'

'Oh – he made quite a knock. Twenty or thirty or something. He had great style. Peter said the only cricket he played was on the lawn with his children so that made his achievement even more impressive.'

'And Miss Pritchard?'

'Well – she was very elegant. She was wearing, I seem to remember, a particularly becoming short white skirt.'

'And she came down because she was a friend of Peter?'

'I imagine so. She did not appear to know Mr Duckham very well. I had the impression she was quite shy with him.'

'She was at supper at your house with them all?'

'Yes. And she stayed for the night I believe. I left her talking with my son that evening and she seemed to reappear for breakfast.'

'You have other sons or daughters?'

'One son who died in the war. It was after his death that Peter was born. It has meant, I'm afraid, that he has an old father.'

'Your wife – ?'

'Died ten years ago.' The old man interrupted before Burden could begin his next question. 'I think Peter saw Duckham as something of a substitute father. More the right age. Able to give him proper advice. That sort of thing.'

'Did you see Duckham again after the cricket match?'

'No.'

'He didn't return the invitation?'

'Yes. I was invited to their house one Saturday. Then there was some sort of a quarrel between Duckham and my son and I made some excuse not to go.'

'You didn't want to see him?'

'It was very silly of me. I think I could have helped them forget all about it. Instead of that, of course, it just made things worse. Very stupid.' There was a sudden vehemence in the old man's voice as he castigated himself. 'A stupidness. It is hard to forgive one's real mistakes.'

'Your son told you about the quarrel?'

'In a way. Not directly of course. We don't – we didn't talk directly about things like that. He was upset about something. He came down one weekend for a game of cricket. He was drinking afterwards in the pub. That's when he talked about it. With some of the others. I was there because of the cricket.' The Canon seemed very briefly and invisibly to smile. 'One half of bitter every Saturday evening as President of the Club.'

'Peter was upset?'

'Oh yes. And angry.'

'Did he easily get upset about things?' Ash Nyren looked up at the face interviewing him and saw it clearly for the first time: a closed face; a thin mouth; careful eyes – sitting in judgement on his son.

Burden rephrased the question. 'Had you ever seen him upset like this before?'

'When his previous company went bankrupt and he lost his job.'

'He must have been very worried.'

Nyren paused before answering. He began to see traps in front of him. 'Anyone is worried if he is unemployed.' Was Peter an anxious type, he wondered? He was certainly a brooder. They'd called him that at school. Even written it on some of his reports.

'Did you ever visit him in London?'

'No. His flat was very small. Just two rooms I believe.'

'Miss Pritchard was his girl-friend?'

Again Nyren paused. Yes and no both sounded dangerous. 'They were not engaged.'

Burden stood up from his desk. 'You've been very kind to cooperate at such a distressing time.'

Nyren stood up from his chair and Burden noticed again how scruffy he appeared.

'I hope you are being looked after properly?'

'My luggage was mislaid. A young man at the airport said he was sorting it out for me but I haven't heard from him yet.'

'You should tell Greyhound about it.'

'I don't like to fuss about little details.'

Burden opened the door for him. 'Do you think the quarrel between Duckham and your son could have upset their concentration?'

The question took Ash Nyren off balance. It was a question that had been haunting him, and he did not know the answer. 'I am sure they were too experienced to let that happen,' he told Burden. But he was thinking to himself, Duckham was too experienced to let it happen, not Peter. Peter did get worked up about things, and he did lose concentration. And in such a mood he did make mistakes. Ash Nyren knew that from watching him at cricket or chess, driving a car, playing piano. He remembered him thumping the piano once in rage when he had played a succession of wrong notes.

*

Stella Pritchard opened her eyes briefly in the silence of siesta, the ever attendant Trixie at her bedside.

'There is someone waiting to see you,' the little girl told her. 'She's been waiting all day. Do you want to see her?' The girl was suspicious. She didn't want to lose proprietary rights.

Stella smiled and took her hand. But by the time a nurse had called Julia Duckham Stella's eyes were closed once more and she was sleeping.

'It's all right,' said Julia. 'I'll stay with her.'

The nurse disappeared, the door closing Julia and the little girl into shuttered half-light. 'Hello,' Julia whispered to the little girl. But the girl put a finger to her lips to hush her. The small room was filled with rasping open-mouthed breathing that sounded like death's door. There was no resemblance here to those newspaper photographs of a pretty young girl. Stella Pritchard's head was half-shaved and bandaged, her remaining hair matted with dry blood. The face hung loose, like that of a drunken woman, the flesh vibrating with each irregular breath. Once she paused so long between breaths that Julia thought she had surely passed away. But then the rasp recommenced, and Julia and the little girl breathed again with her.

Julia drew up a chair, took off her jacket and prepared herself for vigil. Through the shutters she could see a thin strip of sunlight at one end of a shaded courtyard, and later as afternoon grew into early evening siesta faded with that sunlight and the city sounds returned: cars and noisy motor-bikes; a traffic cop's whistle; songs from a juke box in a bar; the laughing of young voices.

I I

'Time me fifty seconds. Gear down and landing checks.'
    'Spoiler switches.'
    'On.'
    'No Smoking sign.'
    'On.'

– Three monotones like a dirge swopping the responses of the check list: Captain Duckham, First Officer Nyren and Flight Engineer Raven.

Three engineers, two Englishmen and an Italian, feed the voice-recorder tape through special play-back equipment in a sound-proof lab at the Royal Aircraft Establishment in Farnborough. They have been playing the final few minutes of the thirty-minute loop over and over again without reaching any conclusions.

'*Established on the ILS. Four thousand feet.*' Nyren calling up Taormina-Peloritana.

Air Traffic Control replies from the airport: '*Roger Tango November. Call me on Outer Marker.*'

On the flight deck Nyren confirms instrument landing system: 'Glide slope alive.'

A lower voice interrupts in an amused mutter: 'Miracle number two!'

'Shut up, George!' Duckham.

There is a pause of about four seconds, then the sound of a bleeper.

'Outer Marker.' Another short pause, and Nyren's voice again: 'We're two hundred feet high.'

'Sod it!' A silence. 'It checks out on my side. I'd say it looks good. Confirm glide slope your side.'

'Check on the glide slope.'

The lower voice, again a mutter and barely distinguishable: 'Bloody marvellous. I bet they changed the slope and forgot to tell anyone.'

'OK. Let's have a bit of hush.'

Nyren calls the airport. '*Tango November over Outer Marker.*'

'*Roger. Tango November you are clear to land.*'

A pause. Then Duckham's voice: 'Disengaging auto pilot. Full flap.'

'Full flap.'

'Fifty. Fifty. Two greens.'

'Check list complete up here. Let's hope they've got it together downstairs.' Another joke from the Flight Engineer.

'Let's have hush again. Eyes up for contact, Peter. I'm staying right on the instruments. George, you better give me an altitude check over the Middle Marker.'

'Roger.' A laugh. 'Now we'll see what his runway visibility is really like.'

A pause, then the bleeper again: 'We're fifty foot high I'd say.'

'As near as dammit then.'

Almost immediately Nyren's voice calling: 'I have approach lights. Half right. Twenty right.'

A pause. Then voices suddenly overlapping.

'Shit!'

'Whoops! Sorry skipper.' That was Peter Nyren.

'Overshoot!'

'Flaps two five.'

'Positive climb. Gear up.' A pause. 'We're lifting like a whale. Give us the lot, George. Let's get back in the sky. Peter – tune in to Oscar Echo on both.'

'Roger.'

'Speed OK. Flaps to one four.'

'Where's that beacon, Peter?'

'Beacon's tuned in. Identing Oscar Echo.'

A pause. Then an exclamation.

'Judas!'

'Air speed and rate of climb all over.' Peter Nyren's voice alarmed and jerky. Interference and noise on the tape.

'Losing air speed and altitude.' The thumping of the aircraft is clearly audible on the tape. Turbulence or a systems failure?

'Fly attitude, Peter.' Duckham's voice reimposing calm.

A warning bell shrills, scaring even the three engineers listening to the tape in the lab.

'Engine fire number two.' The warning bell stops as someone cancels it.

'Another false alarm. It has to be.'

'Probably.' Duckham still calm. A short pause of decision 'Carry out fire drill on number two.'

'For Christ's sake! It's a birdie!' Whose voice that?

'Fire drill, George.' Duckham again.

'Essential power to number three.' The Flight Engineer 'Close number two thrust lever.'

A pause. Then Duckham terse and loud: 'Peter!'

'Yes, sorry.' Peter Nyren in a shaky voice. 'Closing numbe two thrust lever.'

Flight Engineer: 'Shutting start lever.'

Nyren: 'Pulling fire handle.'

A pause. The Flight Engineer calls: 'We're on battery. Number three's tripped on overload.'

'Shed some load and get us back on generator.' Duckham.

A pause – of what – two seconds? Then Duckham in a sudden shout: 'Fucking Christ Jesus!'

The sounds die away to a moan on Duckham's blasphemy and the tape stops.

Three engineers look at each other across the lab. The loop of tape is designed to hold thirty minutes of conversation, cancelling as it re-records. On Tango November something had stopped the tape dead before the crash ever happened. Preliminary examination indicated the same stoppage on the 'Black Box' Flight Recorder. The last four, five or six minutes of Tango November are silence.

The Italian has a list of words to look up in his dictionary. None of them will prove to solve any problems for him: *hush, whale, whoops, shut up, dammit, skipper, shit, sod, fucking Christ Jesus, Judas* and *miracle*.

12

Sharlie was early for his appointment with the other journalist. Quarter to one, the voice had said; under the elephant in the Piazza del Duomo. Sharlie came into the square from the arch, crossing the road behind a bus. The man was waiting, gesticulating a message to some car parked in front of the cathedral. He didn't look the part with his heavy mouth and jaw. His lips were so swollen it was like he had a bee-sting.

He hadn't yet seen Sharlie. Maybe he's just noticed a friend passing, Sharlie was thinking. Then 'bee-sting' saw him, nodded and turned nonchalantly to meet him. Was there something in his face; something in the way he moved? Sharlie slowed up trying to think. You don't ambush people in broad daylight in the middle of the Piazza del Duomo, even in Catania. Anyway, he was another journalist. Wasn't he?

The square was scattered with people; the sun was shining; the city full of the smells of lunch. Innocuous. Sharlie was five paces from 'bee-sting' when he noticed the phalanx: three men from that car heading across the square to cut him off. Sharlie had already had one tooth broken. He wasn't walking wide-eyed into any more trouble. Nor was it time to linger over questions.

He dodged 'bee-sting' and ran for the corner of the square, looking back once. All four men were after him. He turned down the steps into the fish market, slipped on the wet paving and cannoned into a stall of shell-fish – mussels, oysters, limpets and sea-snails in an avalanche. He was up and running again, the four men close behind, the yells of the shell-fish trader filling the market. Two merchants went for him under the arcade, all three of them sprawling into a barrow-load of sea-food. Fish this time – octopus, a pail of live eels and the severed trunk of a large tuna slithered with Sharlie on the pavement. There was a cleaver in a wooden board where he stood up again and he ran now cleaver in hand, the crowd scattering in front of him. He burst out into the open under the railway back towards the waterfront where he alone knew how to hide and seek.

He was stinking with fish, bruised from the falls, but laughing at himself for the hell of it all. Quite like old times. A pity he didn't have a number to call Citto in Rome. Citto would have liked the barrow-loads of fish. And I bet they really were journalists, Sharlie was thinking. Four customers for my photographs I've lost. 'Bee-sting' must think I'm nuts.

Citto walked from the Metro station towards the Piazzale Enrico Mattei and his last Roman appointment. He seemed to be the only living creature in the whole expanse of EUR, surrounded and dwarfed by empty boulevards, gardens, lake and palaces sleeping in the hot afternoon.

In retrospect Citto would blame himself. A day and a half of open questions and search had been too long. He had become conspicuous and though he was not yet conscious of a pursuer or a tail his movements had in fact been under close observation since that early morning. At least he had finished his researches, and so far as the spider's web was concerned he had joined up the two remaining corners. Notwithstanding the quasi-military status of Taormina-Peloritana as a NATO emergency field, it seemed from documents in the two departments concerned that concessions for the ancillary services at the airport – fuel, catering and maintenance – had been made over to three private companies: Servizi TP for the fuel; Panetellana for catering; Air Mecanico for the maintenance. Telephone calls to Messina and Palermo had connected the names: Secretary of Servizi TP was the young Flavio Consoli; Pantellana turned out to be the maiden name of Flavio's mother; and the Chief Executive of Air Mecanico was the *paterfamilias* himself, Avvocato Consoli. The remaining names on the boards were connected with the other members of that initial consortium which had dreamed up the airport in the first place.

Nothing illegal about it, of course – unless negligence or corrupt practice had contributed in any way to the crash of Tango November. But it was the fear of such criminal responsibility that was feeding panic in Rome.

Citto reached the top of the Piazzale. The car park sloped away from him down towards the twenty green-glassed storeys of Mattei's skyscraper. Citto turned to look across the deserted wastes of lake and lawns. No one following him. No one walking in the streets or gardens.

The Ministry clerk was waiting, as promised, sitting in the shade of a pine tree at the top of the car park. They exchanged money and message without preamble: 100000 lire from Citto to the young man; and a name in return, but no address.

'Preuss. He lives in Venice,' said the clerk. 'Teaches at the University. He'll be in the book. There's no address on the papers. I only worked out who he is from the initials.'

Citto wrote down the name, watched the young clerk depart across the road and round a corner and out of sight, then retraced his own steps downhill to the Metro station. That was nice and easy, he was thinking.

The car must have been freewheeling for he only heard it

at the last moment, as the driver banged in the clutch to fire the engine. Even then Citto was still unaware of danger, turning only in surprise for the car park had seemed uninhabited. It was a battered-looking BMW, ten yards away and heading straight for him. He could see two faces in the front seats screwed up in concentration or fear. Nothing more than kids they seemed. No one had ever taught Citto how to run away from car assassins, but whatever instinct made him react was entirely correct. He ran at the car, like a *bandillero* at the bull, jumping away when it was too late for the driver to turn. Citto lay sprawled on the tarmac. He picked himself up, his mind a total blank, silent and blind. Kids having a game, he thought to himself. And they nearly killed me. He felt an oppressive panic: strange aggressive faces in a strange empty city, with home so far away.

Then he heard the car turning behind him and he ran. The car park was divided into wide avenues by lines of low hedge. Sharp hedge Citto found when he tried to jump one. He waded out knee-deep in thorns as the car turned yet again at the top of the slope. At the bottom end of the car park were the lawns and the lake, and a chain across the avenue to prevent cars passing. But the chain had been left unpadlocked for a gardener's trolley. Citto reached it a few yards ahead of his pursuer, and took to the grass. The car ploughed through the chain, thumped on to the lawn, churning up grass as it tried to follow Citto's zigzag flight. Citto kept to the line of lake towards the road bridge, tubby and awkward, scuttling like a fat hen, his briefcase banging against his body. He was at the end of his limited energy. It came into his mind that he could stop running and let whatever happened happen. He wanted to stop. He wanted to give up. Then he saw the lake beside and below him, and he rolled down the bank into the water. The car skidded behind him, swerving away from the lake back on to the lawn. It waltzed around a tree, turned hard on two wheels tearing over the grass through a bush, and away.

Citto pulled himself out of the water. He stood on the bank and wiped his spectacles peering around at the emptiness. EUR, deserted as a city after the holocaust, had absorbed the little drama without a reaction. Three hundred yards away up on the hill across the lake a couple were standing, seemingly watching him, but without gesture or movement.

Citto listened as the roar of that car faded in the distance. They hadn't tried to kill him for a game, and to be here waiting for him they must have known where he was coming. Did that mean the young Ministry clerk had set him up? Was the name he'd given just a fiction, this Preuss? Citto crossed the gardens to the Metro station, noisily wet, leaving a trail of water drying fast on the hot asphalt path behind him.

A mile away towards San Paolo two frightened youths abandoned the BMW and any intentions they might have had of picking up their money. The man had offered them 200000. 'Doesn't matter what happens,' he'd told them. 'Just hit him hard with a car.'

The Metro platform was as deserted as the world outside, and Citto, standing in a shaft of sun, pulled off his jacket and squeezed water from his trousers. By the time a train arrived he was halfway dry, and when he climbed back into inhabited streets he looked quite normally crumpled, like a tourist back from a bathe out at Ostia. Even the centre of the city looked thin in the early afternoon – a straggle of German tourists drooping to a bus; a postcard stall; a couple of *carrozze*, horses sleeping in their nose-bags.

Citto's hotel was a little flea joint a hundred yards from the station. He paid his bill, collected his pyjamas and shaving kit, and left by the narrow alley at the back of the building. Then realized he should have operated in reverse, paying his bill at the last possible minute in case the shirt-sleeved *padrone* had been primed to brief anyone on his departure. The man had asked: 'Leaving town?'

'Going home,' Citto had told him with a nod. Now, as he walked two blocks to the station he was sure he had a tail.

There was a through train for Venice at four o'clock. Citto had ten minutes to check this Preuss's address and number in the Venice phone book. He dialled an *interurbano* in the praying hope he was at home. When the man answered Citto had neither time nor energy left for planned dialogue. He wanted to know if the man was real and if he would talk. All he could hope with was statement and direct question. It came out more like a telegram. '*Ingegnere* – I am a journalist. I believe you gave evidence to the feasibility study on Taormina-Peloritana and that your evidence was suppressed. I am arriving in Venice at midnight tonight by train from Rome. If you can talk to me I will be in the bar on the station.'

There was a long pause at the other end, then an amused voice replied in lilting Veneto dialect: 'You work fast. I had expected maybe a week or two before someone traced it all back. What is your paper?' And when Citto told him – 'All right. I'll be there. How shall I know you?'

Citto described himself: 'I'm fat. I wear round steel glasses, and a light grey suit – very crumpled.'

'And I shall be in a red sweater, drinking Grappa.'

The *gettoni* ran out and the line cut off. The young Ministry clerk hadn't been bluffing after all. Citto wondered if he would suffer any consequences.

The train was four minutes off departure. Citto had bought no ticket. His tail would discover too easily where he was going. He sauntered the length of the concourse as carefully as he could. Three, two, and one. The train jerked into motion a half minute late and Citto ran from an adjoining platform. He looked back as he climbed aboard, but there was no movement in the crowd. No one running to catch the train with him.

Why should they bother, he thought as the train threaded its way out of the city. A fast car on the autostrada would catch them by Bologna. Or they'd have a friend to ring in Florence with his description. If they were really following him it would be very difficult to stay hidden.

He had passed and repassed over the events of the last two hours in wonderment and disbelief. Most things he could have invented, but not that car and its squealing, tyre-thumping pursuit. One near-hit might have been a prank or a mistake. But turning round to come again, that was deliberate, premeditated, nasty. Young frightened faces those two kids had had. Citto wondered how much money they'd been offered.

The train was in two sections bound for Venice and Munich. Citto chose the German half of the train and sat himself in compartment otherwise full with Bavarian nuns on their way back from the Eternal City. Their low guttural chattering had him sleeping before they'd left the city limits, and he wok only twice in five hours, at Florence to buy a drink, and at Bologna to change into the Venice half of the train.

The platform at Bologna was dark and cool. One could feel the change in latitude, and the presence of mountains to the north and south. Citto bought himself a cardboard plate of hot lasagne and a bottle of wine from one of the barrows, and stood eating in a corridor crowded with a party of tired and jaded children returning from a *colonia*. When the kids left the train at Ferrara Citto found an empty compartment and watched the scattered lights across the flat-lands of the Po delta, wondering whether he would ever bring himself to come north and work out of his *ambiente* with people he did not understand. His brother had done it far away in Germany. But then his brother was a realist. He didn't imagine things like hostility and alienation. Citto had always been a dreamer. A bad-dream dreamer. Until he was ten years old he had spent more time alone in the hills with sheep and goats than with lessons or other children in a classroom. It was the village priest who had told his mother to encourage books and learning. What would his priests say now if Citto wrote to tell them where that learning had brought him: to near-death from a car in the middle of a wide and empty Roman park.

Citto smiled through the window at a moonlit sheet of water. There was church money in the airport. One of the names in the consortium handled holy money on the island, investment moved around the markets as discreetly and anonymously as Mafia capital. Citto wondered, not for the first time, whether he should think of such things with amusement or a prayer. His faith and his gratitude were not always comfortable to live with.

The red sweater was waiting in the bar on the station, a bottle of Grappa and two glasses in front of him, the self-mocking smile of a lonely man when he turned to greet Citto.

After the Grappa they walked out of the station, across the piazza, over a vast hump of bridge into a maze of narrow alleys and passages. Citto tried hard not to look around with too much interest but all in vain.

'Your first time in Venice,' Preuss observed. 'See it while you have the chance. Your grandchildren won't have that privilege. Socialism came too late.'

Citto smiled. The red sweater was watching him.

'You found my name very quickly.'

'With some help,' said Citto.

'Do we know how this crash happened?'

Citto shrugged. 'I have my ideas.'

'About the airport?'

'The plane was trying to land there.'

'Don't worry. I hold no brief for it. The brief I held was for objective rational analysis. And you know how highly that is praised in our poor country.'

'They removed your name from the report.'

'Not just my name. They removed my name because of everything else they had removed.'

'Your case was against the airport then?'

'You have seen the airport and you have seen the crash. You have drawn your own conclusions.'

'Taormina-Peloritana is no nearer to the mountain than the airport at Catania.'

'Which proves what? I know Fontanarossa is your local airplane station. But you can't tell me it is either safe or well sited.'

Citto gestured vaguely towards unseen Alps. 'There are airports in Austria and Switzerland built in the very middle of mountains.'

'Not volcanoes, dear boy. Volcanoes have very special characteristics. So far as you Sicilians are concerned the characteristics are fire and earthquake. So far as aeroplanes are concerned the characteristic is turbulence.'

'Was that what you wrote in the report?'

'I made two general points against the existence of the airport and detailed points against the actual plans. If you are interested in minutiae,' he said.

'That is why I came. I have been studying minutiae for two days.'

Red sweater touched his arm in apology. 'I am sorry. Arrogance is unforgivable and I am always guilty.' He smiled his lopsided smile.

They were crossing a humped bridge over a canal, black empty water, narrow black empty alleys in front and behind them, and but for the slapping of water silence everywhere.

'Another airport was unnecessary unless it had been sited to replace and improve on Fontanarossa. That would have meant taking it south of Catania and away from the mountain.'

'So the case you made in the report was that the airport should never have been built?'

'There was no social or economic justification. And it was sited in just about the worst possible place.'

'So why do you think it was built?'

'You don't need me to tell you that. A lot of people made a lot of money out of it. There was land to buy, runways to lay, buildings to put up, roads to improve, an industrial estate to develop. And generous grants to help it all along.'

'Why didn't the other members of the committee share your opinions?'

Preuss shrugged. 'Various reasons. Some genuine, some not so genuine. There were only five technical experts. Everyone else was political.'

'Was the committee rigged?'

'Not blatantly, no. That is – not until I made my own opinions clear.'

'They were worried about your opinions even though it was a minority opinion?'

'The report was published. My criticism could have attracted a lot of attention. There was opposition to the whole idea. Especially locally.'

'Conservationists in Taormina?'

Preuss smiled. 'That sort of thing. Hopeless, isn't it?'

Preuss stopped on a bridge. The moon was framed down a narrow canal, the world momentarily pure black and white. A clock chimed somewhere. Five minutes fast, Citto hoped with a glance at his watch.

'When you were – dismissed – you made no public statement?'

'I am not possessed of that kind of courage.'

'They threatened you?'

'Not violence or anything crude like that.'

'Blackmail?'

'I suppose so.'

'There is no need to tell me. But the question will be asked if you present your evidence to the American and English investigators.'

Again that smile, brief, contorted and sad. They walked on leaving the moon and the water, losing even the sky in a narrow alley between two palaces.

'What were the detailed criticisms in your report?'

'A plea for good instrumentation. An airport in a position like that needs all the visual and radar aids available. ILS, VASI and precision approach radar. They're not really very expensive. It would all have cost less than the money they spent on promotion and presentation. You might say it's an unpopular part of the budget.'

'They have ILS.'

'ADF beacons. Very unreliable.' Preuss turned to Citto. 'There were storms that night, I believe.'

Citto nodded.

'An ADF beacon is like a dead leaf in a storm, blowing around all over the place.'

There were more bells ringing in the city. Citto looked at his watch again. His return train left in half an hour from across the lagoon.

Preuss took his arm, a gesture, it seemed, of restraint. 'You are welcome to stay. Tomorrow I could show you our doomed and beautiful city.' That self-mocking smile was back in his face. Agony from somewhere. Citto could recognize agony, though he wasn't much good at analysing it.

'You have evidence that ought to be given to the crash investigation. Why not travel back with me?'

'Now? Good Lord, one cannot travel quite that abruptly.'

'I'm sure the investigation will pay your expenses.'

'It's not a question of expense, dear boy. I have to prepare myself psychologically.'

'But you will come?'

'I don't know. Tomorrow. The day after tomorrow. The investigators will be there for a long time.'

Preuss led him now at a somewhat increased pace, turning back through a succession of alleys, crossing a succession of bridges. 'You know your train leaves from Mestre. We must find you a taxi.'

'There were points of detail you were going to tell me about.'

'Ah. The airport again. Yes. There's an industrial development on the access road with a lot of modern street lighting.'

'I know it.'

'There was a danger in certain conditions that some of those lights could be mistaken for the runway approach.'

'What conditions?'

'Coming out of low cloud when the pilot has to see everything at the last minute. Especially if the roads were wet and the lighting reflected. It only takes a split second to make a wrong decision and sometimes a split second is all a pilot has.'

Citto smiled. 'I think you were a pilot yourself.'

'A long time ago. Little planes with guns. Since then I've never had the nerve to fly again.'

They skirted a garden and crossed a last bridge, in front of them the tall block of the car park at the end of the causeway. There were a couple of late-night taxis by the bus-station.

'You didn't see much of Venice.'

'I think you should come with me,' Citto said again. He wondered later whether he had said it to ease the pain of that lopsided smile; or whether it was premonition. A lot of things he wondered later.

'I'll see you in a few days' time. I will come down with my offerings. They silenced me too easily last time, didn't they? I should have made a little scandal.' Preuss tapped Citto on the arm as they shook hands. 'One needs company to find one's courage.' And the red sweater smiled, one corner of his mouth turned down in self-mockery.

The taxi ran the length of the causeway, a spit of flame from an oil refinery on the mainland reflected in the lagoon. The train was waiting in the station at Mestre. Citto read the destination boards as he walked up the platform. Vienna, some of the carriages had come from. Trieste. Tarvisio. All roads wending south to Rome. He used his spare cash to buy himself a berth for the night, hoping he would lose in sleep the menace he had felt growing in all things around him that day. Peasants we were born and peasants we should have stayed, his Stuttgart brother would have told him.

13

'I am Julia Duckham.'

Stella looked at the face staring at her in the darkness. She couldn't see the expression in the eyes nor determine the inflection in the voice. But she understood the name.

Julia had been sitting by the bedside for nearly twelve hours, dozing off regularly through the evening, and awaking each time from a frightened dream. Never of Mike but always of despair. She began to fear that semi-conscious state of mind. Sleep was no blessed oblivion. She had watched the little girl falling away reluctantly on Stella's pillow. And when Trixie was asleep Julia laid her in the cot. Some time later a nurse had brought supper, and told Julia there was a free bed in the next room whenever she felt tired. They were glad enough of some English-speaking help.

Stella had woken in the early hours, without a sound, her eyes opening suddenly and trying to focus.

'How are you feeling?'

Stella was watching her.

'Do you want the light?'

The bandaged head moved in a gesture that could have been either yes or no. Julia decided on darkness.

'I am Julia.'

No response.

'And you are Stella. We met at the cricket match.'

Stella couldn't think what to say. She decided the face and voice seemed kind.

'You are the only one of the crew left alive. The hospital has let me help look after you.'

'Why?' Stella asked. 'Why should you want to look after me?'

'It seems the only thing I can do. There's nothing else. Except waiting for the funeral. The town is full of people waiting like that.'

'Where's Trixie?'

'Sleeping.'

'What happened to her?'

'She has a broken arm. And she is shocked.'

'There is no one with her?'

'They are all dead. A whole family.'

Stella closed her eyes. 'How many of us are dead?' She meant Tango November and all who had flown in her.

'There are only six survivors.'

'It wasn't his fault.' Stella's eyes were still closed.

'How do you know?'

'But you know it wasn't, don't you? It couldn't have been.'

Julia took her hand. They had assumed him in the third person. She wondered if that implied anything: I know; and you know that I know. She couldn't be sure. She would never be sure unless she was told exactly how and when it had happened; and where, and how often, and why, and with whom else. How many girls? Did she want to know? Isn't that why she was here, sitting on the girl's bed, waiting for her secrets?

'Do you know what happened?' Julia was referring to the crash.

Stella shook her head. 'It was all chaos. Confusion. It seemed to go on for a long time.' She paused. 'We saw the sunrise. We thought we were safe then.'

'Was there something wrong with the plane?'

'I think so. I don't know.'

'They will be asking you.'

'Who?'

'The people investigating the crash. They're trying to blame him.'

'What do they say?'

'Just about everything they can think of. That he drank too much. That he was after money because he changed jobs. That he was quarrelling with Peter Nyren' – Julia plunged on while she still had the courage – 'that he was having an affair with you.'

Stella turned her head looking for Julia's face. Julia continued quickly: 'They'll say anything and everything if they want to blame him.' She was still holding Stella's hand. 'I'm glad you said it wasn't his fault. I mean – I'm glad you believe it wasn't.'

Stella closed her eyes trying to concentrate. She couldn't follow what the woman was saying.

'You're the most important person really. What you say. You're the only member of crew. The only one who might have known what was happening. They'll have to listen to you.'

'I need to drink,' Stella whispered.

'I'm sorry.' Julia stood up. 'I'm talking too much.' She turned on the bedside lamp, angling it into the wall to dim the light. Stella saw her clearly for the first time: her eyes wide with shock and her face hollowed out with distress. Stella wondered how long she had been sitting there with her.

'What is the time?'

'It's one o'clock in the morning.'

'Monday?'

'Wednesday.'

'Wednesday? When did it happen?'

'Saturday morning.'

'I've been here all that time?'

Stella remembered talking with her father. She had thought then it was Sunday. 'How long have you been here?'

'Only this afternoon.' Julia pressed the bell on the wall. 'There's nothing here for you to drink.'

Two nurses came and Julia backed away to the door as they set to work stripping and changing Stella. She saw wounds down the girl's side, raw and scraped like burns.

Stella watched her leaving. 'Are you going?'

'Not if you want me to stay.'

Stella's head moved again with the gesture that was neither yes nor no.

Tino G. had left the world of lost songs and pictures in his mind. His body was hurting and the music had gone. If anyone had told him that the pain meant life for him he would have found it difficult to summon either laughter or anger. For the moment he had forgotten everything. Corinna; the airplane; the red sunrise; the advance and retreat of death. All he had now was the pain in his body, different pains he was beginning to identify and place – abdominal pain, pain when he breathed, and strange sensations like exaggerated hunger and thirst and a bladder that seemed to be bursting and about which he could apparently do nothing. None of it was really unbearable and the nurses would not give him drugs for they relied now on his consciousness of pain to tell them if anything else was going wrong.

Late in the evening he woke to find a visitor. An old man leaning on a stick, watching him from under bowed head and shoulders. It was only when the man talked that Tino G. recognized the doctor's voice that had kept him company for half a day inside the broken aeroplane.

'Do you mind me coming?' the voice asked. 'Maybe I remind you of bad things?'

Tino G. shook his head.

'They say you are all right now.' The old man smiled. 'Just hurting all over.'

Tino G. nodded.

'I am glad to see you recover.'

'You saved my life.'

'I do not think so. You saved your own life. You decided you would live. That's what is important. The will to survive.'

Tino G. shook his head. 'I thought I was dying. I knew I was dying. I was expecting to die.'

Turi looked at flowers on the table, newspaper cuttings, telegrams. The boy spoke behind him on the bed.

'Crazy, isn't it? A week ago no one knew me. Today I get offers for a contract with two recording companies. You know what one of them's for? For writing songs about aeroplanes. Flying and falling.'

'The newspapers say you come from Sicily?'

'My mother. She wanted me to come. And now I'm here and my feet haven't even touched ground.' The boy paused, his face drawn and tired. 'I'll come back again. To walk around.'

'Then you must promise to visit me.'

'Yes.'

'I have a nice house. A vineyard. A lemon garden. A terrace where to sit and drink in the evenings.'

Tino G. smiled at the picture. He felt himself falling away into sleep again. Blessed sleep. 'Do you have any children?' he asked the doctor, but his eyes closed before the old man answered.

Turi watched the boy sleep. I had a son, Turi was thinking. For three days I had a son.

That evening in Taormina the investigators had listened to a recording of the voice tape flown back to them from England. The voices confirmed that Tango November had had trouble making visual contact on the approach; that the landing attempt had been aborted; that during the first minute of overshoot the crew had had to face turbulence and a fire-warning on the number two engine.

In climb-out, thought Raille, like all the other number two engine fire-warnings on the 119. There was no conclusive proof that the warning had been false. The engine had been too badly burnt in the crash to give any immediate clues.

Raille and the systems analyst from California sat half the night in a hotel bedroom studying a full-size plan of the Flight Engineer's panel, trying to guess the sequence of events that would have followed the engine shut-down. What had caused the flight recorders to pack up at that very moment? It was clear from the voice tape that number three generator over-loaded as soon as the number two engine had been shut down. They would have gone on to battery temporarily while the engineer shed some of the power load: galley power; one of the HF sets; a reduction in cabin heating and lighting; weather radar; booster pumps – in that order according to the company manual. Raille looked at the panel. The engineer would have been in a hurry, he thought, in the middle of a fire drill. The galley power switch was on the top corner of the panel, easy enough to find. Selecting one of the HF sets would have been more difficult. He'd have had to look for it. Supposing he went left hand and eyes to the HF set and right hand by feel to the galley switch? There were two switches together on that top corner, on different planes but very close: battery and galley. He was moving fast, in a bit of a flap: he could have hit the wrong one. He could have turned off the battery instead of the galley. Without battery or generator they'd have been flying blind without lighting or instruments, and the flight recorders would certainly have packed up. Raille propped up the panel plan and tried the movement, mistaking the battery switch for the galley.

The Burbank analyst shook his head. 'Not possible – the switches are different shapes and colours.'

Only if you look at them, thought Raille. The battery switch was square and red; the galley power a black tadpole. They could feel much the same if you were in a hurry. Unlikely perhaps, but certainly possible. An interpretation of Murphy's Law – if a mistake is allowed to be possible then sooner or later someone will make it.

Whose bright idea to line those two switches so close together?

'Looks to me more like the battery failed,' said the Burbank analyst. 'It had been charging high, remember.' The Flight Engineer's note on that blood-stained pad. 'It could have died under load.'

Needless to say the ultimate proof, the battery itself, had been totally destroyed in the crash. Another of the unknown quantities.

But what if the Flight Engineer had made that mistake? He also would have assumed it was the battery gone. With no lights on his panel he couldn't have spotted his error. What would have happened? They'd have had the flashlights out, and eventually the engineer would have got them back on to generator. Presumably at that stage he had forgotten to reconnect the flight recorders.

How long would they have been flying blind? A minute? A couple of minutes? Quite enough to lose them their way.

14

One member of the search-party crawled from his bivvi tent into another dawn to seek out a secluded, down-wind and out-of-earshot spot for his morning voidings. He picked a patch of ground where he could see and evade the attentions of ants. He crouched squatting, hanging on to a bush with one hand, staring up at the blue sky and coming to the slow realization that this clearing on the hillside was no natural open space. The scrub had been torn, the ground marked as though something had been dragged across it with force.

His evacuations complete, the engineer followed the marks down the slope and saw, half-buried in the soil, the lumps of torn aluminium missing from Tango November's left-side wing.

An hour later his team found the point of original impact high on the ridge above the camp site – an outcrop of lava breaking the even slope of the ridge. It was even possible to match the damaged fragment with marks on the rock, and calculate the angle of collision – a steep angle suggested by the fact that impact had occurred halfway across the width of the underside of the wing. The plane must have been climbing to clear the ridge in some desperate last-minute manoeuvre.

Whatever the scenario the margin of disaster was not much more than ten feet; and the final downfall of Tango November a hillock of lava haphazardly formed in some eruption three or four hundred years ago.

Isolated pieces of the jigsaw were beginning to drop into place. Some guides from the volcano had been interviewed. Yes they had been up on the mountain Saturday morning, and very cold and wet it had been. Snow, sleet, hail, the lot.

Yes, they had heard an aeroplane. Very close, and very low. They'd heard it twice, they thought. Once to the north and vaguely overhead, Once to the east, when the sound of the engines seemed to be coming from somewhere down in the valley below them. But then that could have been an impression caused by atmospheric conditions.

The storm? All to the north and west of the mountain at the time they heard the aeroplane. Everything was clear to the east because they'd seen the dawn and the sun breaking out of the sea.

The lower slopes of the mountain? Patches of cloud all over it – like looking at a frozen lake with little islands where the ground showed through. Only the top few hundred feet of the mountain had been completely clear of cloud.

The sunrise? Blood red and dramatic. Quite frightening really. Violent.

15

Taormina-Peloritana was slumbering in the warmth, apparently oblivious of the dramas unfolding on its behalf up and down the length of Italy. Civil operation was still forbidden, though word had it that the airport was about to reopen. A skeleton staff were keeping buildings swept and the Traffic Controllers took turns in the tower, fulfilling their military duties. The airport administration with Servizi TP and Pantellana were manning their combined offices anticipating the resumption of traffic, and helping feed the day's cancellations into Fontanarossa or Reggio Calabria.

Somewhere beyond the Aero Club an oil-tanker and trailer arrived along the avenue of knee-high oleanders. But there was, to anyone sitting on the terrace of the club bar, no more than a buzz of insect in the air and a faint and inconspicuous drone of machinery as the tanker manoeuvred into position.

863 cubic centimetres of desmodromic Ducati exploded into that tranquillity with the effect of a dozen machine guns. Every inhabitant of the field walked to a window or a door, and one vigilant pair of eyes recognized both motor-bike and boy, and telephoned the recognition to a private number on an orange farm thirty miles away under the southern slopes of the volcano.

Sharlie was only belatedly aware of the noise he had made. He had been following Tomacchio's oil-tanker since early morning through the villages under the volcano, across the valleys to the north, and up into the Peloritani hills. He'd had to stop in the last town for petrol and had then momentarily lost track of the lorry, only guessing at its destination. He killed his engine now and free-wheeled across the empty airport car park trying to appear uninterested in his surroundings. But behind his visor he was quartering the ground for that elusive tanker, and when he placed it behind the Aero Club building his hurried sequence of action was neither disinterested nor inconspicuous. He had to work his way as close as possible to the lorry and its operation. Citto had briefed him and Sharlie knew that the point of evidence was the positioning of those long black hoses unreeled from the tanker. He moved as casually as was possible and without showing himself to the driver, running off a dozen exposures from various positions to describe the tanker's operation. He couldn't make sense of it himself without knowing the location and functions of all the stop-cocks and attachments but by the time he returned to the bike he was confident he had enough evidence for Citto to work on.

He rode as quietly as the beast would allow out of the car park and down the link road, pulling the bike up a side-track to wait for the lorry.

Flavio Consoli was unlucky with the telephone that morning. His mother was on the line gossiping with one of her ten sisters and by the time Taormina-Peloritana rang through to him Capo Tomacchio and his lorry had already left the airport.

Flavio listened to the narrative of crisis: a photographer who had been seen recording the arrival of Avvocato Consoli at the Fontanarossa airport two days ago was now photographing the activities of a petrol lorry at Taormina-Peloritana.

Flavio had neither the experience nor the natural 'cool' to cope with so immediate a situation. He had reacted successfully on Saturday morning by soliciting Tomacchio's help and advice. But now the Capo was at the sharp end of the situation and there was no way of talking with him. The man who had telephoned was one of the catering managers. At least Flavio knew enough about the fiddles he pulled to be able to rely on his discretion.

'Do you know the villages further up the hill?'

'The empty ones?'

'Yes. Number three as you come to them. Above the road off a hairpin. The lorry stops there for a job. Take your car and catch up with him.'

'What do I tell him?'

'Tell him he's being followed. Tell him about the boy on the motor-bike.'

'Anything else?'

'Tell him to do everything normal. Tell him to carry on as

though nothing had happened. And tell him I'm on my way. I'll watch the motor-bike. Tell him whoever the boy is I'll buy him off.'

Two minutes later the Dino was tearing up dust and gravel along the track between the orange trees, and Flavio was thanking God for having sent his father away on business that morning into the city.

The empty village was tucked away in a fold of ground near the top of the pass: a piazza; a church, ugly and modern, marked with rusty iron-work; deserted houses in rows up the hillside their doors and shutters broken; cracked streets and brick steps growing dry burnt grass – desolation without a sheep or a goat or a dog or a madman to break the silence. A mis-conceived attempt to resettle peasants on an arid hillside; or more probably just another excuse for the buying and selling of land, and the pocketing of government grants.

Sharlie had smiled when the lorry turned off the main road, for he now guessed the story his camera would record. He drove the bike into the long grass and pulled it up on its centre stand. He took three quick pictures of the track from the main road to place the location, then changed the half finished film in case he ran out of exposures at a more critical moment. After all Citto was paying for these rolls. He slipped the half finished film into the map-pocket in the front of his leather coat.

He heard the lorry stop where the track was closed by a pole barrier; he heard the rattle of chain and padlock, then the lorry straining again up the hillside. Sharlie climbed straight up the slope and cut off the corner, scrambling fast on banks of thistle and twisted thorn. He was already in the far end of the village as the tanker backed alongside the church. He watched as the driver unrolled a length of hose from the lorry into a side entrance at the rear of the building. Sharlie needed to be nearer. He worked his way up a concrete drainage channel into the main street, the Madonna and child in coloured enamel watch-ing him from above each gaping door – icons spared by God-fearing vandals. A broken shutter creaked, and a thin black snake whipped away angry in the grass under his feet. He could see the shimmer of fumes around the church door where petrol was leaking from the pipe and evaporating in the sun. He wondered what size of storage tank there could be inside that shell of church.

The tanker engine was throttled up for pumping and the noise prevented Sharlie from hearing the arrival of a car in the piazza. Nor was he particularly alarmed or uneasy that he could no longer see the driver. He assumed the man was in the church waiting for the pump to complete its work.

But Capo Tomacchio had walked out as the car appeared. He recognized the blue Audi and the catering manager from the airport. He'd been expecting trouble ever since he started out that morning. This of all weeks the Consoli could have relinquished their run. Greedy bastards.

'Have you seen the motor-bike anywhere?' he asked when he heard the story.

'Down on the main road. In the grass.'

Tomacchio glanced at the tanker still pumping away at the side of the church. That boy with the camera was somewhere around hiding in the houses. He pulled the car door open. 'Run me down there. Then get on back to the airport.'

Slow the little sod up, thought the Capo. Give Flavio Consoli time to catch up with him. Immobilize him. But not right here on the doorstep. Delayed stoppage he wanted. The Audi dropped him by the motor-bike where the track joined the main road, and when the car had gone Tomacchio grabbed a handful of gravel and tried to open the petrol tank. There was a flip lid across the cap, but a lock underneath. Tomacchio squatted instead to unscrew the sump filler. He funnelled his dirt into the hot oil and ran in two extra handfuls for good measure. He was back up the hill into the village three minutes later to turn off his pumps and roll up his pipes.

Sharlie had his pictures, two dozen of them: fuel siphoned out from tanks at the airport, driven uphill to the deserted village and stored here presumably for resale. That appeared to be the operation. He now watched the lorry pull away across the cracked paving of the piazza, down the track back to the main road. Airport and village had taken forty minutes out of the day's run, and no one any the wiser. The Capo would be down in Milazzo by lunch-time and back home with his load of petrol for supper. There seemed no point in cataloguing the rest of the day's journey and there was anyhow a risk of being spotted on that lonely road over the top. Sharlie decided to turn back with his pictures. It was not a happy decision. If he had been following the tanker he'd have spent the next few hours driving slowly.

Sharlie rode back down the pass and through the town in the valley with only a vague sensation that the bike was misbehaving. Running a bit sluggish. On the far side of town he noticed a flamboyant green and orange Dino passing in the opposite direction and he wondered briefly if it was the same car that had met the Avvocato Consoli at the airport yesterday. If he'd had a mirror on the motor-bike he might have seen the Dino turning in the road and taking up station a hundred yards or so behind him.

I'll stop him out in the country, Flavio was thinking, and either buy him off or frighten him off.

Sharlie was happy. He'd done the job well and now the road was wide, straight and open beyond the town. He dropped down a gear to accelerate the cobwebs out of the engine. The oil pressure warning light was on, and the engine straining, but Sharlie hadn't noticed the light and the bike ran on, building up to 170 kph before the boy finally realized that something was really wrong. By then it was too late. His left-hand fingers went groping out for the clutch about a tenth of a second too late. The engine had seized, and the back wheel had locked. He was out of control, broadside and falling. He felt his leg break as it hit the road with the full weight of the bike. His Levis shredded along the asphalt. He shut his eyes with the pain. Christ, he was thinking, I've ruined the bike.

From the car behind Flavio watched in disbelief. It seemed to him afterwards that he had witnessed the whole incident in slow motion; the sudden trail of smoke; the bike starting to slew; the back wheel drawing out a thick black line on the road. Then the fall, motor-bike and rider spinning round each other down the road still travelling at something over 100 kph.

An approaching lorry pulled across the road to avoid them, and the Dino braked to a standstill behind. The motor-bike bounced with a cloud of dust into an orange garden. Sharlie instead spun on down the asphalt head first into the concrete kerb. His body flipped over, rolling into burnt grass and dust, coming to a stop slumped between two oak trees.

The lorry-driver ran towards him kneeling in the dirt over the crumpled heap of road-torn denim and leather.

Flavio moved the Dino towards them, stopped and climbed out.

'You'll have to take him,' the lorry-driver shouted. 'He needs a hospital very bad.'

Flavio had no choice. It was law in Italy where public ambulances were few and far between. They carried the boy to the Dino and folded him into the low and awkward passenger seat. Flavio noticed beyond his sense of shock the broken camera bag lying at the side of the road.

'I'll take it,' he said. 'There might be his papers in there.'

'It just happened, didn't it?' said the lorry-driver. 'No one touched him.'

'A puncture maybe,' said Flavio. 'I'll tell the cops in town. They'll want to pick up the bike themselves.'

'You'd better have my name,' said the lorry-driver. 'Don't want them to think it was anyone's fault.'

Flavio turned the Dino back towards town. There had to be a first-aid post somewhere. He turned up his lights, held a white handkerchief from the window, and leaned on the horn – the conventional signs for a private car doubling as an ambulance.

He looked at the boy slumped in the seat beside him: the visor was broken, the face below it pale, almost blue, and blood running in streams from under the helmet. Flavio had placed the camera bag on the boy's lap. There were rolls of film inside and a camera damaged in the fall. It wasn't difficult to prise the camera apart and extract the film. Flavio pocketed the cassettes then let the bag fall on the floor at the boy's feet.

The Dino must have been visible or audible to everyone in town as it came blasting up the road, and sure enough a police car met them, drawing alongside to have a look, then preceding them with its siren wailing to clear the traffic as they made for the *pronto soccorso*. But all they could do when they arrived was lay the boy on a stretcher and wait. Another ten minutes passed before a doctor was located and the boy's breathing grew shallower and his pulse weaker. Sharlie's heart stopped beating just two minutes after the doctor's arrival and when they cut

the helmet off his head they found the skull visibly and irrevocably broken.

It was half past eleven on Wednesday morning. Stella
Pritchard, Trixie, the retired army Major, his wife, the Twickenham sales executive and the Durham GP were alive; Tino G.
and the Northumberland shopkeeper more or less alive.

In Rome Citto was waiting for the bus out to Fiumicino and
the lunch-time flight back home to Catania. In Venice Ingegnere Preuss had been reading pages of an old report deleted
three years previously by the personal intervention of a
Minister. In Taormina Larry Raille had received a sixty-word
cable offering him transfer and promotion into NASA. On
the mountain the search-party was on its way back to civili-
zation, and in the wreckage of Tango November engineers
were unravelling the last structural and mechanical evidence.

Sharlie's mum was told of her son's death when she came
home for lunch from her dirty work-bench in a dirty factory.
Her yell of despair was heard right across the city harbour,
above the hooting of a ship, the noise of cranes, the screech
of wagons shunting on rusty rails.

Part Four

I

'You joined Greyhound in March of this year?'

Stella Pritchard nodded from her bed and Burden, eyes down on his clip-board, made the necessary note. He was interviewing for the first time outside his pensione room and he felt a little disorientated. After the tranquillity of Taormina the bustle and the noise of the city had given him a headache.

'Can I ask you when you first met Peter Nyren?'

'I think in May some time.'

'You flew together?'

'Yes.'

'I don't wish to intrude on your private life. If there are questions you would rather not answer – '

'It doesn't matter, does it? Everyone's dead.'

'You went out with Nyren – ?'

Stella cut him off again: 'He took me out some evenings. There was nothing more to it than that. He was very shy.'

'Would other people in the company, your friends and his friends, would they have considered that you were his girl-friend?'

'I expect they imagined we were sleeping together.'

Burden stared uncomfortably at his clip-board trying to phrase his next question. The girl, lying in bed and watching the fan on the ceiling, asked and answered it for him.

'He used to hold my hand and kiss me good night. Otherwise he never touched me.'

Burden was still silent. The interrogation seemed to have escalated out of his control. He couldn't even see the girl's face. She was lying flat on a high bed, and he was to one side in an uncomfortably low armchair.

The girl spoke again: 'If you're wondering what my feelings were you can write down that I liked him. I wouldn't have objected if he had touched me or seduced me or whatever.'

Burden coughed to clear his voice. 'Did you ever visit his home in the country?'

'He asked me down for a weekend. There was a sort of charity cricket match on the village green. Something to do with his father. He's the local vicar.'

'Was that the Saturday when Captain Duckham came with his family?'

'Yes.'

'You must have known Duckham as Fleet Captain.'

'In the distance. We had never flown together.'

'So this cricket match was the first time you met him?'

'Yes.'

'And you were playing as well?'

'We used to play cricket at school.'

'Did you meet his wife there?'

'Just to say hello.'

'And his children?'

'I suppose so. There were a lot of children. I don't really remember. I expect I was nervous about meeting Duckham.'

'Like meeting the boss?'

'Sort of.'

'But you made friends during this cricket game?'

'We ended up batting together. It was more comedy than cricket. I was at one end and he was at the other and we used to meet in the middle and talk between overs. He was chatting me up if that's what you're asking. But it was all a joke. I mean we had everyone laughing at us.'

'Was Peter Nyren playing?'

'He was playing for the village.'

'He didn't object to this – this chatting up?'

'Why should he? We had everyone laughing and clapping. He thought we were a great success.'

'You stayed down there for the weekend?'

'I stayed until Sunday. I wasn't really invited. I mean Peter's father didn't really know. He was quite surprised to see me next morning.'

'And the relationship was still the same between you and Nyren?'

'We didn't even kiss good night.'

'You mean you quarrelled?'

'No. I meant what I said. We didn't say good night to each other. If you want to know why, I thought he was going to come and spend the night with me.'

Another screwball, Burden was thinking.

'Sunday afternoon he drove me home. He could have stayed the night at my place but all the other girls were there. He was shy about that sort of thing.'

'You shared a flat?'

'A house.'

Burden referred to his notes. 'In Redhill.'

'We all worked out of Gatwick.'

'Are you all air hostesses?'

Stella nodded.

'All with Greyhound?'

'There's one girl from British Caledonian.'

'And Nyren I believe lived in London?'

'He had a room somewhere off the Finchley Road.'

Burden sifted through his notes again. 'Frognal.'

'He used to work out of Luton. Before he came to Greyhound.'

'Can I ask you what your feelings were towards Nyren?'

'I don't know. How would I know? We didn't even sleep together.'

Burden was silenced again. He fitted a new sheet of paper to his clip-board, then began again, as carefully as he knew how. 'A certain rumour has been made known to me concerning yourself and Captain Duckham – '

The voice from the pillow cut in, soft and expressionless. 'We slept together a few times.'

Burden was lost for words or a question. Dixie Duckham strikes again, he was thinking. 'Can I ask over what period this happened?'

'From June onwards.'

'All the time?'

'Once a week, once every two weeks. Just as it happened.'

'Was this when you were flying together?'

'Only the first time. We didn't do it on the aeroplane if that's what you're thinking.'

She was reading him without even looking at him. If Stella had been able to see him now she would have found him blushing furiously. Pretty hostesses straddled on his lap in an aeroplane loo. The thought had occurred to him not a few times.

She went on. 'It was a stop-over. Casablanca from Monday morning to Friday evening.'

'This was after the cricket match I take it?'

'Two weeks after.'

'Do you think Duckham arranged it that way?'

'It's not possible. Casablanca is the trip everyone wants to do and there are only two a week. Mondays and Fridays. It's on strict rotation.'

'How often did you fly with Duckham after that?'

'Two or three times.'

'And with Nyren?'

'About the same.'

'Were you ever in Casablanca with Nyren?'

'No.'

'I take it Duckham came to your house a few times?'

'No. Never. Not with the place full of other Greyhound girls.'

Burden was lost for phraseology again. He wasn't even sure that the questions he wanted to ask were relevant to the investigation. Again the girl seemed to read his thoughts.

'We used to do it in his car.'

How and in which particular ways? Burden wanted to know, but he dared ask no more.

'Were you in love with him?'

'I enjoyed making love with him, if that's what you mean.'

'I imagine you would have preferred a more lasting relationship.'

'What does that mean?'

'You never talked together about the possibility of a divorce?'

'Good heavens no.' Stella closed her eyes. The man was beginning to exhaust her. 'I wouldn't have wanted anything like that. Anyway he was very much in love with his wife. He wouldn't have dreamed of leaving her.' Her head moved as though she was trying to look around the room. 'She's here.'

'Mrs Duckham?'

'She's looking after me.'

Burden also glanced round as though he expected to find her behind a curtain.

'They're very short-staffed. She's a trained nurse.'

Extraordinary, thought Burden. Extraordinary how women behave. He couldn't conceive how people lived in such a way. It was all so untidy. He looked at his sheets of notes. He'd completely lost his way. Dixie Duckham, fifty-three years old and knocking off twenty-year-olds in his car. The man was more than a screwball. He was some kind of freak. And his women along with him.

'Did Peter Nyren know what was happening between you and Duckham?'

'Yes.'

'Did you ever talk about it?'

'Yes.'

'Was he upset?'

'I don't know. I suppose so. He was just a kid really.'

'Did you quarrel about it?'

'No.'

'Did he quarrel with Duckham?'

'They were already quarrelling. About something else.'

'How did Nyren find out about it?'

'One of the crew out in Casablanca spreading the good word.' Her head moved again. 'Have we finished?' Her voice was very thin and tired.

'I have to ask you about Friday night. The flight. The crash.'

'Not now,' she whispered.

'I'll come and see you again.'

Burden stood up, and they looked at each other for the first time since he had sat down. He was embarrassed at the way they had talked, and he tried to rationalize it.

'I'm sorry the questions are so personal,' he said. 'It's the fact of you and Duckham and Nyren all being together on the same flight.'

'Personal feelings wouldn't have made any difference to anything.'

'I'm not saying it did.'

'When they're on the flight deck they're just pros doing a job.' Burden nodded.

'He was the best pilot of all.'

'Duckham?'

'Yes.' Stella closed her eyes again. 'You can tell the good

ones. There's never any fuss. It's always quiet. Taking off, landing. Even when things go wrong they never fuss.'

Her eyes stayed closed and Burden stood watching her awkwardly for a moment before backing away to the door.

There was a woman outside waiting in the corridor. Julia Duckham, less bedraggled than when Burden had interviewed her three days ago, apparently calm, her face made up, her hair brushed into a bun.

'I was trying to listen outside the door. I couldn't hear anything.' She stood in front of Burden as he tried to turn away. 'Can I ask you what she said?'

'All information required by the investigation is considered confidential unless ultimately published in the report.'

'He was my husband. You have no right to conceal anything from me.'

'You must talk with her yourself if you want to find out what happened.'

'There was something. That's what you're saying, isn't it?'

'I'm not saying anything.'

'You can't do that.' Her voice was no longer calm. She cornered him against the wall by the lift. 'You said a lot of things the other day when you didn't even know whether they were true or not. And now that you do know you're suddenly not saying anything.'

Person-to-person, full-frontal anger scared Burden. He hadn't had to face it many times in his life. It made him quite weak at the knees. And of course it was true what she said. He had tossed things at her the other day that were at the time nothing more than second- or third-hand gossip.

'It would appear that your husband had been having sexual relations with Miss Pritchard.'

Burden saw her composure deflate. That well-adjusted face began to fray at the edges. Her alarm or dismay or whatever emotion it was gave him an unwanted but uncontrollable feeling of satisfaction. He tried to frown it out of his head and tried to mitigate what he had said.

'It seems to have been a very casual and insignificant relationship. A self-indulgence,' he could not help adding.

The lift arrived and he stepped quickly inside to leave Julia staring at the closing doors.

Eight years. Eight years without a real quarrel, eight years without tears. Eight years being happy and only the illness of children or an occasional overdue airplane to worry about. Fool's paradise.

Julia walked into Stella's room. The girl was waiting for her, eyes on the door.

'I had to tell him things.'

'I know.'

'I must tell you.'

Julia nodded.

'It was nothing. It was just nice making love with him.'

'Jesus Christ. You think I don't know that.'

'That was all it was. It was nothing. Like having a cigarette or a drink. It didn't mean anything.'

Julia sat on the bed: 'The first time he took me out he told me he felt like making love to every pretty girl he passed in the street. That was warning enough, wasn't it?'

There was a long silence.

'He told me – he said – "one day my life is all going to blow open and reveal itself for what it really is."'

2

Sharlie was dead. A traffic accident statistic. A broken naked boy. A pile of clothes with identity card, driving licence, a single thousand lire note, a penknife, a battered plastic bag of broken camera and lenses. One roll of film had been found still intact inside the leather jacket by hospital staff and it was enclosed with the rest of his belongings in a large polythene bag to await the next-of-kin.

Identification of the body was made that afternoon by Sharlie's mum. She had been driven forty miles to the hospital in a police car. Apart from the professional solace offered by the police driver and a nurse at the hospital, her only comfort was from members of the family: Nonna Lisa, Laura and Laura's brother Pietro. They sat together in a waiting-room, the two older women hand-in-hand crying together, the young brother and sister side by side on a wooden bench staring at the floor. Laura was thinking of Sharlie yesterday high on his mountain picking mushrooms with *Cantallaluna*, happy, laughing, all that tightness from Rome disappearing from his face. Pietro, it had to be admitted, was thinking of his motor-bike.

Citto joined them late in the afternoon, blundering into the waiting-room at the hospital peering through a pair of steamed-up glasses as though unwilling to believe the news he had been given. The News Editor from the paper had met him when his plane landed from Rome. Even at this stage of proceedings neither of them believed the death to be an accident.

He will blame himself, Laura thought when she saw Citto. He'll be saying to himself, I sent Sharlie after that lorry; I am responsible for his death.

Laura watched him sit with the mother and take her hand, trying to comfort her. Sharlie was a good boy, Citto was telling her. Honest, brave, hard-working. *Un bravo ragazzo*.

A courageous boy, Citto would have liked to say. He would have liked to tell this mother that her boy had discovered anger and courage before he died. But Citto didn't want those mother's eyes turned accusingly on him. You again, they would say. Always leading him into trouble. And now into death.

A nurse brought the plastic bag with Sharlie's clothes and effects. There was a form to sign, a list to check. The mother did not want to see it, and Citto took the bag to check its contents. It was just as well that he did so, for some unthinking fool in the nether regions of hospital or morgue had packed the split and bloody remains of the boy's crash helmet. Citto asked the nurse to wrap the torn jeans, leather jacket and the helmet separately. The mother could be spared those details. Citto would take them himself together with that roll of film. He was thinking about forensic examination and evidence.

He visited the local traffic police as journalist and friend, and put his questions. They listened politely to his theories; made notes on the possible culpability of the man with the green and orange Dino. Citto asked them about the motor-bike.

'Examined: found defective; engine seized at very high speed. No signs of a collision.'

Can the bike be photographed?

'It was taken away by a garage pending instructions from next-of-kin or the insurance company.'

The name of the garage?

'Autoboom.' It was a breaker's yard on the coast in Giardini.

Citto returned to the hospital, picked up Pietro and drove fast and furious in the fading light down the valley towards Taormina.

Giardini liked to call itself the lido of Taormina, sited as it was on the strip of land between the sea and the rock on which Taormina stood. In reality it was nothing much more than a railway station, a jumble of pensioni and a long straggle of small specialist garages: coachworks, car electricians, tyre dealers, mechanics.

Citto and Pietro found the bike under a tarpaulin in a breaker's yard along the road towards Naxos, a couple of men already at work by lamplight, separating the engine from the frame.

Who had told them to break up the bike?

'We're just taking out the engine that's all.'

On whose authority?

'I don't need bleeding authority to work in my own yard.'

But Pietro had the bike's documents with him, and when Citto threatened to walk round the corner to call up the Carabinieri the two men stopped their work and faded away.

Vandals? Or saboteurs?

The bike was badly bent, worn and almost molten down the one side where it had slid on the road. The front wheel was twisted, and the whole machine impregnated with tufts of dry grass and earth.

Citto left Pietro mourning over that grim wreckage, guarding it against further desecration. Citto was thinking, there were a dozen men up in Taormina equipped and trained to examine mechanical wreckage. He drove up the hill and around the town to the hotel where the investigators had set up their centre of operations.

But Citto's only link with the air crash investigators was not yet back from his day's work. The English doctor, they told him, would return at nine o'clock. Two hours to wait.

Citto wandered into the narrow hillside streets, his frantic movement running down, his mind beginning to fill with

Sharlie. How many times they had haunted these steps and alleyways together lying in wait after a tip-off about some celebrity staying in the San Domenico, Sharlie prowling, camera tucked into one hand as though it were a knife or a gun. He never missed exposure or focus shooting on the turn. It was pleasing just to watch him at work.

What had happened this morning? Sharlie must have got his pictures for he was on his way back when he crashed. Citto still had that cartridge in his pocket. Had it been used? Citto had searched for more films in that black hospital bag and in the remains of Sharlie's cameras and camera bag. The boy would have travelled with at least half a dozen rolls, but there were no signs of them. They couldn't all have been lost in the spill.

Citto found a studio up one of the alleyways off the main street, the photographer an elderly man of doubtful nationality. He was closing up for the evening but agreed to develop the cartridge for an exorbitant fee. He mistook Citto's urgency for furtiveness. Citto waited in a purple-draped studio, wondering at the portraits displayed on the walls – elderly Teutonic gentlemen and the traditionally beautiful local boys posed semi-naked by the sea, or framed in the pillars of the Greek theatre. The old photographer would be disappointed if he thought he could steal some prints of porn from Sharlie's roll of Kodak.

Capo Tomacchio was tired. Tired, dirty, hungry and thirsty. He drove the heavy tanker and trailer through his yard gates, parked, locked up, and climbed the iron steps on to his terrace above the old boiler house. Unloading could wait until the morning. A black shape leapt at him at the top of the stairs in a frenzy of barking, mad green eyes pulled up short and head high at the end of a chain. The Capo muttered affection and a curse and the Alsatian subsided. He had no nose, that dog. You had to talk to him before he recognized you. Tomacchio glanced across the terrace at the house: lights in the kitchen and the sitting-room. His wife in the kitchen, his daughter in the sitting-room with the gramophone or the TV or some boy-friend. Young Renzo no doubt: aggressive and political, useless except as a mechanic.

Renzo must have heard him coming. He was on his way out as Tomacchio entered and they threw casual good nights passing each other in the kitchen.

The Capo called after him across the terrace: 'She's dropping oil from somewhere.' Renzo could be fixing that when he came in next morning. It would give Tomacchio an extra twenty minutes in bed.

'Bloody old fuss-pot,' thought Renzo down in the yard. He took the lamp from his bicycle and squatted down by the lorry. Best find the leak while it was still warm and dripping. It'd take all morning tomorrow for the yard was pock-marked with oil stains old and new. The leak was on the differential and he pushed a dry tray under it. By the morning he'd have an idea how much it had been losing.

It was as Renzo returned to his bike that he heard the Dino climbing the hill into the far side of the village. It had to be Consoli. There was only one young blood in this part of the world who drove six cylinders with quite so much throttle blipping, air horn blowing, and tyre-squealing. Renzo stood listening to it. Was he coming to take Giuseppina out for the evening? Was that why she'd told him he'd better leave? Renzo's bike was in the old distillery office just under the yard gates. He waited there as the Dino turned into the street and parked outside. Little sod, Renzo thought. I'll murder him if he takes her out.

He heard Flavio ring the bell on the outside of the gate, and pictured him pushing his face up to the wall to talk into the speaker grille. The flabby lazy voice was trying hard to sound urgent: 'I've got to see you,' Renzo heard it say. 'I'll wait in the yard for you.'

See who? The remote-control door lock buzzed and clicked and Renzo smelt after-shave as Flavio pushed his way into the yard not two feet from where he was standing. He's not going upstairs, Renzo thought, because he's scared of the dog. Flavio was the one human that old Alsatian always recognized. Flavio had kicked him once, hard in the head and the body, and like elephants old wolf-hounds bide their time and never forget.

It was not Giuseppina but Tomacchio himself who appeared in silhouette along the terrace and down the iron steps.

Renzo thought he should go now, but it would look a bit

odd appearing suddenly out of the darkness. He waited as the two men met, wondering what conspiracy the two of them were hatching out. Their first words froze him.

'He's dead.' That was Flavio in a low voice.

'Who's dead?'

'The kid on the motor-bike.'

'So? He had an accident.'

'Did you have anything to do with it?'

'What happened to him?'

'I was right behind him.'

'You didn't time that very well then.'

'Did you have anything to do with it?'

'I wasn't there, was I?'

'*I* was there, you bloody fool. And if there's anything the cops are going to find out about it I've got to know.'

'Don't you bloody fool me, young man.'

There was a pause as they seemed to move further from the house and even nearer to Renzo. Tomacchio spoke again.

'You haven't told me what happened yet.'

'His back wheel locked up. He must have been doing a hundred and eighty.'

There was a short pause and Renzo sweated in the silence and the darkness. Eavesdropping on this kind of secret carried a death sentence. Who in God's name were they talking about?

'I put gravel in his oil. His engine must have seized.'

'Holy Jesus.' There was another, longer silence.

Tomacchio spoke: 'Seems to me you'll have to tell your dad. He can hold the cops off.'

'Tell him? Are you mad? He'd kill me. He would literally tear me to pieces.'

'It's his game, isn't it? Just because you're running it for him and part of it goes wrong, he can't eat you for that.'

Another silence. Tomacchio tried again. 'I'll go and see him myself if you're frightened of him.'

'He doesn't know what we're doing.' From Flavio's tone of voice that was a major confession.

The longest silence of all now. Renzo couldn't see where they were, nor what they were doing.

The Capo's voice was angry and hard. Renzo knew that tone. It meant what it said: 'If it goes wrong for me I'll drag you down.

I'll hurt you and him so bloody hard you won't know what's happened. Do you think I'd have got myself involved in this twopenny-ha'penny fiddle if I'd known your old man wasn't in on it? I thought I was doing him a favour. I sure as hell haven't any reason for doing you favours.'

There were sounds of movement, then Flavio's voice uneasy through its lazy slur. 'Where are you going?'

'To get my coat.' Renzo could see Tomacchio climbing the steps back on to the terrace.

'What for?'

'We're going to drain that bloody tank.'

'Tonight?'

'And you're going to drive me there.'

Two minutes later the Capo reappeared along the terrace and down the steps, carrying not only coat but hunting gun.

'What's the gun for?' Flavio was sounding queasy.

'Get in the car and drive.'

The two men passed Renzo out into the street. Flavio's aftershave and the older man's sweat.

When the roar of the Dino had faded out of the village Renzo eased his bike quietly out of the wicket door and cycled home. You're involved, he was telling himself. You talked to that journalist. Today's the day they were following the tanker. He thought of the tubby little man with the stammer hoping he was not the victim, and then spent the rest of the evening wondering if he shouldn't tell someone what he had overheard. But native caution prevailed. Communist or not this was still Sicily where eyes and ears had learnt instinctively to keep their secrets.

There was music in Taormina that night, piano and orchestra drifting from the columns and amphitheatre on the edge of the town high above the sea: a Japanese pianist, a Dutch orchestra, a German conductor, ignorant of each other's languages, uninvolved personally in the tragedy, but gathered under the moon to play a Mozart piano concerto in an open-air theatre excavated three centuries before the birth of Christ. Of such complexity and compassion, thought Ash Nyren, is the Kingdom of Man.

The old Canon was perched high in the auditorium, hunched

up, one elbow on one knee, listening to the music. Yesterday his stubble had been shaved and he'd been dressed in someone's baggy clothes. People had been looking for him and those American students had told them where to find him. He had been lodged in a room under a roof where the sun punished him from morning to evening, and where he looked out on a burnt hillside of cactus.

He listened to the cadenza below him losing itself in the darkness.

K 491. Brahms was more to the Canon's taste; or even the second movement of Beethoven's Third Symphony that had opened the concert. The audience inside would doubtless prefer the Rachmaninov concerto still to come. The middle-class citizens of north-eastern Sicily had bought the expensive tickets and had arrived, elegant and attentive in large cars, paying their respects to the victims of the smashed aeroplane that lay unseen on the dark mass of volcano now framed so perfectly and so improbably in moonlight above and beyond the four Corinthian capitals.

Outside on the hill Canon Ash Nyren decided he forgave Mozart for K 491. It held melancholy into the finale. There was no gay tripping or light skipping here. The old Canon recognized the despair of a recurring Neapolitan sixth.

God's strength, he was thinking, is based solely on the arbitrary nature of death. Man against God.

Citto found the English doctor as the investigators dispersed from their evening meeting. They were scattered in groups round a small interior cloister in the San Domenico at the opposite end of the town from the Greek Theatre. No music filtered in here, only the sound of a fountain and the pattering of rubber-soled waiters carrying drinks.

Mac was in fighting mood that night. He'd been held up all day sorting the remains of five carbonized and fragmented bodies and trying to establish some method of identification. He was falling behind on his detailed autopsies and he had asked for a postponement of interment and repatriation. To no avail. He was told that the funeral arrangements had been finalized for the Saturday, which left Mac with at the most two days to complete his evidence.

'If seats, seat-belts and cabin fittings had been fifteen per cent more resistant,' he had announced at that evening's meeting, 'we would have found a one thousand per cent improvement in the casualty figures. I believe it is of the utmost importance to collect specific data to support this aspect of the investigation so that public pressure in England and America can be brought to bear for the revision of minimum safety regulations.'

Boy, that had gone down like a stone. How they hated that phrase 'public pressure'. He had collected a very old-fashioned look from Ralph Burden over their coffee. Only Larry Raille had supported him with anything approaching whole-heartedness and the two of them were still talking together in the cloister when Citto arrived to interrupt them.

The little Italian, blinking, stammering, struggling with his English, was no champion advocate. But he had facts, and even evidence of a sort. Burden was called to join the little group and Citto told his story from the beginning: the stopped clocks and the petrol lorry at the airport on the morning of the crash, and the lines of inquiry he had followed both on the island and in Rome. He told them of Ingegnere Preuss with his own controversial evidence on the siting of the airport. And he told them finally of the events of that day and the death of the young photographer on his motor-bike. The evidence was the film from the half-finished roll found in Sharlie's pocket, for Sharlie had worked well that morning. He had covered the lorry at the airport to show up the positioning of pipes and stop-cocks, and his last three exposures identified that derelict purpose-built village high in the hills. Even without the missing films there was a clear enough indication of malpractice.

'Why should they be interested in that particular fuel?' asked Raille.

'It's paid for by the military,' Citto replied. 'Part of the agreement to have the field available as a NATO standby. The Italian Air Ministry pays all the bills for emergency equipment.'

Mac interrupted him: 'You really think the photographer was killed?' Mac remembered Sharlie taking pictures for him in the city morgue. He had felt badly enough about the boy's subsequent dust-up with the police. Now he was dead, and the idea that the death might not have been accidental worried Mac as much as it worried Citto. The journalist didn't have to request their participation. They were all of them alarmed.

'Better have a look at this motor-bike,' Raille suggested. 'If you know where it is.'

They sat in the breaker's yard at Autoboom for forty minutes watching Raille work with a lamp and spanners on the bike: Mac, Burden, Citto and Pietro. Ralph Burden had his misgivings. He could see the impetuous Mac leading the investigation into all kinds of trouble with the local authorities. This talk of dark and dirty deeds had no place in Burden's well-ordered routine. Even Larry Raille had felt a twinge of that same misgiving, but he was glad enough to be offered diversionary activity. He had cabled polite refusal of the offered transfer and promotion, and had as a result already suffered one torrid call from his wife in Washington. The further away he stayed from a telephone the easier he felt. And a motor-bike did make a change.

He worked his way backwards through the sequence of disaster: the wheel locked solid, the bottom of the rear tyre worn to the cover with friction on the road, the final drive chain immovable, the gear-box distorted and jammed. Finally when he'd dismantled the forward of the V-angled cylinders, the piston and cylinder wall could be seen fused together, the original point of the seizure. He unbolted the oil pump and filters. They were buried in grit and small stones. Oil flow had been effectively cut off from the engine.

At which point Burden insisted that the bike with all its attendant parts be handed over to the police. 'It would seem right,' he said in his best Department manner, 'to adjourn for the day. We have opened many new complications.'

'It's a long time until tomorrow,' said Citto. 'Evidence in our country has a habit of disappearing.'

Mac looked at the journalist: 'Officially we can adjourn. Unofficially we can have an informal look round – ' Mac's blood was up. If someone had really killed the photographer he wanted to see what the boy had been photographing in that odd-looking village up in the hills. 'How about it, Ralph?'

Burden shook his head. 'I'll stay here with the bike and talk with the police. I think it is advisable to allow them to make the next move.'

Mac turned to the American. 'You coming, Larry?'

Raille was cleaning his hands with petrol and a rag. He had visions of his hotel room, and an insistent transatlantic telephone. 'Why the hell not. We're only tourists.'

3

For six miles on the climb the headlights behind them had been normal enough: something to keep an eye on; nothing in particular to get alarmed about. Flavio had been watching them in the mirror; Capo Tomacchio, slumped in the low passenger seat, from the window beside him.

'Cut your lights before you turn off.'

It was the elder man's first comment in twenty miles. Flavio had felt the Capo's anger as heavy in the air as the sweat and oil from his driving overalls. If my surname wasn't Consoli, he thought, this ape would have had me rolled up in a ditch by now with a broken head.

Flavio turned off the lights as they approached the side road for the deserted village, then used the handbrake to stop the car at the barrier. The Capo hauled himself out of the cockpit to swing the pole skywards. Flavio could hear cicadas in the grass and far away the oscillating drone of the other car lower down the pass, changing tone as it turned in sweeps through the hairpins.

The Dino climbed the track in moonlight round the shoulder of hill up into the piazza. They stopped by the church.

'What happens to the petrol when we open the taps?' Flavio was talking in an undertone as though the ghost village might come suddenly to life.

'It'll seep away. The paving is cracked. There'll be nothing of it left by tomorrow.' The vestry door was stiff on its hinges and the Capo kicked it open. 'You wait here and keep listening.'

Tomacchio disappeared inside, the glimmer of his torch

fading from sight. Flavio waited in the black silence. It was like a kid's game all this excitement, though he could think of better companions than Capo Tomacchio to share it with. There'd be trouble with him when this fuss had all blown over. Maybe I ought to run off with his daughter, thought Flavio. What a pair of ever-lasting tits – and enough money to make life everlastingly comfortable.

He saw the lights of the other car still weaving through the bends. Probably a commercial traveller on his way home to Milazzo. But then the note of the engine suddenly changed, slowing up somewhere near the side-turn for the village. It seemed to stop for a moment, then reverse. Flavio watched the headlights swing out into the valley, and uphill on the track towards them. He banged on the door to warn Tomacchio.

'That car's coming up here.'

'Goddam!' The Capo was outside before Flavio had finished speaking.

'Did you find the tap?'

'Bloody thing's rusted. It's only half open. Running out like a kid peeing. Take all night to empty.'

Flavio saw him reach into the car for the shotgun.

'You're not going to use that, are you?'

'Keep out of sight, sonny-boy. Stay here with the car, ready to move.'

'We can't use guns – ' But Tomacchio was gone. Even the sluggish Flavio felt suddenly alarmed.

The track to the village was closed with a pole. Citto parked the car and the three men moved off on foot in line abreast to cover the width of the track, their torches picking out the unmistakable double tyre-treads of a heavy lorry in the gravel.

The three men felt no presence of danger. There was a low moon and a distant moonlit sea in a long white horizon. There were sweet damp smells left over from Monday's storm and a buzz of crickets. They were not to know that their three wavering spots of torchlight were being held in a gun-sight.

Tomacchio had thought he would be dealing with one man. One corpse was possible, three impractical. He'd seen the dark crimson of a battered Giulia and knew that these three were no policemen. He squeezed the near trigger and the night exploded. Voluntarily or involuntarily the three spots of torch-light disappeared.

Lying in the dirt by the roadside Citto decided that the shot had been fired from the bank above them. He'd been aware only of the noise and a stinging sensation in his face. He thought his glasses were broken and there was warm blood coming from somewhere. He looked round. The other two were lying across the road from him. Dead?

Then he heard the American swearing. Was the English doctor hurt?

'Are you all right?' That was Raille calling over the road to him.

'He is hurt?'

Citto saw the American prodding his colleague. 'You all right, Mac?'

The English voice was muffled and outraged. 'I've torn my bloody trousers.'

There was a silence; maybe a few seconds, though it felt much longer to the three men on the ground.

'I'm not sleeping here tonight,' said Mac.

'So what do we do?' That was the American.

Turn round and go home, thought Citto. Guns is guns.

'Anyone for kamikaze?' That crazy Englishman was getting up, flashing his torch on to the bank above the road. The gun roared again, into the road in front of them as before, and this time Citto saw flame from the barrel maybe ten yards from where he was lying. Mac was down again, in more of a crouch than a sprawl. They heard the gun break for the re-load.

'Next time he does that – ' said Mac. 'Two barrels. We have to make him fire twice then charge him.'

Bloody fool, thought Raille. He's seen too much television. There's only one rule with guns: get out of their way, and stay out of their way. 'I'd say,' he said over his shoulder, 'that whoever it is doesn't want us up in that village. If we turned around and went away he'd probably let us go.'

'What? Let him scare us off with that noise?'

Raille called out loud in stentorian tone: 'Whoever you are, we're moving back to our car.' He looked across at Citto.

Citto repeated the words in Italian, stuttering dreadfully as he tried to communicate determination.

Capo Tomacchio recognized the voice and the impediment – the tubby little journalist who had tried to interview him on Sunday. His companions were presumably foreign newsmen. He saw shapes moving on the road. They seemed to be crawling back down the hill on their hands and knees. Would they go away? They'd call the police. How long would it take the police to arrive? Half an hour to get up here? That sodding fuel would still be draining. Best set fire to the whole issue. Lay a fuse to the tank and blow it up. But immobilize their car first. He needed time.

He moved along the bank, not caring about the noise he made, for he was sure they were not carrying guns. Stocky though he was, he could move fast, a great deal faster than Citto and Larry Raille on their hands and knees. The Capo found their car parked on the slope below the barricade, unlocked, but without the ignition key. He didn't have time to fiddle with wires. The wheels were set askance and he released the handbrake, letting it run back gently into the ditch by the side of the road. It would take them all night to dig it out.

Tomacchio doubled back, still on the bank and off the road. Two minutes later he had rejoined Flavio in that weed-strewn piazza. They had to devise a delayed fuse that would not blow them both up in the process of igniting those storage tanks in the church.

Mac had not moved back up the road with Citto and Larry Raille. He had seen the gunman moving uphill again into the village, and he followed, keeping to the edges of the road, his silhouette below the cover of the banks. He was a degree more apprehensive than before. He knew nothing about the layout of the village, nor how many men were there and with how many guns.

Flavio and Capo Tomacchio were both out of sight behind the church when Mac paced carefully into the piazza. The tall Englishman kept to the iron railing at the side of that strange open space. The dead village lay under a low and waning moon, the weeds in the square throwing long exaggerated shadows, the door and two windows of each house like the mouth and eye-sockets of skulls. Twice men moved at the far end of the piazza and twice Mac froze, naked against the unshadowed moon-facing façade of the church. It was at the far corner of that façade that he first smelt the fuel, an overpowering cloud of vapour.

He moved back along the façade to the main door of the church. It was not locked and he edged it carefully open, each crack of warped wood or rusted hinge echoing like so many gunshots round the village.

The inside of the church was bare; no altar, no pews, incense or candle to suggest the presence of Christ and his angels. The moon slanted in at three windows, low angles of light to show a vaulted ceiling, some artisan's forgotten masterpiece, admired by no one except the birds and the bats. One black doorway led to what would have been a vestry. He could smell the petrol so strong now that a cigarette would have blown the roof off. He inched his way into the darkness, obliged now to use his torch. The paving was cracked where the ground had subsided. Mac could hear the trickling of fuel and the sound led him to large storage tanks at the far end of the building – 15000 gallons or more in each he estimated.

Outside in the village Tomacchio's fuse was ready – a line of dry grass and sticks soaked with petrol and running from the vestry door across the corner of the piazza to where the Dino was parked. But it was a night of unending problems for Tomacchio. Neither he nor Flavio were smokers, and neither of them possessed a lighter or a box of matches. Tomacchio rolled up a page of newspaper and soaked it in petrol. They uncovered the engine of the Dino and disconnected one of the plug leads. Flavio started the engine and after a few blank moments and some thumping shocks up Tomacchio's arm the loose spark ignited the newspaper.

Mac heard the car, but could see nothing. It wasn't until the car actually moved that he found a low ventilator grille to give him some visibility outside. He saw then the narrow snake of fire approaching the church across the piazza. The car disappeared from his view in a wheel-spinning frenzy leaving him staring at that advancing flame. His brain seized up. The burning trail was some five yards short of the church, spluttering and crackling, accelerating in a whoosh each time it reached a pool of petrol. Some of the tall dry weeds in the piazza were burning, like trees in a forest fire from where Mac was watching on ground level. Then his brain moved again and he turned and ran for the church door. I'm not going to make it, he thought. I stood there like an idiot staring at it and now I can't get out. He slipped on the broken paving into a pool of petrol, lost his torch then could no longer find the dark arch into the nave of the church. He was soaked in fuel, his mind and body anticipating explosion. He scrabbled a way round the wall until he found the gap, then ran for his life up the empty shell of that would-be temple. The main church door was closed. He had shut it carefully himself when he'd entered and couldn't now find the latch to open it. He threw himself at it and fell out on to the steps back into the moonlight and a quiet night. It seemed from this side of the church that nothing had happened. Only the sound of the sports car far away racing down the hill.

Mac was halfway across the piazza and running when it blew. There were two explosions, the first when the flame hit the petrol on the floor. Mac threw himself flat, turning his head to watch as the tank blew up. He saw a window grille disappear, arcing somewhere high over his head; the inside of the church lit up. The explosion must have blown through the walls for the flame was already inside the main body of the building and reaching for the roof.

Citto and Larry Raille were struggling with the ditched Giulia when they heard the six-cylinder roar of the Dino and the explosions of the petrol in the cellar. The Ferrari reached the barricade before the two men had time to react, its blazing headlamps bucking up on to the bank to avoid the obstruction of road pole and ditched Alfa. Even through his cracked lens Citto could pick out the lines of that low-slung sports car. He didn't need to see the driver's flushed and fleshy face to know who it was. But the second man was hidden, ducked down below the level of the window and out of sight. Citto watched the lights recede and disappear.

The American was already gone, running back uphill towards the village, yelling anxiously for his colleague.

Explosion and flame high in the Peloritani hills passed unnoticed, and it was two o'clock on Thursday morning before the three men had walked down the pass and up the new link road to the nearest telephone – the airport call-box at Taor-mina-Peloritana.

Another four hours passed while the police gathered them and their evidence, and inspected the burnt-out church in the hills. The decision to arrest Flavio Consoli and his unknown companion was not made until Mac himself telephoned the young Magistrato at his home in the early morning, but by then too much had already happened.

4

Flavio dropped Tomacchio outside the gate of his yard at shortly after midnight. Flavio himself was blissfully uncon-cerned with the realities of the situation. The explosions and the fire had greatly excited him and Tomacchio had some difficulty in making him realize that the journalists, if that is what they were, would have seen and identified his car.

'You need a lot of help,' the Capo said. He tapped his fore-head. 'And someone to think for you.'

Not that Capo Tomacchio had the slightest intention of leaving the matter to chance or to Flavio's doubtful initiative. As soon as the Dino had gone he called up the Consoli house-hold, using the telephone down in the workshop so as not to alarm his wife and daughter.

'If anything goes wrong for me,' he told old man Consoli, 'I'll land you all in it, you and your son and everyone else in that God-forsaken consortium.'

It was an unwise threat to have made to someone of Consoli's stature and influence.

'I'll meet you in an hour's time,' Avvocato Consoli told him, calm and quiet. 'At my office in town.'

Avvocato Consoli sat brooding in his study formulating strategy and waiting for his son. Flavio could see light in the study as he drove down the long approach track through the orange trees. He knew there would be trouble, but what still escaped him was the overall blackness of his own situation.

There were no pulled punches tonight. The Avvocato had had a full account of events from Tomacchio. He didn't have to wait for confession. He beat his son in fury with a pair of drumming fists all the way from the courtyard back to his study –

'Everything and everyone endangered for the sake of a few hundred thousand lire a week – '

It was the insignificance of the money involved that pained the old man most of all. 'Insanity,' he kept shouting. It wasn't even pocket-money. Flavio was pushed into an armchair and told the course of action he would follow. Phone calls were made: to the wife of a cousin's cousin in Reggio Calabria; her Neapolitan brother who owned a luxury car business; another distant relative of that same cousin who taught at a small village school in the Swiss Ticino; finally the periphery men, two heavies roused from their beds and given a rendezvous.

Upstairs in bed, Signora Consoli listened to the continual pinging of the phone on her table. She resisted the temptation to listen in, but the yells of her outraged husband told her that her precious boy was in bad trouble. When Flavio came hurrying upstairs she heard wardrobes and drawers opening and closing. By the time she had plucked up enough courage to move it was almost too late. Flavio was on his way down to the courtyard with two suitcases. The mother clung to him in desperation: Flavio, the only focus to her life, leaving home. The Avvocato pushed his wife to one side. Time tonight was counted in minutes; seconds even.

The poor Signora would spend all night and all next day on her knees and in despair seeking miracles from her God.

Capo Tomacchio had left soon after midnight for his meeting with the Avvocato. He wasn't looking forward to the confrontation. There'd be hard talking, and a lot of recriminations, but the hard-bitten truck-driver reckoned he held enough of the consortium secrets to guarantee his own protection. It never occurred to him – until an hour too late – that the meeting might never take place, and that the arrangement had been made to get him away from his home and family. The realization came when he returned from Consoli's deserted office to his parked car and found it slumped in the gutter with all four tyres slashed.

Tomacchio's wife climbed out of bed when the front-door bell rang some time before one o'clock in the morning. She assumed her husband had mislaid his keys, and the gruff voice on the door-speaker certainly sounded like him. 'It's me,' the voice said, and she pressed the button to unlock the yard wicket. Her first signal of alarm was the dog's continued frenzy of barking on the terrace outside. Why hadn't her husband called up as he always did to hush it? And when the dog did stop, it was with a sudden snarl, a yelp and a choking whimper.

The door on to the terrace was always unlocked, and she hurried now into the kitchen to bolt it. The kitchen was in darkness, and two men already inside. When she screamed Giuseppina woke up and ran for the telephone, but the wires had been cut. There was a third man in the bathroom and a line of blood drops on the floor. The dog it seemed had taken someone's ounce of flesh.

Giuseppina knew neither of the two men but their message was very clear. Get dressed and pack a suitcase, or your mother will be hurt. She did as she was told. She even swallowed the pills they gave her. 'Sleeping pills,' they told her. 'They won't do you no harm.' Kidnap and ransom, she was thinking, and that idea terrified her. When they took her outside she asked what would happen to her mother. 'The same pills that you have swallowed,' she was told. 'We will stay with her until she sleeps, and make sure she's quite comfortable.'

The third man had slipped out of the house again but neither mother nor daughter had seen him. Only when they brought Giuseppina down into the yard and she saw the Dino waiting in the street did she begin to realize what was really happening. Flavio, sweaty-faced and puffy – with a torn and blood-stained trouser-leg. She knew then that she was being abducted, in time-honoured fashion, but did not realize the added complications to her state of kidnap. She was only relieved in that moment to see a face she recognized.

'I shan't hurt you,' Flavio told her as he accelerated away. They were the last words she heard for twelve hours. By the time they reached Messina – and her first opportunity to protest to the outside world – she was deep in sleep. The Dino drove on to the 1.40 ferry unchallenged and with five minutes to spare. By half past two they were on to the southern tip of the Autostrada del Sole and travelling north at 210 kilometres an hour. The car was changed at five o'clock on a forlorn piece of waste ground beside a factory on the edge of Naples. The brother of a cousin's wife's cousin was waiting there for Flavio on the old link road between the two autostradas. He helped him move the sleeping girl from the Dino into a Porsche. The two men exchanged cars and documents, and Flavio drove on northwards, rejoining the autostrada and passing Rome soon after six. The Porsche Carrera was cruising at 230 and only four times on the journey had to slow for roadworks or congestion in the Apennine tunnels: Florence disappeared at half past seven; Bologna at a quarter past eight; Milan soon after nine.

The police had started their search for the young Consoli at seven o'clock, unaware that they were also looking for a kidnapped girl. More than an hour passed before confirmation was obtained that an orange and green Ferrari Dino had crossed on the ferry in the middle of the night. By then the young Magistrato had arrived to take charge of the inquiry and police departments up and down the length of the peninsula were given details of the fugitive Dino. Airports as far north as Pisa were circulated with Flavio's name and passport number. No one believed it possible that he could arrive at any other border crossing before midday.

The young Consoli, tired, almost inebriated with driving, crossed the Swiss border on the autostrada checkpoint above Chiasso at ten o'clock that morning. Since changing cars outside Naples he had driven 530 miles in five hours with only one stop for petrol. The girl beside him was still fast alseep.

5

Scandal and outrage unrolled like a long slow wave through that Thursday. A death; an abduction; a fuel racket: Tang November was back in the headlines and TV cameras an reporters returned to the narrow picturesque streets of Taormina.

The three-nation team of investigators held a press conference that same morning in an attempt to reimpose objectivity on their proceedings. All in vain. Journalists were only interested in Mac and Larry Raille as protagonists of last night's drama, and the result of the drama was a generally accepted assumption that Tango November had lost her way after the blackout of all lights and landing aids at the airport, in turn caused by the combination of a power cut and the lack of fuel for the emergency generators.

But, even if true, that was, as the investigators knew, only one small piece of the jigsaw. It did not explain how the aeroplane had come to crash on the opposite side of the mountain. It did not analyse the effect of a duff generator and an inoperative engine. It did not interpret the partial failures of voice and flight recorders. Nor did it take into consideration the possibility of error or miscalculation on the flight deck, which now seemed to Burden on the personal evidence available to him an inescapable factor in this accident.

The search-party had found the missing piece of wing, and the mountain guides had heard the plane somewhere below the crater. The two pieces of evidence tied in with Tino G.'s red sunrise. It seemed that Tango November had circled the mountain anti-clockwise and had flown clear of the storm clouds before hitting the lava ridge and losing control. So why had Duckham flown around the mountain at so dangerous an altitude, and why hadn't he turned eastwards for the open sea when he came out of the cloud?

'Bloody hell,' Raille said to Mac after the press conference, 'I wish you'd left us with a hi-jacker on the flight deck.'

Sharlie's surviving photographs had linked Tomacchio and his petrol lorry with the fuel racket at Taormina-Peloritana, and it did not take the young Magistrato long to connect the abduction of Giuseppina Tomacchio with the disappearance of Flavio Consoli.

Not that Capo Tomacchio was giving anything away. He feigned bewilderment and ignorance as he sipped coffee on his terrace that morning. 'The Consoli boy was infatuated,' he supposed.

The young Torinese Magistrato was unconvinced. 'Consoli was busy evading arrest and yet you say he took time off to organize a complicated abduction? He must have had some very strong motive for taking your daughter.'

'Love or lust.' Tomacchio shrugged. 'He was a very arrogant young man.'

'You had business arrangements with him.'

'Not with him. With Servizi TP. A contract to service generators and fuel installations at the new airport.'

'One of your tankers was at the airport yesterday.'

'Yes. I was there myself.'

'Photographic evidence suggests you were drawing off fuel from the tanks supplying the emergency generators.'

The Capo nodded. 'There was a fault to be checked. I knew the airport was out of service. It seemed a good time to work on it.'

'I believe fuel for the emergency circuits is paid for by the military.'

'I wouldn't know about such things.'

'It might explain why someone thought it worthwhile to siphon off regular weekly amounts.'

'I wouldn't know. Like I said I was only checking a fault.'

'And what was it, this so-called fault?'

'Fuel flow. That's why the tank had to be drained.'

'But it wasn't drained completely – '

'The level had to be lowered below the interchange between the two tanks.' The Capo explained patiently. 'There are two separate electrical circuits, two generators and two tanks. One system for non-essentials like internal lighting and heating, the second circuit for emergency instruments, clocks and runway lighting. The two tanks are connected in such a way that if fuel starts to run low priority goes to the emergency generator.'

'But last Saturday it was apparently the emergency generator that failed.'

'Exactly. That's why I was checking for a fault.'

The young Magistrato could not help but smile. How many times in his short period of office on the island had his interrogations been led in these elegant and intricate Byzantine circles. There was enough evidence, or coincidence, to hold this Tomacchio for further questioning, even to construct a charge.

But better to slacken the rope for a day or two and watch just where this stocky, tough old lorry-driver would lead them. He'd surely go chasing for his daughter.

The Signora woke from her barbiturate sleep well but weeping, and once the police had taken her confused statement they left the premises, the young Magistrato returning to his office with a new file of evidence for the Tango November inquiry.

Mechanics and lorry-drivers resumed the day's work, and at midday the boss sent for Renzo.

'You know what has happened?'

Renzo nodded.

'You care for Giuseppina?'

Renzo did not reply. The Capo took an envelope from his pocket.

'There's money in there. You spend what you have to and find her. You follow that young puppy's trail and bring my daughter back home and I'll make things good for you.'

Renzo said nothing. But he took the money. He telephoned Citto's newspaper from the bar down the street, returned home to pack a small suitcase, and left the village on the afternoon bus.

Six miles down the road Mac had returned to his basement room in the small hospital where Sanju and Turi met him with a different character of drama. 'A black comedy,' the Indian told him, for their meat lorry and Carabinieri had disappeared. When Turi drove Mac down to the produce market they found lorry-driver and Carabinieri contemplating an empty railway siding. The four wagon-loads of refrigerated bodies had vanished, 'shunted in error' during the night, attached to a fruit train and now lost somewhere in the vast complexity of the Italian State Railways.

Turi led Mac away from the huddle of railway and police officials before the wild Englishman committed some act of irrevocable violence. He walked him instead through the market, stopping at each merchant to ask about the loads dispatched by rail from yesterday's business. There was not one of them who did not know Turi and they were all ready to help him, where with anyone else they might have been reticent. Even in these rich lands on the east coast wholesale fruit and vegetables was monopoly country, the shadow of Mafia if not the actual presence. Turi pieced together something of a picture: wagons had departed last night for Switzerland and Germany, and a whole train in the early morning for Milan and Turin.

Mac watched the little old doctor nosing out the information, head bent over his stick as he dutifully admired a box of grapes or a basket of tomatoes. He could have walked off with enough produce to stock a shop from the offers he had – '*pighiasse, Dutturi, pighiasse*.' It was a colourful mess of a market, mountains of green, red and yellow peppers, melons and water-melons of all colours and sizes, purple aubergines in baskets, the last of summer's peaches, the first of the autumn apples. And above it all, as nowhere else up or down the coast, hung the mountain. Etna rose out of this town without gentle slope or easy contours, smoke from the central crater lying with the wind horizontal towards them, a perpetual omen in the sky. Mac had been a lot closer to the mountain, nearer to the crater, higher on its slopes. But he had never felt its threat so strong.

The omens were for him, he thought. He was now responsible for the disappearance of 180 bodies and he'd lost the evidence he needed for his report. In this atmosphere of intrigue he could be forgiven his instinctive suspicion of conspiracy.

6

It was midday before Burden arrived back at the hospital in Catania. After his previous confrontation with Julia Duckham he was not surprised to find her waiting for him when he stepped out of the lift. They walked in silence up the corridor and into Stella Pritchard's room.

Stella was lying, as yesterday, flat on her back staring into the ceiling. She glanced only briefly at Burden and Julia as they came in. There was a young girl sitting with her on the side of the bed and Burden recognized Trixie from the photographs and stories in the newspapers.

Julia closed the door, leaning against it like a sentinel or a bodyguard. Today's interview it seemed was to be conducted with an audience and Burden, remembering yesterday's unpleasantness, chose to raise no objections. He busied himself instead with his briefcase and clip-board.

'I should like to go through the events of last Friday so far as you remember them.'

Stella's head moved on her pillow. A nod. Stella could see Julia by the door watching her. The two women hadn't talked any more. Truce or peace or neutrality – neither of them really knew what had been established.

Burden cleared his throat and spoke again from his chair. 'You had a couple of days off, I believe?'

'Wednesday and Thursday,' Stella replied. 'I went up to Harrogate to see my parents.'

'And you arrived back on Friday?'

'After lunch. I caught the Yorkshire Pullman. I was home about three o'clock and I went to bed.'

'Your duty began at ten-thirty in the evening. I take it you use the train between Redhill and Gatwick?'

Stella didn't reply for a moment. She turned her face away from Julia. 'Captain Duckham had arranged to give me a lift.'

Burden flipped over his pages of notes. He couldn't remember whether he had an exact time for Duckham's own departure from home. Stella answered the question.

'We met at eight o'clock. We thought we would stop on the way.' She did not say why or what for.

Julia was motionless and composed still leaning against the door. She remembered Mike's words that Friday lunch-time: 'I'll leave early, love. Get some paperwork done.'

'And did you stop on the way?' That was Burden, clearing his throat again.

There was another long pause. 'We used to meet by the station then drive up the hill. We had a place to pull off the road in a country lane. Somewhere behind Nutfield.'

Probably a nice big car, thought Burden. Reclining seats. A radio. Well – there was an eight-hour no-drink-before-flying regulation, but no laws on sex. Mac would probably claim it increased concentration and efficiency.

'We sat and talked,' said Stella. 'Not for very long.' She was

215

remembering how tired Mike had looked. She didn't want to tell that to the investigator. 'We didn't feel like – doing anything else.'

Julia heard Mike calling her into that black-painted dressing-room after lunch. 'Come and help me sleep,' he had shouted, and they had made love while Clara was playing next door. The last time they had ever made love, but now Julia could hardly remember what they'd done or how it had happened. Was she telling the truth, the girl, about not doing anything that evening?

'You then drove on to Gatwick?' asked Burden.

'Yes.'

'You must have arrived early.'

'No. Not particularly.'

'So you had been talking in the car for quite a long time.'

'I don't know. We were listening to the radio. And I was telling him about what one of the girls had been saying that evening at the house. Something about her boy-friend. I just used to prattle on about things like that. He seemed to like listening.'

Stella was remembering exactly what Mike had said: 'I don't feel like flying tonight. I feel like a tired old man.' Again they were not words she wanted to repeat to this inquisitor. 'How about breaking rules and having a drink?' Mike had suggested. The Plough in Smallfield. But in the pub he had just grinned and ordered two tonics and ice. No gin. No vodka.

'Do you remember when you arrived at the airport?' Burden asked.

'Ten o'clock,' she thought.

'You arrived together?'

'He used to drop me off in the tunnel under the terminal. Then he'd go and park the car and we'd arrive separately.'

'And that's what happened on Friday?'

'Yes.' Stella pictured the Crew Room. It had been crowded when she arrived. There were two planes turning round and their own plane still to arrive. Two crews signing off, three crews signing on. That's when she saw Peter.

Burden was thinking in the same direction. 'When was it you found out that Peter Nyren was flying with you?'

'When I signed on.'

'Had you seen him recently?'

'About two weeks ago.'

'You went out together?'

'We'd arranged to go to a concert. I mean we had arranged it a long time ago. There didn't seem much point in cancelling it.'

'In London?'

'A prom. Peter used to go to a lot of them.'

'Was it a nice evening?'

The insinuation did not escape Stella. 'The music was very good and we had a nice meal.'

And afterwards? Burden wanted to ask.

Poor, confused Peter, Stella was thinking. 'What would you say if I asked you to come home with me?' he had asked 'I don't know,' she had replied. 'Are you asking me?' And when Peter had shrugged in moody fashion she had told him to drive her to Victoria for her train home.

Burden shifted on his chair. 'Did you talk to each other in the Crew Room on Friday evening?'

'We said hello.'

'That's all?'

'There was quite a crowd, and I was saying hello to the other girls as well.' Stella remembered the expression on Peter's face when Duckham walked in a couple of minutes after her. He had sunk himself back into a magazine, his face set in the brooding pout that Stella had come to know.

'Did Duckham talk to Nyren in the Crew Room?'

'He came over and said hello.'

'You were with Nyren, were you?'

'No. I was watching. I knew about the quarrel. I wondered if they were going to make it up because of flying together.'

'Did they?'

'Peter said hello back. That's all.'

'And Duckham?'

'He said something about the delay and the cut-off time. You know – when it gets too late and they have to call up another crew.'

'I suppose you were all hoping that would happen.'

'One or two people said we might get an early night. Mike told us the cut-off time was two hours fifty.'

'When did he say that?'

'He came and said hello to all of us. The cabin crew I mean. He always did that.'

'Did he say anything in particular to you?'

'No. Just that there would be some short-tempered passengers around tonight, and to be careful with them.'

Burden turned a page of his notes. Duckham had come within five or ten minutes of his cut-off time. If he had known what the weather was going to be like he'd have probably packed it in. He had had no indication in his briefing about bad weather in Sicily. But then that, unfortunately, was only to be expected. One more of the shortcomings of lesser-known and lesser-used airfields. Ralph Burden could suddenly feel himself in Dixie's place that evening, praying silently for the delay to extend so he could go back home and sleep. How often Ralph himself had prayed that way on Norfolk evenings as the clouds rolled up from the south-west to blot out an evening's mission.

He looked up. Mrs Duckham was watching him, waiting for his next question. Had Duckham screwed this Stella Pritchard that Friday evening? And was it important? Burden wondered. It would surely have made him more tired. And what about post-coital guilt; anxiety; depression; self-disgust. Perhaps Dixie Duckham didn't suffer those reactions. Burden turned back to his questions.

'Did the crew all wait together during the delay?'

'For the first quarter of an hour or so. We didn't know what was happening really. About the delay I mean. Then it was confirmed — and Mike went off to work in his office.'

'And you all stayed on in the Crew Room?'

'Yes. With George telling his jokes.'

'George?'

'George Raven. The Flight Engineer.'

'Did you know him well?'

'I don't think anyone did. I mean everyone knew him enough to say hello. But no one really was a close friend or anything like that. Not that I know of anyhow.'

Burden turned up his relevant notes. 'He lived in Brighton, didn't he?'

'I don't know.' Stella did know. She'd seen him there once in a club, holding hands with a younger man. But that was no business of the inquisitor.

'He had some strange hobbies.'

'I wouldn't know.'

Burden read from his notes. 'Hang-gliding, sky-diving, scuba-diving.'

'And motor-bikes.' Stella remembered George arriving or departing in strange bulky waterproof outfits.

The George Raven file had been passed back to Burden by Mac, and Mac had left one queried comment scribbled in the margin: 'Compensatory personality – doubtful reaction under extreme pressure?' This Raven was the one crew member Burden could not successfully picture. He turned back to Stella. 'Would you say he was an unpopular man?'

'I don't know. He probably thought he was quite popular. I suppose other people quite liked him – in small doses.'

'You don't know what Duckham thought about him?'

Julia saw Stella smile suddenly, a brief illumination of eyes and mouth that faded quickly as though it seemed to hurt her. 'He once said that being shut up on the flight deck with him telling stories was like the Chinese water torture.'

Burden looked at the photograph in Raven's file – a tight-skinned, fit-looking face with thinning hair. Like any old British face staring from a newspaper after winning the George Cross or having murdered little girls.

Burden pulled out his time chart with its neat columns and predictable information. 'Can you remember when you first made contact with the passengers?'

'We were sent over to the Departure Lounge after about an hour and a half. Just to calm things down a bit.'

'Were there any trouble-makers?'

'Not really. Just people getting fed up and drinking too much.'

'So you didn't see the flight crew again until you were on the plane?'

'No.'

'Did you get to see them on the plane?'

'Captain Duckham came into the cabin soon after take-off to talk to one of the passengers.'

'Because of some trouble?'

'Oh no. Just some bigwig on his honeymoon or something. They're always worse on charter flights. As though they've got to let everyone know that they're really above it all.'

'I take it the plane was divided up so far as your duties were concerned?'

'Yes. I was in charge of the front galley. They were mostly Americans in the front section. They were really tired.' Stella paused. 'I remember there was a boy with a guitar. He was from New York. I got him to play some songs to cheer everyone up.'

'Tino G.,' said Burden.

'Who?'

'That's his name. He's still alive.'

Julia saw Stella's brief smile once more.

'But he was right up front.'

Burden nodded. 'Yes. He was very lucky.'

'Is he going to be all right?'

'They think so.'

Stella smiled again. It really was a lovely smile if you could imagine it without the scars, and framed in a proper head of hair.

'If you were in the forward galley you must have had some contact with the crew?'

'There were four of us in the front.'

'Did you go on the flight deck at all?'

'Only at the end – to clear their coffee cups.'

'Can you remember when that was?'

'We were preparing to land.'

'At Taormina?'

'Yes.'

'Was there ever any suggestion you weren't going to land at Taormina?'

'Not that I know of.'

'Can you remember any conversation on the flight deck?'

'Not when I was in there. They were reading the let-down charts.'

'Did you have the feeling that anything was wrong at all?'

Stella remembered Peter Nyren's moody-looking face. But that was surely not relevant. 'Everything seemed normal.'

'So you took the cups and left?'

'Yes.'

'And then?'

'I cleaned up the galley and stowed everything. Then I went into the cabin to help check safety-belts.'

'Were there any problems?'

'In the cabin?'

'Anywhere.'

'There was a loose cupboard in the galley. It had to be tied up with a piece of string.'

'You tied it up?'

'One of the other girls had to sit underneath it. I didn't want everything falling out over her head.'

'There were two hostess seats in the front galley?'

'Yes. And two by the front entrance but they weren't being used on Friday night.'

'Why?'

'Company policy. If there are spare seats in the cabin the folding seats are not to be used.'

'Any particular reason?'

'No one likes them. They're dangerous.'

'So you were sitting in the cabin?'

'When everything was checked, yes.'

'Whereabouts?'

'Halfway down the front section. A rear-facing seat. Where the partition goes when they make up a first class.'

Burden referred to the 119 plans. 'Row 6.'

'We keep that seat free if there's room because it means there's a hostess next to the emergency exit.'

'Company policy again?'

'Sort of. The front window-exits are very stiff to operate. They get jammed very easily.'

'And the fourth hostess was with you?'

'Yes. On the other side. We were both on the aisle.'

'And both in rear-facing seats?'

'Always. Yes.'

'Because they're safer?'

'Yes.'

Burden looked again at the Greyhound 119 plans. Each of the emergency exits had facing seats on either side to increase access room from the gangway. But like all the seating it was on quick-change mountings. Tango November had been flying military charters in Germany on the Thursday and Friday, and the military contracts specified rear-facing configuration with a minimum leg-room between the seats four inches longer than the maximum pitch allowed in commercial aviation. The seating had been changed at Gatwick before the doomed flight. Remembering the mess of twisted seats in the wrecked cabin, Burden wondered how much of the death and injury had been caused by the inadequacy of those quick-change mountings.

He looked back to his time-chart. 'Do you know at what stage of let-down you actually sat in your seat and strapped in?'

'No. I have no idea.'

'What was the sequence of events from then on as you remember them?'

'Everything seemed to happen together. I think the first thing was the sound of the engines changing and the plane pulling up into a climb.'

'Did you have any impression of the plane banking at all?'

Stella paused. She was trying to think herself back into that cabin. 'I can't remember. I don't think so.'

'You didn't see anything from the window?'

'No – it was dark cloud all the way down.'

'You must have been conscious of the movements of the plane after you started climbing again.'

'Not really. It was almost straightaway that I saw Trixie here in the gangway.'

The little girl looked up for the first time.

Burden smiled at her. 'Out of your seat were you, Trixie?'

She did not reply. Burden saw her take Stella's hand. Then Stella spoke again.

'She undid her belt. She was having a game, weren't you, Trixie?'

The little girl nodded.

'I undid my belt and got up to take her back to her seat. So she started playing the game with me. I chased her most of the way up the aisle.'

'Towards the back or the front?'

'The back. I caught her once but she slipped away.' Stella's voice altered. 'I think I got a bit cross with you then, didn't I, Trixie?'

The girl nodded again.

'It was just about then that the lights went out.'

'The cabin lights?'

'Yes.'

'All of them?'

'Except for the torch lamp.'

'How long?'

'I don't know. It must have been quite a time because I know I was getting scared then. We were bumping all over the place and I'd never seen all the lights go like that.'

'But they came back on?'

'Only the emergency ones.'

'Where were you placed at that moment?'

'About halfway down.'

'And Trixie?'

'She got frightened by the dark and stopped running and I managed to grab her. I was taking her back to her seat when we seemed to get into a bad rough patch. Everyone was scared by then.'

'What did you do?'

'I was by the toilets in the middle of the plane. I pulled Trixie down and we both sat on the floor. I jammed us in with my legs and my back against the walls. That's where we stayed. I don't really remember any more.'

There was a long silence, then the little girl spoke for the first time. 'There was the sun.'

Stella remembered. 'Oh yes.' She paused. 'A red sun. Yes.' Julia saw the outline of that smile again. 'It seemed to fill the whole plane. I suppose we came out of the clouds and the sun was coming up and with all the lights off it filled the whole plane with a red glow.' She was remembering more. 'Yes. People were clapping. That's right. Everyone was happy. Everyone thought we were all right. They clapped the sunrise. I began to get up and that's when the plane went diving down again. Down and then up. And down more gently in a long slow circle.'

'Mama was coming,' said Trixie.

'Yes.' Stella seemed to nod.

'Her mother?' asked Burden.

'She got out of her seat to come and fetch Trixie.'

The 'hi-jack' lady who had lost her arm: Maria-Grazia Ragonese, 55th Street, 11219 New York.

'People started screaming.' Stella shut her eyes. 'I suppose they could see the mountain out of the windows.'

There was a long silence.

'You don't remember any more?'

'No.'

Burden stood up with his papers and his briefcase. 'The fuselage broke just where you were sitting. You were both very lucky.'

Stella turned her face to him. She was crying. 'It's not fair,' she whispered. 'All those others. They could see what was happening. They were trying to hold hands, some of them. It's not fair, is it, to die like that?'

7

On the lunch-time news television cameras had shown a predictable traffic jam of reporters and photographers by the locked gates outside the Consoli orange groves. A few intrepids had climbed the stone walls and dodged the dogs to approach the house. But they had found it barred and shuttered, more than probably empty.

Citto instead spent a more fruitful hour and a half in the newspaper archives. Marriages, births, social gossip and telephone directories: he was tracing Flavio's relatives through the mother's side of the family. A solid, wealthy shop-keeping dynasty that had spilt off the island into Calabria and north to Naples earlier in the century.

Citto chose a girl secretary from upstairs, one of the innocents with a soft innocuous voice. The Signora had heard his stutter once on the telephone and it was not, as Citto knew, a voice easy to disguise. He coached the girl in a little speech: 'It is essential I speak with Signora Consoli. I have news of her son, and he has a message for her.'

Citto had a list of thirty-five relatives to call and by the fifteenth repetition the girl secretary was beginning to get the giggles. They came lucky on number seventeen. A Signora Consoli was called to the phone, a voice palpitating with anxiety. Citto, listening in on an extension, recognized the self-effacement and innate apology in her tone. He gave the girl a thumbs-up, and the secretary, overcoming the giggles, read out the second part of her speech: 'My brother will call on you at five o'clock, Signora. Will you be there?'

'Oh yes. Yes of course.'

'It is important not to say anything about this. Your son is in great danger – '

'Oh my God!'

And down went the phone on Signora Consoli's sob of anxious despair.

'That's awful,' giggled the young secretary. 'That's an awful thing to do.'

Citto dismissed the girl and wandered out on to the *Circumvallazione* to find his car. Not for the first time in the five days he he failed to spot two radio cars keeping watch on his movements.

Half an hour later Citto met Renzo off his village bus in Acireale. The little town, usually so crowded, was lost in siesta and the two young men sat at a table in the piazza, Citto lunching belatedly off Costarelli's renowned and extraordinary ice-creams while Renzo drank a nervous succession of coffees and brandies and told Citto what Tomacchio had asked him to do.

'How much money has he given you?'

'Two hundred thousand.'

'That won't get you far if you have to start bribing people.'

'It is not my intention to bribe anyone,' said the young Communist. 'If people don't tell me what I want to know there are other ways of making them talk.'

'You can't take gangsters on at their own game. That's the way to get killed.'

'I'm not carrying a gun.'

'Going to fight them with your bare fists, are you? And expect them to play to the rules of boxing?'

Renzo laughed. 'Is that how you broke your glasses?'

Citto fingered the cuts on his face. 'That, my friend, was your Capo's shotgun.'

Renzo nodded, still grinning. 'I told you he wasn't much of a shot.'

'You know it was him then, up on the mountain last night?'

'Maybe.'

'And yet you're prepared to take his money to go looking for his daughter.'

'I have my own reasons for looking.'

Citto stood up. 'Time to start earning it then.'

'I thought you told her five o'clock?'

'And give her time to set up watch-dogs?'

Citto paid the bill and the two men walked up the hill into a narrow street of eighteenth-century palaces. It was a town of palaces; a town of impoverished aristocrats still trying to live on tithes, still puzzled by the collapse of their once so comfortable feudal economy.

The Signora's cousin lived in one of the larger palaces near the top of the hill, an echoing covered courtyard behind doors large enough to admit two tanks in line abreast. Living quarters were on the first floor and an apprehensive maid was waiting for them on the wide stone stairway. Citto had announced himself in the door-speaker as '*polizia*'.

'There's no one in,' said the maid.

'Signora Consoli is in,' Citto replied. 'Tell her a girl rang up about an hour and a half ago. We have a message about her son.'

'You're not the police then?'

'No, my love.'

They were shown into a drawing-room of great elegance and formality – frayed carpets, tapestries, peeling frescoes and spindly-looking furniture, a museum that no one surely used for living. Neither Citto nor Renzo trusted themselves to the chairs and they waited standing in the middle of the room gazing at the naked cherubs on the ceiling.

Signora Consoli arrived, peering at them as though she had emerged from a very dark room. Praying in a chapel, Renzo thought. He smelt priests in this house.

'Your sister said five o'clock.' Signora Consoli looked at them both in turn not knowing whom to address.

'The sooner we start,' replied Renzo, 'the sooner we find your son.'

Alarm or fear came creeping into the lady's face taking up their accustomed place in the crevices around her eyes. 'What has happened to him?'

'He's been kidnapped.'

The Signora sat down, one hand to her mouth. 'I don't understand. I thought he had done the kidnapping.'

Renzo nodded. 'Yes – he took the girl. Now someone else has kidnapped him.'

The giggling secretary would have disapproved of this second lie. But it was working.

'Does my husband know?'

It was Citto's stuttering turn to draw the lady on. 'You probably realize that your husband has too many other worries to spend very much time on your son.'

'I don't understand who you are.' The lady remembered that soft stutter on the telephone some days ago.

'The girl has been kidnapped along with your son. We're only interested in her. We have to know where to start looking for them.'

'But what happens to my son?'

'If we find them we set them both free. I've told you, we're not interested in him.'

'But he – abducted the girl.'

'It's the girl's safety we're concerned with. Not her virginity.'

The Signora shook her head. 'I don't understand what you want from me.'

'We think you might know where Flavio would have gone.'

'How could I know? They don't tell me anything.'

'Were there any telephone calls this morning?' Citto asked.

'I don't know. I don't know anything.' The Signora was distraught. 'We left very early. My husband sent me here. He was going to the airport.'

'Was your son driving his car last night?'

The Signora nodded.

'The Dino?'

She nodded again.

'It's a very obvious car. He would have tried to change it.'

'How do you mean?'

'An orange and green sports car. The police would have picked him up straightaway. He'd have been looking for another car.'

The Signora seemed to see light, or glimmers of it. 'I know where he would have gone for a car. My cousin in Reggio Calabria, his wife has a cousin in Naples who sells sports cars.

It was he who sold the Dino to us – you know, at a trade price. If Flavio wanted another car that's where he'd have gone.'

'And his name?'

'I don't know his family name. His business is called Highway. There was a sticker in the car.' She pronounced it *higvay*, and Citto asked her to write it down.

The Signora was thinking onwards, remembering the ramifications of that Reggio half of the family. Wasn't there an even more distant cousin teaching somewhere in Switzerland? She thought suddenly, and aloud: 'That's where I would have sent him.'

Citto and Renzo left the palace a few minutes later with a list of half-remembered names but no addresses. 'It's a good start,' said Citto. 'And if you're lucky it'll be enough.'

The Signora watched them leave from an upstairs window. I've done wrong, she thought. If they're friends of the girl they are not Flavio's friends. But if my boy is in trouble what else can I do? At least they will find out where he is. That man with the stammer was right about one thing. Flavio's father would do no more to help his son. She had heard him last night after the Dino had gone telephoning Rome. 'I've got him away,' he had said. 'If we can find a country without extradition he can take the rap for the lot. With a big enough noise no one will think to look any further.'

The Signora turned away from the window back to her prayers in a shuttered room.

The town was coming to life again: conversation in the streets, lights in the twilight, the inevitable smells of coffee and cigars, lines of lethargic traffic in the piazza below. Citto and Renzo cut across the slope of the hill, zigzagging down in right-angles through narrow alleys to where the car was parked. Renzo was silent as they walked.

'You don't have to follow this through, you know – .' Citto stuttered like a stuck gramophone record.

'It's you who sound scared,' said Renzo.

Sharlie, Citto was thinking of. The two pieces of blood-stained crash-hat.

Citto drove fast back towards the city An ATI flight left for Naples at half past six and they made Fontanarossa with half an hour to spare. There were seats available and the first two tens of Tomacchio's money disappeared for Renzo's ticket.

Citto bought newspapers at the bar: the evening edition from town, and the afternoon's from Rome. 'Our National Shame', read one of the headlines, and the picture underneath was a by now familiar silhouette, the half-burned broken-backed shell of Tango November.

'I'm going to shit myself,' Renzo said as Citto took him to the gate. 'This is the first time I've ever been up in one of these machines.'

Ingegnere Preuss had been under observation at his home on the Calle del Paradiso since Citto's visit to Venice on Tuesday night. Preuss would have laughed at the melodrama of such an idea had someone openly suggested it to him. But within himself he was afraid. He was a loose end; a controversial and exorcized chapter in draft copies of a report; initials in the footnotes; a name that could, as the Sicilian journalist had demonstrated, be dug out of files. If I was them, thought Preuss – whoever 'them' may be – I wouldn't leave me or my copies of that expurgated chapter lying around. Taormina-Peloritana had been a very large project. He had seen the budgets and could guess at the kick-backs. Bribes and ease-money all up the line to the highest possible levels. When reputations on that scale were endangered one not very distinguished and bachelor academic was surely expendable.

So his thoughts had run since Citto's visit, sapping his zeal for public honesty and voluntary heroics. But when he heard the radio news that Thursday his courage returned. The smell of scandal was now out in the open. As a potential witness he could surely consider himself immune. Interference with him would be tantamount to an admission of guilt.

He walked almost jauntily to the travel agents over the Rialto and bought himself a railway ticket south. When Citto rang him in the early evening Preuss was able to say with honest bravado, 'It's all right, dear boy, I'm on my way.'

Citto was tired, hungry, grubby and unshaven. He hadn't been home now in four days. His shirt was black and his suit stiff with sweat and dirt from last night's adventures in the hillside village. He drove through the evening rush-hour wondering, as was his gloomy habit, what everyone did in this city to be able to run such sleek and expensive cars. On any level of consciousness his mind was too distracted to notice the two radio cars, blue and red, interchanging with each other as they kept station on him.

Laura had telephoned him at the newspaper. Sharlie's funeral was on Saturday and the family had asked him to be there. Citto wondered whether the mother had seen the papers these last two days, and if so how much she might have read between the lines. The coroner's verdict had been postponed, though Citto had a feeling they would never pronounce finally on the accident. That silted-up oil pump was only half a story. The police were already suggesting that it had been caused by an accumulation of dirt over a period of months; at worst a prank by young kids who knew no better.

So was it fair to plant a doubt in the mother's mind? Would she want to live the rest of her life wondering if someone had killed her son? Citto had seen those sad relatives in the streets of Taormina. They would certainly live with doubts, and the anger and grief of suspecting that Tango November need never have crashed.

Citto raised both hands off the wheel in supplication at the windscreen, or at God up there somewhere in the sky.

God does not exist, Citto's mother had told the priest when her husband's body had been found two days dead on a hillside, their precious flock of sheep irrevocably lost. Citto had been nine years old, his father thirty-five. Heart attack, the doctor had said. Poverty, worry and the fear of failure, Citto had later decided.

Citto found himself near enough home to park and walk. There was never room for the car in his own narrow street. As he turned the corner and out of sight the two radio cars settled down around the Giulia like chickens to roost five and ten yards away.

The concierge called from her basement kitchen as Citto unlocked the street door. He waited as she waddled up from her quarters in a haze of frying oil holding a bunch of bills and periodicals.

'Your cleaning lady came twice and couldn't get in,' she complained. 'She's coming again tomorrow so I hope you're going to be home.'

Citto's cleaning lady came twice a week in the early morning, usually well before he ever left for work. But who knows when he would start tomorrow. He slipped the spare key off his ring and gave it to the concierge.

'We were wondering where you'd got to,' she said eyeing his dishevelled and dirty clothes, the cuts on his face, his cracked lens.

'Working hard,' he told her and nodded good night knowing he had left her curiosity unsatisfied. She'll read about it in tomorrow's paper, he thought, and in an article under my name. She'll be carrying it under her arm all day showing it to everyone. One of my residents, she'd be telling them all.

Citto climbed the stairs past the smells of a half-dozen suppers without provoking any feelings of hunger. He wasn't looking forward to his empty flat and the thoughts that would pursue him there. It was difficult to believe that Sharlie was already thirty hours dead.

Citto stopped suddenly a half-flight below his landing. There was one simple and routine precaution he had always adopted: a thin rectangle of cardboard pinned out of sight on the top of the door. Set with its short face outwards it would lever on the door post and turn itself when the door was opened. If it was not reset one corner of the cardboard remained protruding, visible to the practised eye. The cardboard tell-tale was pointing warning from his door tonight. Maybe he had forgotten to reset it. Or had they been to search through his papers? Was there someone waiting for him, watching him now through the spy-lens?

He stood for a long time gazing at his front door, then turned and walked back slowly downstairs. He waited a moment before unlocking the street door. The concierge had returned to her cooking. There wasn't a sound on the stairs above him. Coward, he told himself as he returned towards his car. Even the battered old Giulia looked suddenly dangerous to him. It was illegally parked, but he left it, veering away across the road and back towards the city centre. That bloody shotgun last night, he thought; that's what unnerved me. Or the two pieces of Sharlie's blood-soaked crash-hat.

He took a taxi back to the office and told the News Editor that his car had broken down. He didn't want to sound quite the bloody fool he felt himself to be. He was given the keys to the only staff-car available and he drove out of the city north along the coast with an idea of visiting Mac and Larry Raille in Taormina.

'The three musketeers', they had called themselves last night walking down the pass from that deserted village. The two Anglo-Saxons had spent half of that long trek talking and speculating about Tango November, and the other half shouting obscene songs or hurling curses at the tail-lights of the two cars that swept past their waving thumbs and arms. Not that I blame the cars, thought Citto. I wouldn't stop on that lonely road for three wild-looking men in the middle of the night. Citto had walked in silence most of the time, his mind half-conscious on the edge of exhaustion. Once or twice he had found himself asleep as he walked; at other times faces had come to him: an old shepherd who used to follow and frighten him in the hills when he was a boy; a professor who had befriended him at University, a man, Citto realized, with the same lopsided smile as Preuss far away in Venice; then Sharlie's face as Citto had first known it, the bright-eyed waterfront delinquent, sharp and laughing and full of life. Sharlie who had been his pupil, at times even his only friend. Poor Sharlie, poor Sharlie's mum, poor Sharlie's Nonna Lisa; poor whole damn world of dead and dying.

Citto gave up the idea of Taormina. What could he talk about with an Englishman or an American? He turned aside down the narrow walled lane into the fishing village and the crowded harbour piazza full of scooters and scooter-trucks. The man with the mattresses was back. They were piled behind his blasting pop-song loudspeaker, plastic-covered, as many as there had been however many days ago it was that Sharlie had bought them whisky and ice-creams in the bar. With my money, remembered Citto. The last three tens of Sharlie's lifetime's spending.

There was a light on Nonna Lisa's terrace: the old lady, Laura and her brother sitting there? Citto didn't see them. Even them he couldn't face. He turned the car on the rough track and drove back out of the village stopping only to buy himself a bottle from the harbour bar. A mile or so into the country he pulled the car into a gravel layby, locked the doors from the inside, climbed on to the back seat and folded himself up for the night with the bottle by his side.

8

Information had been relayed earlier in the evening to an ex-directory number in Naples and the ATI flight from Catania was consequently met at the Campodichino airport by two men – one on a small motor-bike and one in a car, both supplied with a rather vague description of Renzo. The description seemed to fit at least two of the passengers off the aeroplane and the car and motor-bike split up to cover both possibilities.

Renzo had permitted himself the luxury of a taxi for the first time in his life. A few minutes with a telephone directory had given him the address of Highway Concessionaires and he wanted to be sure of reaching their showroom before they shut up for the night. But as the taxi crossed the city in a crawl of rush-hour traffic so Renzo became slowly aware of the high-pitched persistent buzz of a *motorino* somewhere behind them. There seemed no good reason why the motor-bike wasn't joining its two-wheeled companions over- or under-taking the snarl of cars and buses. When the high-pitched buzzing stayed with them through the traffic lanes on the sea-front Renzo decided the motor-bike was tailing his taxi. He waited till the traffic flow halted again in the one-way tunnel under the headland, then paid off the taxi-driver and walked back towards the tunnel entrance, disappearing into the darkness in search of a second taxi, and leaving the motor-cyclist struggling unsuccessfully to extricate himself.

Renzo stopped his second taxi round the corner from his destination. He paid the driver but asked him to wait.

Highway was still open, a luxury salon for luxury cars, Ferraris, Porsches and Jaguars displayed under multi-colour lighting, their wheels deep into thick pile carpet. The manager looked up through a one-way window in the office wall as Renzo walked into the showroom. A drooler, the manager decided when he saw Renzo's cut of clothes. They usually came in this time of the evening on their way home from work, gazing with impotent passion at the objects of their fantasies. They'd be tolerated for a few moments if they were clean; sometimes even allowed to sit in driving seats. But eventually they would need to be shamed to the door, handled, as it were, by remote control. It was company policy not to waste time or brochures on such people.

'Can I help you?'

Renzo looked round. The voice, disembodied, had come from one of the walls. Renzo rocked one of the cars on its suspension and banged hard on the roof as though to test its thickness of steel. A new XJS Jaguar. He swung open the door and climbed inside.

Trouble, the manager was thinking – a *lazzarone* with too much drink inside him. But you could never be absolutely sure. They'd once chased away a ragged man in jeans, and the bloke had walked thirty yards up the road and spent ten million on a Mercedes.

'Can I ask you your price range, sir?'

The silly damn fool leaves the ignition key in the cars, Renzo was thinking. He got back out on the carpet. 'I was wondering about a second-hand Dino,' he said to the wall. 'Do you have any in stock?'

'There would certainly be nothing under seven million, sir.'

Renzo had decided the voice was coming from the mirror-wall behind him. He turned towards the door beside it as he spoke. 'To be more exact I was thinking of a second-hand Dino with a fancy paint job. Orange and green. Something like that.'

The manager had three 'security' buttons on his desk: one to lock the office door, one to lock the showroom doors, and one alert plugged into the nearest police station. He locked the doors but left the police button well alone. He had picked up an orange and green Dino in the middle of last night – a direct swap for a high mileage Porsche. A family favour carried out in secrecy. He'd been told to keep the Dino hidden away for a few weeks. He had no idea why, but he didn't want trouble with the law.

The young man in the showroom had tried the office door and found it locked. He was walking back towards the cars.

'If you would like to call in the morning our second-hand manager will be able to help you.'

Renzo climbed back into the Jaguar and started the engine.

'Nice and quiet, isn't it?' he said to the mirror.

'You will have to leave, sir. We're closing. If you come back in the morning –'

'Second-hand Ferrari Dino, green and orange, and Catania number-plates. I'm quite sure you have one.'

The manager was still at his desk, one hand on the telephone wondering who on earth he could call up for help. The Jaguar was moving, creeping forward towards a half-million lire's worth of special plate-glass. The manager shut his eyes. But there was no crash of glass or crump of steel. He heard the young man's voice again.

'What did you do? Lend him another car?'

Do a bloody favour for the family and see where it lands you, thought the manager. The Jaguar was creeping back on to its carpet.

'You'd better start talking, it's getting late.'

There was a silence. What the hell, the manager was thinking. I've done nothing wrong. I don't mind telling this bloke about it. Except that the family might find out.

There was a sudden roar of engine from the showroom. The Jaguar, front wheels off the carpet, back wheels on and spinning, gyrated slowly round through 180 degrees until it was pointing at the mirror-wall and door.

'Whoever you are you'd better realize I'm going to start smashing this place up if you don't talk.'

'I don't know what you want.'

'I want to know what sort of car you gave him. The documents, the number-plate, the whole lot.'

The Jaguar moved again, towards the mirror and the office door. This time there was no gentle creeping. The car accelerated hard through a row of rubber plants and into the mirror. The whole wall cascaded in over the manager's desk, the desk itself shunted by the car and pinning him, still in his chair into the opposite corner of the room.

They looked at each other face to face for the first time across a glass-strewn desk and crumpled bonnet. Renzo stayed where he was, in the driving seat.

'Did he come here?'

The manager was staring in catatonic silence. Renzo revved the engine and eased off the brake to pin him even tighter to the wall. The chair began to splinter.

'Did he come here?'

The manager shook his head. He was pale and his voice tremulous. 'Out of town.'

'Who made the arrangement?'

'His father telephoned.'

'Was there a girl with him?'

The manager nodded.

'Did she say anything?'

'She was asleep. I had to help carry her.'

'Where?'

'To the other car.'

'She was sleeping?'

The manager nodded. The girl, he was thinking. That's where this boy fits in. An abduction.

'What car did you bring for him?'

'A Porsche Carrera.'

'Colour?'

'White.'

'Registration?'

'I don't know, not without looking it up.'

'So look it up.' Renzo backed the car off and the manager fell forward out of his chair. He picked himself up and walked to a filing cabinet. It was the first time he had moved since the young man came in. He felt his trousers and shirt wet with perspiration, his knees sore where the desk had hit him.

'What else did the old man say when he rang up?'

'Just to fill her up with petrol. Yes – and have all the documents for going abroad. Insurance and everything.'

'For what country?'

'Switzerland.'

The manager found the registration number in his files and read it out.

'Where were they going in Switzerland?'

'I don't know.' The manager was alarmed, sheltering by his filing cabinet. 'I really don't know.'

'You have relatives in Switzerland.'

The man paused before answering. 'There is someone. He teaches. Some little village in the Ticino.' The manager named the village.

'And his address?'

'I don't know. Honest to God, I don't know.'

Renzo climbed out of the Jaguar. 'If you were more polite with people you wouldn't get your walls knocked down.'

Walls, thought the manager. He was looking at twenty million lire of bent Jaguar.

The taxi was still waiting for Renzo round the corner and forty minutes later he was back at the airport checking in for the late evening flight to Milan. Linate by 23.20 was, it seemed, as near and as fast as he could get to the Swiss frontier.

9

Preuss left home at ten o'clock that evening carrying a small valise and dressed immaculately in a lightweight charcoal suit. He was after all making his first appearance on a public stage. He was a witness. Eventually there would be journalists and photographers; even television cameras. He patted good-bye to his front door, little finger and first finger on the wood, the horns of superstition as though he was off to the mountains for a weekend's climbing.

He walked to the station through empty narrow alleyways, up and over the even narrower and darker canals. His jauntiness of afternoon had passed away and the natural caution of a secretive life crept back into Preuss's blood with the damp of the night. He even convinced himself for a while that he was being followed: footsteps on the paving behind him or shadows on the walls, and always someone to observe his progress at each intersection of alley or canal. He looked at them carefully as he passed but they appeared quite normal. No baroque little dwarfs with knives; no men in shabby macs or lodens. In fact some of the faces were quite familiar. By the time he emerged from the maze on to the canal front by the station he was laughing at himself once more, despising his cowardice.

The train was late and the platform already crowded with a party of student tourists who had failed to find seats in the carriages that started from Venice. There would be a scrum for the pickings on the Trieste half of the train and Preuss resigned himself to an uncomfortable night. Couchettes and berths had all been booked.

He was instead the beneficiary of a double coincidence that should have prolonged his life. One of the art-historians from the University was just vacating a sleeping car when the second half of the train finally arrived. Preuss met him on the platform exchanging pleasantries. The art-historian had been to Moscow for a month of research.

'I'm going south,' said Preuss. 'I change at Rome in the morning if we get there in time. The train is late.'

'Late,' hooted the art-historian. 'My sleeping-car is a whole day and a half late. We were eighteen hours standing still in Cop. You have a seat, Ingegnere?'

No, he had no seat.

'I tell you what, then. I've made friends with the Russian car attendant. You can't help making friends if you have to travel together for four whole days. He will let you sleep in my berth. You'll have it to yourself. The carriage goes on to Rome.'

Introductions were made and favours happily offered. Preuss was installed in a berth of inegalitarian opulence where he might have happily stayed, sleeping to Rome and the comparative safety of daylight.

After an hour or so of travel and quiet reading he set out to explore the length of corridor outside. The Russian conductor had already retired to his bunk and the carriage seemed empty – a long, carpeted hallway where the usual noises of a train were inaudible. There was a strange mixture of smells, something like coal fires and sauerkraut. He wondered who could be travelling behind all these locked doors – spies, diplomats, escapees. Tractor salesmen more like.

He paid a visit to the toilet at the end of the coach. Even here the sounds of the outside world were muffled, insulated by a double thickness of ventilator, presumably against the Russian winter. How strange, thought Preuss, to wash one's hands with Russian soap and dry them on Russian towels on a simple journey down to Rome.

Then he heard the sounds of the train suddenly more clear as though a window or a door had been opened somewhere letting in the noise. He stepped back into the corridor.

Preuss hardly saw the two men. He felt himself seized, thumped hard somewhere in his midriff and propelled through the doors into the adjoining carriage. They held him in the recess by the exit, his arms twisted behind him as they searched his pockets. Preuss was doubled up with pain staring at the open door in front of him where the noise and the wind were rushing in a black void.

They seemed to hold him there for an eternity and he was thinking all the time, why am I not fighting them? Because, he rationalized to himself, I do not believe that these men are foolish or evil enough to harm me. Citto would have recognized the slight down-turn of mouth, the ghost of self-mockery. And ghosts were all that remained to Preuss.

As he tried to straighten up one of the men propelled him with a foot in the small of his back. Preuss saw lights scattered over a flat landscape as he tipped head-first through the open door and into the gale. He had two distinct thoughts as he fell: an angry regret that he had not sent a copy of his chapter to that journalist in Sicily; and an impression that somehow his body would catapult across the Polesine into the estuary of the Po and die embraced by the sea that was trying so hard to destroy his beloved city.

He bounced instead at eighty miles an hour on hard metal tracks, a body bursting open like a sack of stained *vinaccia* as it ricocheted into the reeds of a drainage ditch beside the railway.

10

The death of Preuss strategically mistimed, tactically ill-planned and clumsy, was by any criterion an unlikely 'accident'. In Italy it was no longer publicly acceptable that people fall unaided from buildings or from trains.

Avvocato Consoli was a realist. Until now a cover-up had been possible. Someone instead had over-reacted, a colleague in the consortium or some exposed official or politician. No hope this time of sitting tight and letting the scandal fade away like countless others into the Italian tapestry. Tango November was a foreign plane with foreign deaths – Anglo-Saxon investigators, Anglo-Saxon journalists, Anglo-Saxon insurance assessors and opinion. The other men involved would protect themselves with the influence or immunity of office. They would certainly not endanger themselves to shield a mere upstart lawyer from Catania. But they might, at such an anxious moment, be prepared to speed the exile of a voluntary scapegoat.

Flavio and Giuseppina were asleep on separate floors of the one-time farmhouse that Flavio's distant cousin had rented for them outside the small Swiss village where he worked. Flavio was sleeping on cushions in the living-room, disappointed by the girl but with, he imagined, time on his side. Giuseppina had successfully prolonged the effects of the barbiturate until the evening and when Flavio had arrived to claim the ultimate fruit of abduction she had peered at his naked body through very sleepy eyes. 'My God,' she'd mumbled, 'what a tiny cock.' Thus challenged Flavio had found mind incapable of mastering his matter. Under cover of her – feigned – sleep he had retired limp and puzzled to the distant cousin's gift of whisky and the pine log fire in the living-room.

The farmhouse, Giuseppina had noticed, was lost in trees above a wide valley. In the daylight she had seen a village a mile away across the fields below them, high mountains all around, terraces of vineyard on the hillside. She imagined she was somewhere in north Italy. Not that it greatly mattered. Her bedroom door was locked and her clothes had been taken away. There was nothing she could do about escaping and even if she shouted there was no one to hear her. The distant cousin she had not seen.

Giuseppina lay awake most of that night trying to analyse her feelings towards Flavio and his fleshy face: boring, boorish, stupid. He was certainly rich. But then she wasn't exactly poor and, with or without lovers, she did not fancy passing the rest of her life's nights pinned under his heavy body. She hadn't known many men: an uncle had once tried to deflower her on a drunken picnic; village boys had kissed and pawed her; a schoolmaster had nuzzled her. Only Renzo's hard and grimy hands had held her with any authority – but what was Renzo? A mechanic. An honest mechanic, who'd never taken a bribe or argued himself a bonus in all his working days. Why else would her father employ him? She had got to know him at school, holding hands at the back of the bus on the way home from Acireale each afternoon. He had given up school a year before anyone else. No one knew why, though people said he'd quarrelled with one of the teachers. His politics were certainly very unfashionable.

Giuseppina heard the fast mechanical rattle of a train down in the valley. All day and all night they'd been passing, and each time they passed she would hear the bell on a level-crossing or a station ringing away like a priest at mass. This time the bell made her feel sleepy and as light began to silhouette the mountains she fell asleep with all her thinking still unresolved.

At about the same time Renzo of the hard and grimy hands arrived in the village a mile away across the fields, climbing off the early morning stopping train from Bellinzona. He left his suitcase in the station and set out on foot as the world awoke pacing each street and courtyard of the village in search of a white Porsche Carrera with a Naples number-plate.

A fourth protagonist was closing in on the village also from the south and at a speed at times in excess of 900 miles an hour. The Avvocato Consoli was travelling in the rear seat of an MRCA prototype, an 'observer' on a routine test flight. Less than an hour after take-off at Ciampino the plane landed at an airfield some thirty miles from the Swiss border. A chauffeur-driven Mercedes complete with bodyguard was waiting for the plane and the car with its three occupants crossed the Swiss border unchallenged at Ponte Tresa shortly after six o'clock.

Except for the wood smoke from chimneys the little Swiss village came to life much as Renzo's own village back home in Sicily: men with carts or tractors riding to the fields across the valley, or to their pastures higher up the hillsides; the cars of dark-suited men scurrying off down the valley to their work in the towns; the smell of baking bread as the long shadow of mountains gave way to the sun.

Renzo had found no white Porsche, and when the petrol station opened below the village he walked down the road to ask the attendant whether he had seen such a car around yesterday.

The man laughed at him. 'You think I got time to look at cars? I have to run this place on my own. Petrol, servicing, repairs. You tell me if I got time to remember individual cars.'

The village doctor, sweeping leaves in his patch of garden, was more helpful. Renzo made out he was looking for a friend; a friend who'd been bitten by a dog and who might have requested treatment.

'Yes,' replied the doctor. 'He's on vaccine. A tourist. He's out on one of the farms across the valley.'

There were half a dozen farms dotted about the slopes on the far side of the valley. They were connected to the village by a track over the railway and the fields, but Renzo took a longer way round, climbing the main road for a mile above the village, crossing railway and river where the valley narrowed and where he was well out of sight from village and farms. He walked back through the larch woods high on the hillside and eventually spotted the Porsche tucked away behind some out-buildings on one of the smaller farms.

Renzo would have moved faster had he known how little time was left to him, for as he slipped out of the woods and into the deserted farmyard so the Avvocato's chauffeur-driven Mercedes was entering the village past the petrol station a mile away.

The farm kitchen was tidy and empty, undisturbed by the new tenants except for two half-empty packets of biscuits and a tin of milk on the table. Renzo found the Consoli boy in the shuttered living-room asleep on the floor in a roll of cushions and blankets, the fire long dead, the room reeking of stale cigar smoke and surgical alcohol. An elaborate collection of bottles and bandages littered the only table. Renzo smiled. Capo Tomacchio had been right. The old Alsatian had had his retributive pound of flesh.

There were two suitcases on the floor and what looked like Giuseppina's clothes draped over a chair. But no sign of the girl. Renzo climbed a creaking wooden staircase and found an upstairs bedroom locked, with the key in the door. He opened it. The girl was sleeping curled up in the quilt, her long hair spread all over the bed.

Not that Renzo had time to linger or to daydream. As he bent down to claim Giuseppina with a kiss he glanced out through the low window and saw a large car on the track crossing the floor of the valley towards them. The limousine looked too clean and hurried for any farmer and Renzo obeyed his intuition. He left the girl asleep, ran downstairs and out of the house and scrambled in and out of the yard buildings until he had found a suitable weapon. The Mercedes was crossing the river forty yards below him as he hurried back into the farmhouse shouting and prodding Flavio awake at the business end of a pitchfork. The young Consoli, weak from his vaccine and doped with whisky and sleep, was in no mood for argument. He preceded the pitchfork upstairs and into Giuseppina's bedroom. The girl woke up to find both Flavio and Renzo barricaded into the room with her.

'Come on you love-birds,' they heard the Avvocato shout from downstairs. 'It's time to move again.'

Avvocato Consoli was not expecting trouble at this stage of his journey. The bodyguard, friend of a friend, had been brought along merely to subdue the girl if that proved necessary. It took five minutes of confused shouting through the door to establish that Flavio was being held prisoner by a determined young man armed with a pitchfork. The Avvocato would have felt in that moment like disowning and relinquishing his contemptible son, if Flavio did not have a specific role still to play. Time was short. There were funds to draw from a bank in Zürich. A plane to catch. A further connection to make in Lisbon. Flavio was to 'disappear', leaving a rather dirty and obvious trail behind him. He did not know it, but he was, besides his other crimes, in the process of absconding with airport funds. Avvocato Consoli was preparing himself in the role of outraged father.

He bargained through the door. He wasn't carrying much money, he explained. He offered 10000 Swiss francs. Too bad, he was thinking, if the girl gets left behind. He would have to find some other means of silencing Capo Tomacchio.

Renzo was equally unprepared for such a situation. It had been his intention to drive Flavio back to the frontier and hand him over to the Italian police. That was the bargain he had made with Citto. But he wasn't going to get the boy back into Italy with the Avvocato waiting outside the door. He accepted the money, not for himself, but on behalf of the girl who had suffered the indignity and shame of abduction.

The notes were passed under the bedroom door and Flavio allowed, with the help of the bed-quilt, to climb down from the bedroom window. Only Giuseppina had reservations, for when she surrendered the quilt she was left naked and with nothing to cover herself. Flavio disappeared through the window and out of her life with even stronger regrets about his loss and last night's failure.

The quilt gave way when he was still halfway from window to ground. He fell painfully on his dog-bitten leg and had to be carried to his father's car. The Porsche was entrusted to the bodyguard and two minutes later Renzo, watching from the bedroom, saw both cars rejoin the main road and disappear at high speed northwards towards the Gotthard Pass and Zürich.

Renzo stayed on in the bedroom with the naked though now no longer protesting girl. He did not need the pitchfork to complete the scenario of hi-jacked abduction and by the time they came downstairs hand-in-hand to look for breakfast Giuseppina had been irrevocably 'dishonoured'.

Later that morning Renzo walked over the fields to call Capo Tomacchio from the village and tell him that his daughter was safe.

'Good boy,' Tomacchio shouted up the telephone from Sicily. 'But don't waste any more money on aeroplanes. You can both take the train home.'

'Maybe for Christmas,' Renzo replied. 'We're staying here to get ourselves married.'

Renzo put the phone down on his prospective father-in-law's yell of anger. He walked out into the village street to buy food for lunch, then strolled downhill to chat with the old man in the garage. It seemed to Renzo by the time he rejoined Giuseppina at the farmhouse that he had already found himself a new home and a new job.

Tomacchio's apoplectic rage proved to be his last free speech for many years. He was arrested by direct order of the Procuratore later that day.

I I

Earlier that morning the middle-aged woman who acted as Citto's cleaning lady had left her home by the old port. She walked to the two blocks of apartments and offices where she did most of her work and collected Citto's front-door key from the concierge at seven o'clock.

A few minutes later an explosion destroyed the third-floor landing. The cleaning lady had been shielded from the blast by the half-open door and miraculously escaped injury. The interior of the flat was destroyed by the explosion and the fire that followed.

The concierge downstairs told the police that Citto had been home the evening before. She described his manner and appearance as 'strange and secretive'.

Half an hour later traffic police attempted to move an old and battered Giulia parked illegally in a side road a quarter of a mile away.

Duplicate keys were used to open the door and start the

engine, but as soon as the wheels turned an explosive charge was detonated. The police driver inside the car was killed and five onlookers in the street injured badly enough to be taken to hospital.

Citto had been uncomfortably asleep and hung-over on the back seat of an office car in a quiet country lane. He was woken by banging on the windows and when he climbed out of the car he found himself surrounded by two jeep-loads of police.

Unshaven and dirty, smelling of whisky and unsteady on his feet, he was treated like some kind of dangerous fanatic. Police later announced that he had been found in 'suspicious circumstances' and detained for questioning. After cross-examination he was said to be suffering from persecution-mania, and later that same day was charged with leaving explosive booby-traps at his home and on his car.

A day of black comedy was completed by Swiss frontier officials at Chiasso when they examined four apparently misdirected Interfrigo vans. Instead of the expected crates of fruit and vegetables they found mutilated human bodies labelled and wrapped in plastic bags. For some hours the Swiss police believed they had uncovered some grotesque atrocity. Luckily for the Italian authorities the four vans were still in the no-man's-land of the Chiasso marshalling yards and the bodies were successfully reclaimed after embarrassing explanations at the highest levels of government in Berne and Rome.

Military teams worked through the night to lay the bodies in coffins and five Italian Air Force G-222s flew the remnants of Tango November's payload into Taormina-Peloritana exactly a week after their originally scheduled arrival.

12

The funeral procession descended from the airport in mid-morning, crossing the valley to climb another hillside towards the chosen cemetery. The army lorries carrying the coffins had been draped in black and peasants in the lemon gardens and vineyards stood up from their work to bare their heads as the bodies passed. A band and a church bell played the lorries through a crowded village street where women stood crying on the pavements. Even the boys and girls on their motorized cycles were silent and watching.

Relatives of the dead were waiting along the new gravel paths at the far end of the cemetery. They stood in small groups by each grave while loudspeakers relayed a short service, the appropriate prayers being read alternately by a Catholic and an Anglican priest. Canon Ash Nyren had been asked by Greyhound Flight to conduct the Anglican half of the service but had refused, saying simply to the puzzled American who had sought him out, 'I am no longer a man of God.'

He was standing now, a lone untidy figure to one side of his son's empty grave. Today was the first time he had been conscious of other men and women involved in the tragedy. They had all gathered together outside the town gate in Taormina waiting for buses to carry them here. Ash Nyren had never seen so much distress. It frightened him; made him angry. He was used to a village family here and there; a sister or a mother; widows. His own wife with a telegram on another sunny September morning thirty years ago.

Nyren watched a woman, one arm around her husband trying to comfort him. She was oblivious to them all, kissing the collar of his jacket, touching his cheek as though his frozen face was about to break apart, breathing on his hands. She steered him to the bus, where briefly his consciousness returned and he stood aside to help her up the steps. Apart from Nyren they were the last to board that particular bus. There was no room for them to sit together, but she held his hand over two rows of seats all the way to the cemetery. And when she lost him later in the crowd he stood quite still looking it seemed at people's knees until he was reclaimed.

I can't help you, thought the old Canon. I cannot help any of you. There is nothing to say. There are no answers. You just spit in the sky; shake a fist.

The plots in the cemetery annexe had been laid out in alphabetical order and there was no one near him that he knew. He had noticed Julia Duckham somewhere far away. There seemed quite a crowd around her and Ash Nyren felt a momentary resentment that his son should have so little to show for his twenty-nine years. One aged and confused father. The Nyren line was dying in solitude at one end of this hot white-stone cemetery. Three centuries of priests and soldiers and the only event left to record, his own death.

> *'And though after my skin worms destroy this body,*
> *Yet in my flesh shall I see God.'*

He wanted none of that drunken poetry said on his behalf.

There was chaos for some minutes as the coffins were off-loaded from the lorries. Groups of soldiers, sailors and airmen were carrying them to the named and numbered graves. Inevitably mistakes were made which distraught relatives were trying to sort out as photographers and cameramen moved in to record their distress.

Julia watched it all in a blank haze, her children on either hand, her sister behind, her step-daughter to one side. Other people had joined them, she knew not from where: some of Mike's old colleagues who had flown out from London with Pam and the children; the bearded English doctor who had come to shake her hand; even that investigator who had asked all those unpleasant questions. It was Mac who told her that this 'Raffles' Burden had been with Mike flying Mosquitoes in the war. Why hadn't Burden told her? She didn't want his deviousness here hovering over Mike's graveside. Perhaps he had come to spy on Pam and the children; perhaps he thought they were also relevant to his investigation.

But Burden's motives were quite genuine. He felt he owed a final salute to his old fellow-combatant, and he stood stiffly to attention when the final prayers were read.

*'Man that is born of a woman hath but a short
time to live, and is full of misery . . .'*

The bodies were blessed and lowered in batches of ten as the
priests and military teams moved along the gravel paths. But
Ash Nyren said his own farewell and slipped away before they
reached him. Peter's coffin was lowered by four Italian airmen
and with no one in attendance.

Mac too was leaving the ceremony, angry and troubled to
see his bodies – his evidence – placed so finally out of reach. It
was he who saw the old Canon leave, plunging away behind
the crowds, his arms and legs swinging as the previous time
he'd seen him, left with left and right with right, just like
Groucho Marx.

That same afternoon on the far side of the city Sharlie
Barzizza was buried, a mother, a grandmother, an aunt, an
uncle and two cousins accompanying him from a mid-town
church to the cemetery.

Citto's request to be allowed to join them had been turned
down by a local prison governor for Citto was not, within the
meaning of the law, a member of Sharlie's family. He spent the
afternoon instead under further interrogation trying to answer
questions so absurd and far-fetched that he was tempted at
times almost to laugh. He peered and blinked at his accusers
through thick lenses and stammered his replies, but they were
neither moved by his vulnerability nor convinced by his
protested innocence. It was as well for Citto that he did not yet
know of the Ingegnere's death. He could cope with the privations
of a foetid crowded cell drawing on the stoicism accumulated
from twenty generations of disease, drought and earthquake.
But to feel a direct responsibility for two men's deaths would hurt
him; weaken him irreparably for the rest of his life.

Autumn descended upon the Veneto and the Polesine in
wild grey squalls. On the Monday after his death, and after
elaborate but inconclusive forensic examination, Preuss's body
was carried bucking and tossing in a black gold-scrolled launch
across the lagoon to the cemetery island of San Michele. He
was buried in a circle of umbrellas – colleagues and pupils

from the University. To them his death still seemed an inexplicable and tragic accident.

A story leaked to a newspaper had tried to suggest that the Ingegnere had been inebriated when he fell from the train – vodka drinking with the Russian car conductor. But the level of alcohol in autopsy was minimal.

Subsequently and more strangely a suicide note had been discovered, a typewritten confession from the Ingegnere that he was being blackmailed for reasons of his homosexuality and had thus decided to take his life. But police in Venice found evidence of a break-in at the Ingegnere's flat and the 'confession' was destroyed without its contents being made public. As with Sharlie, the coroner's verdict had been postponed.

13

It took Ash Nyren two days to walk up the lower mountain slopes. He slept rough, eating grapes from the vineyards or chestnuts from the woods, and drinking water from village fountains. On the third morning he reached the tree-line and found the jeep tracks that carved a zigzag path up to the lava summit. He climbed all day under the sun, passed occasionally by groups of tourists and guides riding in the jeeps. The mountain had always attracted strange foreigners and though they remembered him later no one was in any way troubled by the sight of a shaggy old Anglo-Saxon plodding up towards the crater.

He reached the summit in the middle of the night, guided the last few hundred feet by the occasional glowing hiccup of red explosion above him. Ash Nyren had expected resolve to weaken in the face of exhaustion and pain. Indeed, if he had removed his shoes he would have found his feet raw with broken blisters. But he arrived quite calm and still determined, his only worry being that animal instinct of self-preservation that might yet inspire fear.

He sat for perhaps half an hour sheltered from the wind

behind a rock, feeling the heat in the ground, smelling sulphur fumes, hearing a growling in the earth and watching the intermittent bursts of flaming gas and stones from that large strange hole in the ground. Each explosion lasted for perhaps three seconds and was heralded by a much longer and crescendo glow. He would need that light to guide him, and the strangeness of sound and sudden heat to draw him on.

In the dark and against the wind he saw and heard no one. A small party of German tourists had arrived with a guide. They had toured the whole area of crater photographing the display and now settled down to wait for the sunrise. They noticed Ash Nyren when he stood up. He was silhouetted in the glow that preceded an explosion, appearing it seemed from nowhere, an image to haunt most of them for the rest of their lives. At first he was motionless, just a figure standing and watching, shaking one fist in the air. Suddenly they saw him run, a wild splay of uncoordinated arms and legs like a human windmill. For a moment he made no progress, blown backwards almost by that subterranean force. Then his silhouette shrank and receded still wild and uncoordinated, but moving away from them fast towards the glowing hole in the ground. And into that glow he fell, stumbling head first and arms flung as the gas and stones came up in a roar, disappearing from their sight in a brief scatter of flame.

When the sun came up his dog-collar and jacket were found stowed out of the wind under a rock. The old Canon had left a note inside the jacket – one scrawled sentence of no apparent significance.

> *King Arthur is not dead but is resting from his wounds on the slopes of Mount Etna.*

14

Four months passed. Tango November had been picked clean, a half-buried carcass in the winter snow, her wings and engines crated and lifted out by Skycranes, her instruments and systems packed in polyurethane and flown to laboratories far away. The broken-backed fuselage remained, appearing and disappearing as the snow fell and melted and fell again.

Lanterns on adjoining lemon trees threw wild shadows where the two men were working. The incessant sound of water flowing and falling governed the urgency of their movements as they pulled loose earth into channels with long right-angled shovels guiding the flow from the aqueduct. Old Turi and his even older *massaro* had one hour's water left and thirty trees still to irrigate.

Mac would have liked to join in but he knew any attempt to help would only interfere with a routine perfected by years of practice. He moved away not to disturb them, ducking his six and a half feet through the trees, placing his feet with care in the darkness. It was mid-winter and though the orchard was full of lemon scent Mac felt frost not so far above. He climbed steps in the wall and saw the mountain rising over the trees, a white moonlit cone in the black sky. Old Smokey covered in snow. Mac could pick out the ridge where Tango November had lost her left wing, and the dark shadow of dead ground beyond it where the plane had finally fallen.

Landing was aborted when interruption of power supply at the airport caused failure of all ground instruments and runway lighting.

The senior members of the three-nation investigation had reconvened in Taormina to discuss the first draft of the Italian government report – Burden, Mac and Larry Raille, who had arrived complete with strident wife on what she told them was a second honeymoon, a celebration.

There was nothing much to celebrate within the investigation. The outline draft of the report was too full of reservation and qualification. *One minute into overshoot the flight crew were led to shut down number two engine after a fire-warning. The single remaining generator overloaded and a subsequent battery failure probably affected all essential flight-deck instrumentation. It is impossible to establish the duration of the failure but the combination of incidents seems to have caused the pilots to lose their position.*

Thus the bare outlines. There were countless pages of analysis discussing each of the technical failures in detail. But they only told half a story. It was the general scenario that had escaped them, Mac thought, the human element that could not be read out on instruments, X-rayed or photographed in ultra-violet.

Even the timing was wrong. The journalist had seen the airport clocks stopped on 05.40. But two of the crew watches on the crashed plane had stopped at 05.37, and the mushroom man had heard the plane over his head high on the mountain at 05.35. Prognosis: ground instrument and lighting failure occurred after the crash and in no way contributed to the emergency.

But the melodrama of corruption and intrigue had fogged that issue. The world, even Italy herself, preferred to believe in traditional villains. Capo Tomacchio was in prison; Flavio Consoli had fled to South America: they were the culprits, and the scenario was accordingly fitted around them. It seemed that nothing would be learnt from the disaster.

The failure of components in number two engine was almost certainly provoked by the suddenness of the lighting and systems failure at the airport, which caused the crew to adopt a last-minute emergency climb-out procedure, which in turn ignored stress limits on the power-plants that might otherwise have been observed.

Not a word about fire-warnings on that notorious number two engine. Not a word about the electrics, for surely the time had come to stipulate a fail-safe emergency wind-driven generator for all civil aircraft. Not a word about the nitrogen fuel-inerting system that would have prevented the outbreak of fire. Not a word about the ADF beacons, so dangerously inaccurate in dirty weather. Not a word about the lack of emergency breathing apparatus in the cabin. Stronger seats and smoke hoods would have saved 150 lives.

The 119 still flew unmodified; landing aids and lighting layout at Taormina-Peloritana had not been improved;

minimum cabin safety regulations laid down by the American FAA and British CAA had not been challenged.

Greyhound's own company report had paradoxically blamed their own flight crew. Administration, safety standards, aircraft and aircraft maintenance had all been exonerated.

Ninety per cent of the time, thought Mac, even ninety-nine per cent, flying the big jets could be less frightening and less taxing than driving a London bus. It was during the ten or the one per cent of time that pilots earned their money: when flying aids failed to give them adequate information; when turbulence pulled them out of the sky; when their machinery started to play up; when they had to come down at night or in cloud to land at primitive airports in the middle of mountains; when they were overtired, frightened or lost.

'*Tango November, you are clear to land . . .*'

They had heard the tape that morning in the conference room. It had sobered up the esoterics of investigation listening to three dead men approaching their moment of truth. Not surprising that Duckham's last recorded expression was a despairing blasphemy.

'Fucking Christ Jesus!'

Mac shivered in the darkness. The two lanterns were moving far away through the lemon trees, the water still cascading. Mac climbed down on the far side of the wall and followed the rough path across the dry bed of a river. The village was outlined on the other side, a scattering of lights along the line of the village street, and on this side of the houses the glow of a charcoal brazier on Turi's terrace where supper was cooking. Mac smelt sausages and chestnuts. He could hear the stuttering staccato of the tubby little journalist, and the slight shy laugh of the pretty girl with him.

Julia Duckham was up there somewhere, probably in the house talking with Turi's wife. Julia had been studying Italian ever since September. Mac couldn't quite figure out why. Something to do with her husband being buried here. A sort of obligation she felt.

Mac had visited her a month or so after their return to England. A courtesy call, or so he had kidded himself, though he was the last person to make gestures of that sort. A week later he had driven down again, this time to build the bonfire and let off the fireworks he had promised the kids on his first visit. After that he had become an almost regular visitor. Not that there had been an iota of intimacy between them, not even soft talk. In fact Mac was convinced he would never bring himself to make a move. His whirlwind seductions had no place in her set-up, not with kids and a dead husband. If there was a decision to be made she would make it herself. She had only travelled out with him now to visit the grave.

Graves. Mac picked his way through boulders in the river-bed and scrambled up the far bank. He looked back at the mountain and saw a brief glow of explosion on the crater, and he remembered the wild-haired priest who walked like Groucho Marx.

Citto heard the rusted hinges of the iron gate at the bottom of the garden and saw the tall English doctor appear along the path under Turi's fig-trees. This Mac had changed since September – less exuberant; care or trouble in his eyes. Everyone had changed, Citto thought: old Turi, tired and talking of retirement; Nonna Lisa, sad and silent, staring at the sea all day; Laura, buried into her books and her studying.

And Citto himself had changed. Five weeks in an Italian prison were enough to change anyone. God help those, he thought, who spent half their lives inside. The newspaper had supplied good lawyers – but no publicity. The whole affair had been low key and muted, silent and invisible to the point of nightmare. It was little Laura who had kept him sane, visiting him once a week with her serious smile.

Citto had been saved the delays and inconsistencies of Italian law by the vigilance of the young Torinese Magistrato and with the help of an attempted bomb outrage at a Communist Party office in Brescia. Forensic evidence, spotted by the Magistrato in a law journal, linked the unusual type of friction detonator used in Brescia with the explosions at Citto's apartment and in his car. All three incidents were subsequently attributed to one of the militant right-wing groups, the vendetta against Citto having been doubtless suggested to them by persons unknown in Rome.

Citto had been released without charges. But he'd nevertheless found his status at the newspaper subtly changed, as though the period of imprisonment had somehow sullied him. Perhaps his own attitudes had changed. Maybe he had lost his fervour and the mildly crusading zeal he had previously displayed. Certainly he had lost all sense of purpose and direction. His Tango November involvement had started as something of a crusade. Somehow somewhere it had gone wrong and Citto felt himself to be at fault. Preuss had told him about the deceptive lighting layout round the factories to one side of the airport. His theory had been passed on to the investigators but the weather conditions – the wet roads of that September morning had never been repeated. In the four months since that storm it hadn't rained once. Diabolical, thought Citto, if young Flavio Consoli and Capo Tomacchio had been innocent of any involvement in the crash. Poetic justice was no substitute for the truth, and Citto knew that the whole truth had eluded them all. The real culprits had escaped.

He stood over the brazier turning the sausages, watching Laura's face across the glow as she fanned the charcoal. If she would come with him, he thought, he would apply for another job somewhere on the mainland. Follow the rainbow north like Sharlie had tried to do.

Mac joined them over the heat, and the women came out from the house wrapped in shawls. They had thought they would eat indoors, but somehow no one moved and they stayed on the terrace facing the mountain, the moon high behind them over the village. The two lanterns returned across the river, Turi and his old retainer with their tools and their boots, and the job completed. Old Turi washed under the pump and climbed the steps from the garden with two jugs of wine drawn off from a barrel in the cellar below the terrace.

They ate and drank, and Turi brought up more jugs of wine. They turned the charcoal out on to the stones and made a fire with old prunings from the lemon trees. And in the darkness where they couldn't see or be seen too clearly they talked of many different things: of grapes and lemons and harvests; of children; of Renzo and Giuseppina married and living in Switzerland; of the $5000 Sharlie had posthumously made on his pictures of Tango November. They talked in the end and inevitably of death and dying – Turi who had watched it happen too many times; Julia trying to cope with it as a calamitous violation of her own and her children's lives; Citto who remembered his father and mother and Sharlie and

Preuss's sad lopsided smile; Turi's wife who long ago had lost her only child.

Mac did not join in. Death was his profession. Too late now to become like Turi and concern himself only with the living. Each time Mac looked up away from the fire he saw the outline of the mountain, and each time he saw it he waited for that glow on the crater to explode and die away. Once every forty seconds, he reckoned, like a slow mammoth heart-beat.

King Arthur is not dead but is resting
from his wounds on the slopes of Mount Etna.

The next day over a hotel lunch the investigation disbanded, the evidence now left to the Italians for their ministerial and legal reports, to be published after two or three or four years, by which time memories and the risk of legal complications would have faded.

The Italians thanked their British and American collaborators, and Priscilla Raille, uninvited guest, toasted her husband's last investigation. The other men dutifully raised glasses to wish him luck in outer space: NASA's trouble-shooter designate for the manned space-labs of the future, solving technical jigsaw puzzles in solitary splendour fifty miles into the sky.

Here's to the 119, thought Raille as he raised his own glass. Let's hope the 'albatross' gets lucky. Almost unnoticed the FAA had issued a service bulletin suggesting the repositioning of sensing elements in the number two fire-warning system. But a service bulletin was a long way short of a mandatory air-worthiness directive, and as for those battery and galley power switches, they remained in close proximity, red square, and black tadpole, inviting Murphy's Law and another 'unlikely' disaster.

Raille's successor was smiling at him across the table. A Board member of reasonable disposition who would probably ask no difficult questions. Apart from Burden he was the only man round the table not conscious of failure. And even Burden felt some regret for he knew that Duckham would not escape criticism in the final analysis. Notwithstanding pages of mitigating circumstances and notwithstanding their concern not to apportion blame, the crash would be classified in most minds as 'pilot error'.

That afternoon two taxis drove them all to the airport, and on the way both cars made a detour to a small cemetery high above a village.

The hillside was cool in the afternoon sun, the crowded jumble of mausoleums, headstones and wall-tombs white as the almond blossom in the gardens below. Larry Raille, his wife, Ralph Burden and Mac Pherson were standing by the brass plaque that recorded the facts of the crash in English and Italian. Julia Duckham, walking away down the gravel path towards her husband's grave, heard the American woman reading the words in her hard brittle voice.

'In memory of one hundred and eighty-seven passengers and crew in Golf Foxtrot Echo Tango November who died on our mountain.'

The cemetery annexe was well kept with flowers and shrubs – courtesy of the Tango November Disaster Fund. Dutch orchestra, Japanese pianist, Beethoven, Mozart and Rachmaninov: $1000 for the cemetery; $2000 for Trixie in New York; $15000 for a private numbered bank account in Lugano – 'administrative expenses' incurred by a local politician.

Julia laid her flowers on Mike's grave. There was only his name on the stone, no inlaid photograph like the Italians used. She would have preferred that. Something to keep his reality alive – his smile here in the sunlight.

The valley filled with sound, the slow whistling roar of giant turbo-fans, a black shadow floating over the hills. 200 tons of shining silver and 300 lives hanging in the air as a DC-10 settled to land thirty seconds short of threshold on runway two nine Taormina-Peloritana. In the daylight; in the sunshine; without problems. The pilot could have done it standing on his head.

Epilogue

'Tango November you are clear to land'

Duckham felt the first shudder of turbulence, the outside edge of the storm that according to the weather radar was centred somewhere on the flank of the mountain to their left and beyond the airport. It was time to get the feel of the plane before landing.

'Disengaging auto pilot.'

She tried to snatch forward as the auto pilot uncoupled and Duckham eased back on the wheel to catch it. The flat tiredness of the last few hours was lifting as adrenalin took over: sweat on the palms; heart-beat accelerating; his brain reviewing the unknown factors, the permutations of possible difficulties – doubtful ground visibility, a storm and a mountain.

'Full flap.'

Peter acknowledged with a grunt. Duckham glanced over at him. He was still brooding like a sulky kid, and not it seemed in the least perturbed by the landing approach. After all he had been here before and in the daylight. He could visualize it all.

'Full flap.'

'Fifty. Fifty. Two greens.'

'Check list complete up here,' said George. 'Let's hope they've got it together downstairs.'

'Let's have hush again.' Duckham didn't want his crew distracted in any way. 'Eyes up for contact, Peter. I'm staying tight on the instruments. George, you better give me an altitude check over the Middle Marker.'

'Roger.' The Flight Engineer laughed. 'Now we'll see what is runway visibility is really like.'

The amber light and bleep signalled the Middle Marker beacon. George Raven took the third bleep as centre. 'We're fifty foot high I'd say.'

'As near as dammit then.'

Peter Nyren called out contact. 'I have approach lights. Half right. Twenty right.'

Duckham looked up from his instruments for the first time and saw the comforting glow and pattern of a double line of orange lights twenty degrees or so to starboard. He peeled the plane over watching and straining for the runway lights beyond. Then was suddenly uneasy about those orange lines.

Both he and Peter saw it simultaneously, a factory emerging from the cloud, a factory yard, four simple orange street-lamps reflecting deceptively into double lines on the wet asphalt.

'Shit!'

'Whoops,' said Peter. 'Sorry, skipper.'

The real runway lights appeared, ten degrees left. But they couldn't get back anywhere near them. Bloody half-arse airport. It was even worse than the street-lighting layout at Basle.

'Overshoot!'

The three men reacted simultaneously. Duckham pulled back to rotate; George Raven applied power; Peter operated the flap controls.

Sorry, skipper, Peter had said. The first non-broody remark since they'd met in the Crew Room, Duckham thought. It had taken a mistake to shake him out of it.

'Flaps two five.'

'Positive climb. Gear up.'

Peter acknowledged and raised the wheels.

Duckham could feel the plane lifting sluggish, beginning once more to thump in turbulence. His mind's eye was full of storm and mountain. 'We're lifting like a whale. Give us the lot, George. Let's get back in the sky. Peter – tune in to Oscar Echo on both.'

'Roger.' They were aiming now for the Outer Marker on the opposite approach path, the ADF beacon Oscar Echo. Over the beacon they would turn north on a two-minute timed leg. Only then would they be definitively clear of high ground.

Peter was tidying up flaps. 'Speed OK. Flaps to one four.'

Duckham nodded. 'Where's that beacon, Peter?'

'Beacon's tuned in. Identing Oscar Echo.'

They hit the bad rough quite suddenly with a thump that took Duckham right out of his seat up against his straps.

'Judas!' That was George. His seat didn't hold him too good in turbulence especially when he was swivelled frontwards to monitor.

'Air speed and rate of climb all over.' – Peter watching the instruments and beginning to sound jumpy. They were bumping hard enough now to throw their loose kit to and fro on the floor. 'Losing air speed and altitude.'

'Fly attitude,' Duckham told himself. Take it easy and keep your eye on the one instrument, he meant. When it starts to get bad most of the instruments go berserk. Only the artificial horizon stays clean and gives you any idea of what the aeroplane is actually doing.

A warning bell shrilled.

Not now, thought Duckham. Please God not now.

Raven reached up to cancel the bell: 'Engine fire number two.' Even George's voice momentarily lost its professional cool.

'Another false alarm. It has to be.' Peter looked across to Duckham.

'Probably.' Duckham shrugged. 'Carry out fire drill on number two.'

'For Christ's sake! – It's a birdie!'

Duckham ignored Peter and repeated the order. 'Fire drill, George.'

George Raven carried out item one of the fire drill, diverting power demand away from the fire-affected engine and generator: 'Essential power to number three.' Down to one generator, he was thinking. Just for a false fire warning. 'Close number two thrust lever.'

There was a pause, then Duckham terse and loud: 'Peter!'

'Yes, sorry.' Peter took it up in a shaky voice, both hands over to the central console as he buffeted in his seat. 'Closing number two thrust lever.'

George cut off fuel. 'Shutting start lever.'

Peter reached for the fire controls. 'Pulling fire handle.'

The number two engine was running down. Then warning lights flickered on the panel as the one remaining generator overloaded and switched itself out of circuit.

'We're on battery,' called George. 'Number three's tripped on overload.'

'Shed some load and get us back on generator.' Duckham remembered the Engineer's earlier misgivings about the state of the battery.

Get rid of galley power and one of the HF sets, thought George, and he reached simultaneously for the two switches. But as he turned them the lights died.

'Fucking Christ Jesus!' Duckham turned with a shout to look back over his shoulder. Apart from a torch lamp in the ceiling the flight deck was in total black-out.

'The battery must have gone. The bloody battery – I can't see to do anything –' George Raven was staring at where his panel had been. He could see nothing; illumination, warning lights, indicators, everything had gone.

'Get some flashlights out!' Duckham faced front again. The quick turning of his head had made him dizzy and in the dark he could hardly see the instruments. The ones that were visible seemed to be inoperative. 'Chrissakes, George, I've lost everything. Get a torch on the artificial horizon. I can't see bugger all.'

Duckham could no longer 'feel' what the plane was doing. The dizziness was still with him and he felt vaguely nauseous. The turbulence was thumping them now like a wild horse trying to throw a rider. Duckham had to keep the plane flying straight and climbing. It felt to him as though they were banking right. But that could be his head. 'What are we doing Peter? I can't feel it. Are we turning right?'

'Feels straight to me.'

'Are we climbing?'

'I think so.'

'Get a torch on the altimeter and air speed.'

George Raven was out of his seat on hands and knees, bracing himself against the turbulence, looking for the lamps. He had a pair of them in his bag, but the bag had been turned inside out in the buffeting. He was trying to think what could have failed. He knew he hadn't made a mistake. He had never made an operating mistake in his whole career. It must be the battery. It had been charging high all the way out. Nickel-cadmium. Those bloody things could catch fire under high charge. And what about that warning on number two? They hadn't completed the fire drill yet. The whole back of the plane could be ablaze for all they knew. Closed-circuit TV you needed with engines at the back, at least so you could see what was going on.

Peter had pulled out one of the emergency battery lamps and was using it as a hand-held torch, pinpointing what was left of the instruments. 'Looks like we're climbing.'

Duckham was trying to fly the plane 'seat of his pants' and on the standby horizon midway between the two pilots. He still had his pressure instruments, air speed, vertical speed and pressure altimeter, with the old-fashioned liquid compass on the ceiling. But the plane was hammering like a pneumatic drill in the turbulence and he still felt giddy and sick. 'George, get me some more light on the instruments. Altitude and air speed.'

'They're up and down like yo-yos. I think we're climbing through six five. And it looks like two-fifty knots.'

'What in fuck's happened to the electrics?'

'Overload. Then the battery went. I'll try and get back on generator.'

'Keep your torches on what we're doing for the moment.'

George was back on his seat facing forward, one hand out to keep a flashlight on the instruments and controls.

'What are we steering, Peter?'

Peter shifted his torch on to the standby compass in the ceiling. 'Can't tell. It's spinning all ways.'

'I'd say we've kept it more or less straight.'

'I think so.'

'We should be somewhere over Oscar Echo by now if we had our ADFs. I think we'll keep straight on and make height. I've had enough here. If we can get power back and a radio working we'll try and get clearance for Malta.'

'Roger.'

'George. Try and get us some juice back.'

Duckham sounded calm and matter-of-fact, but he didn't fool himself. The storm was throwing them around like a ping-pong ball on a fountain. They couldn't really tell what attitudes they'd been flying during the last few minutes. He still felt the plane right wing low and was trying to stop himself from over-correcting. They were disorientated and lost, and given the chronic instability of ADF beacons in storm conditions even their original fix on Oscar Echo might have been wildly inaccurate. In which case they could be quite literally anywhere. They might break from cloud straight into the side of the mountain at any moment. Duckham had to force himself to keep his eyes down on the little instrumentation left to him. You could get hypnotized anticipating disaster through the windshield – like speeding down a motorway in fog faster and faster, waiting for the tail-lights of a lorry to come up and hit you.

George turned the flashlight back on his panel. He had to shed power load and try to reactivate the number three generator. Cabin lights and heat, the weather radar, two booster pumps; he switched them out one after the other. He'd already disconnected galley power and one of the HF sets. He moved the flashlight to check them; HF set off; galley power on. But he'd turned it off. He checked the switch; the spring was all right. Then he saw the heavy red switch next to and below it. The battery was off. Even then he didn't realize what had happened. The battery switch has bust, he thought. No, it was OK. He flicked it on and lights and instruments came back to life. What the hell had happened to it?

'Good boy!' Duckham's eyes were over the instruments checking each reading.

Peter turned, grinning at George in relief.

Good boy? I'm fucked if I didn't hit the wrong bloody switch, George was thinking. Battery for galley, so help me. He tried the number three generator again and this time with the load shed it reconnected without trouble.

'Check on that fire,' called Duckham.

'Number two fire lever – light's out. Fire extinguished.'

'If there ever bloody well was one.'

'Altitude check, Peter.'

'Climbing through eight five.'

'Two more lovely thousand and we're clear.' George meant the height of the mountain at 10800 or 10900.

Peter remembered the sight of its smoking cone clear of the clouds just eight or nine minutes ago. It already felt like a hundred years. How the hell do we know where we are, he was thinking. Why is Duckham so sodding unperturbed?

There was suddenly more light coming from outside, and the turbulence was easing. Duckham felt the plane lift lighter. An upcurrent, he thought. We're somewhere near that damn mountain. 'Altitude?'

'Nine eight.'

'Bearing one nine five.' Peter's voice, abrupt and censorious. 'I don't think we know where the fuck we are.'

You're late, thought Duckham. You should have picked up the bearing as soon as the juice came back. That's your job. But he said nothing for the moment. The boy was nervous enough.

'Bearing one nine five,' Peter repeated.

Duckham acknowledged. 'I know, I've seen it. No point in turning now. We need height. We'll keep climbing in a straight line.'

They were flying more or less south-west instead of north-west, into the mountain instead of away from it depending on their original position and attitudes over the last two or three minutes. The drift would have been gradual: a storm-affected heading on Oscar Echo beacon that could have been as much as twenty to thirty degrees out; then flying blind when Duckham had imagined they were right wing low. He must have over-corrected. Something like a gentle but continuous ten degree turn. Four to five minutes – even on two engines and full climb they could have made twenty to twenty-five ground miles. We're bang over the mountain, he thought, and we need another 500 feet.

'Jesus Christ!'

The red flash and thump were simultaneous. Number two engine blown up, thought Duckham; or else we've hit the volcano. But they were still flying. Still climbing. Two fifty knots. All instruments OK. He looked up.

The cloud had broken, like flying out of the end of a wall. A blood red sun was halfway out of the sea on the horizon, its glow filling the whole cockpit with lurid crimson light. The thump must have been an air-pocket on the edge of the clouds. They were over the lower northern peaks of the mountain with about 200 feet clearance if they kept climbing straight. The main ridge of crater was a mile or so to starboard and above them. They were going to make it. The sky ahead was clear for ever.

'Hallelujah!' That was Peter beside him. He was smiling, almost laughing.

Duckham eased himself forward out of the seat cushion. He was soaking wet, as though he'd been standing under a shower, his arms and legs suddenly weak as muscle and mind relaxed. It was the most beautiful sunrise he had ever seen.

'Shepherd's warning,' said George looking at the sky. It was my balls-up, he was thinking. I'll have to tell them when we're down. I switched battery for galley. There'll be a sodding report to write. A sodding great black mark against my name. Better keep the flight recorders tripped out, he thought. That way no one'll be able to check up too closely.

Clearance for Malta, Duckham reckoned. That sun will get rid of the cloud by the time we get back. Bugger the schedules. Greyhound will survive.

He watched the mountain floating below them, the crater still to starboard and spewing smoke. The ground in front of them fell away almost perpendicular. Another two seconds and they'd be clear.

That bloody smoke, Duckham thought suddenly. It disappears, down over the edge. Leeward side. We're flying with the wind and we haven't got height. What if the gale that was helping lift them over the mountain pulled down on the other side with equal force?

Anxiety started pumping round his arteries again, tired mind and tired body calling *pax*. He had anticipated it by a second or two, the plane by rather less. It started to shudder. Duckham's brain seemed to be moving in slow motion as though working its way through paragraphs in a text-book. Clear-air turbulence around a volcano that could snap off wings and engines – the 707 over Mount Fuji, he thought. Fly attitude, he told himself.

They hit the down-draught beyond the edge of the ridge, like falling into a hole in the ground. The initial drop was about 500 feet straight down. George Raven, unstrapped, was thrown up on the ceiling. Then the plane bounced steady and level at 9500 feet, ninety tons deadweight shuddering through the frame and the wings. There was a deep wide valley below them and ridges coming up on the far side.

Ride it, you bugger, thought Duckham. His eye was now o

the altimeter, his whole body waiting for the airflow to lift them again. The highest ridge in front of us is at six five or six six, he thought. We've still got room to fly.

The altimeter was holding at nine five – but holding like an ironic smile. Duckham could feel the pull, gentle, inexorable. Then the digits started spinning – quite slowly, like the indicator in an old-fashioned elevator: nine four, nine three, nine two, one, nine, eight, seven, six, five . . . they seemed to be flying straight and normal. Only the altimeter and the vertical speed indicator told them they were sinking, slow and gentle and terrifying, like falling in a nightmare. All they could do was wait for the bottom of the down-draught. It would lift them before the floor of the valley, but would it lift before they fell below the level of the ridges beyond?

'You all right, George?'

George Raven was on the floor, dazed and trying to pull himself back on to his seat. Peter was transfixed, eyes staring through the wind-shield watching the lower slopes of the mountain with their cappings of cloud floating up towards them.

Eight two, eight one, eight, seven nine . . .

The valley lay tangential to the mountain, running left and northwards. We could try to turn with it, thought Duckham, but there was barely room and if they banked hard they would lose too much air speed. They were condemned to that ridge in front of them, two miles away and closing fast as the elevator went on down and down.

'Christ! Do something!' Peter blowing his cool in a mutter.

Duckham knew what he was thinking. Nose down, turn, and fly out of it down the valley. But if the spiral kept on down they would never pull out of a dive, not before they hit that green valley floor 2000 feet below. It has to lift, thought Duckham. The air has to lift over that ridge and pull us with it. Law of nature. Law of life and death.

The down-draught stopped at five thousand nine, the top of that ridge perhaps 300 feet above them – pine trees and lava in a jumble of skyline just above the cloud. They were lifting again. Two sixty knots at an angle of climb. Six thousand, six thousand one, six thousand two. Tango November seemed to move like a tired heron flapping across the sky.

Duckham could see where they were going to hit. A protrusion of rock above the trees as small as a small lorry.

Right rudder.

'We're going to hit,' Peter yelled.

It was the sort of easy shaped lump of rock a kid would scramble up on a Sunday walk and it took the underside of the left wing with a thump and an explosion, turning the whole plane through thirty degrees like a car broadsliding in a corner.

'You've killed us!' Peter yelling again.

Duckham pushed the wheel right forward. The ground beyond the ridge fell away steeply – tree-tops and a gentle slope twenty miles down to the sea. Clear sky for ever.

They were left wing low but still flying. Duckham used right rudder and ailerons. Tango November was yawing, hanging in the air, an acrobat swaying off-balance on the tightrope.

Duckham looked back through his side window as he dragged on the wheel. Ten foot of the left wing was sheared off like a torn arm, fuel and hydraulics spewing from the arteries. The ailerons had gone and there was no lift from that left side. They were slipping left wing down in a long arc that was turning them back into the high ground and the mountain.

Air speed dropping. Nose down for speed and some semblance of control. Full right rudder to counteract the drag on the left. Ease back on the wheel as they made air speed.

There was nowhere to go. Clear sky and sea were passing to starboard and out of sight.

'I can't get her out of the turn. We're going down.' Duckham heard his voice ridiculously calm and measured.

In and out of wisps of cloud now, still seeming to float above the world a thousand feet clear of reality.

'Landing gear down. We want somewhere to put down. Somewhere flat.'

Going through the motions, thought Duckham. There's no fields on this mountain. They were heading back at it now, the ground rising to meet them.

'Landing gear checks, Peter.'

Peter's voice was barely audible: 'Three greens.'

Oh Christ Jesus it can't be happening to us. This is when life is meant to come flooding back through the mind. All thos years in a split second. Tell me something, Duckham was thinking. Tell me what it was all about. But he couldn't get his mind to move. Born Rangoon, 1922.

Peter was stuck like a kid on a roller-coaster, mouth open, staring at the wind. George was doing something with his seat. God help the passengers who can see it all happening. Is there time to tell them? He didn't even have one hand free. Come on, cloud, close us in and make it decently unexpected.

Right rudder and trim. Nose up to flatten out. Two hundred feet. One fifty. One. Fifty. They were floating no more. The world was hurling itself past them in a violence of trees and rocks.

Peter was making some noise like a moan, his hands and feet stuck out in front of him like a baby in a high chair. George was frantically screwing down the safety bar on his swivel chair.

Keep your eyes down, Duckham told himself, or you'll freeze. He had picked a few hundred yards of somewhere that looked flat. There were lives to be saved if he could take off some of their speed. Spoilers, reverse thrust and turn the fire levers at the last possible moment. Three jobs to do. Think about them. One, two and reach forward for the fire levers.

Peter's moan had turned into something else. George had lost his safety bar. His hands were scrabbling for it.

Duckham felt the under-carriage hit the trees. He had to keep flying it or the left wing would dip and they'd cartwheel. His right foot was hard down on the rudder. Three jobs; five moves. Pull for spoilers; select reverse thrust; wait for the reverse operating light; then pull back throttles and reach forward for the fire levers.

Mike Duckham reached with both hands, his mind clear: only one and three; number two was already shut down.

George was screaming, his chair swinging loose. They were on to the ground, the fuselage tearing and jumping under them. Slow down. Please, dear Lord, slow this bugger down.

Duckham pulled and turned the fire levers. The three jobs were done.

The light darkened outside. He looked up and saw death in a black lava slope one hundredth of a second away.

you would like a complete list of Arrow books
ease send a postcard to
O. Box 29, Douglas, Isle of Man, Great Britain.

CITY OF THE DEAD

Herbert Lieberman

CITY OF THE DEAD will shock you and grip you to the very last page

CITY OF THE DEAD starts where the others leave off

'Once again his gaze drifts past the Chief to the reconstructed corpses, the gobbets of flesh and bones still in trays all about him . . . "Why the hell do you do it" ' ?

He does it because it's his job. Paul Konig is Chief Medical Examiner, New York City. Each day's grisly workload of strangled whores, battered babies and dismembered corpses is just routine to him. Contemptuous of the police, the public and his fellow doctors, he presides over the morgue like a monarch. But things can go wrong even for Konig, when he finds he's up against a dead-end in the most gruesome multiple murder case in his career.

'I became afraid – literally afraid, to turn the page' *New York Times*

'The toughest, most harrowing, most gruesome novel in a long time' *Publisher's Weekly*

Two Thrillers from Jack Higgins

TOLL FOR THE BRAVE

Ellis Jackson had woken up hugging a twelve bore-shotgun.
In the next room, his mistress and his best friend lay naked on
the bed, their heads blown to pulp.

Active combat, a Viet Cong camp and the callous treachery of
his interrogator and lover, Madam Ny, had all taken their toll.
Back in England, Ellis had finally cracked.

Or had he? Maybe things weren't as simple as that – in any
case, Ellis wanted some answers. Making use of his highly
developed talent for survival, he found them: and they proved
he wasn't mad.

It might have been easier to take if he'd *really* been out of his
mind.

NARROW EXIT

Paul Henissart

Tunis. Shortly after a shaky government welcomes Arab terrorist Salah Al Houaranni, Israeli counter-intelligence pulls off one of its most spectacular coups: the guerilla leader is kidnapped from under the noses of his own guards.

Then Alex Gauthier, head of the Israeli espionage network in Tunisia, misses a vital transmission. And within hours Operation Flood is in ruins.

The three commandos and their prisoner wait on a lonely beach for a submarine that never appears – and Gauthier must risk breaking his cover to prevent their capture.